Threading the Needle

**Center Point
Large Print**

Also by Marie Bostwick
and available from Center Point Large Print:

The Cobbled Court Novels
A Single Thread
A Thread of Truth
A Thread So Thin

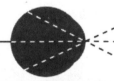

**This Large Print Book carries the
Seal of Approval of N.A.V.H.**

A Cobbled Court Novel
Book #4

Threading the Needle

MARIE BOSTWICK

CENTER POINT PUBLISHING
THORNDIKE, MAINE

This Center Point Large Print edition
is published in the year 2011 by arrangement with
Kensington Publishing Corp.

The text of this Large Print edition is unabridged.
In other aspects, this book may vary
from the original edition.
Printed in the United States of America
on permanent paper.
Set in 16-point Times New Roman type.

ISBN: 978-1-61173-118-7

Library of Congress Cataloging-in-Publication Data

Bostwick, Marie.
    Threading the needle / Marie Bostwick. — Center Point large print ed.
    p. cm.
    ISBN 978-1-61173-118-7 (library binding : alk. paper)
    1. Female friendship—Fiction. 2. Quilting—Fiction. 3. Connecticut—Fiction.
    4. Large type books. I. Title.
PS3602.O838T57 2011
813′.6—dc22
                                              2011012680

Though the fig tree may not blossom,
Nor fruit be on the vines;
Though the labor of the olive may fail,
And the fields yield no food;
Though the flock may be cut off from the fold,
And there be no herd in the stalls—
Yet will I rejoice in the Lord,
I will have joy in the God of my salvation.

—Habakkuk 3:17–18

With thanks to . . .

Mary and Hugh Bargiel, owners of the Strong House Inn, a charming B&B and quilting haven in beautiful Vergennes, Vermont, who inspired me to write about an inn catering to quilters and whose hospitality (and cuisine!) brings guests back again and again.

Cindy Bosson, owner of Flora and Fauna, in Litchfield, Connecticut, the lovely gift shop that inspired For the Love of Lavender, for generously sharing her time and knowledge about creating herbal soaps and cosmetics.

"The Team" (you know who you are), for their ongoing support and endless patience.

Liza, for helping me find my focus.

The Reading Friends who love New Bern as I do and whose expressions of encouragement are my greatest reward.

Prologue

New Bern, Connecticut—1966

Madelyn Beecher stood on the icy sidewalk in front of Thomas Edison Junior High School, exhaling a frosty vapor as she scanned the faces of the chattering children who streamed past before they boarded the yellow buses that stood idling by the curb or formed into little clumps and cliques for the walk home from school.

As the crowd thinned out, Madelyn tightened her grip on the brown paper bag she held clutched in her left hand, shifted her book bag to a more comfortable position on her shoulder, and frowned, causing a small indentation to form between her brows, a line about three-quarters of an inch long, like the top of an exclamation point. When she grew older and frowned more frequently, this line would become permanent and more pronounced. Repeated, fruitless attempts at its eradication would pay for a family ski vacation in Vail for Dr. David Miner, one of the most prominent cosmetic surgeons on New York City's Upper West Side. But, at age twelve, that little line did nothing to mar Madelyn's looks.

She was pretty, with a clear complexion, high cheekbones, brown eyes rimmed by thick lashes, and light brown hair that she would later dye blond. However, like many young girls, Madelyn could only see the flaws in her face and figure.

She was the tallest girl in her class, half a head taller than most of the boys. She found this embarrassing, so she tended to walk with her shoulders hunched in a futile attempt to appear shorter. Yet a year or two from growing into her long limbs, Madelyn's grandmother, Edna, often accused her of being so clumsy that she could "trip over a piece of string," a cruel but not entirely inaccurate barb. Madelyn thought her forehead too high, so she kept her bangs long to cover it and to shield her eyes, which reminded her too much of her deceased father. Sometimes, when she looked in the mirror and saw his eyes staring out from her face, she would begin to cry.

As a child, Madelyn was pretty. As a woman, she was beautiful, with a face cameras loved and a body men craved. She would not pass very far into adolescence before realizing that her physical appearance brought her attention and gave her power. But on this day, still clinging to the remnants of a short and rocky childhood, Madelyn would happily have traded her face, her body, and her life for those of her best and only friend, Tessa Kover.

It was twenty-nine degrees on that February afternoon. The radio said another snowstorm would blow in after sunset. Mr. Walters, the school custodian, didn't put much faith in weathermen, but he figured they had at least half a chance of being right and so he decided to sprinkle a layer of salt on the walkways before he swept the gymnasium.

He donned the plaid wool jacket and matching cap his wife had given him for Christmas and headed outside with a bucket of salt just as the buses were pulling away. He saw Madelyn Beecher standing outside with her coat unbuttoned, holding a brown paper lunch sack. Mr. Walters knew why she was waiting. In his thirty years as a school custodian, he'd seen plenty of friendships between preteen girls, though the relationship between Madelyn Beecher and Tessa Kover was more intense than most—at least on Madelyn's part. Girls could be funny that way.

"She's already gone home, princess."

Mr. Walters, who had no children of his own, called all the girls at Edison "princess" and all the boys "son." None of them minded.

"Tessa was one of the first ones out the door when the bell rang. Think Ben Nickles was walking her home."

"She wouldn't walk home with Ben Nickles," Madelyn insisted. "He's a creep. Besides, we always walk home together."

The old man tossed a handful of salt onto the

steps and shrugged. "Well, he was carrying her books. Whatever it was, she's long gone. Probably home by now."

He looked up at the sky. "Feels like the weatherman was right. Feels like snow. You should head home before it starts."

The frown line between Madelyn's brows deepened. She sighed. "See you tomorrow, Mr. Walters."

"See you tomorrow, princess."

He watched Madelyn shuffle down the sidewalk with her shoulders drooping.

"Hey! Princess!" he called out. "Button up your coat, will you? It's cold!"

Madelyn waved at him and went on her way, coat still undone. Mr. Walters shook his head as he tossed more salt onto the walkway.

"Poor little thing," he mumbled to himself. "Doesn't anybody look out for that child?"

Tessa and Madelyn were born in the same week in March. The previous year, to mark their twelfth birthdays, Madelyn made a pair of semi-matching friendship bracelets for her and Tessa to wear, stringing fishing line with aquamarine-colored beads salvaged from old necklaces that she'd bought at tag sales. It had taken months to find enough.

The girls lived three doors apart from each other on Oak Leaf Lane, in New Bern, Connecticut. It was a pretty street and aptly named, lined with big Victorian framed houses and oak trees with strong branches that stretched streetward to create a canopy of green every spring.

Madelyn moved there at the age of nine, after the death of her father. She and Tessa became friends the way children often do, with the prodding of some well-meaning adult who assumed that two girls of the same age, living on the same street, had enough in common to become friends. This turned out to be true even though the adult in question never stopped to consider just how different Madelyn and Tessa were.

Tessa was as petite as Madelyn was tall. She, too, was pretty but in a sweet, girl-next-door way with blue eyes, brown hair that refused to hold a curl, and a sprinkling of freckles across her nose. As an adult, Tessa would grow to just a hair over five foot three and had to watch her diet carefully to keep from putting on weight. As a seventh grader she hadn't yet reached the five-foot mark, and after an uncharacteristic bout of begging, she had convinced her mother to let her start wearing high heels.

Every day after walking to school, Tessa took off her red snow boots and exchanged them for a pair of heels she'd stowed in her book bag. Later in life she would develop foot problems and would exchange her three-inch heels for two-inchers but never gave them up entirely, except when she was working outdoors. Then she would slip into a pair of comfortable, well-worn clogs, which might explain why she went on to become such an avid gardener; that was the only time her feet didn't hurt.

Madelyn, always self-conscious about her height, wore flat-bottomed Keds sneakers she purchased at Goodwill and embellished with beads, sequins, and embroidery floss scavenged from her grandmother's sewing box. A widow on a fixed income, Edna Beecher's means were more limited than her neighbors', but she wasn't as poor as she pled, just miserly, and rarely gave her granddaughter any spending money. Madelyn got most of her outfits secondhand from tag sales, thrift shops, or, if no one was looking, by riffling through bags filled with old clothes that neighbors left on the porch for St. Vincent de Paul to pick up.

Tessa was bright and studious, brought home straight As on her report cards, and was a favorite with her teachers.

Madelyn, though equally bright, was a painfully slow reader. She struggled in school, barely passing her classes. In those days before most educators knew about learning disabilities and differences, Madelyn was labeled by her teachers as an "underachiever." She believed this to be true.

Madelyn lived alone with her grandmother,

Edna Beecher, a woman who prided herself on speaking her mind and took no trouble to disguise the fact that she considered being saddled with the care and expense of her orphaned granddaughter yet another in a long line of bad breaks fate had handed her.

Tessa shared her home with her mother, father, an amiable older brother named Joseph, and a golden retriever predictably named Rex. Never in all the time Madelyn spent in the Kover home, which was considerable, did she hear Mr. and Mrs. Kover raise their voices or say anything unkind to each other. Joseph and Tessa got into arguments but not often and not of any lasting duration.

Tessa was a good little girl, loved by her family and held up as an example by her teachers. Surprisingly, this did nothing to decrease her popularity among her peers. Everyone liked Tessa; they always had. And that was a problem. Tessa had never known anything but approval and success and was, therefore, frightened by the idea of failure or disapproval. Because of this, she was an unusually compliant child, doing and saying what was expected, avoiding risks, coloring inside the lines.

Unlike many good little girls who revel in their goodness, Tessa had dreams of adventures and chances, whims and wildness, and secretly admired people who seemed not to care what others thought of them. This was what attracted her to Madelyn—until her adolescent need to belong trumped her desire to be different.

Having been wounded early in life and often, Madelyn was simultaneously cautious and careless. She held herself aloof from anyone she felt might hurt her. It made for a lonely existence but freed her from the expectation that she ever should or could win the approval of others. Madelyn possessed a sort of calloused courage, a personality that was fiercely independent and undeterred by outside opinion. She did what she wanted, when she wanted, without asking permission or pardon. Even as a child, one of Madelyn's most oft repeated phrases was, "That's the deal. And anybody who doesn't like it can just go to hell."

Hearing Madelyn say those words shocked Tessa and made her feel a little bit wicked, a sensation she didn't find as unpleasant as she supposed she should.

Tessa liked having sleepovers at Madelyn's house because, under Edna's nonexistent supervision, the girls were permitted to eat nothing but potato chips and hot chocolate for dinner, watch horror films that gave them nightmares for weeks, and stay up till all hours playing with the dollhouse or stay out till all hours having adventures.

Not long after arriving in New Bern, Madelyn found a worn, dusty, and furnitureless Victorian dollhouse in Edna's attic. She carted it down to her room and set about fixing it up, beginning with a stop at the hardware store. When she told the owner what she was up to, he gave her a book of outdated wallpaper and carpet samples. With a murderously sharp craft knife and no supervision, Madelyn cut them into the precise sizes and shapes needed to repaper and recarpet every room in the tiny house.

Tessa donated a family of dolls to the project—father, mother, brother, and sister. Gathering scraps from her mother's sewing room, she stitched together tiny patchwork quilts for each of the doll beds. The quilts were simple, tiny squares of blue, red, or pink checkerboarded with white, but Tessa was happy to have something to contribute.

It was Madelyn who had most of the ideas and did most of the work on the project. She had a gift for that kind of thing, spending hours scouring the tag sales and junk shops for tiny furnishings, sometimes making her own. Her most impressive creation was a miniature chandelier fashioned from wire and a pair of old crystal earrings she bought for ten cents at the Methodist Women's White Elephant Sale.

The girls spent hours playing with the dollhouse, arranging and rearranging the furniture, acting out their lives and lacks, childishly testing out the roles they supposed they would live. Adventures, on the other hand, were how they tried on the roles they *wished* they would live. One in particular stayed with Tessa all her life.

Upon a moonlit night in their eleventh summer, Madelyn and Tessa climbed out the bedroom window, shimmied down a porch column, and spent a wild night chasing through woods and fields, catching fireflies, feasting on strawberries stolen from a farmer's garden, sneaking into a pigpen and then luring the pigs into the open by offering them ears of half-green corn—also stolen from the farmer.

Tessa was hesitant about releasing the pigs, but when Madelyn reminded her of the awful fate that awaited the adorable piglets unless someone intervened, Tessa went along with the plan. *Charlotte's Web* was one of Tessa's favorite books. She reasoned that, given the opportunity, Fern would have done the same thing. As she held out an ear of corn and backed slowly out of the pen with two pigs following behind, she felt not guilty but adventurous—and a little bit brave.

The next morning, Tessa's legs began to itch. By the afternoon, she was covered with red spots from knee to ankle. Her father went over to Edna's yard in search of poison ivy but couldn't find any. Her mother wanted to take her to the doctor, but Tessa protested, worried that the doctor might start asking questions she'd rather not answer. Tessa was a terrible liar and she knew it. Madelyn was the one who'd made up a story about Tessa coming into contact with the noxious weed while they'd been running through the sprinkler in Edna's backyard.

Mrs. Kover furrowed her brow and turned to her husband. "I just don't know. What if it gets worse?"

"Oh, she'll be fine," Mr. Kover said dismissively. "When I was a kid I used to get poison ivy all the time. Get some calamine lotion. She doesn't need a doctor."

"It's not that bad, Mommy. I hardly itch at all."

"There. You see? She hardly itches at all." He smiled at Tessa and ruffled her hair. "That's my big girl."

Later that day, Mr. Kover sat Tessa and Madelyn down on the front porch steps and took their picture. The girls wore matching blue pedal pushers and white midriff blouses. Each had one arm slung over the shoulders of the other. Tessa tucked her free hand firmly under her thigh to stop herself from scratching her legs and grinned as wide and bright as sunshine in August.

Madelyn enjoyed playing at the Kovers' as much as Tessa enjoyed playing at her house, though for different reasons.

Madelyn thought of the Kovers as a "regular family" and envied their "regular family" lifestyle, which included game nights, annual camping trips to the North Woods of Maine, and home-cooked sit-down dinners served at six on the dot. Madelyn was especially fond of Mrs. Kover. Being naturally maternal, Sarah Kover fussed over Madelyn as if she'd been her own, urging her to finish her milk and wear warm sweaters, and avoid crossing her eyes; French braiding her hair, and even sewing the matching pedal pushers and blouses Madelyn and Tessa wore in the photograph. Mrs. Kover was the only adult who seemed to have any influence over Madelyn, though the girl's willingness to be influenced had its limits.

Madelyn went to the Kovers' nearly every day after school and quickly learned that if she passed through the Kover kitchen around 5:45 P.M. and commented about how good everything smelled, she would be invited to stay and eat. However, in recent months, Madelyn began to notice that her dangled hints for dinner invitations often went unheeded. When she rang the Kovers' door as usual on a Saturday morning in late January she was met not by Tessa but by Mrs. Kover.

"You're up bright and early, Madelyn. But I'm afraid Tessa isn't home. She went to Jillian Eversoll's for a sleepover last night."

Jillian Eversoll? Why would Tessa want to stay overnight with her? Jillian had small, piggy eyes, and just the week before, she'd tattled on Madelyn for passing notes to Tessa during English class.

"Oh. Will you tell Tessa that I dropped by?" She turned from the door to face the snow-drifted street and the prospect of a whole day with no one but Grandma Edna for company.

"Why don't you come inside for a minute, Madelyn? I just took a loaf of banana bread out of the oven. Would you like some?"

Mrs. Kover made hot chocolate and set a cup in front of Madelyn along with a plate of warm banana bread spread with melting butter that dripped onto the girl's fingers, then sat across from her at the table with her own cup of cocoa.

Sarah Kover was blond and had a warm, motherly smile. Madelyn thought she looked a little like the actress who played Samantha Stephens on *Bewitched*.

"So, Madelyn, how is school?" Mrs. Kover blew on her cocoa to cool it.

Madelyn shrugged. "Okay."

"Do you like Mrs. Bridges? You know, she was my teacher when I went to Edison. She's been teaching math for about as long as I can remember."

"I don't think she likes me very much."

"Why do you say that?"

"She called Grandma in for a conference last month to talk about my grades. They aren't very good. Grandma was mad. She said that Mrs. Bridges said that I'm not living up to my potential and that that's just another way of saying I'm lazy."

Mrs. Kover pressed her lips together, as if keeping them closed required some effort. "I'm sure Mrs. Bridges didn't mean it like that. I think that was just her way of saying that, with a little more effort, your grades will improve. You're a smart girl, Madelyn. I'm sure Mrs. Bridges was just trying to encourage you."

"That's not the way Grandma saw it."

Mrs. Kover wrapped her hands around her cup and frowned, resting both elbows on the table, which was something Grandma Edna had told Madelyn that ladies didn't do. Madelyn mentally chalked up one more thing on her growing list of things Edna was wrong about and propped her own elbows up on the kitchen table.

"No. Well . . . sometimes older people don't always . . ."

Mrs. Kover faltered, sighed, and changed the subject. In the entire time Madelyn had known her, she never heard Mrs. Kover say anything bad about anyone else.

"Give yourself a little time, Madelyn. Things will get easier."

Madelyn licked some butter from her fingertips

and nodded, not because she thought Mrs. Kover was right but because she liked her.

"What about friends? Have you made any new friends this year?"

"Tessa's my friend."

Mrs. Kover smiled, keeping her teeth hidden under the tight bow of her lips. "I know. But there are a lot of other nice little girls in your class, you know. Besides Jillian, there's Allison Treash, Lisa Sweeney"—she ticked the list off on her fingers—"Mary Louise Newton. Oh, a lot of girls."

Madelyn shook her head stubbornly. "Tessa is my friend," she repeated.

"Madelyn, have you ever heard the phrase 'putting all your eggs in one basket'?"

Madelyn had, but didn't say so. She didn't like the direction the conversation was heading.

"I'm worried that's what you're doing with Tessa," Mrs. Kover said gently. "Tessa has always had a lot of friends. And that's best, I think. When you concentrate all your attention and affection on just one person, you run the risk of . . ."

Madelyn kept her expression blank, her eyes fixed on Mrs. Kover.

"I just think it would be a good idea if you spent at least some of your time with someone other than Tessa. Do you see what I mean?"

Madelyn didn't, not because she couldn't but

because she didn't care to. She liked her eggs where they were, thank you.

Tessa is my friend, she thought. *Anybody who doesn't like it . . .*

Madelyn was annoyed with Tessa and wondered why she hadn't waited for her. Maybe she had a lot of homework and wanted to get started on it early. Madelyn knew how Tessa was about things like that. She'd rather eat a bug than miss turning in a homework assignment. Yes, that probably explained it. She decided to forgive Tessa. Madelyn could never stay mad at her for long.

It started to snow. Madelyn hoped it would snow hard enough so school would be canceled the next day. Then she and Tessa could go sledding or, better yet, stay inside and play with the dollhouse.

By this time, the once-empty dollhouse, in true Victorian style, was fairly bursting with furnishings. But every few weeks, Madelyn would add something new to the décor. When she did, she always showed Tessa first.

Today it was a new mirror for the parlor she'd made from an old gold compact. Madelyn had unscrewed the bottom half of the compact, removed the hinges, reglued the loose rhinestones around the edge, and polished them with rubbing alcohol to make them shine. Though a bit gaudy, the refurbished mirror was the perfect size to hang on the wall behind the miniature sofa she'd found and recovered in red velvet the previous fall. Madelyn couldn't wait to show it to Tessa.

She turned the corner onto Oak Leaf Lane, running the last three blocks to Tessa's house, holding the paper bag with the mirror inside in her left hand and her book bag in her right, the sound of her footsteps muffled by the snow.

Coming closer, she saw a boy in a blue snow parka—or rather, the back of him—leaning up against the white clapboard wall of Tessa's house with his head bent down, his feet spread shoulder-width apart. Between those feet, Madelyn saw another pair of feet, clad in red snow boots.

Ben Nickles had Tessa pinned to the wall!

She ran faster, her heart racing and her breath coming in short gasps. Leaving the sidewalk and running across the yard, she saw that Ben had his lips pressed against Tessa's. Tessa turned her head to the left, but Ben moved with her, pushing his face up close to hers. Madelyn saw the pink tip of his tongue snaking into Tessa's mouth before he shifted his weight and moved his hand down to the front of Tessa's coat and clawed at the front of her jacket.

Madelyn let out a yowl as she closed in on them, swinging her book bag over her head like a lariat. Ben lifted his head and turned around just in time to get hit square in the jaw with the full force of Madelyn's bag. The blow knocked him off his feet and backward into the snow.

"What the heck!" Ben yelled as he grabbed his jaw and glared at Madelyn. "What did you do that for?"

Tessa gasped and knelt next to Ben in the snow. "Are you all right? Let me see."

Ben grimaced and then wiggled his jaw back and forth. "I'm okay. I wasn't expecting it. That's all."

Still kneeling, Tessa looked up at Madelyn with blazing eyes. "What was that about? Are you crazy or something?"

Ben, rubbing his jaw, let out a short, mirthless laugh, as if indicating that the answer to her question should be obvious.

"I was trying to save you," Madelyn said. "He was *attacking* you!"

Tessa rolled her eyes. "He was *kissing* me!"

Ben looked up at Madelyn and smirked. "What's the matter, Maddie? Jealous? Of me kissing Tessa? Or of Tessa kissing me?"

Tessa's cheeks turned red. Ben laughed. Madelyn didn't understand his joke, only that she was the butt of it. She hated for people to call her Maddie. She waited for Tessa to come to her defense by saying something cutting to Ben, but she didn't. Instead Tessa helped him get to his feet.

"Madelyn, you've got to quit following me around like this, okay?"

"I wasn't following you around," she said. "I was waiting for you. So we could walk home from school together. We *always* walk home together."

Tessa let out a heavy sigh. "Yeah, I know. Look. That was all right when we were little, but we're going to be thirteen next month. We're too old for that now."

Madelyn frowned, puckering her forehead as she held up the brown paper bag. "But I brought something to show you. Something new. For the dollhouse. Do you want to come over and see it?"

"The dollhouse!" Ben guffawed. Tessa looked at him. Her cheeks flamed an even brighter shade of red.

"I told you," Tessa said in a voice that was nearly a hiss. "We're too old for that stuff now. I can't spend all my time hanging out with just you. You've got to quit waiting around for me after school every day and you've got to quit coming over to my house every afternoon. People will think we're weird or something."

Madelyn squared her shoulders. "Well, I don't care what people think. You're my friend." She hefted her book bag onto her shoulder and glowered at Ben. "Nobody had better say anything bad about you in front of me!"

Tessa threw back her head, squeezed her eyes shut, and let out an exasperated growl.

"Not me, Madelyn! You! *You're* the one everybody is calling weird, and they're right. You are! You follow me around like a stray puppy. You eat dinner at my house practically every night of the week. My father says we ought to start charging you room and board! My family can't do anything without you butting into it. You still play with dolls. And you steal clothes from the charity bags people leave on their porches! It's practically the same as digging through their trash.

"You're weird, Madelyn! You are. You always have been. Don't you get it? You're embarrassing me!"

Madelyn blinked her big brown eyes. "But . . . you're my friend."

Tessa glanced at Ben, who raised his eyebrows into a question, before turning back to Madelyn. She swallowed hard and then, without looking Madelyn in the face, shook her head firmly.

"When you moved in with your grandmother, my mother said I *had* to ask you over to play. She said I had to be nice to you because you were an orphan and nobody wanted you. She made me be friends with you, so I was. But," she said softly, looking up at Madelyn with a pained expression, "I don't want to be your friend. Not anymore."

The tears that had pooled in Madelyn's eyes spilled over and ran silently down her cheeks. Tessa bit her lower lip and blinked, trying to keep herself from crying too.

"I'm sorry, Madelyn. You're not . . . it's not that I don't like you, but . . . you're just too much. You try too hard. I don't want to hurt you. . . ."

Madelyn's nose was running. She swiped at it with the back of her hand. "Shut up," she said in a raspy voice. "Just shut up. I don't have to listen to you anymore. I want my bracelet back."

Tessa looked confused.

"The friendship bracelet I made for you. I want it back."

Tessa pulled up the sleeve of her coat to expose her wrist and hesitated a moment before pulling off the bracelet and handing it to Madelyn.

"I'm sorry."

Eyes still swimming with tears, Madelyn glared at Tessa, shoved the bracelet inside the pocket of her jacket, and ran away without saying another word.

Ben laughed, made a megaphone of his hands, and called after her. "What's the matter, Maddie? Breaking up too hard to do?"

Tessa stood silently with her fists clenched at her sides, watching Madelyn's retreat.

When Madelyn was out of sight, Tessa spun around and, making a windmill of her arm, slapped Ben as hard as she could across the jaw in the exact spot Madelyn's book bag had hit him a few minutes before.

"Ow!" Ben covered his jaw with his hand. "What was that for?"

"For being mean to her! And for making *me* be mean to her!"

Tessa made a fist and punched him as hard as she could in the shoulder three times. "And that's for trying to stick your tongue in my mouth! And that's for grabbing my boob! And that's for being such a pervert!"

Ben backed away from her, but she followed him, kicking him in the shin with her red snow boot. Keeping one eye on the furious girl, he bent down to pick up the schoolbooks he'd abandoned in the snow. "You're crazy! You know that?"

He retreated across the yard at a pace that wasn't quite a run. Looking over his shoulder he yelled, "And weird! You're just as weird as your girlfriend!"

"Well, I'd rather be weird than a perverted creep!" Tessa yelled back. "Hey, Ben. Let me give you a tip. Next time you try to kiss a girl, think about brushing your teeth first. My dog has better breath than you!"

When he was gone, Tessa wiped her tears on the back of her sleeve, picked up her books, and went inside. She ran upstairs to her bedroom and didn't come out of her room for the rest of the night. Mrs. Kover left a cheese sandwich and glass of milk on a tray outside her door. It went untouched until Rex found it, wolfed down the sandwich, and lapped up the milk as far as his tongue could reach, then knocked over the glass with his paw to get at the rest, and lay down next to the empty tray and took a nap.

Chest heaving from the exertion of running across the snowy yards, Madelyn slid open the heavy wooden garage door, tugged on a piece of grimy string to turn on the overhead lightbulb, and walked past Edna's DeSoto to the wooden worktable under the side window.

She pulled Tessa's bracelet out of her pocket, then took off her own, laid both on the worktable, and smashed the beads over and over and over again with a hammer until there was nothing left of them but a tangle of twisted fishing line and a pile of pale blue dust. She swept the glittery remains into a rusting dustpan, dumped them into the trash, and dried her eyes before going inside.

After closing her bedroom door, she dumped her coat and books on the floor, then flopped backward onto the blue and white patchwork quilt that covered her bed. She lay there, dry-eyed, and stared at the ceiling some minutes before reaching her decision.

Rising from her bed, she crossed the room and

picked up the dollhouse. The miniature furniture was scattered by the abrupt movement and the ever-smiling members of the doll family toppled onto the floor in a heap.

Edna, who was walking to the bathroom to take the afternoon dose of her liver pills, frowned as she met her granddaughter in the hallway.

"What are you doing with that thing?"

"Putting it in the attic. I'm too old to play with dolls anymore. It's all just make-believe anyway."

Edna snorted. "I was wondering when you'd finally figure that out."

The next day, Tessa failed to turn in her homework and Mrs. Bridges had no choice but to give her detention. Concerned about this uncharacteristic lapse on the part of her favorite student, the teacher called Tessa's mother and asked if everything was all right at home.

When Mrs. Kover explained about the situation with Madelyn, Mrs. Bridges said, "Well, I'm sorry she's so upset, but between you and me, it's for the best. Madelyn isn't the sort of girl Tessa should be spending time with.

"Forgive me if I sound harsh, but I've been a teacher for thirty-six years. I've seen girls like Madelyn before. Once they hit high school, they turn wild. Get themselves into all kinds of trouble and bring other girls, good girls from good homes, girls like Tessa, along for the ride. You're lucky this friendship ended when it did.

"Mark my words, Sarah, Madelyn Beecher will come to a bad end."

1
Madelyn

August 2009

I try to resist the urge, but as I sit in the offices of Blackman, Janders, and Whipple, located on the forty-eighth floor of the Mancuso Tower, a cathedral of excess located on Fifth Avenue at Fifty-sixth Street, I can't stop myself from adding it all up in my head and marveling at the true price tag of what Sterling used to call "a lifestyle." How did I fail to see it before? And how am I going to live without it?

How am I going to live at all?

The Oriental rug that sits under the antique mahogany partners desk of my attorney, Eugene Darius Janders, is hand-knotted silk and worth thirty thousand dollars at least—enough to buy a new car. It's very fine, though not as fine as the one in the library in our house in the Hamptons. I mean, the house that *used* to be ours. And if I added up the rest of the furnishings in Gene's office, it would probably be enough to buy a nice little cottage in the country for cash. Not a cottage in the Hamptons, mind you, but someplace quiet and removed from the city. Connecticut, maybe.

Then there's his wardrobe. Gene's suit is summer-weight wool, tan, two button, side-vented, custom made, probably in London, priced somewhere between five and seven thousand, which, even in New York, is enough to pay a month's rent for a two-bedroom apartment in a very decent part of town. His blue paisley tie, designed by Brioni, retails for one hundred and ninety-five dollars—enough to buy a week's groceries. I think. It's been a while since I did my own grocery shopping.

And the shoes. Oh, the shoes! Hand-tooled calfskin, individually and exquisitely custom made by John Lobb for a very small, exclusive clientele—the trust-fund set, celebrities, the upper echelon of Manhattan's successful lawyers, men like Eugene, a few brokers and money managers, including my husband, Sterling Baron, once one of New York's most successful fund managers, now one of its most notorious— men who don't balk at spending five thousand dollars for shoes. Only the very well-heeled can afford to stride down the sidewalks of New York in a pair of made-to-measure Lobb loafers.

Forgive me. That was a terrible pun, I know. But these days I have to take my humor where I can find it. At the moment, nothing about my life is especially funny.

Four months ago Sterling and I spent, for more than it takes to buy a pair of Lobb oxfords, a weekend in the Boathouse Suite at The Point, a very exclusive resort on the shores of Upper Saranac Lake, and we did it without even looking at the bill.

Was that only four months ago? That seems another lifetime, another life . . . because it is.

Exclusive. What a word. I used to think it meant limited to a small number of the "best" people, but I've recently come to realize it means limited to whoever can pay, a club to which my membership has just been rescinded, as Eugene was now explaining.

"Bottom line is, Madelyn, you're broke."

I laughed nervously. "You mean broke like I'll have to rent out the house in the Hamptons this summer? Or broke like I'll have to apply for food stamps?"

"Madelyn, haven't you been listening to anything I've said?"

"I've been trying very hard not to."

"You don't *have* a house in the Hamptons anymore. The feds have seized it, and the condo in Vail, *and* the Bentley. The only reason you're still in your apartment is because I convinced the judge to give you until the end of the month to move out."

I felt a pressure in my chest. For a moment, I wondered if I might be having a heart attack, but I'm only fifty-six and in perfect health. I wasn't dying; I was panicking.

"But where am I supposed to go? Can't you get the judge to change his mind? I had nothing to do with this! I didn't cheat the investors out of their money, Sterling did. The investigators have cleared me of any wrongdoing. I knew nothing about it."

It's true. I didn't know anything about it. Sterling was rich when I met him, rich when I married him, and as time went on, he just got richer. He never talked to me about his business. There was no point, he said; matters of high finance were way over my head. "You can't be smart *and* beautiful, Madelyn, so why don't you stick to beautiful? That's what you do best." When we first married, he said it with a laugh, but after a few years, with a sneer.

Sterling was one of the most successful fund managers in New York. Even in years when the market was down, Sterling's investors made ten percent minimum. Nobody cared how, not until Bernie Madoff was exposed and suddenly the success of money managers with the Midas touch, people like Sterling, was called into question.

I didn't even know Sterling was under investigation until we came home from our

34

weekend at The Point. I remember everything about that weekend, how strange it felt, not because we hadn't been there before—we go to The Point at least two or three times a year—but because of the way Sterling was acting. He was . . . how shall I explain it? Attentive. He looked at me, looked me in the eye the way he hasn't looked at me in years. I wondered what he wanted. I kept waiting for him to say something, or do something, or ask for something. But he didn't. He just kept looking at me. And he held my hand when we walked to dinner. He hadn't done that since . . . well, not for a very long time. And he didn't bring his cell phone along. He didn't make or take any calls for the entire weekend. Maybe that doesn't seem unusual, but that's because you don't know my husband. Once, we went to dinner at the White House and Sterling left during the salad course to take a call from his secretary. Of course, he was sleeping with his secretary at the time, but that particular call, I believe, was about business.

Anyway, Sterling didn't talk on the phone once that weekend. He talked to me. He listened to me. And for a little while, it was nice, almost like it was in the early days, when he cared, back in the days when I cared too. So long ago.

We didn't talk on the drive home. Sterling seemed to pull into himself. I kept going over the weekend in my mind, thinking that maybe, just maybe, we might be happy, that Sterling had undergone some transformation, decided to be a real husband to me. I wondered if that could be true. And I wondered if it wasn't too late.

Returning home, we were met by stern-faced FBI agents who handcuffed my husband and took him away while I stood watching, hoping I'd wake up from this nightmare soon. I didn't.

Sterling seemed unfazed. With his hands behind his back, half hidden by the starched whiteness of his French cuffs, he calmly told me to call Mike Radnovich and cancel their golf game and then to ask Gene to meet him at the police station.

Gene has never liked me. The feeling is mutual, but he's very good at his job. If anyone could get us out of this mess, it was Gene.

"Seriously, Gene, can't you do something? Talk to the judge, get me some more time? You did it before. I didn't do anything wrong, so why am I being punished? Where do people expect me to live? On the street?"

Gene leaned forward, his forearms resting on his desk. "Madelyn, don't you get it? No one cares. Over the years, Sterling took twenty billion dollars from his clients, told them he was going to invest it for them, all but guaranteed them a minimum ten percent annual return, and then sat on the money. Compared to Madoff, Sterling is small potatoes, but still . . . a billion here, a billion there, sooner or later it adds up to real money. People are angry and they're looking for someone to blame."

None of this was news to me, not anymore. Gene had given up referring to the charges leveled against Sterling as "allegations" weeks before. Eugene Janders is a brilliant litigator, but he's not a magician. Even his talent has its limits. After looking at the evidence, Gene said that Sterling's only chance of not dying in a prison cell was to plead guilty, display remorse, and hope for a lenient judge.

He was probably right. Even so, I couldn't help but notice that Gene offered this advice right after our bank accounts had been frozen. You can call me cynical (and you'd be right), but I couldn't help but wonder. Would Gene have been quite so ready to throw in the towel if Sterling still had access to an almost unlimited supply of cash to pay for the services of Blackman, Janders, and Whipple? Sterling's admission of guilt might be his best shot for a lighter sentence, but it was also the cheapest way for Gene's firm to rid itself of an unwinnable case and a client whose pockets weren't nearly as deep as they'd been. It was all very convenient.

"Sterling kept the game going by reeling in new fish and using their money to pay off his longer-term investors. As well as," Gene said after a dramatic pause—he had a habit of always

speaking as if he were addressing a jury—
"financing his lavish lifestyle . . . and yours.

"A lot of people have lost a lot of money,
Madelyn. Little old ladies don't have enough to
pay rent at their assisted living communities.
Folks who were looking forward to a secure
retirement on a golf course are realizing that
they're going to have to keep working for years
to come. Parents who had scrimped and saved to
make sure their kids could go to college are
filling out applications for educational loans that
will leave them in debt for years. Families are
losing their homes. Charities that entrusted their
endowments to Sterling are being forced to cut
back programs or even close—"

"I know that!"

Gene shook his head sorrowfully and
continued, ignoring my interruption. "And every
time those people turn on the television, or boot
up the computer, or flip through a tabloid, they
see a picture of Sterling coming through the door
of his private plane—with you behind him. Or
Sterling at the helm of his yacht—with you
sitting next to him. Or Sterling, in his custom-
made tuxedo, walking down the red carpet at a
Broadway premiere—with you on his arm,
wearing a diamond choker from Harry
Winston—"

"I don't have it anymore! I had to give it up. All
my jewelry, everything Sterling ever gave me.

Even my engagement ring," I said through gritted teeth. The loss of the ring didn't bother me. If I hadn't had to surrender it to the court, I'd have happily thrown it in Sterling's face.

"No judge who cares about public opinion," Gene droned on, "and that's all of them, is going to stick out his neck to help the wife of Sterling Baron right now. No one cares about your problems, Madelyn. People have problems of their own."

"I understand that! And I feel terrible about it, but it's not my fault. If I'd known what Sterling was up to, I'd have left him, or stopped him, or . . . something, but I *didn't* know! I'm as much a victim of his schemes as anyone else," I said, ignoring the twitch at the corner of Gene's mouth.

"I've lost everything too. What am I supposed to do now? Where am I supposed to go? The government has seized all our assets, frozen all our accounts."

"So you were paying attention."

"Yes!" I snapped. "I know I'm not a Rhodes Scholar, Gene—Sterling was always so quick to remind me—but even I can understand words like 'Madelyn, you're broke'!"

Gene reached into the breast pocket of his jacket.

"Don't bother getting out your handkerchief, Gene. I'm not going to cry."

He stared at me, to see if I meant it. I stared back.

"Just tell me what I'm supposed to do now. What have I got left? There must be something."

Gene's eyes flitted over the surface of his desk as he looked for and eventually found a blue file folder. "There is," he said, opening the file. "You've got an account in your name, and your name only, which is a good thing, at the Connecticut National Bank."

"I do? Oh, wait! I do! I remember now. The money I'd saved before I married Sterling. I'd forgotten. It's been sitting there all this time?"

Gene nodded. "And gaining interest."

"Really? It can't be that much, though."

"It isn't," he said. "Connecticut National is pretty conservative. Still, your average return over the last thirty years was a little more than seven percent, which means your little nest egg is now worth $119,368.42."

A hundred and twenty thousand dollars. Less than the cost of my surrendered diamond choker. Less than the annual maintenance fee on the penthouse apartment I had to vacate by the end of the month, leaving everything behind—my furniture, my paintings, my china—everything but my clothes and what few possessions I could prove had been mine before my marriage.

"Cheer up, Madelyn. It could be worse. You could have invested your money with Sterling.

Then you'd really be broke." Gene started to chuckle, but I shot him a look filled with such loathing that he dropped his eyes and mumbled an apology.

"I was just trying to help you see the bright side."

"I'm sure."

He cleared his throat and shuffled the papers in my file. "I've got some more good news," he said officiously. "I lit a fire under my associates, got them to hurry along the probate of your grandmother's estate. It's done. You can claim your inheritance free and clear. Good timing, don't you think?"

My inheritance?

"What are you talking about? She cut me out of her will years ago, even before I met Sterling."

I felt a flush of heat in my chest. Even from the grave, Edna Beecher, the meanest, most disapproving old woman who ever walked the earth, could still upset me.

"She was bluffing? I can't believe it. How much did she leave to me?"

Gene held up his hand. "No money. She split that between her church and the Humane Society. Not that there was much to begin with. She left you the house—"

"The house? On Oak Leaf Lane?"

"Yes." Gene drew his brows together. "Did she have another house?"

"No . . . I just . . ." I said quietly, laying my hand over the warm place on my chest, "I'm just surprised. It's known as Beecher Cottage. Our family is distantly related to Harriet Beecher Stowe, the famous abolitionist who wrote *Uncle Tom's Cabin*, and her father, Lyman Beecher, and Henry Ward Beecher, her brother, preachers who were nearly as famous as Harriet in their day. They lived in Litchfield, east of New Bern.

"You see what pious Yankee stock I'm descended from," I said with a hollow laugh. "My grandmother was almost as proud of her Beecher heritage as she was disappointed in me. The cottage is the last remnant of that heritage. I never thought she'd leave it to me."

"According to her will, she didn't want to," Gene said, picking up a yellowed paper and scanning it. "But it seems the old lady couldn't bear to leave the family house in the hands of strangers, so, as the last Beecher standing, she felt she had no choice but to leave it to you. Along with many admonitions about avoiding the bad end she felt sure you'd come to." He lifted his gaze. "Shall I read them to you?"

"No, thanks. I've heard them all—a million times."

Gene closed the folder. "Ghostly harangues aside, it's all good for you. Gives you somewhere to go."

"Somewhere to go? Where?"

Gene blinked and shook his head slightly, as if amazed by my denseness. "New Bern, of course. You need a place to live and now you've got one—Beecher Cottage."

The hot spot on my chest grew hotter and larger, spreading up my neck to my cheeks. "New Bern? I'm not going back to New Bern!"

"I don't see as you have a lot of choice, Madelyn. You've got to live somewhere. Why not New Bern? I hear it's very picturesque. Lots of trees. Lots of scenery . . ."

Lots of memories.

"Most people would be thrilled to inherit a nice cottage in Connecticut."

"I'm not most people!" I snapped. "And I'm not going back to New Bern! Call a Realtor. Tell them to sell the house. Tell them I'll consider any offer."

Gene took off his glasses, revealing his impatience. "Don't be an idiot, Madelyn. The housing market has hit rock bottom. Or hadn't you heard?"

"Yes," I said, loathing Gene at least as much as he loathed me, "but there's got to be someone out there who is willing to buy it if the price is right."

Gene shook his head. "I talked to your grandmother's attorney, Franklin Spaulding. He told me that there hasn't been a real estate closing in New Bern for the last seven months. Nobody is buying, not at any price."

"But . . . there has to be . . . surely there's . . . I can't live in New Bern. . . ."

Gene smacked his hands against his mahogany desk. I jumped, startled.

"Madelyn! Will you listen to yourself? Not five minutes ago you were asking where you were going to live and what you were going to live on. I've gotten you a check for a hundred grand and a house and all you can do is gripe! If not for me, you'd be living in the state women's prison. I think a little gratitude is in order here, don't you?"

"I'm sorry, Gene," I said stiffly, knowing he was right, hating him for it.

I've been around the block enough times to know that the truth isn't always enough to protect the innocent. If I'd had a lawyer less talented than Eugene Janders, it was possible Sterling and I would both be living at the Metropolitan Correctional Center.

"I don't mean to appear unappreciative, but this is hard for me. I haven't had time to adjust."

"You'd better adjust, Madelyn, and quickly, because the party is over."

His tone was unsympathetic and his speech was frank. Clearly he thought this would be our last meeting and felt no need to mince words.

"You had a good ride with Sterling. When he married you, I thought you'd last a couple of years. Five, if you were lucky." He looked me up and down, slowly, insultingly. "Clearly you possess talents that can't be seen with the naked eye."

Four months ago, he'd never have dared to look at or speak to me that way. The balance of power had shifted. He knew it. I knew it. I said nothing.

Gene stood up at his desk. The meeting was over. He handed me a manila envelope.

"What's this?"

"A check, made out to you; a deed to the house; contact information for Wendy Perkins, the Realtor who is holding the keys; and a bill for legal services."

I looked at the papers. My jaw dropped open. "Nine thousand dollars?"

"I gave you a discount. No need to thank me."

I didn't.

I picked up my purse and my papers and turned to walk across Gene's hand-knotted silk rug, out the door, and into a future that would force me to return to the one place I'd hoped never to see again—New Bern, Connecticut.

2
Tessa Woodruff

Thirty-four years ago, Lee Woodruff and I promised to love each other till death did us part, in sickness and health, for richer or poorer. As a bride, I'm not sure I fully grasped what that was all about, but I do now. There's a reason they make you take vows—to hold you together through times like these.

It's not the fact that we're celebrating our anniversary over breakfast at the Blue Bean Coffee Shop and Bakery instead of dinner at a white tablecloth restaurant that's bothering me. I don't mind that. But I do mind that there's very little celebrating being done. We've never had an anniversary like this.

Lee rubbed his chin and narrowed his eyes as he stared at the legal pad. "I'm going to have to pull some money out of the 401(k) to pay Josh's tuition."

"That's supposed to be our retirement."

"The way things are looking, we'll never be able to retire anyway."

"Won't we have to pay a penalty if we take it out early?"

Lee looked up. "Can you think of another plan? If you can, I'm all ears."

"Honey," I said gently. "Don't be so hard on yourself. We're not the only ones this has happened to. A lot of people are in the same boat."

Lee picked up his coffee cup. "I should have seen this coming."

"How? You're an accountant, not a fortune-teller. Even the economists didn't see this coming."

Lee shook his head before taking a slurp of coffee. I looked at his plate. He'd hardly touched his food.

"My dad always said a man's first and last job is to protect his family. Right now, I'm almost glad he's not alive to see how far off the job I've fallen."

"Hey!" I said, giving him a nudge under the table. "This isn't all your doing. We've worked hard, side by side, all this time. Up until now, we've done all right. In fact, I think we make a pretty good team."

I smiled, hoping to steer the conversation onto more romantic ground. Lee wasn't picking up on my cues.

"We should have played it safe," he mused. "We should have stayed in Boston and let well enough alone instead of putting everything on the line for a crazy dream."

"Don't say that! I mean it, Lee! Don't ever say that!"

Lee put down his cup and looked at me with surprise. I'm not generally given to emotional outbursts. "I just meant that . . ."

"I know what you meant, but you're wrong. Moving to New Bern, finally working up the courage to start living our own dream instead of somebody else's, is the best thing we've ever done. When I look back and think what our lives were like before we started talking about the farm and the shop and what we wanted out of life . . ."

I shook my head and smeared a piece of toast with strawberry jam. "It's practically a miracle that we got to be married this long."

Lee frowned. "What are you trying to say? You think we'd have ended up divorced if we'd stayed in Massachusetts? You never said anything about being unhappy. . . ."

"I'm saying I didn't even *know* I was unhappy. And so were you. Admit it, you were."

"Well," he said slowly, "I don't know if I'd have put it in those terms exactly."

"How about bored? How about wondering if this was really all there was to life?"

Lee looked at me, a little smile of admission crossing his lips. "Well. Maybe sometimes. But I never thought of divorce."

"Neither did I, but you've got to wonder if, eventually, we might have. It's happened to so many people we know—Lena and John, Caroline and Stan, the Willises from across the street. They all said they'd 'grown apart.' I can't help but think that the problem was that they stopped growing together.

"Maybe this is a crazy idea," I said earnestly, "and maybe it won't work out, but I'm proud of us for trying. And if we end up broke, I can honestly say that I'd rather be broke with you than anyone I know. . . ."

Lee laughed. "Aw, shucks."

"I mean it, Lee Woodruff. I love you. More today than I ever have."

"But only half as much as tomorrow?"

"Are you trying to flirt with me?"

"I am. Is it working? Because I love you, too, Tessa. Now more than ever."

Our kiss was interrupted by the lilt of Charlie Donnelly's Irish brogue. "Ah, the lovebirds!" he called out as he approached our table, holding Evelyn's hand. "Lee is so overcome that he hasn't touched his pancakes. It's true love, I tell you, true love."

Evelyn laughed. "It would be for you, Charlie. I can't imagine the day when you'd ever be too overcome with anything to miss a meal."

Charlie is the owner of New Bern's most elegant restaurant, the Grill on the Green. He's a serious foodie, though you couldn't tell it to look at him. Charlie is as skinny as a rail. Evelyn owns the Cobbled Court Quilt Shop. It's located just a hop, skip, and a jump from For the Love of Lavender, my herbal gift shop. We know Charlie and Evelyn from various community and Chamber of Commerce gatherings, but not well, not enough so you could call us friends. After all these months, we still haven't made any close friends in New Bern. We've got to make more of an effort in that regard.

Evelyn and Charlie have recently returned from their honeymoon in Ireland. Not that they told us this personally—but New Bern is a small town. News travels fast.

"The waitress says congratulations are in order," Evelyn said. "How many years is it?"

"Thirty-four," Lee replied.

Charlie whistled in admiration. "Good for you! I hope we'll be able to say the same someday, and that when we do, we're both still able to walk."

"I'm sure you will," I said. "You look young and healthy enough."

"Being married to Evelyn is making me feel younger every day." Charlie beamed as he turned to Evelyn and gave her a loud smack on the lips.

"Behave yourself," Evelyn said, though not with any real conviction.

"Why? I never have before."

The door to the café opened and Jake Kaminski, owner of Kaminski's Hardware, came in. Jake is a big man, tall but trim, with broad shoulders and a long stride, the kind of guy people call a "man's man," though he's pretty popular with the ladies. Jake was a year ahead of me in school. He did a tour in Vietnam and has a glass eye to prove it. Even so, Jake is considered the most eligible bachelor in New Bern.

Jake lifted his hand when he spotted our group and walked toward the table.

"You're back! Can I get a kiss from the bride?" He gave Evelyn a big bear hug and a peck on the cheek. "How was the honeymoon?"

"Idyllic. Ireland is so beautiful. And Charlie's family was just wonderful. His sisters are just the kindest, sweetest women in the world."

Jake looked at Charlie and raised his left eyebrow. "Sweet? Really?" He winked at Evelyn. "You *sure* they're Charlie's sisters, related to him by blood and all?"

Charlie grinned. "Oh, yes. Grania, Maura, and I share the Donnelly DNA. The girls are carbon copies of my dear old dad, the kindest, most soft-spoken man in the county. Whereas I take after my mother, the woman who nagged him to an early grave."

Jake slapped him on the back and laughed. "Ah, Charlie, I've missed you. Welcome home. You both look great. Marriage must agree with you."

"I highly recommend it," Evelyn said, looking lovingly at her groom. "You should give it a try, Jake. With Charlie off the market, you must be New Bern's last bachelor standing. You'll wear yourself out."

"It's a tough job, Evelyn, but somebody's gotta do it. As far as marriage, the third time was the charm for me. Can't see risking a fourth," Jake said, then deftly changed the subject. "Lee, the water pump you ordered came in."

"Thanks. I'll pick it up later today."

"So, what's going on here?" Jake asked. "You having a secret meeting of the Chamber of Commerce or something? Between us, we own about half the businesses in New Bern. Speaking of business, how's yours? Mine's off."

Lee tilted his head and sucked some air in through his teeth. "Could be better. Tessa and I were just talking about that. Seems like no one is buying."

Charlie's grin faded and he nodded understandingly. "Don't worry too much. I've been in the restaurant business longer than you've been married. These things go in cycles, you know. Things will rebound."

"I hope so," I said. "And soon. If they don't, I'm not sure my store will be around by our next anniversary."

I felt Lee's eyes on me and turned to see him staring at me, his mouth a thin line.

Charlie glanced at Lee and said quickly, "Lee, I hear you're keeping chickens now. Have you got any eggs to sell to the restaurant? Or extra produce . . ."

"Eggs? Sure. We've got a lot of nice tomatoes and zucchini too. Of course," Lee said, "this time of year, so does everybody else."

"Yeah." Charlie laughed. "If you forget to lock your car, you'll come back and find your front seat filled with squash. What about cucumbers? Onions?"

"I've got plenty. Green beans too."

"Good! Bring some over today, will you? After the lunch crowd thins out."

"I'll be there," Lee promised.

"Tessa," Evelyn said, "Margot said you were thinking about taking her lap quilt class. I hope so. It's her first time teaching and she's so excited."

"I think I'm going to have to bow out," I said apologetically. "Business is so slow that I'm going to let my part-time girl go. Soon there'll be no one to run the shop but me. Anyway, it's probably not a great time for me to take up an expensive hobby. . . ."

Lee interrupted me. "Don't be silly. Take the class."

I shifted slightly in my chair and lowered my voice so the others wouldn't hear. "The class is sixty dollars. Plus, I'll need supplies and fabric. I don't think it's a good . . ."

Ignoring my whispered protests, Lee looked at Evelyn and said, "I can help out at the shop if need be. Don't worry. You can count her in."

I don't like having people speak for me. Lee knows that. I'd have said something but I didn't want to have an argument in public—especially on our anniversary. Evelyn and Charlie exchanged an uncomfortable glance.

"Well. Good," Evelyn said. "Come over when you get a chance and I'll help you choose your fabric. You're going to love quilting. It's a great way to get to know people."

We said our good-byes. Charlie and Evelyn left

the café hand in hand. Jake went to the bakery counter and bought a coffee and muffin to go. We waved as he left.

The tension was thick between us. I was still miffed, but for the sake of the day, I decided to let it go.

"Well, that's some good news, isn't it? I bet Charlie can buy up a lot of our extra vegetables and eggs."

Lee wasn't listening. "Why did you do that?"

"Do what?"

"Tell them business was bad, make out like we can't afford for you to take a little quilting class. We hardly know them!"

"But," I puffed, "you said it first. 'Things could be better.' You said so yourself. You're right, they could. What's so terrible about saying so? I don't know what you're so upset about."

"Because I don't want you going around telling everybody our private business! Start saying things like that and next thing you know it'll be all over town."

"They wouldn't do that. After all, they're in the same boat. Every business in town is struggling."

"Maybe, but I still don't like everybody knowing about our troubles, okay?"

"Okay." I shrugged. "Sorry."

Lee cut into his stack of cold pancakes. "It's not like we're destitute, you know. It's not like I can't take care of my family."

"Lee Woodruff, what are you talking about? I never said anything of the kind! I never even implied it. All I meant was—"

Eyes on his plate, he lifted his hand. "Let's just not talk about it, okay?"

Where had this come from? Lee and I have always shared everything from housework and child rearing to bill paying and breadwinning. Now he was acting like the responsibility for bringing home the family bacon rested on his shoulders alone. I didn't get it. Then again, Lee was the one with the accounting degree. If he was so concerned about our financial situation, maybe I should be too.

As if reading my thoughts, Lee looked up from his plate of pancakes and gave me an apologetic smile. "Don't worry so much. We'll figure it out."

"You think?"

"Sure." He raised his mug and clinked it against mine. "Happy anniversary, babe."

"Happy anniversary."

He smiled and gave me a look—*the* look. As always, my heart gave a lurch and my pulse raced. How does he do that?

"So," he said casually, "think you might consider closing a little early today?"

"Why should I? Got something special in mind?"

He grinned. "Yes, ma'am. Meet me in our

bedroom at six and I'll explain it to you in detail. Better yet, I'll show you. Shouldn't take more than a couple of hours."

"A couple of hours? Oh my. Sounds like we might need some provisions. Want me to pick up a bottle of champagne on my way home?"

He shook his head. "Already have one chilling in the refrigerator. Steaks too. I'm making dinner. That is, if you've got the energy to get out of bed and come to the table."

"And if I don't?"

"Then I guess I'll just have to serve you in bed."

"Think that's a good idea?" I asked. "Might lead to all kinds of things."

"It's a risk I'm willing to take," he said, his eyes twinkling as he reached for my hand, turned it palm up, and brushed his lips over the soft flesh of my wrist.

I blushed. Thirty-four years of marriage and he can still make me blush. It's embarrassing. And wonderful.

I leaned my head down and whispered in Lee's ear, "I wish it were six already."

"Me too."

The café was nearly empty. I sipped the last of my coffee and watched Lee finish his breakfast, wondering, not for the first time, how I'd managed to land such a handsome husband and how he managed to get even better looking as the years passed.

Behind the bakery counter, a waitress turned the radio to an AM news station.

"And in national news, Eugene Janders, attorney for Sterling Baron, requested his client's sentencing be postponed. Baron, who was convicted of masterminding a decades-long Ponzi scheme that bilked investors out of billions, could be sentenced to as many as one hundred years in prison. . . ."

"One hundred years," Lee said as he sopped up a drizzle of syrup with a fork full of pancakes. "Two hundred would be better. Sterling Baron? He's married to that friend of yours, right?"

"Former friend," I corrected him. "I haven't seen Madelyn since high school. I wonder how she's faring in all this."

Lee wiped his mouth with his napkin and got up from the table. "Fine, I'm sure. The rich get richer. They always do."

"The news said that the government had seized all their assets and she had to move out of her apartment. Nobody seems to know where she went."

Lee pulled out my chair for me. "She's probably flown off to Switzerland or the Caymans to cash out her offshore accounts and live in style far from the reach of the feds, someplace a million miles from New Bern."

3
Madelyn

The Realtor, Wendy Perkins, who apparently didn't know that rhinestone eyeglasses went out of style in 1968, offered to give me a tour of Beecher Cottage.

"It's got a few quirks," she said. "And a lot of deferred maintenance. The back door sticks. You've got to kick it hard on the bottom before you can lock it. The powder room is tucked under the main staircase. You'd think it was a closet if you didn't know better, and the hot and cold water is mixed up on the faucets."

"I know. My grandfather made a mistake when he was connecting the pipes and never fixed it. Don't worry," I said, taking the house keys from her outstretched hand. "I know every inch of the place. I spent ten years of my life there."

Wendy furrowed her brow, making her sparkly eyeglasses ride higher on the bridge of her nose. "That was before I came to town. But I knew your grandma. So funny that Edna never mentioned you."

I murmured noncommittally. I wasn't surprised in the least.

When I left New Bern, Edna said I was as good as dead to her. She was a woman of her word. From that day forward, I'm confident she never uttered my name again. In my current circumstances, it was for the best. Wendy didn't recognize me, either as Edna Beecher's granddaughter or as Sterling Baron's wife. With luck, neither would anyone else—at least for a while.

I'd resigned myself to the necessity of returning to New Bern, but I didn't plan to stay there one moment longer than I had to. At the first sign the housing market was improving, I'd sell the house and move somewhere, anywhere that wasn't New Bern.

In the meantime, my plan was to lie low and avoid attracting any attention to myself. People were bound to discover my connection to Sterling eventually. But by the time they did, I hoped Beecher Cottage would have a new owner and I'd be long gone. By then, maybe I actually *would* be Madelyn Beecher again.

Had it been possible, I'd have severed my ties with Sterling and the Baron name legally, permanently, and immediately. I should have divorced Sterling years before; heaven knew I had every reason to. His womanizing was legendary.

Sterling wasn't committed to the marriage, but the image it projected to the world suited his purposes and fed his ego. Sterling was having his cake and eating it, too, taking me with him to Broadway premieres and charity galas, smiling as we posed for the cameras, then sneaking away after for a late-night rendezvous with his blonde of the moment. Why would he want a divorce?

Why would I? Until recently, Sterling had been too rich to divorce. Yes, his serial unfaithfulness humiliated me, but you'd be surprised what you can learn to put up with when the price of humiliation is a lifestyle that, once upon a time, I hardly dared dream of—vacations to Tahiti on private islands, beachfront property in the Hamptons, a penthouse, a maid, a cook, a personal secretary, trips to Paris to view the spring couture collections and a blank check to buy whatever caught my eye. Shoes, and bags, and furs, and jewels, and, and, and . . . Anything and everything I wanted was mine simply by signing those two little words, "Madelyn Baron," on a check or credit card slip.

Did it make me happy? For a time. Sterling understood the arrangement and so did I. Yes, I had to turn a blind eye to his infidelities to maintain my lifestyle, but in my shoes, who wouldn't have done the same?

And even if I'd suddenly woken up one morning and decided that I could not tolerate this shameful farce of a marriage anymore (and there were many mornings when I did), a brief reflection on the chain of events that would follow if I presented Sterling with divorce papers quickly convinced me to think about something else.

Sterling is vindictive, and he hates to lose. If I tried to divorce him, I had no doubt he'd sic the legal wolves on me, with Gene Janders leading the pack, and wouldn't call them off until they'd ripped me to shreds financially and personally. And Sterling was not the only one who strayed during our marriage. The frequency and intensity of my assignations were minuscule compared to Sterling's and in every case my infidelity was a direct response to his. I don't believe in romance and I'm not interested in sex. I haven't been for a long time, if I ever was at all. I took lovers not for love, but to exact revenge on Sterling and, I suppose, to prove to myself that I was still desirable—to someone.

If I had tried to divorce Sterling before the arrest, I had no doubts about the outcome. Sterling would come out smelling like a rose and I would be left with nothing but a shredded reputation and a pile of legal bills, and all at an age when the odds of staging a second act range from remote to impossible.

Of course, that's exactly what happened anyway. Don't tell me that God has no sense of irony.

And so, now that Sterling has been rendered powerless to harm me, at least in court, I'm too poor to be free of him. I have all the attorney's bills I can handle at the moment. Divorcing Sterling will have to wait until I can beef up my bank account.

And the best way to do that, the only way I can see, is to focus on sprucing up the cottage so it will sell quickly and I can leave New Bern, this time forever. I want no part of this place. I never did.

But fortunately for me, other people feel differently. For some people, a quiet little village in New England is their dream location. Soft market or no, it couldn't be *that* hard to sell the house. Gene said there was no chance of it, but lawyers are always pessimistic; imagining worst-case scenarios is part of the job. Gene might be a good attorney, but that didn't make him an expert on Connecticut real estate, did it? Besides, he'd never even seen my grandmother's house.

Down market or no, as I drove in the direction of Oak Leaf Lane, I felt optimistic. Even in a bad economy, a beautiful house can always attract a buyer, and no matter the memories connected with it, Beecher Cottage was a truly beautiful old house.

Once.

Sitting behind the wheel of the new, very used Volvo wagon I'd purchased with eight thousand dollars from my fast-dwindling bank account, I drove up and down Oak Leaf Lane twice before pulling to the curb and realizing that the place with the broken fence posts, missing shingles, and overgrown hedges really was Grandma Edna's old house—now mine.

Dear God. What had happened?

I climbed out of the car, took my suitcases out of the back, and stood looking at what had once been the prettiest house on the block.

The grass hadn't been cut in months; the flower beds were choked with weeds. Two windows were broken and the shutters were missing slats. One window was missing the shutters entirely. And the roof . . . the only thing that appeared to be holding the remaining shingles in place was a thick layer of blackish green moss.

If this was what the exterior looked like, I could only imagine the condition of the interior. My plan to spruce up the old place and resell the house in short order crumbled—and my confidence with it. This was going to be a huge project. I stood on the sidewalk making a mental to-do list and growing more discouraged by the second.

Next door, at a house that used to belong to the McKenzies but was now a dental office, a door opened. A woman walked out, glancing curiously at me as she got into her car. Oak Leaf Lane was busier than it had been when I was a child. Half the houses on the street had been turned into offices. Lying low was going to prove harder than I'd imagined. Of course, standing out on the sidewalk surrounded by a pile of Louis Vuitton luggage wasn't exactly helping me fly in under the radar.

I opened the creaky garden gate and carried my bags up the pathway to the porch, noting that many of the bricks were either missing or crumbling to dust and that a web of weeds was growing between the others. The steps were sound. A couple of the boards were unpainted, as if they'd been replaced recently. The porch was a different story. The wooden planks felt soft under my feet, squashy and waterlogged. I walked carefully, testing each board before I stepped, wondering if they would support my weight.

The key stuck in the lock, but after I jiggled it a few times it gave way with a metallic click. I carried my bags over the threshold and dropped them on the floor, raising a cloud of dust.

The foyer was exactly as I remembered: dark, gloomy, cheerless. The wallpaper, with its rows of hideous brownish pink cabbage roses, was as ugly as it had been when I was a child, except now it was peeling in spots. A moldy smell permeated the room and made me sneeze. I reached out to flip on the light switch. Once. Twice. Three times. Nothing happened.

"Great! That's just great!" I kicked one of my suitcases as hard as I could. "Sterling Baron! It's a good thing you're locked up in a nice, safe jail cell! Because if you were here I'd kick you into next week, you stupid, worthless, selfish son of a—"

Maybe I imagined it, but somewhere on the upper floor of the old house, I could have sworn I heard a door slam. In my mind I heard the echo of her voice, her shrieking, incongruously loud and piercing graveled voice, dripping disapproval, as it always had.

"Watch your mouth! I will not put up with that kind of filthy talk, do you hear me? Come here. I'm going to slap you into next week. Don't you dare back away when I tell you to come! If you can't clean up your mouth, then I'll just have to do it for you."

My cheek burned hot and angry from the memory of those slaps and an acrid taste filled my mouth, the flavor of humiliation, soap, and hatred.

I spun around, grabbed an edge of peeling wallpaper, and pulled as hard as I could. A wide, jagged strip came away from the wall with a satisfying rip, exposing a patch of white amid the thorny stems and leaves of hideous brown.

4
Tessa

After breakfast, I walked Lee to his truck, a beat-up green and white heap named Mustang Sally he'd bought for eight hundred dollars and a she-goat.

The tires were newish and there was only a little rust on the bed, which is why Lee thought it was a steal, even though it didn't run. The man who sold it to him towed it to our place. After spending three weeks under the hood and three hundred and fifty dollars in replacement parts, the engine ran, loudly. Idling, Mustang Sally sounds like a snowblower on steroids. When she's in gear it's worse. I think Lee likes it that way.

He also likes Spitz, our black-and-white border collie, who was sitting up in the back of the truck, tongue out, eyes bright, excited about taking a ride. Spitz is another of Lee's quirky finds. He bought her as a pup with the idea that she'd help in rounding up the other animals; border collies are bred to have strong herding instincts. Spitz spends hours pacing back and forth outside the goat enclosure, eyes glued to their every move. But inside the fence, she has no clue, just zooms around the pen, barking at the goats as though challenging them to a race. At first they were scared of her, but now they just ignore her. Poor Spitz. She couldn't herd her way out of a paper bag, but she's a good dog.

Spitz barked as Lee climbed into the truck cab, turned the key in the ignition, and pressed the gas pedal a few times, coaxing the engine to catch.

"Six o'clock! Our bedroom!" He shouted to be heard over the rattle and knock of Mustang Sally's engine. "You, me, a bottle of champagne, and a night to remember!"

I curled my fingers over the edge of the open window, raised myself up on my toes, and puckered my lips for a kiss.

"Six o'clock!" I shouted before stepping onto the sidewalk. He winked as he shifted gears and hit the gas, his engine so loud that people on the street turned to look as he drove off.

Sometimes I find it hard to remember that this manly man in the beat-up pickup, his handsome face tanned by wind and weather, his hands capable and calloused by work, is the same man who used to spend his days sitting behind a computer screen tallying up debits and credits under the sickly glow of fluorescent lighting. He is now, as he was then, a good man, a hard worker, faithful and responsible and the true love of my life. But he's changed since we moved to New Bern, and though Lee may not realize this, it's a change for the better.

Leaving two secure corporate jobs with benefits to grow tomatoes and sell potpourri might sound crazy and impulsive, but it wasn't something we did on a whim. Lee and I discussed it for months before we took the plunge, planning everything out carefully, making budgets and timelines and lists both pro and con. But if it doesn't work out according to our carefully laid plans, I'm worried that Lee will blame me. We made this decision together, but I was the one who started the ball rolling.

Fall's official start was still a few weeks off, but as I walked east on Commerce Street, the morning air felt crisp though the sun was shining brightly. Looking across the street toward the Green, I spied a squirrel scurrying through the grass, pushing aside a sparse blanket of yellowed leaves in search of nuts, finding none, then sitting up on its hind legs and staring up at the branches of the tree expectantly. And just in case I'd missed the signs of impending autumn, an ancient yellow school bus pulled up at the corner and opened its doors with a mechanical sigh. It was the first day of school. I'd forgotten. When I was a child, school didn't start until after Labor Day.

I stopped to watch the kids with slick-combed hair and new backpacks pile onto the bus. One little guy in particular caught my attention. He had freckles and a cowlick, like Josh did when he was little. Judging from the number of times his mother blinked her eyes as she waved to him through the window and the way she clutched at the hand of his baby brother, this was Freckle Face's first day of first grade.

The doors sighed and closed as the last tiny scholar climbed aboard. The mothers waved frantically as the bus shuddered and pulled away with its precious cargo. After Freckle Face's bus rounded the corner and was safely out of sight, his mother's face crumpled like discarded tissue paper and she bent down to pick up her youngest, a chubby, dimple-kneed toddler, and crushed him to her breast. The tiny boy squirmed in her arms and protested, "Mommy! Yer squashin' me!" as the other mothers encircled the woman to offer Kleenex and comfort.

If I wasn't already late opening the shop, I might have crossed the street and joined them. I knew just how she felt. I've stood at the bus stop and the airport, proud and bereft, smiling through tears and waving for all I was worth as my child set out on adventures of his own with barely a backward glance—just as he should.

It all goes too fast. I don't blame her for clinging to her remaining baby as though she'd never let him go. If I could, I'd have done the same.

Josh was supposed to be one of three. That was the plan. But we decided to save up for a nicer, larger house before starting our family. It seemed like the responsible thing to do and, after all, we had plenty of time. But it took longer to get pregnant than we'd supposed, a lot longer. I had one miscarriage before Josh was born and two after.

By the time Josh started kindergarten, I knew there would be no other children. I was disappointed but not bitter. We had Josh, and I absolutely loved being a parent. So did Lee. My only complaint about motherhood was that it passed too quickly. When college catalogs started showing up in the mailbox with Josh's name on them, I had to face facts: Our nest would soon be empty. Those were hard days for me, thoughtful days.

I spent a lot of time sitting and thinking in the two always-empty bedrooms of the four-bedroom house we'd put off having children to buy. What if we hadn't been so careful? What if we had followed our hearts instead of our heads and begun our family sooner? Might those empty rooms have been occupied by another son? A daughter? Twins?

It was too late to do anything about it, but . . . what if? How different might our lives have been if we'd taken a few more chances? Stepped on the cracks in the sidewalk? Not all the time, but sometimes. Would we have been happier? More successful? Cast a bigger shadow? The past was past, but what about the future? On the backside of fifty, was it too late to change?

At the time, I believed it was. But one day, as I was cleaning out a closet in one of those empty bedrooms, I came across a box of memorabilia that changed my mind. Inside, I discovered a picture of Madelyn Beecher and myself, sitting on the steps of my parents' front porch on the day after the pig rescue. My legs were covered with itchy red splotches, but I was grinning from ear to ear. It was such a little thing, but I could still remember how good it had felt to do something wild and unpredictable and just a little bit dangerous.

I dug the picture out of the box and when I went to bed that night, I showed it to Lee and told him all about my wondering and worries, my questions about what if and what now. I was surprised to learn that Lee had many of the same questions, that like me, he'd been wondering what comes after the empty nest. But the biggest surprise came when my husband, the mild-mannered and rational accountant, man of sharpened pencils and creased trousers, admitted to a secret and seemingly irrational desire.

"A farmer? You want to be a farmer?" I laughed, looking at my husband's solid-citizen blue blazer and sober striped tie hanging neatly over the back of a chair, mentally replacing them with dirty denim overalls and a flannel shirt. "Seriously?"

"I used to spend every summer up in Vermont, on Uncle Dwayne's farm. I'd pick apples and milk cows, hoe corn and onions. I loved it. And," he said, looking a little offended, "I was actually pretty good at it."

"I'm sure you were." I'd never pictured Lee as a farmer, but I was sure if he decided to be a farmer, he'd be a good one.

"Uncle Dwayne used to talk to me about taking over the place after he died."

"Why didn't you?"

"Dad convinced me that farming was a dead-end profession. I suppose he was right, but," Lee said wistfully, "I kind of wish I'd given it a try, just to see for myself. . . ."

Doesn't that just take the cake? Lee and I were even more compatible than I'd suspected.

I'd never considered farming as a dream vocation, but I loved gardening, especially herb gardening. A few years previously, I'd begun experimenting with blending the herbs into sweetly scented concoctions and oils to infuse all kinds of soaps, lotions, and creams, but I considered it a hobby. Just like gardening.

Nothing was settled that night. Even at our most impetuous, Lee and I needed time to take the leap. But after months of late-night discussions and dream spinning, we reached a decision.

Lee loved farming. I loved working with herbs.

If we combined those two loves into a reasonable business plan, we ought to be able to figure out a way to make a living doing them—not a handsome living, but enough. Josh's college tuition was safely tucked away, and once he was launched, we wouldn't need as much income, especially if we moved to the country, where the cost of living would be lower. After doing the math and working out a plan, we finally decided to make the break.

We began spending weekends driving around New England, looking for a small farm on a few acres of good soil, with room enough for me to grow my herbs and Lee to grow his crops, plus keep goats and chickens. The farm had to be near a town, someplace I could open a shop. It didn't have to be a big town but it needed to have a real downtown area with good walk-by traffic and well-located storefronts available at an affordable rent. Sounds easy enough, but it wasn't. Lee and I must have visited twenty little towns without finding what we were looking for.

We were just about ready to give up when I received an invitation to a class reunion at my old high school back in New Bern. After my graduation my folks, lured by warm weather and low taxes, had moved to Florida. Consequently, I hadn't been back to New Bern in years or kept in touch with any of my old classmates.

Thank heaven for Sandy Janetta, chair of the

New Bern High reunion committee, and her determination to track down every member of our graduating class. If not for her, we might never have gone to New Bern and never have met Sandy's husband, Bob, a Realtor who knew of a perfect farm on the outskirts of town with sixteen acres of good land, a three-bedroom, two-bath antique farmhouse with a wood-shingled roof and a beehive oven, plus a barn and a big sunroom that would serve as my workshop. Bob also knew that the owners of an antique shop on Maple Street were planning on retiring and the storefront would soon be available to rent. We couldn't believe our good fortune.

As Lee and I drove back to Massachusetts, we laughed and sang along with the radio. Lee reached out to squeeze my hand and said, "I think all those years spent nose to the grindstone are about to pay off. I think we're about to find our happy ending."

I thought so too. And in my heart, I still believe it. Things are bound to get better. Charlie Donnelly said they would, that we were just in a down business cycle. We had a plan, a good one. The bank had increased my line of credit based on that plan, all printed out in colored ink with pie charts and spreadsheets and month-by-month sales projections. Not that we'd met any of those projections since our third month in business, but we would. Eventually. We just had to stick to our plan. I'd never failed at anything and I wasn't planning on starting now.

As I rounded the corner, I shoved my hands in my pockets and looked down, deliberately stepping on every crack in the sidewalk, only lifting my head when I heard someone call my name.

5
Tessa

Wouldn't you know it? The first time I come to work late is also the first time I have customers waiting for me to open.

"There you are, Tessa!" Reverend Tucker waved and his face split into a wide smile, his teeth as white as the clerical collar around his neck. "Good morning! Beautiful day, isn't it?"

The woman who was with him had been standing with her face close to the shop window, hands cupped near her eyes to block the sunlight as she peered through the glass. She was blond and wore a pink and green paisley skirt with a matching pink sweater set. It wasn't until she unfolded herself to her full height, probably close to six feet, and turned her sparkling blue eyes on me that I recognized her.

"You know Margot Matthews, don't you?"

"Yes, of course. Nice to see you again, Margot."

I do know Margot, but not well. She works at Cobbled Court Quilts with Evelyn, but I'd met her at the New Bern Community Church. On my first Sunday there, she invited me to the coffee hour and introduced me around. We exchange greetings and small talk every Sunday. Last week she'd told me about her quilting class and urged me to sign up. I'd promised to think about it but hadn't committed. Soon Evelyn would tell her I was in, but I simply had to wiggle out of it. No matter what Lee said, I didn't have enough time, money, or talent to take up quilting. I'd explain that to Margot, but another day. She seemed so nice. I hated to disappoint her.

Reverend Tucker was nice too. He's about my age, with steel gray hair, glasses that are always slipping to the end of his nose, and a friendly, natural way of expressing himself in and out of the pulpit. But I've always been nervous around ministers, even ones as nice as Reverend Tucker. Seeing a clergyman always makes me think about things I shouldn't have done but did and things I should do but haven't.

What did they want? Were they part of the church welcoming committee? Or the finance committee? Maybe, once you'd attended a certain number of times, they expected you to start paying a tithe to the church? I hated to disappoint them, but right now, ten percent of my annual income was a negative number.

"It's good to see you again, Tessa. Reverend Tucker and I are out doing a little church business and we thought we'd start with you. Do you mind if we come in?"

"Sure. Just let me unlock the door." I fumbled around in my purse, feeling awkward for keeping them standing there while I hunted for my keys, which, naturally, meant that it took me forever to find them.

Margot turned toward my display window. "You've got such a sweet shop, Tessa. I dropped in to see you a couple of weeks ago. You were out, but someone else helped me." Margot screwed her eyes shut and tapped a finger against her lips, trying to jar her memory. "Emily? I think that was her name."

"Emily," I confirmed, grateful for the cover of Margot's chatter. Where *were* my keys? This was becoming embarrassing. "She's been helping me out over the summer." I didn't bother to add that when Emily returned to college in a couple of weeks, I wouldn't be replacing her. I couldn't afford to.

"Well, I just loved the lavender body lotion and peppermint lip balm she sold me. Reverend, have you been in Tessa's shop before? She has the most wonderful products made from herbs she grows herself. Isn't that right, Tessa?"

"Oh?" the good reverend replied. "Sharon's birthday is coming up. Maybe I can get her present here."

"Found them!" I nearly shouted with relief as I yanked my key ring out from a side pocket of my handbag and held it aloft.

I opened the door and walked through the shop, turning on lights. One of the things I love about this space is the large, many-paned windows that face the street. They give the shop a homey, old-fashioned look and a lot of natural light. My feeling is, the more light the better. That's why, before we opened for business, we took down all the old dark paneling and replaced it with a rough-textured white plaster, restained the dark floors with alternating eighteen-inch squares of white and mossy green in a checkerboard pattern that let the natural grain of the wood show through, then painted all the wood and glass display cabinets white. Finally, we'd removed the fluorescent lighting and replaced it with lots and lots of spotlights in ceiling cans, which flooded the room with clean, white light. Walking into this room is like walking over clouds on a clear day, surrounded by sunlight above and around, with glimpses of the green earth below.

Reverend Tucker stopped in the middle of the room, next to the candle display, and looked around. "I remember this shop back when Edwin Hargrove had his antique business here. Everything was so gloomy. The place smelled like mold and wet dog."

The reverend wasn't the first person to mention

this. Apparently, Mr. Hargrove had a shop dog, a golden retriever who liked to roll in mud puddles.

"What a difference," he continued. "It's so bright and it smells so fresh. Not at all perfumey," he said in a slightly surprised tone.

"I use real plants and herbs for my products, no artificial perfumes. Lavender is our most popular scent, but I make products using rosemary, peppermint, lemongrass, bergamot, clary sage, roses, gardenia, and all kinds of spices and citrus peels too."

"Smell this!" Margot said eagerly, taking the cap off a tester of lavender lotion and holding it under the minister's nose. "Sharon would love it."

He sniffed at the bottle. "Very nice. Does this come in some sort of gift basket? I'm not very good at wrapping things."

Three minutes later, I'd made my first sale of the day. Mrs. Tucker would be getting a Lavender Luxury Basket for her birthday, a bottle of lavender body lotion with matching glycerine soap, lavender sugar scrub, and a candle, prettily arranged in a white wicker basket and tied with a purple tulle bow.

"This is perfect," Reverend Tucker said as he shoved his change into his pocket. "Last birthday I bought Sharon a coffee grinder. Didn't go over well."

Margot looked at me with eyebrows raised and

lips pressed together, trying to suppress a smile. I had to look away to keep from laughing. Under his starched clerical collar, Reverend Tucker was a man like any other, one who hadn't heard the "never get your wife anything that plugs in" rule.

"Feel free to come back anytime you need a gift, Reverend. I'm happy to help."

"Thank you, Tessa. I will." He picked up his shopping bag and walked away from the counter, getting halfway to the door before Margot stopped him.

"Reverend? Aren't you forgetting something?"

He looked at her blankly for a moment, and then spun around to face me. "Oh yes! The fund-raiser! The church is hosting a fund-raiser in September, a benefit for the Stanton Center and New Beginnings. Their donations have been down this year, and if they can't raise some money, they'll have to begin cutting back programs."

The Stanton Center is our local shelter for women and children who've been victims of domestic violence and New Beginnings is an offshoot of that, a community center offering counseling, career training, and enrichment classes for victims of domestic violence or, as space allows, any woman who needs help making a fresh start. They do wonderful work. In other circumstances I'd be happy to help, but . . .

"I'm sorry, Reverend, but it hasn't been a very good year for me. I just can't make any donations right now. I wish I could."

"Oh, no. We're not asking for money," Margot assured me. "The church is sponsoring a country fair on our grounds and on the town Green in September. We'll have a used book sale, a quilt show and raffle, cakewalk, carnival games and pony rides for children, a soup-and-salad luncheon, and a silent auction. It's going to be a lot of fun, and since we'll be having it on the peak fall foliage weekend, we're hoping to attract a lot of tourists. . . ."

"And tourist dollars," the reverend added. "We're hoping to raise six thousand dollars over the weekend. Would you be willing to donate an item for the auction?"

"Absolutely!" I said. "What a wonderful idea." I started looking around the shop, searching for items that might attract high bids.

"How about another Lavender Luxury Basket?" I asked, pulling one off the shelf without waiting for an answer. "And you said there will be children? I've got a cute basket with bubble bath and shampoo, a terry cloth towel, and a rubber duck."

"Oh, that is darling!" Margot exclaimed, her eyes laughing. "Are you sure you can afford to donate two items?"

"Sure. It's all for a good cause. Candles are

always popular, especially in the fall. What if I put together a whole basket of those?"

By the time Margot and Reverend Tucker were ready to leave, I'd promised three baskets for the silent auction, as many gallons of peppermint iced tea as they'd need for the luncheon, and a bushel of vegetables for making soup. I was sure Lee wouldn't mind.

"See you on Sunday," Margot said as I walked them to the door. "You know, we really should get together for lunch sometime."

"We should."

"Thank you again," Reverend Tucker said as he shook my hand. "And tell your husband I said thank you to him as well. I hope we'll see him in church sometime."

"Yes," I said, knowing it would never happen. "That would be nice."

6
Madelyn

I am not a big drinker. Not anymore.

Many years ago I learned my lesson the hard way and haven't overindulged since. I do enjoy a glass of wine, two at the most, with dinner, but I haven't had a hangover since I lived in New Bern.

Ironic, isn't it? The first hangover I've had in

thirty-eight years occurred on my first morning back in New Bern, the scene of my last hangover. There's got to be some sort of deep celestial significance to all that, but as the sun beamed through the bedroom window and directly into my eyes, I was too groggy to figure out what it might be.

I rolled on my side and tried to go back to sleep, but the movement made my head pound. My eyeballs were a size too large and my tongue felt like it was made from dryer lint. I groaned aloud before rolling onto my back again, my arm flopping against the mattress and raising a flotilla of dust motes into the column of sunlight.

Moving slowly to minimize the jostling of my throbbing head, I got out of bed, went into the bathroom, and scooped water in my mouth with my hands. I took four aspirin tablets from the bottle in my cosmetics bag and washed them down with a few more scoops of water. The aspirin would soon dull the ache in my head, but it wasn't going to do a thing for my queasy stomach.

It seems counterintuitive to put quantities of greasy food into a nauseous stomach, but the experiences of my misspent youth had taught me that was exactly what I needed to do. But there was no food in the house. That, along with hatred for my husband and an extended wade in the wallow of self-pity, was part of the reason I was in this condition.

After furiously tearing off strip after strip of ugly brown wallpaper from the foyer yesterday and screaming a few more choice words at the absent company who I felt most deserved them— Sterling, the ghost of Edna Beecher, Eugene Janders, the entire federal government, God—I felt no better. Seeking relief, I pulled a bottle of Delamain Extra cognac out of my luggage and poured myself a drink, a big one.

While I was packing my things under the watchful eyes of the federal agent who was there to make sure I didn't take anything that wasn't "mine," I'd spotted the bottle of Delamain sitting on a countertop. When the agent's back was turned I slipped it into my voluminous handbag, but only as an act of defiance. I don't even like cognac.

However, desperate times . . .

Halfway through my second glass, I realized I really should eat something, but the cupboards and refrigerator were bare. By that time, driving to the supermarket on the edge of town was out of the question—the last thing I needed was a ticket for DUI—and the shops within walking distance were already closed for the night. Riffling through my purse, I'd found two tiny bags of peanuts left over from my last airline trip. I sat down in the dark kitchen and ate them one by one, washing each down with a swig of cognac.

Stupid. And now I was paying the price.

I stood over the commode, considered throwing up, decided against it, then pulled on a pair of slacks and a sweater before going downstairs to look through the kitchen cupboards, confirming what I already knew. There wasn't a scrap of food in the house. If I wanted breakfast, I was going to have to go out and buy some.

The thought of wheeling a shopping cart through the aisle of the grocery store was more than I could face. So I fished my darkest pair of sunglasses from the bottom of my purse, hid my disheveled hair under a baseball cap, and walked downtown in search of a café. I knew I shouldn't be spending money eating out, so I promised myself that starting tomorrow, I'd be frugal. Besides, I reasoned, the fresh air might do me good.

It did.

Summer had a few days left to run, but the morning chill made it clear that fall was fast approaching. Here and there, the trees showed spots of yellow and pale orange. A gust of wind in the branches made a rustling sound, as if the leaves were made from paper. The sun shone bright and clear in a sky of brilliant blue that, even through the shaded lenses of my glasses, was impossible to ignore.

Pretty. I had forgotten.

New Bern, with its tree-lined streets, neatly

trimmed hedges, and rows of quaint white-clapboarded, black-shuttered antique houses—real antiques, not ersatz "reproductions" that never quite look or feel like the real deal—was very pretty indeed. A picture postcard for "the good old days." Charming.

It was easy to see why tourists in search of the quintessential New England village and city dwellers looking for a peaceful weekend retreat put New Bern on their not-to-be-missed list. In their shoes, I'd feel the same. And for a moment, even with my head aching and the light filtered through smoke-colored lenses, I did. For just a minute, the length of the village block where the white clapboard houses with trimmed hedges give way to a row of wide-windowed, no-chains-allowed storefronts, I allowed myself to be charmed by New Bern.

But only for a minute.

I heard her a split second before I saw her, a disembodied voice blown around the street corner. Even all these years later, there was no mistaking it—that upper-crust, eastern-seaboard, non-rhotic accent of hers, all absent "Rs" and extended vowels, delivered with the lower jaw slightly jutted and the eyebrows slightly raised, a voice that could only belong to Abigail Burgess Wynne.

"I know I said I'd be there, darling, and I will be. I just want to stop by the quilt shop and say

86

hello to Evelyn. I haven't seen her since she got back from Ireland."

She rounded the corner, cell phone to her ear, walking briskly, wearing good wool slacks, pearls, and a summer-weight cashmere sweater over a starched snow white blouse, not a hair out of place. That had not changed. I hadn't supposed it would.

She was older but not yet old. There were more lines around her mouth and her hair was pure platinum now, pulled into a low knot at the back of her neck, but there was something about her expression, her eyes. . . . Strangely, she looked almost younger than she had at our last meeting.

All these years later, I could remember every wounding word she'd uttered, every stabbing inflection of her voice, the utter loathing in each glance of her piercing, icy eyes.

Now she sounded relaxed, happy, and there was a definite spring in her step. She hustled past me without a glance, took a sharp right turn into the old Cobbled Court, and disappeared, the sound of her voice and the echo of her heels on cold gray stones fading behind me.

I walked past the door of the café until I was sure she was gone, and then stopped, reaching my palm out to rest against a gritty red-brick wall. My heart was racing and the aspirin-dulled pain in my head was back. The rest of me felt numb. I couldn't keep standing there on the street, but I couldn't force myself to go inside the café either. Instead, I made an about-face, fighting off nausea as I retraced my steps back down Oak Leaf Lane. The crisp sunny morning and the chittering birds mocked my retreat.

Three doors from my destination I looked up and saw it—the painted porch of the old Kover house—and the memories . . . all those awful memories came flooding back.

Why was I here? The scene of my most humiliating failures? Of all the cities, towns, and villages in the world, why did I find myself a refugee in the one place that never welcomed me, filled with people and the memories of people who never wanted me? Why? What kind of cosmic joke was God playing now?

Eyes glued to the sidewalk, I walked the last half block to Edna's garden gate with quickened steps, went inside the house and back to bed, pulling the covers over my head to block out the light and the memories—all the memories.

Impossible.

7
Madelyn

I slept off the cognac and dreamed about my dad. I didn't remember my dream, I never do. But it was something about Dad and a ship. Dad on a ship. Something like that.

The ocean is more than an hour's drive from New Bern. Even so, Dad wanted to be a ship captain when he grew up. It didn't work out. Instead, he became a shipbuilder, actually a submarine builder. He worked for the Electric Boat Company, out of Groton, Connecticut, where I grew up. When I was nine he was knocked unconscious by a piece of swinging steel and never woke up. Grandma Edna came to Groton after Dad's accident. She had to. There was no one else.

I kept vigil in the hospital waiting area, a room with gunmetal gray tile on the floors and stiff plastic sofas, where people dozed or wept or drank cardboard cups of coffee bought from the vending machine while keeping one ear tuned for the sound of nurses in rubber-soled shoes, bringing news. They wouldn't let me in Dad's room, not until the last day, when I was told to come and say good-bye. It didn't matter. Dad was already gone. He had been from the moment that slab of metal cracked his skull. The tubes and screens and beeping monitors had only delayed the inevitable.

It was terrible to see him like that, and frightening. I tried to put my hand into Edna's, but she pulled back and closed her fist on empty air, pulling herself in as tight and hard as a pillar of polished marble. We'd scarcely exchanged a score of words since she arrived in Groton but, somehow, I already knew she could never forgive me. Though I didn't know why. Not yet.

I never met my mother. Until Dad died, I didn't know where she was or who she was. Edna lost no time filling me in on the details of my unplanned arrival in this world. The history she imparted was one-sided and colored by hate, but it's all I have to go on. Hers was the only voice in the room.

My father was bright and a good student, good enough to be accepted into the United States Merchant Marine Academy in Kings Point, New York, on Long Island. The competition for admission was fierce and with good reason: tuition was free. The family would never have been able to pay for Dad's education otherwise.

The courses were demanding and the discipline was rigorous, but there was still time for Dad and his shipmates to go into Manhattan on weekends. He met my mother in Greenwich Village, at the

White Horse Tavern, where beatnik poets, writers, and hangers-on liked to drink. In the same year my parents met, the poet Dylan Thomas would collapse at the White Horse Tavern. He died a few days later.

My mother made fun of Dad's short midshipman's haircut and starched uniform, but he didn't care. He was smitten. Every time he could get leave, Dad made a beeline for the city so he could see her.

Edna heaped the whole blame for all that happened on my mother, but I have my doubts. Dad was a good man, but he *was* a man, and young, subject to the same tricks and traps of biology as any other healthy, normal, not-quite-twenty-year-old male. I'm sure my mother didn't have to tie him down to get him to sleep with her, but you could never have gotten Edna to believe it.

I'm not saying my mother was an angel. I don't know what she was; I never met her. Neither had Edna, but that didn't stop her from painting my mother as a conniving tramp who had lured my father into her bed—and probably plenty of other men as well. Scores of them. Who knew which of my mother's revolving door of lovers fathered me?

"You don't look like anyone on *our* side of the family, that's for certain," she'd say. "A girl like that could have put anything over on him.

Tommy was always too softhearted for his own good."

I suppose it's possible, but I *do* have his eyes. As far as my mother being able to put something over on him? That's possible, too.

Within a few months of meeting Dad, my mother was pregnant. Whether Dad was the only one or only one of many, I have no idea. But he insisted on "doing the right thing" and marrying my mother.

I'm a little unclear on what happened next, but I know the wedding never took place. In due course, my mother gave birth, dumped me with Dad, and disappeared, never to be heard from again. Dad dropped out of school to care for me, which made my grandparents furious. It didn't happen until I was three, but Edna insisted that stress over Dad's quitting school caused my grandfather's fatal heart attack.

Dad rented a house in Groton and found a job in maritime construction. Welding hatches onto submarines was as close as he'd ever come to seafaring. His hours could be strange, but the work was steady. The Cold War was good for business.

Dad hired a babysitter, Mrs. O'Dell, to look after me while he was working. Other than that, it was just Dad and I, living in a little house just a few blocks from the Connecticut shoreline. Most of the time, I was happy.

When I was in the second grade, my school held

a mother-daughter tea. Mrs. O'Dell offered to go with me, but Dad took the day off work and came himself. He was the only father there. I remember how funny he looked sitting in a second-grader-sized chair, drinking pink lemonade and eating a pink-frosted cookie shaped like a tulip. I remember all the women in the room smiling as they looked at him, and feeling so proud of him. Dad was very good-looking.

Amelia Jessup's desk sat next to mine. Her mother looked at my father, smiled, and said, "Amelia, aren't you going to introduce me to your classmate?"

"This is Madelyn Beecher," Amelia replied dutifully. "And this is her father, Mr. Beecher." Smiles and handshakes were exchanged between the adults.

Then Amelia turned to her mother, and in that hoarse stage whisper that seven-year-olds have, she rasped, "Madelyn's father came because she doesn't have a mother. But Teacher said we aren't supposed to talk about it."

The silence that followed was blaring. I remember hearing the clock ticking and nothing else. Amelia's mother's cheeks flamed bright red. After a moment that seemed to hang suspended in time, the teacher announced that there was more lemonade in the pitcher and then made a great show of filling everyone's glass.

That was the first time in my life that I

93

remembered feeling shame. Funny thing is, I didn't even understand what I was supposed to be ashamed of. That night, when he was tucking me into bed, for the first time, I asked Dad about my mother.

"Why didn't she want me?"

"*I* want you," he said. "Always did. Always will. Who else do we need? We've got each other, don't we?"

I nodded.

"Well, all right then. That's the deal. Anybody who doesn't like it can just go to hell."

Dad wasn't a man of many words, but the fierce flame of love in his eyes was eloquent. I didn't ask about my mother again.

Dad never spoke to or of his parents. Until Mrs. O'Dell called Edna after Dad's accident, I never knew I had a grandmother. Edna wasn't happy about having to take me in, but felt she had no choice in the matter. She couldn't just hand me over to the state to raise, could she? What would people say?

On my second day in New Bern, I was sitting on the branch of one of the apple trees when I overheard her say that to her three-doors-down neighbor, Mrs. Kover.

"Edna, don't say that. She seems a sweet little girl. And don't you think it'll be nice to have some company? Give it a chance. After all, she's your only grandchild."

"So Tommy *said*."

"She has his eyes."

Edna said nothing.

"Anyway," Mrs. Kover said, "I was just coming over to ask if Madelyn could come to our house for lunch tomorrow. Tessa will be home from camp this afternoon. She'll be thrilled to have a playmate so close to her own age."

That was how I met Tessa Kover. That first summer we were inseparable. But maybe that was because we were so close in age and because summers in New Bern were hot, long, and offered few childhood distractions, at least the organized kind. Back then, mothers didn't spend their lives hauling kids from one activity to the next. They told them to find something to do, to be home for dinner, and shooed them out the door.

Tessa and I had no trouble keeping busy. We built tents in the backyard and staged puppet shows in the Kovers' living room. We made cookies and quarts of vanilla ice cream, sitting in the shade of a spreading maple tree and taking turns cranking the handle of the Kovers' old-fashioned ice-cream maker until the sweat beaded on our foreheads and the soupy custard inside froze into something semisolid. We made daisy chain crowns for our hair and key chains from neon pink and white plastic lanyard, a skill Tessa had acquired at camp.

Was Tessa thrilled to have me for a friend? At the time I didn't care. All I knew was I liked her.

No. I didn't just like Tessa. I loved her. Loved her with that intense, exclusive love that only very young girls are capable of, the slavish devotion of an abandoned pup for its rescuer. Loved her so utterly that if my grandmother commented, as she often did, "I suppose if Tessa Kover jumped off a bridge, you would too," I wouldn't have thought two ticks before answering, "Yes. Absolutely, yes."

When school began and I had a chance to meet other children in New Bern, my attachment to Tessa wasn't diluted in the least. I wanted no other friends. I had Tessa.

Whatever Tessa did, I did. When Tessa cut her hair into a short bob, I nagged Edna until she got out her shears and cut mine too. When Tessa joined the Girl Scouts, so did I. And when Tessa had to get eyeglasses, I faked my school eye test, deliberately mistaking Es for Gs. The teacher sent a note to Edna, who took me to see the optometrist, who was not fooled. Edna was furious. In the parking lot outside his office, she slapped me across the face so hard my ears rang. It was the first slap of many.

Tessa wasn't just my friend; she was my ideal. My idol. I didn't just want her; I wanted to *be* her. I wanted her life, her family, the love and acceptance I'd been denied. Her family was part of the package. They were so happy, so wonderfully normal. That's what I wanted, just to be happy and normal. Just to be like Tessa.

At ten, at eleven, at twelve, at thirteen, I was too young to understand that love isn't a mirror, reflecting back what you're feeling word for word, gesture for gesture. I didn't know that sometimes, that most of the time, love goes unrequited.

I do now.

8
Tessa

September

Lee slipped his arms into his blue blazer and turned toward me. "How do I look?"

"Good," I answered before wiping away a trace of shaving cream his razor had missed. "Definitely the best man for the job."

"Yeah?" He peered into the bathroom mirror and examined his reflection, as if worried that I was just being nice. I wasn't. He did look good. Farmwork had made his shoulders wider, more solid, and his face, bronzed brown from working out of doors, was handsome against the crisp white collar of his shirt. But the sight of him dressed so formally depressed me. I knew he'd rather be wearing overalls and barn boots than a blazer and wingtips.

Lee flicked imaginary lint off his lapel. "Tie or no tie?"

"No tie. It's just a temp job. You don't want to look too anxious."

"I am anxious. I need this job. No point in pretending I don't." He pulled a blue paisley tie out of his jacket pocket and looped it around his neck. "The head of HR is George Kortekass's cousin. He called her and put in a good word for me."

George Kortekass was another accountant in Lee's division back in Boston. It was nice of him to recommend Lee, but I really wasn't keen on the idea of his taking this job; the company was clear on the other side of the state. Still, the pay was pretty decent.

"Here," I said, taking the ends of Lee's tie. "Let me do that for you."

"Thanks." He sniffed and leaned his head closer to my hair. "You smell good."

"It's a new shampoo I've been working on— orange and clove. I thought it might be good for the holidays. What time is your interview?"

"Not until eleven, but I want to get down there early. You never know what kind of traffic you'll run into on Ninety-five."

I finished making the knot and slid it into place under his shirt collar. "Are you sure this is a good idea? Stamford is such a long commute."

"Winter is coming. We need to order heating oil before the prices go up. If there were any job openings closer to home, I'd take them. Nobody's hiring."

"I know. But maybe if I . . ."

Lee made an impatient noise, half sigh, half growl. "We've been over this ten times. It has to be me. A good holiday season for the shop would solve all our problems, and you're the only one who can make that happen. I've got no idea how to make citrus and clove shampoo. You do." He stretched his neck and hooked his finger inside his shirt collar, trying to get more comfortable. "Besides, it's not that far."

"Hour and a half each way."

"It'd just be for a few months." He smoothed the lapels of his jacket and looked at his watch. "Gotta scoot. I'll drop those coolers of tea off at the church before I leave town. Can you collect the eggs before you go?"

"Sure. When will you be home?"

"Dunno."

"Call me when you do. I'll be at the church helping out with the fair this morning, but I'll be in the shop after lunch. I want to hear how everything went."

He nodded and he fished his keys from his pocket. "Wish me luck," he said.

I kissed him on the lips. "Luck."

The weekend forecast predicted sunny skies with temperatures in the low sixties and a slight breeze from the northwest; perfect weather for drinking cider, wearing sweaters, oohing and ahhing over the fall colors, and going to a country fair.

The fair had been pulled together on such short notice that I wondered how people would know it was even taking place. As I crossed Commerce Street, carrying two shopping bags with my auction items, the answer was obvious.

At the west end of the Green, across from the stately white elegance of the New Bern Community Church, someone had stretched three long lines of rope between the trees and hung them with dozens of bright, colorful quilts that fluttered like flags in the breeze and commanded the attention of everyone passing by. And as it was the peak weekend of fall foliage season, the passersby were plentiful.

The fair wouldn't open until ten, but already there were clusters of people wandering between the artfully constructed corridors of quilts, taking pictures of them and each other, like visitors to a museum of masterpieces hung *en plein air*. Every parking spot on Commerce Street was filled and in the time it took me to cross the Green and find the silent auction, three buses pulled up to the curb and released streams of tourists who immediately made a beeline to the Green, drawn forward by the vivid colors and arresting patterns of quilts.

I found Candy Waldgren, who was in charge of the silent auction. Candy and I had served on the high school prom committee. We'd been friendly in school, though not close. Candy was pleasant but nervously energetic, involved in all kinds of church and community activities. Whenever we ran into each other, she'd say we must get together soon, but somehow we never did. I suppose she meant it, but like so many of my childhood friends and acquaintances, Candy had a busy life and a full circle of friends. She didn't have time to add another to the roster, not even an old new friend. It was probably just as well. When we were in school Candy had been something of a gossip. I had the feeling she still was.

"This is so generous of you, Tessa. Thank you *so* much," Candy said, pushing a stray lock of hair off her forehead and tucking it behind her ear before taking my bags. "This was all pulled together so quickly, I've been simply frantic. Next is the library fund-raiser. I don't know why I said I'd chair it, but I suppose someone has to. Mark Simonson was supposed to do it, but he had to pull out because of some unexpected 'work commitments,'" she said, making air quotes with her fingers.

"Work commitments, my foot. Sylvia's divorcing him, that's what. About time too. He's been cheating on her with a cocktail waitress over at the VFW for years. Can you believe it? Poor Sylvia." Candy sighed with momentary pity. "Anyway, once I'm done with all that we've just *got* to get together and catch up on old times."

"Yes. Have you seen Margot Matthews? I'm supposed to help her sell tickets for the quilt raffle."

Candy already was busy refluffing the bows on my donated baskets but she looked up briefly to scan the crowd. "I don't see her. They were looking for help making sandwiches earlier. Maybe try the kitchen?"

Margot wasn't in the kitchen, but while searching for her I did find Jake Kaminski, who was setting up the dunk tank. He said Margot had run to the quilt shop.

"Why don't you wait at the raffle table? She'll be back in a minute." He crouched into a pitcher's stance and threw a baseball at the bull's-eye as hard as he could. He hit his target at dead center, releasing the spring-loaded dunk seat with a startling slam.

Jake straightened up and grinned. "Not too bad for a one-eyed man, eh?"

"Not too," I agreed.

I made my way back toward the quilts, past

carnival booths that volunteers were scurrying to finish setting up, a roped-off area for the used book and tag sale, and a booth where Charlie Donnelly was already selling lemonade and cookies to hungry tourists.

The raffle table sat at the end of the center aisle of quilts, under the branches of a large tree still loaded with bright orange leaves. Seeing no sign of Margot, I took a stroll through the aisles of quilts, pausing before each one and marveling at the variety of colors, patterns, and styles. Some were simple, using only two or three fabrics to make bold statements; others were perfect mishmashes of color, with scores of scraps that I would never have imagined going together but that somehow did. A few of the quilts were very modern-looking, asymmetrical and abstract arrangements of shapes whose meanings and messages could only be guessed at. But most were very traditional collections of squares, rectangles, and triangles arranged into an orderly geometry of stars, hearts, and flowers, patterns created and crafted by women since colonial days and before, then shared among generations of mothers, daughters, sisters, and friends without credit or copyright.

The traditional quilts appealed to me most. I liked the history behind them and the balance. My Yankee roots were showing; we New Englanders prefer to live life in proper proportion and good order. Or maybe that's just what *I* prefer and I've generalized it into a regional disposition that suits my personal taste. Who can say?

I returned to the table just in time to see Margot approach carrying a big cardboard box. She smiled when she saw me, lifting her fingers from the edge of the box and fluttering them in greeting.

"Can I carry something for you?"

"Oh, no. It's not heavy, just bulky."

Margot set the box on the table and started unloading it. Inside was a roll of raffle tickets, a cash box, a glass fishbowl, some class brochures for Cobbled Court Quilts, and, of course, the raffle quilt.

It was a square quilt, meant to hang on a wall rather than cover a bed, with nine multicolored blocks of red, yellow, orange, blue, brown, and green maple leaves on a white background, separated by panes of beige, with four borders surrounding the leaf blocks: a thin band of black, then a wider border made up of scraps of the fabrics that had been used in the leaves, then another black border and, finally, a wide border of a printed leaf fabric that incorporated the colors used in the large leaf blocks. I helped Margot unfold the quilt and hang it on a wooden frame so people could see it.

"Gorgeous!" I exclaimed. "Who made it?"

"I did. A couple of years ago. The fund-raiser came up so quickly that there wasn't time to make a new quilt, so I decided to donate this one."

"It's beautiful. I'm going to be the first to buy a raffle ticket. I've never won anything in my life, but who knows? Maybe I'll get lucky."

I fished a dollar bill from my pocket, put it in the cash box, and tore a ticket off the roll.

"And if you don't," Margot said, "you can always make one like it."

"Sure, if I had your talent and a couple of years with nothing to do but sew. Maybe I should buy two tickets."

I sat down on one of the folding chairs and began filling in my name and phone number on the back of my ticket. Margot sat down next to me.

"It's not as hard as you think. Evelyn always says, 'If you can sew a straight line, you can make a quilt.' Nearly all of these," she said, tipping her head toward the rows of beautiful, colorful quilts, "are made of straight lines. Nothing more. You should give quilting a try, Tessa. I wish you'd reconsider taking my class."

"That's sweet of you, Margot, but I'm just not creative." I dropped one half of my raffle ticket into the empty fishbowl and put the other half in my pocket.

"Yes, you are! You're very creative! Look at

what you did with For the Love of Lavender. The space was so dark and gloomy before. You've transformed it."

I shook my head. "I *reproduced* it. From pictures in a magazine. Right down to the paint colors and the plates on the light switches."

"Well, what about all those wonderful potpourris and lotions you make?"

"That's just gardening and following a recipe. It's a whole different thing."

Our conversation was cut short when a woman approached the table to buy a ticket. Over the next two hours, Margot and I sold seventy-eight raffle tickets. In between customers, Margot kept at me about quilting, overruling my every objection.

When I told her I couldn't leave my shop during the day to take classes, she suggested that Emily could watch the shop while I did. When I told her that today was Emily's last day before returning to college and admitted I couldn't afford to replace her, Margot said that I could join their quilt circle, a small group that included Margot, Evelyn, Evelyn's mother, Virginia, Ivy, who also worked in the shop, and Abigail Spaulding. The group met on Friday nights after work. Margot had an answer for everything.

"We need fresh blood in the quilt circle. Now that Abigail's niece, Liza, has moved to Chicago, we're down a member. And, actually, I already talked to Evelyn and the others about you. They think *you're* the perfect person to take her place. So do I," she said with a triumphant little smile, then crossed her arms over her chest and looked at me pointedly.

"You know something? I used to think that Evelyn Dixon's business savvy was the reason Cobbled Court Quilts is so successful, but now I'm beginning to wonder. I think you're her secret weapon. You just don't take no for an answer, do you?"

Margot giggled and dropped her arms, her posture changing from obstinate to amiable in the time it took to crack a smile. "I didn't spend ten years learning marketing in Manhattan for nothing."

Margot blinked twice, pausing for a moment before speaking. "Salesmanship aside, it would be good for you. I'd like to get to know you better, and I hope you don't mind my saying this, but . . . I think you could use some friends right now. Am I right?"

I didn't say anything, just dipped my head to one side to signal assent.

"You won't find a better group of women in the world than in our quilt circle. We're all as different as we can possibly be, but everybody has something to offer. We've been through a lot together, but what is said in the circle *stays* in the circle.

"You get all that and quilting too. You'll love it. Maybe you don't see yourself as a creative person, but if you've got an ounce of creativity in you, quilting will bring it out. Plus it's a great way to put aside your troubles and focus on something positive and productive. Quilting can even be therapeutic. It's *way* cheaper than therapy," she said with a self-deprecating laugh, "and a lot more fun. So? What do you say?"

I looked at the glass fishbowl where seventy-eight red raffle tickets already covered my lone and unlikely slip of chance, then glanced back at the maple leaf quilt.

"You think I could learn to make one of those?"

"Absolutely."

I was quiet for a moment, replaying her reasons in my mind.

"Friday night, you said?"

"Friday nights," she confirmed with a nod. "Six o'clock. You could come tonight if you wanted."

"No, not tonight," I said, thinking of Lee and his interview. Tonight I wanted to be with my husband. "But soon. You've convinced me."

9
Madelyn

Returning to New Bern has aged me—on many levels.

I'm long overdue for a round of Botox, but that sort of thing is far out of my budget now. Maybe it's just as well. It never worked on that deep frown line between my eyebrows anyway. And another thing: Those injections hurt. They do. Don't let anybody tell you different. I don't miss that part one bit.

But I do miss my hairdresser. Deeply. My roots look awful. I can get away with backcombing over my part for another week or so, but then I'm going to have to pick up a bottle of dye at the drugstore or something. There are limits to how far I'm willing to succumb to the "natural look." But for today an altered appearance suits my purpose.

When I called to schedule a Friday morning appointment at the bank, I gave my name as Beecher. Eventually the bank manager is bound to figure out my connection to Sterling, but I'm hoping to buy myself some time before that happens—time enough to win him over and convince him that, my unfortunate marital status notwithstanding, I'm a good risk. I need a loan. I need it badly.

Just because I don't pay a mortgage on Beecher Cottage doesn't mean that I get to live here for free. The property taxes are high, and according to a letter I received from the town last week, they'll be higher next year. Utilities for such a large house aren't cheap either. The estimate for my winter heating oil nearly stopped my heart!

And then there's maintenance. Over the last few years of her life, I doubt Edna spent ten cents maintaining Beecher Cottage, preferring to leave that legacy to future generations—i.e., me. I've already spent over a thousand dollars on plumbing. I'm not talking about remodeling the dated bathrooms; this is money I've had to spend just to make sure the toilets flush. Don't even ask about the roof; I wish I hadn't. But those watermarks on the upstairs walls and ceiling are there for a reason. We've had a dry summer and fall, but come spring, when the snow melts on the eaves and April showers start to shower, what am I going to do?

In its current condition, Beecher Cottage is all but unlivable. But performing even the most basic and necessary repairs on the house will empty my bank account by a third—I've got estimates to prove it. With zero money coming in and lots of zeros going out for taxes, utilities, and repairs, how am I supposed to live?

I've got to sell Beecher Cottage; I've just got to. It's the only solution. But I've no hope of selling the house at any price unless I remodel it first. Remodel, not repair. New roof, new bathrooms, new kitchen, new appliances, new paint, wallpaper, and carpets—new everything. And, as everyone knows, new everything doesn't come cheap.

And so, with her crow's feet and worry lines in full flower, her hair backcombed and swept into a ponytail to hide the gray, and wearing the most nondesigner, nondescript outfit she owns, Madelyn *Beecher* is walking downtown to try to borrow one hundred thousand dollars from the New Bern National Bank.

The bank sits two blocks south of the Green, about a mile's walk from my house. The stone exterior is solid and serious, the interior cool and formal, with tall ceilings, ornate woodwork, wrought-iron teller cages, and marble floors that echo when walked upon. Employees work at desks on the outer walls of the lobby, their activities overseen by the bank manager, whose walnut desk sits on a raised platform in the center of the room surrounded by a carved wooden railing with a swinging gate that subordinates must unlatch before entering this holy of holies. Everything about the structure is designed to inspire confidence and a certain level of awe. Inside the sacred confines of New Bern National, no one speaks above a murmur, and no one questions the manager, Mr. Fletcher, a well-fed man, not quite sixty.

Until I saw his face, I didn't realize that Mr. Fletcher was, in fact, Aaron Fletcher, one of the few boys whose attentions I had utterly rejected in high school, partly because my taste trended toward athletes but mostly because his superior attitude irritated me. Apparently, Aaron was unchanged.

He rose halfway from his chair with an acid smile and gestured for me to take a seat in one of the low chairs opposite his desk.

"Madelyn. Or should I say Mrs. Baron?" he asked in a voice slightly louder than necessary, a tone that attracted surreptitious glances from customers standing in the tellers line. "How nice to see you after all these years. How can I help you?"

The moment he called me Mrs. Baron, I knew I was in trouble, but I had to at least *try* to win him over. I smiled as sweetly as I could and murmured some nonsense about it being good to see him as well and how impressed I was that he'd risen so far but that I wasn't really surprised, that even in high school it was apparent he was destined for big things. When I ran out of compliments, I leaned a little closer, close enough for him to spy a glimpse of cleavage (yes, I was that desperate), and made my request.

He listened, sort of, with his eyes glued to my décolletage. When I was finished, he looked up and proceeded to subject me to a ten-minute lecture on the links between the soft housing market, the credit crunch, toxic assets, bank failures, the Wall Street meltdown, rising unemployment, sinking tax revenues, and, if I recall correctly, the falling test scores among eighth graders in math and science, and the "shenanigans"—he actually used the word "shenanigans"—of Bernie Madoff and *people like him.*

The writing was on the wall. Aaron Fletcher was not going to give me a loan. Not today. Not ever. I gathered up my things.

Aaron rose from his chair and placed his hand on a stack of papers in the top tray of his in-box. "I've got sixty applications for home equity loans here, Mrs. Baron. All from honest, hardworking people who've done nothing wrong but have lost their jobs or their savings because of the greed of others. I doubt I'll be able to help more than one in twenty. Most of them owe more on their homes than the homes are now worth."

"Yes, I understand, Mr. Fletcher. Thank you for your time."

Being polite was an effort, but I made it. When you live in a small town, politeness is more than just good manners; it's a survival skill.

"Do you understand? Do you, *Mrs. Baron?*" He was grandstanding now, playing to the crowd of onlookers. His fleshy jowls wobbled as he moved to the other end of the desk and laid his hand on another pile of papers even higher than the first.

"This is the paperwork on loans that are in foreclosure or about to be. Some of them belong to my friends and neighbors, people I've done business with for years."

He glared at me. "These are decent folks. People my grandkids go to school with! For one reason or another, they can't make their house payments. Either they lost their jobs, or their mortgages adjusted to higher rates, or some fly-by-night operation put them into a loan they didn't understand and weren't qualified for in the first place . . ."

I had had enough. I circled around the desk, trying to make my exit. Aaron moved his beefy body between me and the wooden gate that separated the king from the commoners, then reached out a pudgy finger and poked me— poked me! Right in the chest. As though I were an errant spaniel or a disobedient child.

So much for good manners.

Advancing toward him, raising myself up to my full height, which gave me a good two inches on the fat financier, I put my face up next to his, so close he must have felt the heat of my breath.

"Loans?" I spat, pushing deep into Fletcher's personal space and forcing him to back away. "The kind of loans your bank bought up in bundles without a second thought because there was money to be made off them and the opportunity was just too good to pass up?

"People losing their homes because they've lost their jobs *is* a terrible thing. My husband obviously added to the misery of a lot of people and that's why he's in prison, paying for his crimes. Of course, I don't understand all the ins and outs of what he did or how he did it. After all, I'm no financial expert. Not like you, Mr. Fletcher.

"I wonder . . . a couple of years ago when you were raking in record profits, did you stop to think that maybe it wasn't a good idea to make a loan to newlyweds with twenty thousand dollars in credit card debt who were both working for minimum wage? Did you stop to wonder why the paperwork on the loan application for a man who makes a living changing oil and rotating tires listed his income as a hundred thousand a year? Did you ask yourself what would happen when the two teachers who could well afford the five and a half percent teaser rate for their newer, bigger house woke up one morning and found the rate had adjusted to nine?"

I glared into his piggy little eyes, daring him to answer. He opened and closed his mouth, a strand of saliva strung between his upper and lower lips stretching and shrinking, but no sound was forthcoming. I was too angry and too loud. Tellers and customers stared, some with grim smiles on their faces. I lowered my voice. But not by much.

"You know what they say, Mr. Fletcher, money is the root of all evil. And there are plenty of people guilty of perpetrating that evil. But not all of them are behind bars." I reached out and pushed the dumbstruck banker out of my path with a sweeping gesture.

A man waiting in the teller line clapped and called out, "Damn straight!"

A couple more patrons joined in as I stormed out of the bank. Their applause filled me with a sense of righteous indignation—right up until the moment I went through the door and was hit by a blast of chilly autumn air and the realization that before the sun went down, everybody in town would know that Madelyn Beecher Baron, New Bern's most infamous prodigal daughter, had returned.

10
Madelyn

I stood on the street feeling stupid. And angry with myself. By tomorrow half of New Bern would know about my run-in with Aaron Fletcher. A quarter of them would claim to have witnessed it personally. I could have kicked myself. Instead, I kicked a pebble and watched it skitter down the sidewalk in the direction of the Green.

As I'd walked to the bank earlier, I'd noticed a bit of a bustle on the west end of the Green, near the church. There had been more than the usual number of cars parked nearby and quite a number of people setting up tables and tents, plus two men stringing long lengths of rope between trees. In summer, New Bern plays host to all kinds of events, everything from al fresco concerts and 10K runs to craft fairs and poetry readings. It was a bit late in the season for it, but I supposed this was just another one of those.

But this event was larger than New Bern's usual community function, much larger, with all kinds of different areas for crafts, and food, and carnival games. It took up the entire western half of the Green and spilled over onto the grounds of the church. The fair didn't appear to be quite ready for business—people were still scurrying about setting up tables—but a crowd had already gathered. A few fair-goers wandered past the booths, but most were gathered near the trees, looking at rows of colorful quilts hung on ropes like freshly laundered rainbows.

My pipe-dream plans for the day—hiring contractors to begin remodeling Beecher Cottage—had been blown out of the water, so I decided to join the festivities. Why not? I had nothing else to do. The fair was a welcome distraction and there was no charge for admission. Good thing; I only had four dollars in my pocket.

I didn't want to be recognized, so just to be safe, I put on my sunglasses before walking across the grass to see the quilts.

Grandma Edna was a quilter, a pretty good one too. All of her quilts were handmade, very traditional. I liked it when Edna worked on her quilts. Quilting seemed to calm her—or perhaps making all those teeny stitches required so much focus that it sapped her ability to focus on my many failings. In any case, Edna was happier when she was quilting. She tried to teach me how to quilt once but got furious and started screaming because I kept trying to make changes to the patterns. I was never very good at following directions.

At the end of one of the rows I saw a card table with two chairs and a sign saying QUILT RAFFLE TICKETS—$1. A pretty quilt would have been a nice addition to one of my empty bedrooms, but I couldn't tell which was the one being raffled, nor was there anyone selling tickets. I decided to investigate the rest of the fair and come back later.

For two dollars, I bought a glass of lemonade and a simply enormous cookie from a man with a charming smile and an even more charming Irish accent. The cookie, loaded with macadamia nuts and some sort of butterscotch bits, was delicious, crunchy but chewy and warm from the oven. The lemonade, tart and sweet, was made from real lemons. It might not have been the breakfast of champions, but at that moment, sound nutrition was the least of my worries.

Beecher Cottage was still a drain on my fast-dwindling bank account, a millstone around my neck. I couldn't sell it without remodeling it and I couldn't remodel it without money. Of course, I could try other banks, but I suspected it would be the same story everywhere. Loans were hard to come by now—doubly so if your last name happened to be Baron. My Plan A was dead on arrival. I had to come up with a Plan B. How?

I walked across the street to the church grounds and into a roped-off area where a tag sale was being held. I hadn't been to one since my marriage. Sterling had forbidden me to buy anything at a tag sale, thrift store, or even high-end consignment shop.

"What will people think if they see my wife going around in somebody's old clothes? I don't want to see you wearing anything but the best."

Funny. When he first made this pronouncement, after our wedding, I thought it was because Sterling wanted *me* to have the best, but now I realize it was because he wanted *other people* to see me wearing the best. It was always about him. His image. His reputation. His wealth. His wife. What a pathetic excuse for a human being he is.

Defiantly, I joined the others who were already

sifting through piles of cast-off clothing, jewelry, books, and an odd mishmash of old glassware, throw pillows, toys, tools, typewriters, and appliances. I spent half an hour at it without finding anything that made me want to part with my money. It was disappointing but not surprising.

The best sales, the ones where you can unearth real treasures amongst the trash, tend to be estate sales, the ones where *everything* is up for grabs. Sometimes family members of the deceased are so stunned by grief or so anxious to clear out the house that they don't realize that Aunt Thelma's old dishes were actually Limoges or that the ugly old portrait of some long-dead ancestor whose name no one can remember was painted by a renowned folk-art painter. You never know what you'll find hidden up in somebody's attic.

So far, I hadn't found any riches among the refuse. I was about to give up when I stumbled upon something truly priceless—an idea—and it didn't cost me a dime.

As I walked by a table of children's items, I heard a conversation between a young couple that piqued my interest. I drew closer and feigned interest in a pile of old toys.

"It's such a cute little village," the woman said, looking around the Green as she absently leafed through a stack of boys' shirts. "Too bad we can't stay here."

The man, who I assumed was her husband,

said, "I tried. But there's no room at the inn. There's no inn, period. You'd think that a town like this would have a ton of hotel rooms. The closest place I could find a vacancy is the Walden Inn, but the prices . . ."

He let out a low whistle and I knew why. The Walden Inn is very beautiful and very, very expensive. Their "standard" rooms start at five hundred a night and junior suites can be double that. It is the hotel of choice among the Manhattan elite looking to spend a weekend in the country, but it is far beyond the means of ordinary mortals.

"I wanted to stay in New Bern," he continued apologetically, "but the only place with rooms available is that motel. If you want, I'll call and cancel our reservation in Kent."

"No, no," she assured him. "It's worth driving a little farther to stay somewhere nice. If you're having a romantic weekend in New England, you have to stay at a cozy, romantic little inn," she said with a flirtatious smile. "Don't you think?"

"Absolutely." He put his arm around her waist and they went off to investigate the used books.

No room at the inn . . . No inn period . . . A town like this . . .

The man's comments played and replayed in my mind. How had I not thought of this before? New Bern had no inn!

The only real lodging in New Bern was the

121

Yankee Motel. Built in the mid-fifties and not refurbished since, it had all the charm of a cardboard box and was situated right next to the highway, three miles from the center of town. People only stayed there because there was nowhere else to stay.

Beecher Cottage, on the other hand, simply oozed charm—or it would once it was fixed up. Best of all, it was in a great location, just a short walk from the Green, the shops, the museums—all the places visitors came to see!

I opened and closed my fist, adding things up in my mind. Beecher Cottage had five bedrooms, two with private baths. If some work was done to the attic and the old guest apartment above the garage was fixed up, it would be possible to add two more. Maybe three. Eight potential rooms, each paying, say, two hundred dollars a night . . .

Why, if I could fill those rooms even half the time . . . even a third! I could transform Beecher Cottage into a profit-making enterprise. And providing lodging could be just the beginning. Unlike many Victorian-era homes, the main floor had large public rooms that flowed well. Imagine the kind of income I might generate by hosting small weddings or conferences. Getting a zoning change shouldn't be that difficult; half the houses on Oak Leaf Lane were already designated as commercial anyway. And once they realized that having an inn within walking distance of downtown could help support their enterprises, I was sure the other business owners would . . .

Other business owners?

What was I thinking? I didn't know the first thing about business. I hadn't punched a time clock in three decades. And when I *had* worked, I'd only been hired for my looks, not my brains. Even if I had the business acumen of Conrad Hilton, where would I get the money? Transforming Beecher Cottage into a bed-and-breakfast would require a cellar-to-dome renovation, and an even bigger loan than the one Aaron Fletcher had just turned me down for.

No. It was a crazy idea—a pipe dream. Impossible.

I clenched my fist in frustration. This time my fingers closed on something. I looked down and saw that I was holding a very small, very worn miniature sofa. It was Victorian in style, with a dark stain, ornately carved legs, and a curved back, upholstered in faded red velvet, the perfect size for a dollhouse—for *my* dollhouse. The dollhouse I hadn't seen since I'd abandoned it in Edna's attic all those years ago, leaving it to rot with the rest of the junk . . .

I picked up the tiny sofa with both hands and stared at it.

No, I thought. It wasn't the same sofa. It couldn't be. Not after all these years. And it couldn't be a sign either. Could it? No. I don't believe in signs.

An older woman with iron gray hair, wearing a stick-on name tag with the church logo printed on it in blue ink and her name, Darlene, written in red marker, walked past.

"Ma'am? Pardon me. Darlene?"

Hearing her name, she turned around. "Can I help you with something?"

"Yes, how much is this?"

"Everything on that table is one dollar."

"I'll take it." I pulled one of my two remaining dollars from my pocket and handed it to Darlene.

"It's a sweet little sofa, isn't it? Do you have a dollhouse?"

"I do . . . I mean, I did. Not anymore."

Darlene smiled vaguely. "Oh. Well. With new upholstery and a little TLC, it'll be good as new. It's a shame the way people throw away perfectly good things without a second thought. We live in a disposable society. . . ." Darlene tsked her tongue in disgust. " 'Use it up, wear it out, make it do, or do without.' That's what my mother always used to say. And back in my day, that's what we did."

"Yes," I said. "In mine too."

I thanked Darlene and headed across the Green with the little sofa clutched in my fist. I passed the quilts and gave a thought to the raffle, but only fleetingly.

I had places to go, people to see, treasure to unearth.

11
Tessa

I told Emily that I'd be back at the shop as soon
as my shift at the fair was over. Ivy and Dana,
who also work at the Cobbled Court Quilt Shop,
were right on time to take over from Margot and
very excited about the apparent success of the
fair.

"Just look at this crowd!" Ivy exclaimed. "This
is great!"

"It is," Dana echoed in a softer but no less
enthusiastic voice. "Really great!"

I'd never have guessed it if Margot hadn't told
me, but both women—Ivy, blond and blue-eyed,
tiny in stature but big in personality, and Dana,
dark of hair and complexion, even shorter than
Ivy and definitely more timid—had been victims
of domestic violence. Ivy and her two children
now lived in a house on Proctor Street. Dana was
still living at the shelter. What kind of monster
could possibly hurt these two wonderful,
intelligent women? It boggled the mind.

"It was really nice of you to help out," Dana
said with a shy smile.

"I was glad to. I only wish I could do more."

"You've done a lot," Ivy said. "Everybody has.
If the turnout stays this strong through the

weekend, maybe we won't have to cut back any education programs. I hope we can save the GED classes at least. Wouldn't you know the year I finally have time to take my high school equivalency exam is the year they threaten to close the prep classes because of budget shortfalls."

"It won't come to that," Margot said brightly. "Look how well everything is going!"

She got up from the table to make room for Ivy and Dana. "I've got to get back to the shop. You know how it is, the minute we're shorthanded is the minute everybody decides they need fabric for a new quilt. Oh! Speaking of that! Tessa is the newest member of our quilt circle!"

"Terrific!" Ivy exclaimed. "Have you decided what your first project will be?"

I pointed to the raffle quilt. "That. Assuming my raffle ticket isn't the winner. It looks pretty complicated, but Margot seems to think I can do it."

"Sure you can," Ivy said. "Margot will help you. We all will. When you come in the shop to pick out your fabric, just holler if you need some advice."

"Thanks."

That was the second time someone had offered to help me pick out fabric. What was all the fuss about? How hard could choosing fabric be anyway? Especially since I planned on using the same fabrics as the raffle quilt. It was pretty just as it was. Why change anything?

"See?" Margot said. "You're already making new friends. I told you! Well, I should get back. Tessa, do you want to walk with me?"

"Oh. Thanks, but no. There's something I need to do first."

The wooden doors that separate the church vestibule from the sanctuary are thick and heavy. As they swung slowly closed, the voices, laughter, and bustle of the fair were muffled to a whoosh of white noise.

I grew up in this church. So did my parents and grandparents and great-grandparents. Given that, you might suppose I made a beeline back to church as soon as I moved home, but you'd be wrong. It wasn't that I had anything against church, quite the opposite. I have fond memories of this building, of stories told with flannel board figures, of singing and climbing Jacob's ladder in Sunday school, of snuggling between my parents and falling safely asleep during long sermons, of Easter Sunday and new dresses with stiff petticoats and hats with daisies on the brim and white patent leather shoes with a purse that matched, of hayrides and bonfires with the youth group and getting my first kiss from Billy Jessup when the pastor wasn't looking, and, of course, of my wedding day.

But after that and in spite of good intentions to the contrary, I rarely went to church again—any church. I'd fallen out of the habit at college, as had Lee. After Josh was born, we'd started attending a church near our house, thinking that's what parents do, I suppose. But we never felt comfortable there, so after a few months, we quit going.

Still, you'd have thought that I would have gone back when I moved home, for nostalgia's sake if nothing else, but no. Family tradition, fond memories, good intentions—none of that brought me back to church. Desperation did.

When we decided to move to New Bern, the housing market was hot. Even though we weren't going to move until Josh finished high school in Massachusetts, we went ahead and put in a nearly full-price offer on our farm in New Bern because we were worried that someone might buy it out from under us. By the time Josh graduated, the housing market was cooling—rapidly.

We'd figured selling our house near Boston would take three weeks at most. After three months without an offer, our Realtor called to suggest dropping the price and burying a statue of a saint upside down in the yard. "I know it sounds crazy," she said. "But I've been in this business a long time and I've never seen it fail."

We agreed to the price reduction but said no to burying a statue in the yard.

"Was she serious? I mean, what's next? Voodoo dolls and rabbit's feet?" I asked Lee, sharing a laugh later that day.

Lee grinned. "Now that the market is slowing down, maybe she's taken up a side business selling religious artifacts to desperate home owners."

"Maybe. But I can't imagine how desperate you'd have to be to consider entombing a plastic saint in the rosebushes a viable part of your real estate marketing plan."

Months later, after more than a year of making double mortgage payments, paying remodeling costs for the shop, which had gone twelve percent over our estimates, realizing that business was way below our projections and that our investments were going down even as college tuition was going up, I could imagine what that kind of desperation felt like. I was there. I was inches away from driving to Massachusetts with a ceramic saint and a shovel. But first I decided to try a more conventional method. I went to church and prayed that someone would buy our house.

It worked.

I went to church on Sunday. On Monday, the Realtor called with an offer on the house—not a great offer, but an offer. We accepted it.

Now, was that a coincidence or an answer to prayer? I wasn't sure; I'm still not. But I decided that it'd be ungrateful to show up at church, pray, get what I asked for, and then never return—somewhat akin to showing up for a dinner party empty-handed, then leaving right after dessert and never sending a thank-you note.

And there was something else.

That first day, I sat in the same pew my family had occupied for so many years, sixth row back on the left, and found something I never expected and still can't quite explain. I suppose peace is the most straightforward description, but there's more to it than that—refuge, sanctuary, awe. And thirst, the need for more.

It was that need, more than obligation or gratitude, that drew me back a second time and draws me back today. I can't pass by without entering in. Especially today.

With the door closed in this hushed and empty space with its tall windows streaming sunlight, simple unadorned walls, and rows of high-backed pews, I moved instinctively to my accustomed place. My steps were muffled, nearly silent, as I walked up the carpeted aisle to the sixth row and knelt with my head bowed in the wooden pew that has been polished smooth and gleaming from contact with the arms and elbows and backsides and knees of generations of supplicants and seekers like me, and I prayed.

There was so much to pray about.

I prayed about the shop, the farm, the bills, and

the mortgage. I prayed for Josh, for his protection and happiness and future. I prayed about missing him and for strength not to let him know how much. And I prayed for Lee, for his interview, that he'd get the job, and that this would somehow close the distance I felt growing between us. I prayed about everything. Not eloquently, and not with any great faith that my prayers would really change anything, but sincerely and, yes, a little desperately.

I was so focused that I didn't hear the door open or footsteps on the carpet. When Reverend Tucker touched me lightly on the shoulder, I jumped.

"I'm sorry, Tessa. I didn't mean to startle you."

I laid my hand over my thumping heart and let out a little laugh. "That's all right, Reverend. You just caught me by surprise. Hey, what happened to you?"

His hair was plastered down on his head and his clothes were damp from his white collar all the way down to his black tennis shoes, which actually squelched when he took a step. I really must have been concentrating not to have heard that.

He blinked a couple of times, as if wondering what I was talking about, then reached up to touch his wet hair.

"Oh, that. I took a shift in the dunk tank."

"You should go put some dry clothes on. You'll catch cold."

"I'm all right. It's warm for September and I'm halfway to dry already. I'll go to my office to change in a minute, but I wanted to check on you first. Are you all right?"

"I'm fine. Just had a few things on my mind."

"Then you've come to the right place. 'Come to me, all who are weary and heavy-laden, and I will give you rest.' Matthew 11:28. I haven't any advice or counsel that even comes close to that, but if there is anything I can do for you, you only need to ask."

"Thank you. I appreciate that."

He smiled gently and nodded. The movement made a drop of water drip from his hair onto the lens of his eyeglasses.

"So?" he asked, taking off his glasses and drying them ineffectually with the tail of his damp shirt. "*Is* there anything I can do for you? Anything you want to talk about?"

I pressed my lips together for a moment before answering. "Sometimes I wonder what God must think of me. I don't darken His door for years and when I finally do, it was only because I had a cartload of problems to be solved. Don't you think that ticks God off?"

Reverend Tucker tipped his head back as far as it would go, as if the answer to my question might be printed somewhere on the soaring ceiling of the sanctuary.

"There was once a man who had a thoughtless

son who took his inheritance and wasted it all on foolishness. When the son had spent every dime, he became hungry, desperately so. Realizing how foolish he'd been, he was ashamed to go home. But desperation and hunger finally led him back to his father's house, where he hoped he might find work as a servant.

"When he saw his son coming, the father's joy was so great that he ran down the road to greet him. The father didn't ask where his son had been, or what he had done, or why it had taken him so long to come to his senses. He didn't care what had driven his child through the door. He was just happy to see him."

Reverend Tucker put his water-streaked glasses back on his nose.

"That's what I think God thinks of you. He doesn't care what brought you here or what condition you arrived in—hungry, doubting, desperate, damp." He glanced at his bedraggled clothes and shrugged.

"Makes no difference to God. He's just happy you're home."

12
Madelyn

The railing was dusty and strung with cobwebs. How long since anyone had climbed these stairs? Opened this door? Entered this cold, dark, unfinished space? Years, certainly. Decades, possibly.

I still remembered where the attic light switch was. I snapped it on and a naked overhead bulb, the old-fashioned kind with the glowing filament visible through a clear glass dome, pierced the darkness with bright light that faded to shadows near the edge of the room and severed at sharp angles near the sloping ceiling, a landscape of silhouettes and shadow shapes cast by forgotten furniture and relics of the past.

It was quiet, eerily so. I stepped through the door, toward the light, and turned in a slow circle. There were no ghosts in the attic, but there was a claw-foot bathtub, two chairs with torn upholstery and sagging springs, an ornately carved armoire missing a section of scrollwork that, when opened, revealed a stack of fine-loomed linen sheets edged with lace and embroidered vines, and a half dozen round boxes each holding three or four hats trimmed with ribbons and feathers, peek-a-boo veils and clusters of fruit, and even a papier-mâché bluebird perched jauntily on the rim of a straw boater banded with a blue and white ribbon.

Who could they belong to? I'd never known Edna to wear hats, and these were so tiny, too small and too feminine, ever to have sat atop that big head with its gunmetal gray curls sprayed into immobility.

Hidden under dusty sheets I found three bureaus with rubbed finishes, missing pulls, and mirrors spotted black by age and fungus. One of the mirrors was cracked from edge to edge. Next I found two nightstands, some broken lamps, and a gateleg table piled with boxes of papers and photograph albums. I didn't take time to look through those. Under paint-spattered tarpaulins, I discovered piles of boards, nails, and tools, cans of paint, rolls of wallpaper, and unopened boxes of shingles. There were carpets, too, rolled up and stacked like cigars in a box, dirty, frayed, and in varying states of disrepair. There were stacks of flowerpots, mostly cracked, a copper weather vane, corroded green, and two stone lions with distinctly Oriental faces.

I found several oil paintings leaning against the back wall and flipped through them, hoping to come upon some undiscovered Matisse or Renoir that could change my fortunes. No such luck. But some were pretty, landscapes mostly, and once they were cleaned, the gilded frames would be lovely. There were several ornate metal bedsteads stacked up against the same wall, some with footboards, some without, and so covered in grime that it was impossible to tell if they were made from brass, iron, or something else.

Next to that, stashed under a stiff gray oilcloth, I discovered a small oak cabinet with a black metal base. The finish was still smooth. I opened the lid and fiddled with an interior mechanism until I heard a click. An ink-black sewing machine decorated with flowers and swirls and lettering in gold rose from the recesses of the cabinet.

There was a small bench sitting nearby. I pulled it up to the cabinet, sat down, and pumped the metal foot treadle while using my hand to turn the flywheel. At first, it seemed to be frozen, but after jiggling the wheel back and forth and carefully applying a slight pressure, the wheel started to turn and the needle moved up and down—slowly and stiffly, but a little oil and a good cleaning might do wonders. Interesting.

The darkest corner of the attic was dominated by a large mound covered in white sheets. Pulling them back, I found a full-sized antique brass bed, complete with mattress and box spring. It was beautiful, decorated with medallions that, at first, I thought were porcelain but which a bit of rubbing showed to be mother-of-pearl.

Good Lord! An antique brass and mother-of-pearl bed in perfect condition! What must that be worth? It was no Renoir, but still quite a discovery. And there was more.

The mattress was heaped with half a dozen old quilts, including the blue and white pieced quilt that had graced my bed when I was little. Most weren't in very good shape. Some were stained, and one so badly torn that the batting was exposed. It looked as if some sort of animal, a mouse maybe, had been nibbling at it. What a shame.

The chances of repairing them to any kind of usable state seemed slim, but you never knew. Maybe I should drop by that quilt shop that now occupied the old Fielding Drug building. I'd met a chatty woman in the grocery store who told me about it. She worked there. What was her name? Margaret? Margie? Something like that. I knew where the shop was, tucked back in Cobbled Court. It couldn't hurt to take the quilts by the shop and get an opinion.

Carefully, not wanting to do any further damage in the unlikely event that any of them were salvageable, I refolded the quilts, then walked back to the center of the room, under the light, brushing the dust off my hands as I turned in a circle one last time, squinting to see if I'd missed anything.

Where could it be?

I remembered exactly where I'd put the

dollhouse all those years ago, back when I still believed in ghosts. I remembered standing on the top step of the staircase with the door open, near but not actually in the attic, and sliding the dollhouse with its inanimate inhabitants across the floor just to the left of the door. That's where it had been, but it wasn't there anymore.

Maybe Edna had given it away or thrown it away, along with all other traces of my existence. That's what she said she would do, and I had no reason to doubt her. Except for the blue and white quilt, there wasn't a single artifact of my childhood anywhere in the attic. Edna had always been thorough.

It didn't matter. I wasn't interested in what was missing from the attic, only in what was present. A normal person cataloging the detritus of Edna's attic might be seized by an urge to phone a garbage collector—and an exterminator—as quickly as possible. Not me. As I stood in the middle of that dim, forgotten cavern, among those broken, dirty, outmoded relics, the last earthly evidence of people long dead and buried, I saw possibilities. And hope. Not much, but some.

There might be something to all this. Or not. Maybe finding that miniature sofa was a sign. Or maybe it wasn't. Only time would tell. There were many questions to be answered before I let myself get too excited about all this.

Signs or no signs, I still didn't know the first thing about running an inn, or any other kind of business. I was totally ignorant about anything even remotely related to the subject. But thanks to the advice and tutelage of Millicent Fleeber many years previously, I knew just where to go and who to see in order to dispel my ignorance.

I took a last look around the attic, mentally cataloging the contents before turning off the light, going down the stairs, and heading back downtown. Remembering that the library closed early on Fridays, I jogged the last quarter mile. When I presented myself at the reference desk, I was out of breath. The librarian asked if I wanted a glass of water.

"No," I gasped, holding my hand out flat to wave off her concern. "I just have a question. Can you tell me where the business books are shelved?"

13
Tessa

October

Cobbled Court Quilts stays open until seven on Thursdays. A bunch of bells tied to the doorknob signals the arrival of customers to the quilt shop, but the jingle was drowned out by the laughter of the women standing clustered near the checkout counter.

Just as happy to go unnoticed, I quietly headed toward some bolts of autumnal fabric and began looking for the leaf print I'd seen on the raffle quilt. I didn't see it anywhere.

Evelyn spotted me from across the room. "Good evening, Tessa!"

"Hi." I smiled and gave a little wave. Besides Evelyn, I saw Margot, Evelyn's mother, Virginia, who also taught classes and worked at the shop, and two women whose faces were unfamiliar.

Margot ran over to give me a hug. "I'm so glad you found time to come in!"

"I know," I said apologetically. "I've been so busy. . . ."

Margot waved her hand and made a "no explanation needed" face. "You're here now and that's what counts. And you're joining us at the quilt circle this Friday?" I nodded and Margot clapped her hands as if this were the best news she'd ever heard.

"Wonderful! Can I help pick out your fabric?"

Again with the offer to help me choose fabric. Initially, I'd thought that was so odd, but now that I was actually inside the shop, I understood what she was talking about.

Cobbled Court Quilts had three times the floor space of For the Love of Lavender, and every inch of it was packed tight with fabric. The walls were lined with what seemed like miles of triple-decked shelving, each loaded with fabric bolts. The center of the shop held rows of smaller display cases short enough so customers could see across the room, with still more bolts of cloth. The shorter units were piled with baskets of sewing notions, pattern books, and ribbon-tied bundles of fabric in coordinated colors.

I had no idea where to begin. I knew exactly what fabrics I wanted; I'd taken a picture of Margot's raffle quilt and printed it out on my computer. But as I looked around the shop, I couldn't find any of the ones I needed.

"Where can I find this?" I asked, pointing to the leaf print.

Margot squinted and looked at the picture. "I don't think we have that in stock anymore."

"No? Well, what about all these? For the maple leaves?"

Margot looked at the picture again and then turned to look at me with a creased brow, as if she didn't quite understand my question.

"Tessa, I made this quilt three years ago."

"So?"

"So, for the most part, quilt fabric is like fine wine. The manufacturers create a certain number of bottles—or in this case, a certain number of bolts—and when they're gone they're gone. I doubt we have more than a handful of the fabrics I used in this quilt still in stock."

Now it was my turn to be confused. "But . . . I want to make *this* quilt."

Margot grinned and turned to the others, who were also grinning. Suddenly I felt very foolish and out of place, as though I'd just walked in on the meeting of a club I wasn't a member of.

One of the women I didn't know, a short and stocky lady with salt-and-pepper hair and an olive complexion, said, "We're not laughing at you, we're laughing with you. Because we've all been there. Haven't we, Connie?"

"Oh, yes," said the petite brunette who was standing next to her. "Many times."

The first woman held out her hand and wiggled her fingers. "The picture. Come on. Let's see it."

I walked to the counter and handed her the computer printout. She pulled a pair of red-rimmed reading glasses off her head and looked at the picture on the front. The others, Margot excepted, crowded around to have a look as well.

"Nice! Hey, Connie, this is right up your alley," she said, glancing at her friend before turning back to me. "Connie likes piecing big, bold blocks that incorporate complementary colors. Kind of a restrained scrappy look. What do you think, sis?"

"Oh, this *is* pretty. I'd love to see it in spring colors, shades of green—celery, celadon, shamrock, and maybe jade—just to bring in a little touch of blue. That'd give you somewhere interesting to go with the border fabric. Know what I mean?"

I had no clue what she was talking about—she could have been speaking Armenian, for all I knew—but I nodded anyway. She wasn't fooled.

"Never mind." She smiled and put out her hand for me to shake. "I'm Connie, but I bet you already figured that out."

"I'm Tessa. Nice to meet you."

"And this one," Connie said, tipping her head toward the woman with the salt-and-pepper hair, "is my sister, Bella."

"I know, I know." Connie chuckled. "Other than the eyes, we look nothing alike."

"We're half sisters," Bella said as she gave me back my picture. "Connie got Dad's hair and I got his shoulders. If I'd have been born a boy I could have played defense for the Jets. As it is, I teach middle school phys ed."

"And I teach high school chemistry," Connie said. "We come from a long line of teachers."

"Tessa owns For the Love of Lavender, just down the street," Evelyn put in.

"Really?" Connie looked genuinely interested. "I've walked by there a million times but haven't had a chance to stop in yet. It looks so cute from the outside."

"Thanks."

Connie had just said a mouthful. Probably ninety-five percent of the residents of New Bern

143

could have said the same thing. What was I doing here? I should be back at my shop, figuring out how to bring in more customers. And yet . . . they seemed so nice. Margot had been right about me: I really needed some friends.

Back in Massachusetts, my social life centered around work; same for Lee. When we moved, everyone at the office promised to stay in touch, but those promises were short-lived. I telephoned my old friends frequently at first, but as time passed I found we had less and less to say to each other. After a while, I gave up calling them. I told myself that it was normal, that long-distance friendships were bound to fade, but I had to wonder: Had we ever really been friends to begin with? Besides working in the same building, we'd never had much in common.

I never imagined being lonely in New Bern. After all, I was coming home, wasn't I? I supposed I'd just pick up my old relationships where I'd left off. It didn't work out like that. Many of the people I knew in high school had moved to other towns or other states. And those who were still here were too busy to add more people to their lives. At first it didn't bother me. I was so busy settling in, starting a new business that there wasn't time to feel lonely. But now I was lonely. I wanted friends. I needed them.

"This will be Tessa's first quilt," Margot said proudly, beaming like the mother of a child who's just mastered the art of shoe-tying. This information brought forth a round of cooing and congratulations.

Virginia, Evelyn's mother, a tiny little thing with hair as white and fine as spun sugar and bright blue eyes that missed nothing, was holding a fluffy and overweight cat in her arms. Later, I would learn that this cat, though a tom, was named Petunia. Virginia walked to the bowfront display window, set Petunia down in a cushioned basket, and looked at me. "What colors were you planning to use in your quilt?"

"These colors," I said, holding up the picture. Why was it so hard to make everyone understand? "I don't want to make *a* quilt, I want to make *this* quilt."

Virginia narrowed her eyes, which deepened the wrinkles at the corners and made her look even wiser than she already did. "But you can't make *that* quilt. Anyway, why would you want to? Margot already did. If you're just looking to reproduce somebody else's idea, you might as well buy a paint-by-numbers kit. Quilting isn't about replication. It's about self-expression, making it work, and making your own rules."

The doorbell jingled. A voice came from the doorway. "And as we all know," the voice declared, "rules are meant to be broken. That's what I've always thought."

Virginia nodded and turned to greet the newcomer. "Hello, Abigail."

I'd heard of Abigail Burgess Wynne Spaulding, she of the many surnames—who in New Bern hasn't? But I'd never met her. Rumor is that she owns half the town. Rumor also is that, after her recent marriage, she prefers to be called Abigail Spaulding.

She was beautiful for her age (though it was hard to tell exactly what her age might be), elegantly but simply dressed in a pair of light wool slacks, sweater, and a tweed jacket that said old money. She was tall, though not as tall as I'd expected. Her wedding earlier in the summer—or rather her re-wedding—to Franklin Spaulding, her attorney of many years, had been the talk of the town.

When Abigail's niece, Liza, who'd been engaged to Evelyn's son, Garrett, got cold feet and backed out of the wedding, Abigail and Franklin used the occasion to renew their own vows. It was, I'd heard, the wedding to end all weddings, with lobsters trucked in from Maine and music by a twenty-five-member orchestra. Afterward, they'd headed off to Bermuda for what was supposed to be a two-week honeymoon, but they'd liked it so much that they stayed on until fall.

Since Abigail's niece had called off the engagement to Evelyn's son, I wondered if there might be any tension between the two women, but if there was, I certainly didn't see it. They looked to be the best of friends.

"Hello, all," Abigail said cheerily. "Evelyn! Good news! Your wedding present has finally arrived. I'm having it delivered to your house tomorrow afternoon at two. Will you be home?"

"Abigail, you didn't have to give us a wedding present. . . ."

"You're certainly right!" she retorted in pretended offense. "If you're not invited to the wedding, you don't have to send a gift."

I'd heard about that too. Apparently Evelyn's wedding to Charlie had been a very last-minute affair. Though they'd been dating for years, so, really, does that count as last minute? In any case, they'd finally decided to tie the knot and eloped to Ireland for the honeymoon.

"Getting married without me. Tsk, tsk. How could you? However," Abigail said magnanimously, "I have decided to forgive you."

"That's big of you, Abbie."

"Isn't it?" she said with a little smile before turning to face me. "Who are you?" Her expression was pleasant, but I was a little taken aback by her abrupt manner. I'd heard that Abigail Spaulding was a little odd. Guess I'd heard right.

Margot came to my rescue. "This is Tessa Woodruff. She owns For the Love of Lavender."

"For the Love . . . Oh, yes. Yes, of course! You're the one who's joining us on Friday nights, aren't you?" Abigail exclaimed in recognition as she reached out to shake my hand. "I've seen your shop. Very sweet. I keep meaning to go in. . . ."

Story of my life.

"Nice to meet you, Mrs. Spaulding."

"Please, call me Abigail."

"Tessa is here to pick out fabric for a quilt," Virginia said.

"Well, I'm here for the same reason. Ted Belden has talked me into making a quilt for the library auction." Abigail rolled her eyes. "I don't know why I agreed to it. It'd be so much easier, and probably more profitable for the library, if I just wrote a check. But Ted is insistent. I can't think why. It's not as if my quilting talents are particularly legendary."

Evelyn tipped her head to one side. "Maybe not, but you are."

"Oh, stop it."

"I mean it, Abbie. You know everybody in town. The chance to own an Abigail Original will generate a lot of interest, might start a bidding war."

"I seriously doubt that. But," she said, heaving a martyred sigh, "I've already agreed to do it, so there it is. I just can't make up my mind about a pattern. It can't be anything too complicated. I don't have time for that. The auction is the Saturday after Thanksgiving. What are you making, Tessa?"

"This," I said, showing her the picture.

"Oh, this is lovely. I'd have no trouble getting this done in time." She drummed her fingers on her cheek. "Hmm. Christmas colors, I think. Something festive. Tessa, what colors are you using for your quilt?"

"We were discussing that when you came in," Bella replied.

Abigail peered at the photo again. "Well, you really could use anything, couldn't you? Should be fun to make."

When Margot brought up this whole thing I'd thought it would be fun, too, but I was beginning to have doubts. "I wanted to make the exact same quilt Margot did, with the exact same fabrics. But if they aren't in stock, what do I do? There must be a dozen different fabrics in this quilt."

"More like twenty," Connie replied. "It's very scrappy."

I groaned. "Twenty? How am I supposed to find twenty fabrics that look good together?"

"By starting with one," Virginia declared, "and building from there. What are your favorite colors?"

"Green. Blue. Purple. Actually lavender, like the plant."

Virginia shook her head. "Then why in the world were you planning to make an autumnal quilt? Never mind," she said, waving me off before I could answer.

Virginia walked to the opposite side of the room and stood in front of one of the triple-decker shelves, with her hands on her hips. "Something came in last week that might do for your border. Now, where did it go? Oh! Here we are!" Virginia was a tiny thing. She rose up on her toes but could barely reach the top display shelf.

"Let me get that for you." Bella bounded to Virginia's side, pulled down the bolt Virginia pointed to, and then carried it to the cutting table before rolling it out.

"Oh, that's pretty," Connie said.

It certainly was. The collage of leaves in rich shades of green, blue, turquoise, and taupe was veined with threads of gold that glittered, but barely, giving those deep colors a lighter, almost translucent feel, like sunlight shining through treetops. I loved it. Even more than I loved the border on Margot's quilt.

"Do you think this would work?"

"Absolutely," Evelyn assured me. "And with so many colors to play off, you can take this in all kinds of directions, really make it your own."

I reached out to touch the fabric, rubbed it between my fingers. It was so soft. I never expected cotton to feel as smooth as silk. "I love this shade of green," I said, pointing to one of the leaves.

"So," Margot said, "if you use that green as your anchor color, then add a few more shades, maybe pick up a couple of the background colors as an accent, just to give it some punch . . ."

"Like this?" Abigail pulled a fabric the color of a ripe pear off the shelf and laid it next to the leafy print. It was a perfect choice, picking up the subtle veins of gold in the leaves and making the other colors richer without overpowering them.

"Oh, I like that!" Virginia exclaimed. "But Margot's right. We need more green. How about these?" she asked, pulling out two more fabrics from the shelf.

"Or this," Evelyn said, carrying another bolt to the table. "Do you like this sage color?"

"It'd be nice to bring in a little more turquoise, just a touch," Bella added, eyeing a shelf loaded with blue and turquoise fabrics.

Soon everyone was engaged in the hunt for the perfect color combinations, even me. I found two more greens, rejected one as too muddy but left the other, a diamond print a shade or two brighter than emerald, on the table with the bolts under consideration. Twenty minutes later, we had twenty beautiful fabrics that, miraculously, looked beautiful together—my diamond print among them.

"Now we'll need a good neutral," Connie said. "Ivory, leaning a little toward yellow. Like the pages of an old book."

"That's what this reminds me of," I said,

brushing my hand across the bolts. I still couldn't get over how soft they felt. "When I was a little girl, I used to collect autumn leaves, then lay pieces of paper over them and make rubbings of green and blue and yellow and paste them in a scrapbook. I think I had some idea of trying to preserve the summer in them. This is sort of like that, a leaf scrapbook in fabric."

"Well, there you go," Margot said, spreading her hands. "You've got a concept, an image to aim for. And you told me you weren't creative." She clucked her tongue, pretending to scold. "You've been holding out on me."

"Yeah," I deadpanned. "That was it. My latent creativity has suddenly emerged. Margot, you never told me that quilting was a team sport."

"Didn't I? Well, it is. And you're now an official member of the team. We've got jerseys and hats and everything."

Margot was teasing, but from what I'd just seen, there was some truth in what she said. When I walked into the shop that evening, I'd felt like a party crasher. Not anymore. As soon as I'd expressed an interest in quilting, these women I barely knew started scurrying from one end of the shop to the other, carrying bolts, thumping them down on the table, seeking my opinion, smiling when they'd hit the mark, gamely hauling them back to the shelf if their choice was rejected, just as engaged in the process as if they'd been making it for themselves. It was incredible.

I'd yet to sew a single stitch but already I realized there was more to this quilting business than just making blankets, a lot more. And whatever it was—a club, a party, a team—I wanted to be part of it.

14
Tessa

A spool of cotton thread, plus four full yards of fabric and sixteen of those eighteen- by twenty-two-inch fabric cuts that quilters call "fat quarters" made a pretty, and pretty large, pile on the checkout counter.

Bella and Connie had gone off to meet their father for dinner. Abigail was standing at the cutting table, debating the merits of white snowflakes on a bright red background versus scarlet poinsettias on ivory and gold as a border fabric. Margot stood next to her, rotary cutter in hand, waiting for Abigail to reach her decision. Virginia was working at her quilting frame near the big display window while Petunia rubbed against her legs. Evelyn stood at the register, ringing up my order. I stood with pen poised over my checkbook and braced myself for the total.

"Thirty-eight dollars and twenty-four cents."

I frowned. "That can't be right."

"Yes, it can. Four yards of fabric, plus tax, comes to thirty-eight twenty-four."

"But what about the fat quarters and thread?"

"There's no charge for those," she replied with a quick shake of her head. "Part of our can't-miss marketing strategy for novice quilters. We build up your fabric stash to the point where you're really hooked. Once that happens, you're ours for life."

"That sounds kind of sinister."

"Nothing of the kind. Quilting fabric is calorie-free, nontoxic, and made from one hundred percent cotton. It's practically organic. Can I help it if my customers can't seem to get enough of it? We all have our little vices."

"And it's your job to feed them?"

She shrugged. "Somebody's got to."

"Very funny. Evelyn, you can't give me free fabric."

"Yes, I can. I own the joint."

Before I could argue with her, the doorbell jingled. Evelyn looked up and called out, "Hi, Candy. Did you decide to sign up for the appliqué class after all?"

Candy Waldgren said hello to the group, then shook her head. "No time right now, Evelyn. I'm swamped. One of these days I've just got to learn to say no. I'm on committees for the library fund-raiser and the Christmas tree lighting on the

Green, and I'm in charge of costumes for the church pageant. Maybe I'll have time to take a class after New Year's, but right now, I'm just making pillowcases. My grandson is going through a cowboy phase. Do you have any Western fabrics?"

"Right there in the juvenile prints. Let me show you." She came out from behind the counter to help Candy, leaving me to fill out my check.

Lee was right, I shouldn't have said anything about the store being in trouble. She meant well, but I wasn't buying Evelyn's "novice quilter discount" story, not for one minute. I hesitated for a moment before writing in the amount Evelyn had quoted, telling myself I'd figure out a way to repay this unsolicited favor.

Candy quickly chose two fabrics from the shelf, one with a blue bandanna theme, the other with scenes of bucking broncos ridden by hat-waving cowboys. She carried the bolts to the cutting table and let them drop with a thump right next to Abigail's fabric.

Abigail shot her an indignant look, but Candy either didn't notice or didn't care. She asked Margot to cut two yards from each bolt. Margot cast a questioning glance toward Abigail, who twitched her shoulders to indicate her continued indecision. Margot carefully moved Abigail's yardage to the side before unrolling Candy's fabric.

"Two yards, you said?"

Candy nodded. "Yes. Two of each. Actually, make it two and a half. Better too much than too little."

She turned away from the table to face the rest of us. "So, has everybody heard the news about Madelyn Beecher? She's moved back into Beecher Cottage and wants to turn it into a bed-and-breakfast. Tessa, you were friends with her back in grade school, weren't you? After all the stuff she pulled, can you believe she had the nerve to come back to New Bern?"

Madelyn is back in New Bern?

That couldn't be true, could it? A dozen questions circled in my brain, but none of them found their way to my lips. Candy's revelation left me speechless, but it didn't matter. Candy chattered on without waiting for answers to her questions, apparently oblivious to the effect her words might have on others.

"You of all people must know what I'm talking about, don't you, Abbie? After all, she had that affair with your husband, didn't she?"

For a moment that felt far longer, the room was dead silent. Everyone looked at Abigail, who was looking at Candy with an impenetrable stare.

During my senior year, I'd heard whispers about Madelyn, who had dropped out of school and was working as a secretary for Abigail's then-husband, Woolley Wynne, but I hadn't

156

believed them. Yes, Madelyn had, as we called it back then, "a reputation." But she had a policy when it came to boys: "anything but." Woolley Wynne wasn't a boy; he was a grown man. Surely he wouldn't have been satisfied with anything less than everything. And surely Madelyn, just a teenager at the time, wouldn't have carried on with a married man. Would she?

From where I was standing, I could see Abigail's jaw clench and unclench. She smiled benignly and in a voice that was neither warm nor cold, she said, "Candy, I never realized you were a student of ancient history. Or shall we call it ancient rumor? How fascinating. I'm rather more interested in current events myself. So tell me, where did you hear all this?"

Candy swallowed before answering. "From Aaron Fletcher. Madelyn inherited the house from her grandmother, and Aaron said she came to the bank asking for an enormous remodeling loan. When Aaron turned her down, she made a scene. What could she have been thinking? Did she really think that Aaron would approve *her* for a loan?"

"Especially after she turned him down every time he asked her out in high school," I said. "Which, as I recall, was dozens of times. Yes. That was foolish of her."

Candy pressed her lips together and her eyes darted between Abigail and me, her confusion apparent. Out of the corner of my eye I could see Abigail's lips bow into a small smile.

"Well, you know what kind of girl she was, Tessa," Candy said defensively, trying to regain her footing. "You can't blame Aaron for turning down her loan. And I certainly don't blame you for dropping her the way you did."

If Candy thought her words would win me to her cause, she thought wrong. Years ago, I had stood by in shamed silence as Ben Nickles verbally bashed Madelyn. I wouldn't make the same mistake twice.

"You know, Candy, I've come to the point in my life where I think it's best not to lay blame too thick on anybody. Especially if you've never walked in their shoes," I said. "I wouldn't wish Edna Beecher as a grandmother on my worst enemy."

"Well," Candy puffed, "that may be, but, as Abigail says, that's ancient history. According to the papers and blogs, she's even more notorious—"

Abigail put up her hand and cut Candy off. "I haven't the least interest in what the tabloids are saying. I've been targeted by those leeches myself from time to time. You were saying something about Madelyn turning Beecher Cottage into a bed-and-breakfast. Where did you pick up that bit of gossip?"

Candy smiled triumphantly. "It's not gossip.

It's the absolute truth. Cecil told me about it."

Cecil was Candy's husband. He worked in the New Bern zoning department.

"He said she came into the office and asked about changing the zoning on Beecher Cottage from residential to light commercial. When Cecil asked why, she said she was thinking of turning it into a small inn with herself as the innkeeper." She crossed her arms over her chest and tipped up her chin, as if daring anyone to take issue with her account.

"That's not a bad idea," Evelyn observed. "New Bern could use a nice inn. And Oak Leaf Lane is a perfect location."

"Well, maybe," Candy said grudgingly. "But have you driven by Beecher Cottage lately? The place is a complete wreck, ready for a bulldozer. You'd have to be crazy to think about turning it into an inn."

"Crazy," Abigail mused. "Or desperate."

Abigail looped her handbag over her shoulder and smiled. "Margot, dear. Can you put aside my fabric for now? I just remembered something I need to do."

15
Madelyn

In the days following my attic epiphany and rush to the library, my dining room table all but disappeared under the detritus of my research, a collage of pens, pencils, Post-its, legal pads, file folders filled with papers filled with notes and calculations, and books—*Small Business for Dummies*, *Business Plans for Dummies*, *So You Want to Be an Innkeeper*, and a half dozen others.

Millicent Fleeber would have been proud.

I was—I am—a high school dropout. I gave up on school in my junior year, after receiving an F in English. My feeling was this: If I couldn't pass English, which I could actually speak, what hope was there for chemistry?

But after I married Sterling, my ignorance became an embarrassment. The first time I publicly said something that revealed my lack of education, Sterling leaned down, chuckled, and said, "That's all right, Madelyn. You can't be smart *and* beautiful." Everyone laughed. I blushed and wished that the floor would open up and swallow me. The third time Sterling delivered that line, his smile was forced and I noticed some eye rolls being exchanged with the laughter. He came home the next day and thrust a piece of paper at me.

"What's this?"

"A list of the one hundred books everyone should read. Don't say another word in public until you've read ten of them. Gene is trying to get me a spot on the symphony board. But his efforts will come to naught when people hear I'm married to some bimbo who thinks Madame Defarge is a dress designer!"

That made me cry. Sterling didn't care. "Get the books," he said.

My humiliation led me to the New York Public Library and Millicent Fleeber, a doughy-faced, badly dressed, incredibly knowledgeable librarian. Miss Fleeber introduced me to Charles Dickens (and, by extension, Madame Defarge), Jane Austen, William Faulkner, Harper Lee, Vladimir Nabokov, John Steinbeck, Edith Wharton, Robert Frost, Edna St. Vincent Millay, Charles Baudelaire, and my favorite poet, Emily Dickinson. She also taught me that I wasn't too stupid to learn.

It wasn't easy. My reading speed hadn't improved one iota since high school, but Miss Fleeber convinced me that speed didn't matter. "Books are to be *savored,*" she said.

It took me years to finish reading the ten volumes Sterling demanded as payment for lifting my sentence of silence. At the first party we attended after I'd done so, someone wondered aloud if Truman Capote, rather than Harper Lee, was the actual author of *To Kill a Mockingbird*. I joined in the conversation, cautiously at first, pointing out the differences in their writing styles and ending with what I felt was my trump card. "Besides, if he had—even secretly—written a novel that went on to win the Pulitzer Prize, do you think that Capote could *possibly* have kept that under wraps? The man had an ego the size of New Jersey."

That line elicited laughter and nods of agreement from my listeners. Beaming, hoping he'd witnessed my moment of triumph, I turned to look for Sterling. He was standing in the doorway with his back to me, leaning down to whisper something in the ear of a woman with teased hair and plunging décolletage.

Reading all those books didn't help me win my husband's love or respect, but it did instill in me a deep appreciation for libraries in general and research librarians in particular. "Ignorance isn't a chronic condition, not unless you permit it to be," was one of Miss Fleeber's favorite maxims. My visit to the research desk of the New Bern Library proved how true it was.

After a week of reading, calculating, planning, and plotting, I concluded that my crazy plan really wasn't all that crazy. New Bern had always been an attractive spot for regional tourism. The librarians helped me find specific figures on tourism, including where our visitors stayed and for how long. Almost none of the town's tourists actually stayed in New Bern, at least in part because the village was short on lodging.

Numbers don't lie. I'd identified the need, the opportunity, and done the math. So far, it all added up. In three or four years, less if the economy turned around, the Beecher Cottage Inn could be a moneymaking enterprise and, hopefully, an attractive investment for a wealthy someone looking to fulfill their secret dream of becoming the proprietor of a charming little inn in a charming village in New England.

A lot of people have that dream. And a lot of people will be willing to pay for it—so long as their dream comes as a turnkey operation with proven positive cash flow.

This house, this town, this life—it isn't my dream, but it's somebody's. My dream is to sell this house at a price that will let me get away from New Bern, the scene of all my failures, and never come back. But there's a lot to be done between this and that, and today was all about writing my business plan, a task that required intense focus. Otherwise, I'd have looked at the caller identification before I answered the phone and let it go into voice mail—as usual.

"Madelyn?" He paused for a moment, waiting for me to say something. "It's Sterling."

"What do you want?"

"To talk to you. I've been trying to get hold of you for days," he said impatiently. "Don't you ever answer the phone?"

Not when you're calling, I don't.

He'd called nearly every day since I arrived in New Bern. I never picked up. Why would I? It was his fault I was in this mess. But that didn't stop him from leaving messages, make that commands, for me to return his calls. I ignored them. All of them.

"I've been busy," I said. "Working."

"Working? You?"

I thought about hanging up on him. I should have. But in spite of the applause that had accompanied my speech and indignant exit from New Bern National, that smug banker's rebuff still stung. People had dismissed and talked down to me all my life. I'd had enough.

Maybe my plan would never come to fruition, but at least I *had* a plan, and I'd worked it out all on my own. I wanted someone to know that, even if it was only Sterling. Perhaps especially if it was Sterling.

"Madelyn? Are you there? You said you're working. Working on what?" he repeated.

"A business plan."

He laughed. There it was again, the tone I knew so well—the sneer. Some people never change. I should have known.

"*You're* working on a business plan? Don't tell

164

me you found a job as somebody's secretary, not after all these years."

"Not *typing* a business plan, Sterling. Writing one. I've decided to renovate Beecher Cottage and turn it into an inn."

"What?" Sterling laughed, not a polite chuckle but an incredulous guffaw. "Are you crazy? You're not equipped to run a business, especially an inn. It's hard work. And the profit margins are terrible even when times are good. Nobody is traveling right now, Madelyn. Everybody's broke."

"Thanks to you!" I snapped.

"Seriously, Madelyn," he said, the laughter leaving his voice. "You don't know the first thing about business. You weren't even a very good secretary."

"How would you know? You were too busy running your hands up my skirt and down my blouse to find out."

"Don't be ridiculous. You're not smart enough to run a business."

"You're one to talk. You didn't run a business, you ran a Ponzi scheme! You never made an honest dollar in your life. You're a thief, Sterling. Nothing but a thief!"

"Hey!" he shouted before dropping his voice to a half-whisper. "Knock it off, will you? They could be tapping the phones."

I rolled my eyes. "You already pleaded guilty,

Sterling. Remember? And even if you hadn't, do you think they don't have the goods on you already?"

There was a pause. I waited for him to come back at me, the way he always did, to shred me with some scathing retort, but he didn't.

"I didn't call to fight."

"Then why did you call, Sterling? Whatever you want, the answer is no."

"Can we stop this? Just for a little while could we call a truce?" His voice was laced with tension. Holding his temper was costing him some effort, I could tell. He did want something.

"You may not realize it, Madelyn, but I'm trying to help you. Let me help you." His voice softened; it was almost gentle. I wasn't fooled.

Sterling could be charming when he wanted to. No one knows that better than me. Before we were married, he wined me and dined me and so thoroughly dazzled me that even if I'd been inclined to resist, and even if I hadn't seen marrying him as my only available path to security and survival, I would have succumbed to his charm. He was and still is a handsome man. When he gazed at me with that animal hunger in his eyes, I could not help but say yes. Yes to him, yes to everything.

Not anymore.

"Madelyn," he said in a concerned, almost fatherly tone. "Running an inn is real work, not a hobby. I know you must be bored stiff out in the country, but surely you can find something else to do with your time. Take up bridge," he suggested. "Or tennis. Maybe riding. I've heard there are some good stables out there."

"Bridge? Tennis?"

Was he kidding? What kind of fantasy world was he living in? I wasn't a bored socialite looking for ways to fill her time, not anymore. And he wasn't a financial tycoon with a private plane and an estate in the Hamptons. After all that had happened, the lifetime of lies and insults and the public humiliation, he still had the gall to treat me like a big-busted, empty-headed bimbo? Maybe I wasn't the sharpest pencil in the box. But at least *I* was smart enough to face the facts.

"Or you could volunteer somewhere," he continued without a trace of irony. "But an inn? Face facts, Madelyn. You're beautiful. You were beautiful. But you're no Rhodes Scholar. And you don't have a head for business."

"Then I'll damned well grow one! I have to! Sterling, don't you get it? They Took The Money," I said, enunciating each individual word so there would be no possibility of his missing my meaning. "You're penniless and I'm near to it. I've got to do something to take care of myself, and what I've decided to do is open an inn. This isn't some whim of mine, Sterling. I've spent the last week figuring out capital expenditures, operating costs, occupancy rates, and cash flow projections. I know what I'm doing!"

Sort of.

I'd learned a great deal in the last few days. The biggest lesson was that I *could* learn it. Capital expenditures, cash flow projections, operating costs. These weren't just words I was tossing out to impress Sterling—though I admit that part of me did want him to be impressed—I actually knew what they meant! I wasn't a moron. I never had been and I wanted Sterling to admit it, to show me at least a little bit of respect.

Was that so much to ask? Apparently.

"For God's sake, Madelyn. If you wanted investment advice, why didn't you pick up the phone and call me? I could have . . ."

"You?" I laughed. "You think I'd take investment tips from you? What planet are you living on?"

He made a choking sound, trying and failing to swallow back his anger. I'd gotten to him. I was glad.

"I spent forty-one years on Wall Street, Madelyn. Forty-one years! I know everybody who's anybody in New York."

"Been getting a lot of calls from them lately, have you?"

Sterling went on as if he hadn't even heard me.

"The wealthiest people in the world came to me for advice. I managed one of the largest investment portfolios in the country. For forty years, my clients had returns of ten percent minimum. Minimum! I helped thousands of people. Back in the eighties—"

"Sterling, are you crazy?" I asked, wondering if it might be true. "You didn't help people. You took their money, raked a pile off the top for yourself, and then paid out that annual ten percent return with the money of the next poor sucker who came through your door. You didn't *invest* money, Sterling. You *stole* it. That's why you're in jail. Remember? You're one of the reasons everybody is broke!"

He started to shout at me, spitting out all his favorite insults, names, denials, and epithets. Sterling Baron's Greatest Hits.

Everything was everybody else's fault. Everybody else was inferior, wrong, clueless, and out to get him. It was a familiar playback; I'd heard it all before. But this time was different. This time I didn't have to sit there and take it.

I shouted back, determined to make myself heard over the tirade, telling him I was hanging up and not to call me back—not ever. I stood up, ready to slam the phone down.

Sterling stopped for a moment and then called out, "Wait! Madelyn, wait! Don't hang up!"

He was still shouting, but this time it was

different. There was something in his voice that I'd never heard before—fear.

"Madelyn. Please. I'm sorry. Please don't hang up."

An apology? From Sterling? That was a first. I didn't say anything, waiting for him to make the next move.

"I need a favor."

Of course he did. I told myself to hang up. But his voice, the fear in his voice . . . I folded one arm protectively across my chest.

"What?"

"My sentencing hearing . . ."

"I heard they'd put it off again."

"They did. But even Gene will run out of stall tactics eventually. He thinks it would help if you'd come and testify on my behalf."

"You can't be serious."

"I'm going away for a long time. I know that. But if the judge is lenient, I might get as few as ten years. If you spoke at the sentencing, it would make me seem more sympathetic, more human. You know. Thirty happy years of marriage. A family man . . ."

My breath caught in my throat. For a moment, it almost felt like my heart had stopped beating.

"A family man? Our marriage, happy?" I choked. "Oh, Sterling. You really are deluded. No, Sterling. No. Some lies are just too big."

I couldn't bear to listen to any more. I hung up

the phone, leaned against the kitchen counter, and covered my eyes with my hand. Twin teardrops slipped out from beneath my palm. Two for Sterling. Two for me. Two for everything we'd done to each other.

16
Tessa

Picking out the fabric took longer than I'd thought, and then there was that whole scene with Candy Waldgren. I should have gone straight home after I finished. Lee was waiting for me and he was making lasagna. He makes great lasagna. Instead, I drove to Oak Leaf Lane. I couldn't help myself.

Even in the dim light of the streetlamp, I could see that Beecher Cottage was badly in need of a paint job. And a new porch. The shutters were in terrible shape too. There was an expensive, cream-colored sedan parked in front of the house. It seemed like I'd seen it somewhere before.

I pulled to the curb a few doors down from Beecher Cottage, turned off the car, and stared at the ramshackle old house. The living room window glowed with the light of a brass floor lamp that stood near the window. Who had turned it on?

Someone turned on the porch light. The door

opened and Abigail Spaulding walked out, looking tight-lipped and angry. She was followed by a woman, barefoot and wearing a baggy sweater, about my age, with beautiful sad eyes and an expression even angrier than Abigail's.

I couldn't hear what she was saying, but the mute workings of her lips and the jagged movement of her right arm as she gestured toward the street and the way Abigail swiftly descended the porch steps and marched down the walkway gave me the general gist of the one-sided conversation. Abigail climbed into the big sedan and drove off. The woman smiled grimly and turned to go inside the house, slamming the door so hard that even inside my car, I could hear the reverberation.

The whole scene couldn't have taken more than a minute to play out. But even with her unkempt hair, her shapeless sweater, and with the evidence of time and troubles etched into her once smooth face, I knew that Candy Waldgren was telling the truth.

Madelyn Beecher had come home to New Bern.

17
Madelyn

If I'd slammed the door any harder it would have come off the hinges. Who did she think she was?

Angry as I was, I almost laughed at that.

She was Abigail Burgess Wynne, of course! And judging by the incredible gall she displayed in showing up uninvited on my doorstep, she had changed not at all. There she was, trying to run me out of town—again.

When I answered the door, I'd stood there for a moment, absolutely dumbstruck. Though her appearance had changed so little in the years since I'd last seen her, it took a moment to convince myself that the woman standing there really was Abigail.

She smiled and asked if she could come inside. In my shock, I let her—but only as far as the foyer.

"I heard you were back in town, so I just thought I'd stop by and say hello."

"Why?"

She frowned. "You needn't take such a hostile tone, Madelyn. I know that our history together hasn't been exactly . . . shall we say, cordial? But that was a long time ago. Things are different now. Water under the bridge and all that."

She looked down, fiddling with her gloves as she spoke, tugging at each leather finger and then pulling at the wrist and stretching them tight over her hands, smiling one of those obligatory smiles people paste on to help them get past awkward moments.

"When I heard you'd moved back into Beecher Cottage and had plans to turn it into an inn, I just thought I'd—"

"Drop by with a houseplant and a Hallmark card? Quit pretending, Abigail. You're here because you want something. What is it?"

She gave a quick, sharp tug on each of her gloves, then intertwined her fingers and folded her hands together at her waist. "I've heard about your troubles with Sterling."

"Really? I didn't peg you for the sort of woman who reads the tabloids."

"I don't." She shot me a look, then went on. "Besides, one needn't read the scandal sheets to know about your situation. The *Wall Street Journal* has done quite a few stories on you and your husband, you know. So have all the other financial pages. Anyway, when I heard tonight that you were planning on opening an inn I talked to a few people, made a few calls. . . . To get to the point, Madelyn, I understand that you're in terrible financial straits. And, at least to some degree, I feel responsible for your situation."

You do? This should be interesting.

"I don't condone what went on between you and Woolley, but it wasn't the first time he cheated on me, nor was it the last. You were so young and I knew what Woolley was like, how single-minded he could be when he wanted something."

Or someone. Oh, yes. Yes, he could.

I had heard from Woolley's own lips how, for nearly two years, he had wined and dined the beautiful Abigail Burgess. How he had wanted her and how she had resisted, he never giving up and she never giving in, which, of course, only inflamed his desire more. When he'd finally won her, she'd told him point blank that she'd marry him but never love him. He was convinced she was just being coy. He was wrong.

I'd heard the tale a hundred times. It was Woolley's favorite postcoital bedtime story. I'd lie next to him on the rumpled sheets, my skin still hot from the heat of his hands, and listen to him talk about her, how cold she was, how beautiful she was, and how he hated her.

It wasn't true, of course. No man talks that much and that passionately about a woman he hates, especially not when he's in bed with another woman. Woolley loved Abigail and only Abigail. I was her stand-in in his bed, nothing more.

Abigail played her hand well. Even after she'd told him she didn't, couldn't, and wouldn't love him, he kept pursuing her. Abigail's heart was the one thing Woolley's millions couldn't buy, but he never stopped trying.

What if I'd played my hand differently? What if I'd made Woolley pursue me instead of allowing myself to be scooped up and taken home like some abandoned pup, grateful and fawning and oh so eager to please? If I'd been as clever as Abigail, would Woolley have loved me? Would Sterling? Would anyone?

I don't know. I never will. But one thing is certain, I won't let it happen again. I'm not going to be pushed out or pushed around ever again, not by anyone, not even Abigail.

Abigail swallowed hard before continuing. "I should have handled things differently, not taken my anger out on you. But Woolley's unfaithfulness hurt me terribly. . . ."

"You weren't hurt," I spat. "You were embarrassed. Worried that people would see through that little farce you played with Woolley."

"Maybe that's how it looked to you, but that's not . . . I'm not . . ." She stopped for a moment. I could see the muscles twitch near her jaw as she clenched her teeth together.

"That was all a long time ago," she said. "And I'm not here to talk about that. I came to talk about you."

I let my arms drop by my side and looked her straight in the eye but said nothing, enjoying the expression of discomfort on Abigail's face and remembering one of Sterling's maxims of negotiation—the first one to talk loses.

Abigail licked her lips. "Later, after that day in Woolley's office, I . . . well, I always felt bad about how I treated you. You were so young. I know all about how the schemes of powerful men can entrap a young and friendless girl. And then, when I heard you'd ended up with Sterling . . ."

She waited a moment, hoping, I suppose, that by some word or movement I might acknowledge her comment.

I didn't so much as blink.

"Even before his arrest, I knew what kind of man Sterling Baron was. Woolley liked him, but I didn't. Woolley was never a good judge of character."

I smiled a little, realizing that her comment could easily be construed as insulting—to both of us. But Abigail didn't seem to pick up on that.

"When I heard that you'd married Sterling, I felt sorry for you. I saw pictures of you in the papers, at gallery openings and charity galas. You had money and jewelry and clothes and I suppose everyone thought you were the luckiest woman on earth. I knew better. Your eyes were so dead. You were just a fly in Sterling Baron's web. And I always felt that I'd participated, at least in a small way, in your capture.

"Diamonds are cold comfort, poor substitutes for love. I learned that too late. Almost too late." Her voice dropped and softened until it was almost a whisper. "Franklin Spaulding showed me what I was missing."

Did she think I cared? Did she suppose that because we'd both held membership in the sisterhood of loveless marriages to wealthy men, that meant I was interested in hearing about her love life?

"What do you want, Abigail?"

"To help you," she said. "To make amends, I suppose. If I can. I know New Bern is the last place on earth you want to be. And I know that you wanted to sell Beecher Cottage but weren't able to."

"Who told you that?"

"Don't look at me that way. It's a small town, Madelyn. I made a few calls, asked a few questions, that's all." She hesitated a moment. "I sit on the board of the bank. I know Aaron Fletcher."

Of course she does.

"And I heard your name again tonight. I was going to wait a few days to contact you, but then I thought . . ." Abigail reached into the pocket of her jacket and pulled out an envelope.

"Here."

"What is this?"

"A check. For seven hundred and fifty thousand

dollars. Which, I understand, is two hundred thousand more than the price you'd hoped to list the house for. Enough to allow you to go anywhere you want and start over."

I turned the envelope over, lifted the gummed flap, and pulled out the piece of paper that was inside. It was just as Abigail said, a check for three-quarters of a million dollars made out to me, Madelyn Beecher Baron. Nobody besides myself—not Sterling, not the feds—had any claim in it. I could cash it at any bank, get into my car, and escape New Bern forever. It was tempting.

But when I looked up at those ice-blue eyes, I couldn't think of anything but the humiliation I'd suffered at her hands, Woolley's unwillingness to defend me, my inability to defend myself. Never again.

I pinched the check between my thumbs and forefingers and tore it in half. "Get out of my house."

18
Tessa

Babe! I'm home!" I shook out my jacket and hung it up on the rack near the back door. Lee didn't answer, but I could hear him in the kitchen, rattling pots and pans.

I walked toward the sound. "Did you look outside? Halloween's a week away and it's already snowing! Hard!"

I love the first snow of the year. It's exciting. Makes me feel ten years old again.

Lee was bending over by the cupboards, pulling out a blue mixing bowl.

"Josh called, wanting to talk to you." He kicked the cupboard closed. "You missed him," he said, the accusation clear in his voice.

"Oh. I'll call him back." I dropped my shopping bag on the floor and reached for the phone.

"He went to the library for a study group. Couldn't wait any longer."

"Well, then I'll call him later, after dinner," I said evenly. I was late, but not *that* late. Not late enough that I deserved to have Lee jump all over me.

Experience has taught me that when Lee is in a bad mood, which isn't often, it's best to ignore it. His bad moods usually pass quickly. When they don't, I've found that there's no point in trying to draw him out. When he's ready to talk, he talks. Coaxing him to open up before he's ready only makes things worse.

Lee grunted, opened the refrigerator, and pulled vegetables out of the crisper. Was he making a salad? The kitchen didn't smell like lasagna. Or anything else.

"Can I help you with anything?"

"I'm on it."

More banging of dishes and drawers, followed by a furious chopping of vegetables. He hacked at the onions as if he intended to draw blood.

"Well," I said brightly. "I'm going to pour myself some wine. It was a crazy day."

I took two glasses down from the cupboard, filled them with pinot noir, kept one for myself and set the other down on the counter next to Lee. From where I was sitting, he definitely looked like he could use a drink. I perched myself on the opposite counter and started talking. Someone had to.

"I stopped by Cobbled Court after work, picked out the fabric for my quilt. You've got to go in there sometime, babe. You wouldn't believe how much inventory Evelyn has in her shop."

"Huh." He slashed a green pepper in half, gutted the seeds, and started dicing the green flesh with an eye toward vengeance.

"Choosing the fabric was way more complicated than I thought. Thank heaven the other women were there to help me. I needed something like twenty different fabrics. They're really pretty, though. Do you want to see?"

Without waiting for his answer, I hopped off the counter, took the fabrics from my shopping bag, and spread them out on the kitchen table. I smiled and fanned them out into an arc, like

181

colorful spokes on a wheel. They really did look good together.

Lee looked at the pile, then at me, and frowned. "How much was all that?"

"Thirty-eight dollars," I said, silently blessing Evelyn Dixon and her invented novice quilter discount.

"Oh. That's not too bad."

I put the fabric away. Lee turned back to the cutting board, using the blade of the knife to sweep the decimated vegetables into a bowl, then paused to take a sip from his wineglass, which I took as a good sign. He pulled out a cast-iron skillet and put it on the stove—no banging this time.

The mail was sitting in a pile near the telephone. I flipped through it and started to tell him about Madelyn's surprising return to New Bern and her even more surprising plans for Beecher Cottage but stopped short when I noticed an envelope with a past due notice from New Bern Energy.

"Babe, did you forget to pay the oil bill?"

The skillet, now filled with a mélange of onions, peppers, and mushrooms, banged hard against the burner, making me jump. The vegetables jumped too. Several pieces of pepper spilled onto the floor.

"Forget? No! No, Tessa, I didn't *forget* to pay the oil bill. I just didn't pay it, all right? I paid the taxes, the mortgage, Josh's tuition, the electricity, and telephone, Internet, and the house, car, and health insurance. After all that, there was two hundred and sixteen dollars left in the checking account. Two hundred and sixteen! That's it!"

Lee is not a shouter. His pent-up frustration exploded and sparked like a Roman candle on the Fourth of July and fizzled just as quickly. His shoulders drooped. The metal spatula he was holding in his hand flopped against his leg, leaving a grease mark on his pants.

"I didn't forget to pay it. I just didn't pay it, not yet. All right?"

"All right," I said. I moved toward him, took the spatula out of his hand, and set it on the counter. "It's all right. We'll pay it as soon as we can. No big deal."

"Yeah. I'll transfer some more money out of savings tomorrow," he said. "I hoped we wouldn't have to do that again, but . . ." He sighed. "I didn't get the job. They called just before you came in. They had one hundred and twenty-eight applicants for the position. One hundred and twenty-eight! For a temp job!"

"Oh, babe. I'm so sorry."

"Yeah. Well. The commute would have been a killer. I'd have spent half of what I made on gas."

He bent over and started picking mushrooms and peppers up from the floor. I stooped down to help.

"You know," he said, "this is just not the country I grew up in. Back in my dad's day, if you worked hard and played by the rules, you'd be all right, you'd get ahead. Nowadays, the rich just get richer and the poor get poorer. It's not right. I was listening to the radio today and heard a story about the housing bubble. They had clips from a mortgage broker who was blaming greedy real estate investors, a real estate investor who blamed greedy bankers, a banker who blamed greedy home owners, and a home owner who blamed greedy mortgage brokers! I swear, nobody takes responsibility for anything these days! I just don't understand it, Tessa. You work hard all your life, try to do the right thing. . . . Isn't there any justice in the world?"

It was a good question and one I sometimes asked myself. But I didn't know the answer, so I told him what I did know.

"It's their loss. You're the best man for the job, for any job. I love you."

He got up and dumped the spoiled vegetables into the sink, and stared out the kitchen window into a curtain of black shot with white as the snowflakes fell.

"I really thought I had it," he mused. "They only interviewed six people."

"Six? Out of one hundred and twenty-eight? You should feel good about that."

"Maybe. But first runner-up doesn't come with

a paycheck," he said, bitterness returning to his voice before he waved it off. "I'm sorry, hon. Don't listen to me. I'm just having a bad day."

"You get to have bad days." I walked up behind him, put my arms around his waist, and turned my head so my cheek rested against his back.

"I've got a great idea. Why don't you sit down at the table, finish your wine, and tell me all about your bad day while I finish making dinner? By the way," I said, squinting at the mess in the skillet. "What *are* we having for dinner?"

"Vegetable and goat cheese omelets."

"Okay. That sounds good, but what happened to the lasagna?" I took my apron off the hook by the pantry and slipped it over my head before opening the refrigerator and pulling out a bowl of eggs from our own chickens.

Lee carried his wine to the table and sat down to watch me. "Ran out of time. When I went out to the barn to bring in the stock for the night, the pigs were missing. They were out in the garden, scrounging for leftover potatoes. I was able to lure three of them back to the pen with a bucket of slop, but that big one . . ." He shook his head. "She was having no part of it. She saw me coming and ran toward the woods, making a break for freedom. And then Spitz got all excited and tried to help and that just made everything worse. She was just out there running around in circles, barking like crazy. Then the sow got ticked and rushed her. Spitz took off for the barn, yelping, and hid behind the grain bin. It took me over an hour to catch the sow, and then I had to haul Spitz out of her hiding place. I finally ended up carrying her inside."

I smiled as I cracked eggs into a bowl and set the shells aside. "Where is she now?"

"Passed out under our bed, sleeping off the trauma."

I pressed my hand to my mouth, stifling the urge to laugh. Poor Spitz. Poor, pathetic Spitz. "So how'd the pigs get out in the first place?"

Lee let out an irritated snort. "The gate to the pigsty was wide open. Somebody had actually *tied* it open with a piece of rope. And I found empty soda cans lying on the ground near the pen."

"Soda cans?"

Frowning, he nodded and took a gulp of wine. "Yeah. Two of them. Somebody's idea of a joke. Or a rescue mission. Stupid kids."

I couldn't help myself. I couldn't suppress the laughter, not even with both hands over my mouth. I dropped my hands and laughed so hard I had to wipe away the tears with the hem of my apron.

Lee put down his glass and spread out his hands. "What? What's so funny?"

In spite of the carnage Lee had inflicted on the veggies, we had a nice dinner together. I told Lee

186

about Madelyn's return to New Bern, news that he found considerably less interesting than I did.

"I suppose she has to live somewhere, but I'd just as soon it was somewhere else. A penal colony on a desert island, she and her husband and everybody like them. Just drop them off in the middle of the ocean and let them rot."

I steered the subject back to the pigs, specifically to Spitz and her inept attempts at pig herding. Lee gave me a blow-by-blow description of the hapless dog's attempts at driving the porker back to her pen. By the time he finished the story, we were both laughing.

To celebrate the early arrival of winter, I decided to make snow ice cream, running outside in the wind to scoop the drifted snow into a bowl, then mixing it with sugar, cream, and a touch of vanilla. After dinner, Lee volunteered to clean up the kitchen. I went to the bedroom and got into my pajamas, then sat cross-legged in the middle of the bed and phoned Josh.

"Hi, Mom. Hey, what's with Dad? He sounded peeved when I called before."

"Oh, he's fine. The pigs got out. So, how are you? How's school?"

"Good. Everything's good. So far, I'm getting an A in organic chemistry."

"You're kidding! That's great, sweetie! You must get it from your dad. I had to take Geology 101 to fulfill my college science requirement.

Rocks for Jocks, they called it. Just me, the defensive line of the football team, and an aging professor who mumbled as he narrated slide shows of geologic strata. He gave me a C."

Josh laughed. "At least you still remember what strata are."

"Sort of."

"So, Mom, not to change the subject, but I wanted to talk to you about Thanksgiving."

"I know. We need to get your plane ticket soon. We're just a little bit tight on finances right now."

"Well, that's what I wanted to talk to you about. I might not need a ticket. Professor Kleypas and his wife are going to Aruba for Thanksgiving and they want me to house-sit for them. All I have to do is bring in the mail, walk and feed the dog, and make sure the place doesn't burn down. They'll pay me five hundred dollars for the week," Josh said. "And the house is really nice. They've got a pool."

"Oh." I paused for a long moment, trying to let this all sink in. "It sounds like a good opportunity, but . . . I hate to think of you being alone at Thanksgiving. . . ."

Not to mention how much I hated the idea of Lee and me being alone for Thanksgiving.

"What would you do about dinner?"

"Ted's mom already invited me to come to their house." Ted was one of Josh's college friends, a day student who lived at home. "They're having a whole gang of people over, kids whose families can't afford to fly them home for the break."

That was nice of Ted's mother to invite Josh to dinner, but we *could* afford to fly our son home for Thanksgiving, sort of. We had credit cards. Paying them off was another matter, but still . . .

I put my hand up to my mouth and chewed a ragged edge off my cuticle, sorting through my emotions.

We've never had Thanksgiving, or any major holiday, without Josh. It was bound to happen eventually, I'd always known that. Children grow up and move out, creating lives of their own. Roots and wings, that's what a good parent should give their children, so they say. And I know it's true, but at that moment, I couldn't help but wish that I'd bought myself a set of wing clippers a long time ago.

"Mom? It's okay. If you don't want me to do it, I'll tell Professor Kleypas I can't. I just thought it'd be a help right now."

"No, no," I said. "You're right. I'm being selfish. Five hundred dollars is a lot of money."

Josh's tone brightened. "And it might lead to other things. Professor Kleypas hires a couple of students to help with his research every summer. He usually picks rising seniors as lab assistants, but if I make a good impression on him, who knows?"

"Who knows?" I echoed.

"And I'll be home for Christmas," he rushed to assure me. "It doesn't make sense to spend money on a plane ticket when I'm coming back three weeks later. Right?"

"Right," I said hesitantly. "I'll talk to Dad, but I'm sure it'll be fine."

"Hey, is Dad there? Can I talk to him?"

"He's doing the dishes. Hang on and I'll go get him."

"Mom? You're sure you're fine with this Thanksgiving thing, right?"

"Sure," I said, making my voice deliberately light. "I wasn't in the mood to make a big meal anyway. Sometime after you cook your twentieth turkey, the thrill wears off."

Josh laughed. "Yeah, I'll bet."

"Hold on while I get Dad. You'll be happy to know he's in a much better mood now. Josh? Have I told you recently how proud I am of you?"

"Yes. You have. Two days ago, the last time we talked. And every time before that."

I laughed. "Well, it bears repeating. I'm proud of you, Joshie. And I love you."

"Love you too, Mom."

It had been a long day and by the time ten o'clock rolled around, we were both exhausted, but I couldn't sleep. Lee was snoring, and Spitz, who had emerged from beneath the bed and wedged herself between Lee and me, protected on all sides from any marauding swine that might break into our bedroom, was doing the same. But that wasn't what was keeping me awake.

I kept thinking about Josh and how strange it would be to have Thanksgiving without him. In our current circumstances, it was for the best, a godsend really. But it didn't feel like one. Why did we ever let him go to school in Florida? Why couldn't he have stayed in-state? What was wrong with UConn?

I rolled over and punched my pillow, trying to find a more comfortable position.

Still, it said something good that Josh's professor was willing to entrust him with the care of his home, didn't it? Lee said it said something good about me and the way I'd raised him, but Lee gets as much credit for that as I do. Anyway, I'm not sure we're better parents than anybody else. Josh is just a good, responsible kid. Always has been. I miss him.

Spitz twitched and jerked in her sleep, probably dreaming of lions and tigers and pigs, oh my. I rolled onto my back again and cast a resentful glance toward Lee's peacefully dozing form. He never had any trouble falling asleep.

Giving up, I opened my eyes and stared at the ceiling and turned my thoughts toward the day's other disturbing development: Madelyn's homecoming.

What was she doing in New Bern? Was she happy to be back? Was she lonely in that big house by herself? What had she said to Abigail? If I knocked on her door and said hello, would she invite me in? Or slam it in my face?

Alone in that big house, that repository of so many of her childhood memories and mine, was *she* able to sleep?

19
Madelyn

Even folded, the quilts were bulky. I chose the two whose chances for repair seemed most promising, put them into a shopping bag, and loaded them in the car before going back inside to make a pot of very strong coffee. I needed it. I'd hardly gotten any sleep the night before; I'd been too excited. And nervous.

After three weeks of research, three weeks spent reading everything I could get my hands on about home repair, remodeling, innkeeping, and general business, taking a detailed inventory of the attic to decide what could be repaired and reused, what was beyond hope, and what might be sold to raise a bit of extra cash, checking out zoning restrictions and commercial building codes, rejecting my original idea of an eight-room inn as too expensive, then refiguring budgets for a five-room, and adding up projections for expenditures, cash flow, and profits, my business plan was done.

Just before midnight I took a deep breath, punched the equal sign on my calculator, and whooped in triumph.

$81,265.00! Yes! It was possible!

If. *If* I was careful, efficient, imaginative, and just a little bit lucky, and *if* I did as much of the restoration and remodeling work myself as was possible, it could happen. But it was a risk. I'd be betting everything I had left in the bank on this one roll of the dice. But it was a risk I had to take, *wanted* to take.

I stood next to the coffeepot, drumming my fingers on the countertop, impatient for it to brew. I couldn't wait to get started.

The hardware store opens at seven-thirty on Saturday, so I went there first.

As I read the list of tradesmen who I needed to hire, the manager, a bear of a man, handsome, with a neatly trimmed beard and wide muscular shoulders, the kind of man who looked like he'd spent a lot of time at the business end of a hammer (exactly the kind of man whom Sterling was not), looked me up and down in a way that made me uncomfortable.

At the risk of sounding egotistical, I'm used to men looking me over like I was a piece of meat in a shop window, but this wasn't that. I wouldn't have thought twice about that. This man seemed to be studying me, searching me, and not just my body but my face, my expression, the inflection of my voice. It was strange. The fact that one of those searching brown eyes was made of glass might have had something to do with it, but it wasn't only that. He kept looking at me like he knew me.

Of course, since my outburst in the bank, I'd had the feeling that everyone was looking at me that way. It made me feel self-conscious.

Why hadn't I left my Prada handbag at home? My jeans and sweater were generic enough, but my bag screamed two things—"I am not from here" and "I have money to burn." Not the message you want to send when you're trying to negotiate the best price on a plumbing job.

"Seems like a pretty big project you've got in mind here," Grizzly Man said, tugging on his beard.

"It is."

He nodded slowly and made a sucking sound with his teeth. "Why not hire a general contractor and let him deal with it? It'd make everything easier."

"And add fifteen percent to my budget." I shook my head. "I've got to squeeze every cent I can out of this project and do as much of the work myself as possible. Sweat equity. You're a businessman, I'm sure you know what I'm talking about."

I looked at him straight on, intent and unblinking, letting him know that I was someone to be taken seriously.

He gave his beard another tug. "All right, then. I'll get you some business cards. There's a lot of good guys out of work right now. You'll have your pick."

"Thank you," I said, and pulled a shopping list from the depths of my bag. "I'm also going to need prices on paint, primer, stain, varnish, brushes, sponges, and an electric sander."

"Sure thing." He beckoned to one of his young clerks. "Just give your list to Matt. He'll ring you up and carry everything out to your car for you."

"Oh. Thank you . . . but . . . that won't be necessary," I stammered, feeling like a complete idiot. "I'm not really planning on buying anything today. I just want to get prices. I need to check with a few suppliers. . . ."

"You mean with the big box store?"

He turned to a young clerk without waiting for my response. "Matt, go shelve those bags of water softener salt that came in this morning. I'll take care of this customer."

Matt scooted off on his errand while I stood there, blushing and feeling like a kid who'd been caught telling a fib. When the clerk was gone, he turned to look at me.

"Ms. Beecher . . ."

"Madelyn."

"Madelyn," he said with a slight inclination of his head. "I don't want to make any assumptions, but I've got a feeling that you'll need a fair amount of guidance to see you through this remodel. I don't mind taking time to answer questions. We offer our *customers* a level of personal attention that the big box stores can't compete with. On the other hand, I can't compete with their prices. Not entirely."

He trained those big brown eyes, even the glass one, on me to see if I was catching his meaning. I was.

"Now, since you're planning on acting as your own contractor," he continued, in a tone that was direct but not unkind, "I'm going to give you the same professional discount I'd give to any of the contractors here in town. If you do business with me, it'll probably cost you one or two percent more than it would if you were buying from those other guys. But for that two percent, you'll get the best customer service in the state and the peace of mind that comes from doing business with people in your community—the same people who will support you once you open your doors."

He smiled faintly. "As a businesswoman, I'm sure you know what I'm talking about."

He'd seen right through me. I smiled back. I couldn't help myself.

"I'm starting to. As you've probably guessed, I've only been a businesswoman for something less than twenty-four hours."

"Everybody has to start somewhere," he said without a trace of mockery. "If you're willing to put in the work it takes to be your own contractor, it's obvious you're not afraid of hard work. That's about half the battle right there."

"If you don't have a lot of money to invest, you've got to replace it with something. In my case that means time—and elbow grease. And I used to have a kind of knack for scavenging, finding old things and fixing them up again. At least, I think I did. It's been a long time since I've had occasion to test my skills, but I'm willing to try.

"Speaking of that," I said, "do you rent sanders for wooden floors? Beecher Cottage is full of them and they're all in terrible shape. If I could do them myself, it would probably save me quite a lot."

He stared at me and frowned. I thought I'd said something wrong.

"Wow. What they're saying is true, isn't it? You really are broke. That jerk hung you out to dry just like he did everybody else. I'm sorry. You didn't deserve that."

His words caught me by surprise. I'd known it wouldn't take long before my presence in New Bern was generally known, but it annoyed me to know that speculation about my fortunes, or lack thereof, had become fodder of the gossip grapevine. I'd always hated this town, and now I remembered why.

"Do you always make such personal observations about complete strangers?"

The big man ducked his head.

At least he has the good grace to feel embarrassed.

"Pardon me. I was out of line. But, Madelyn, we *do* know each other. Can't blame you for not recognizing me. I didn't have the beard back then and I was about twenty pounds lighter. I can't chase down a hockey puck the way I did back in high school. And, what with the missing eye, I know I look different, but I'd recognize you anywhere. You haven't changed a bit."

Hockey puck?

I mentally shaved off the silver-flecked beard, looked more closely at his face, the remaining eye, the long, angular nose with that slight bump in the middle, a souvenir of the league championship game between New Bern and Litchfield, when he'd taken a hit so hard his helmet got knocked off and then he'd gone on to score the winning goal—broken nose and all.

Jake Kaminski.

My face felt hot.

"Madelyn? Are you all right?"

"I . . . I'm fine. I . . . Late for an appointment. I

just remembered." I grabbed my handbag from the counter and started frantically searching for my car keys.

That stupid bag. Why did I bring that big, expensive, stupid bag? I could never find anything in it.

"I'm sorry. I didn't mean to upset you."

Finally, my fingers felt metal. I yanked the keys out of my bag.

"No, no," I said quickly, blinking as I walked. "I'm not upset. Just late. Thanks for your help. I'll be back . . . another day," I lied, gave him a short, hollow smile, and then lied again.

"It was nice to see you again, Jake."

20
Madelyn

My hands were shaking so hard it was a struggle to fit the key into the ignition. I backed out of the parking space quickly, without bothering to check my mirrors, and came six inches from getting my bumper hit by a beat-up green and white pickup truck. The driver slammed on his brakes and his horn. I lifted my hand in a limp apology and drove away as quickly as possible, taking a right out of the parking lot because it was easier and ending up downtown because I didn't know where else to go.

There was an empty parking spot in front of the Blue Bean Coffee Shop and Bakery, so I pulled in and turned off the ignition. I sat there for a moment, with my elbows resting on the steering wheel and my head buried in my hands.

I'm sorry. You didn't deserve that.

His words echoed in my brain and summoned up a fresh threat of tears. Why? It wasn't like I hadn't thought the same thing a hundred times, a thousand. I'd been feeling sorry for myself for a long time, even before I'd met Sterling. Why should hearing the same thing from Jake Kaminski make my hands shake and bring me to the edge of tears?

Because Jake Kaminski knows you. He knows everything.

I took in a breath and let it out, steadying myself, and shushed the voice in my head. I didn't have time for this. Not now.

I lifted my head and looked at myself in the rearview mirror. "Enough," I said aloud, wiping a smear of mascara from under my eyelashes. "Get hold of yourself. You look like fifty miles of bad road."

I hadn't had anything besides coffee and my stomach was growling, whether from hunger or distress I wasn't sure, but I decided to get something to eat.

I reached over to the passenger side to get my purse from the seat, spotted the big shopping bag with the quilts inside on the floor, and decided to bring it along. The quilt shop was just down the block from the Blue Bean. After I ate, I could walk over and look up that Margaret person, see if she thought the quilts were worth trying to save.

The Blue Bean is really more of a café than a bakery, though they do offer delicious, homemade cookies, muffins, scones, and rolls. I was famished. I ordered a small brewed coffee with cream and a raspberry scone.

It was Saturday morning and the café was full. I spotted a couple getting up to leave and sat down, putting the bag with the quilts on the floor next to me. The previous occupants had left their newspaper, so I took a pen from my purse and started reading the classified listings for auctions and estate sales, circling any that seemed promising.

My coffee cup was about half empty when I heard a giggle and a woman's voice say, "Oh, look who's here! Madelyn, right? I'm Margot. We met at the grocery store. Remember?"

I looked up from my newspaper into the pretty, beaming face of a tall woman with blond hair and eyes the color of sapphires. Margot. Not Margaret. Now I remembered.

"What a coincidence. I was planning on coming to the quilt shop to see you."

"Really?" she said with a giggle, not a self-conscious giggle but a delighted one, as if she was genuinely pleased that I'd wanted to look her up. I couldn't think why she would be; we barely knew each other. What a strange woman.

"Well, it looks like I saved you a trip. I'm here to have breakfast with a friend, but it's so crowded! Would you mind a little company?"

Without waiting for me to answer, she pulled a chair out from the table and sat down, then called to her friend, who stood with her back to us, scanning the room for two empty seats. Margot motioned for her to come join us and started making introductions. She could have saved herself the trouble. The moment the woman turned around, I knew who she was.

Though I hadn't laid eyes on her in more than thirty years, I could still pick Tessa Kover's face out of a crowd.

21
Tessa

The night before, Friday, as we were leaving the quilt shop after my first night as a member of the Cobbled Court Quilt Circle (and a great night it had been, too! I'd already sewn my very first quilt block and couldn't wait to get started on the others!), Margot suggested we get together for breakfast the next day.

"It'll be fun!" she exclaimed. "We can talk about quilts and you can tell me the story of your life. Now that we're in the same quilt circle, I need to know absolutely everything about you!"

Of course, Margot was teasing. I'd never planned on telling her much about my past. Not so soon. Not until I turned around and saw Madelyn Beecher, and Madelyn Beecher looked up and saw me, then ran out the door of the Blue Bean without saying a word.

Margot laid her hand on her chest and blinked back a sheen of tears. "Oh, Tessa," she whispered. "Tessa, that is just so sad. Poor thing."

"I know. I don't blame Madelyn for bolting. We were friends, true friends. I wish I'd realized back then how rare real friendship is."

I picked up my fork and moved my eggs from one side of the plate to the other. I'd lost my appetite.

"I just tossed her over. For what? The approval of a boy with wandering hands and bad breath? A bunch of cliquey girls? Sure, Madelyn was a little weird, but at twelve, who isn't? She didn't deserve to be treated like that. No one does, especially somebody whose only crime was trying a little too hard to be a friend. There are worse things, believe me."

I laughed at my own stupidity. "Do you know how many times my old so-called friends from work have called me since I moved?" I held up two fingers. "That's it. And both of them phoned within the first three weeks after I left—and then only in response to the e-mail with my new contact information. I sent it out to about thirty people, my thirty 'closest' friends. Two called me. That's all."

"Do you ever phone them?" Margot asked.

"I did for a while. Not anymore."

I bit my lip, wondering how much to share. This was just supposed to be a casual get-together for coffee and conversation, nothing more. I didn't want to scare her off by unloading my whole life story. Yet she didn't seem to mind. And I needed to talk.

"It must be hard," Margot said. "You've had a lot of changes in a short period of time, haven't you? New home, new business . . ."

"Two new businesses," I corrected. "For the Love of Lavender, plus the farm. Neither is thriving. Could we have picked a worse time to give up two steady but staid jobs and go into business for ourselves? Could our lives get any more complicated?"

I took another sip of coffee and thought better of what I'd said. "Don't listen to me. It's not like we're the only ones with financial problems. It could have been worse," I said with a wry smile. "We could have invested our money with Madelyn's husband."

Margot frowned, her expression still concerned. "Pity on the people who did. I just can't believe she's married to that terrible man. She has such a nice face."

"After she left New Bern, I guess she started hanging out with the wrong crowd."

Margot nodded. "I'll say."

"But don't blame Madelyn for any of that. There's no way she knew what he was up to," I said emphatically.

"How do you know that?"

"She was cleared of everything in the investigation. If they could have pinned anything on her, I'm sure they would have. But it's more than that. Madelyn is . . . well, she's just not capable of something that low."

I couldn't explain it to Margot, but some things you just know. Some things don't change. Madelyn was the one who raced across the snow, swinging her book bag over her head, prepared to beat the stuffing out of the boy she thought was attacking me. She was the one who threatened to pound anybody who said anything bad about me. Madelyn had guts. And character. And for a long time, she'd been my friend.

"Did you see her face when she saw me?" I asked. "Like a stone. If she never saw me again, I'm sure it'd be too soon."

Margot was listening intently, her head bobbing slowly, but when I stopped to take a breath she said, "That is sad, but that's not what I meant. I was talking about you. I'm sad for *you*. You've been carrying this around for all these years, haven't you?"

That pulled me up short. Sympathy was the last thing I expected, or deserved. I turned my head away and looked at the wall.

"You don't understand. I was so awful to her, so often. Not overtly, not the way I was that day in the snow, but over and over again, year after year.

"After I ended our friendship, she changed. Not in a good way. She started getting involved in all kinds of self-destructive behavior—cigarettes, alcohol, boys. Especially boys. She collected them like merit badges—trinkets she pinned to her chest to prove that she was . . . well, I don't know what she was trying to prove. Maybe that she was worth something to somebody?

"Teenage girls are always falling in and out of love, but this wasn't that. She didn't care about those boys. She tossed them aside as fast as she gathered them up. There was something frantic about her, like she was hoarding hearts. But those boys didn't love her any more than she loved them. They used her and she let them. I don't think anybody loved Madelyn—not ever. Her mother never wanted her, her father died when she was just little, and her grandmother was awful to her, cruel. Abusive, even.

"When I went outside, sometimes I could hear Edna screaming at her. Once, I looked out my window and saw Madelyn's stuff thrown out on the front lawn. Edna was out there, slapping her over and over again, and Madelyn was just standing there, taking it. Like she was used to it. . . .

"I guess she was," I whispered, wiping guilty tears with the back of my hand. "Somebody should have reported Edna. Somebody should have done something. *I* should have done something," I said, finally turning to look at Margot's face, expecting to see the condemnation I deserved. It wasn't there.

"Like what?"

"A million things! Stood up for her. Told her I was sorry. Told her that Edna was wrong about her. I could have been her friend. How hard would that have been?" I asked. Margot didn't answer.

"Do you know something? When Madelyn dropped out of school I felt relieved that I wouldn't have to see her every day, relieved to be able to forget about her."

Margot nodded understandingly. "But you never did."

I let out a short, derisive laugh. "Oh, no. You're wrong. Once I left New Bern, I did a great job of forgetting about Madelyn. I stuffed that all into a closet, put a lock on the door, and resolved never to think of it again. Then I went on with my life and got a job in human resources, where you're pretty much paid to be a friend. There's a lot of explaining of benefit packages and administrative stuff, but mostly I just listened to people's problems and encouraged them to make good choices. I was a professional friend. Another irony."

"Sounds to me like you might not be quite as good at locking the past away and forgetting it as you'd like to believe," Margot said.

"Maybe not. Anyway, here I am, back at the scene of the crime. So is Madelyn."

Margot picked up her cup and wrapped her hands around it, resting her elbows on the table. "So? What are you going to do about it?"

"About what?"

"All these ironies you keep talking about? What you call a coincidence, I call an appointment. Do you think it's possible that God knows about the anguish and guilt that you, and possibly Madelyn, have been laboring under all these years and has arranged for you two to come back to New Bern so you can do something about it?"

"Like what? Kiss and make up? You saw the expression on Madelyn's face when she spotted me. You can't possibly think she's going to forgive me."

Margot's blue eyes bored into me as she quoted a verse I remembered vaguely from childhood

Sunday school lessons. " 'If possible, so far as it depends on you, be at peace with everyone.'

"So far as it depends on *you*. If you reach out to Madelyn and try to make amends, she may rebuff you. But then again"—Margot smiled—"she might surprise you. Either way, you'll have the peace that comes from knowing you did the right thing."

"The right thing? What's that? How am I supposed to know what to do?"

With that calm, knowing smile still on her face, that smile that was starting to annoy me a little, Margot said, "The path to peace is paved with knee prints." Then she took a sip from her coffee cup as though this explained everything.

" 'The path to peace is paved with knee prints'? What are you? The oracle of Cobbled Court? What the heck is that supposed to mean?"

Margot giggled and I smiled in spite of myself.

"Seriously," I said, shaking my head. "What is that supposed to mean?"

"It means that we can know peace in every situation, no matter how difficult, by turning that situation over to God. The apostle Paul said not to worry about anything. Instead, he said we should let all our requests be made known to God through prayer and with thanksgiving. And that when we do, we'll know peace that passes all understanding, the peace of God."

Margot was obviously very sincere, but this just didn't make sense to me.

"Margot, I believe in God, but I have a hard time believing He's personally interested in my little worries. I mean, doesn't He have better things to do? Famines? Wars? Natural disasters? That sort of thing? Who am I to bother God?"

"His child," Margot said simply. "You've got a child, right? If Josh called you, worried, distressed, and sincerely seeking your advice, wouldn't you stop what you were doing long enough to help?"

"Yes, but that's different."

Margot swiveled her head from side to side. "I don't think so. God cares about you just as much as you care about your son—more, even."

She closed her eyes for a moment, summoning another verse from her memory. " 'Before they call, I will answer; while they are still speaking, I will hear.' Isaiah 65:24. That's not me talking. That's what God says about Himself. You believe in God; why not believe what He says?"

Margot was sweet and kind, and she made it sound so simple, but it couldn't be. Could it?

"I'm not sure. I'd like to," I said cautiously. "But . . . what if it doesn't work?"

"Work as in, what if God doesn't patch things up between you and Madelyn? He won't. That's up to the two of you. He's just providing you with the opportunity. It seems to me that God wants you to at least *try* to reach out to her.

"And," she said in a somewhat softer tone, "I

think that's what you want, too, isn't it? Think. You've been sitting here beating yourself up over all the opportunities you had to reach out to your old friend and ease her pain, opportunities you ignored. God has gone to such a lot of trouble to give you another chance," she said earnestly. "Are you going to let this one pass too?"

I looked down at my hands. "No. I don't want to let that happen. Not again."

"Good. Good for you."

"So . . . what should I do? Pray?"

"Good idea," she said, then immediately closed her eyes and lowered her head.

She was going to pray here? Now?

I looked around nervously, afraid of being conspicuous, but no one was looking at us. Feeling a little awkward, I followed Margot's lead, closed my eyes, and ducked my head down.

Quietly, in plain language, as if she were speaking to someone she knew well and respected enormously, Margot thanked God for bringing us together that day, for bringing Madelyn and me to New Bern, for giving me the inclination and opportunity to set right an old wrong.

I prayed, too, not as eloquently as Margot, but I meant everything I said.

"Amen," Margot said, and then looked up at me and smiled. "There. That wasn't so hard, was it?"

I shook my head. "So, now what happens?

Should I be on the lookout for a burning bush or something?"

Margot laughed. "There *are* precedents, but I don't think you'll need something quite that flashy. Just wait and see what kind of doors God opens. It might happen quickly or it might take a while, but God will answer. Trust me."

"Okay," I said, but doubtfully. I was hoping for something a bit more concrete. I looked at my watch. "I've got to go and open the shop. Who knows? I might actually have a customer today. Or two!"

I smiled and stuffed my napkin into my coffee cup. "Thanks, Margot. It's been a long time since I've been able to just sit down and talk with a girlfriend. It was nice of you to take the time."

Margot stopped sweeping invisible crumbs off the table long enough to give me a dismissive wave. "It was fun. Let's do it again soon."

"I'd like that."

I stood up and started to walk around the far side of the table, intending to give Margot a hug. But I stopped short, my path impeded by the presence of a big brown shopping bag.

"What the heck?" I asked, grabbing the table edge to keep myself from tripping over the bag.

Margot peered over the far side of the table, onto the floor.

"Somebody must have left their shopping bag behind after breakfast. Wait a minute," she said, peeking into the bag, "there are quilts in here. Old ones."

Curious, I bent over to look and spotted an old, worn quilt with a blue and white pattern that, thanks to my newfound interest in quilting, I recognized as a double Irish chain. But I didn't need quilt classes to recognize that particular quilt.

I'd seen it a hundred times—two hundred times—before. I'd sat cross-legged on that patchwork, mindless of the intricate pattern and delicate stitching, laughing and whispering, eating cookies, dropping crumbs, making up stories and dreaming up dreams, a lifetime gone, back when we were girls, when Madelyn and I were best friends and the doors between us both were open.

I couldn't believe it.

Before they call, I will answer; while they are still speaking, I will hear.

22

Tessa

Virginia toddled over to the shop's sunny bowfront window, where her quilting hoop stood, and gently shooed Petunia off her chair. The cranky and curiously named tomcat gave her a glare before hopping onto the display window and settling himself into a basket filled with carefully coordinated fat quarters.

"You're going to get hair all over," she scolded. "And you know exactly what you're doing, don't you? Spoiled."

Petunia yawned and rested his chin on his paws before closing his eyes.

"Absolutely spoiled," Virginia mumbled before sitting down and unfolding the quilt, draping it over the hoop.

I positioned myself behind her, so as not to block the light, and waited to hear the old woman's verdict.

"Now. Let's see what we have here." She slid her reading glasses up her nose and leaned over the quilt.

"Well, it's dirty, for a start. But that's easy enough to deal with. A good washing will make a world of difference. But it mustn't be washed by machine," she cautioned. "You'll need to soak it in a tub, use a mild soap, and wring it out by hand. No electric dryers and no hanging it on a clothesline! That would put too much stress on the seams. It needs to be stretched out flat to dry."

"Wash it by hand, dry it flat. Got it."

Virginia glanced over her shoulder. "Good. But washing is the last step in the process. The seams are coming loose, here and here. See?"

I leaned closer and noted the places she pointed to.

"Now, if this were my quilt, I'd probably replace the whole binding. It's terribly worn, especially at the top. See how thin the fabric is there? Won't be too long before the batting will start showing through. Especially if she plans to actually use it on a bed."

"I don't know what she plans to do with it."

"Well, let's go ahead and replace the binding," she said, turning back to the quilt. "It'd be best to use an antique fabric. Probably something from the turn of the century."

"You think it's that old?"

"Judging by the style and type of fabric used, simple and straightforward, not a lot of flowers and folderol, I'd say so. It's no older than that. See? It has a bias binding. If it was made prior to 1900, they'd probably have used a straight binding."

"Virginia, how did you learn so much about quilt restoration?"

She grinned and waved off the question. "Oh, if you live long enough you're bound to pick up a few things. I mostly learned out of necessity. If you live to be my age, the quilts you made as a youngster start wearing out. I had too much time and money invested in them to throw them away, so I learned how to fix them up."

"And you think this one is worth fixing up?"

"Oh sure," she said confidently. "There's plenty of wear left in it. Plus, it's a beautiful quilt. The hand-quilting is pretty near perfect. Couldn't do better myself.

"These days my stitches are getting a little wobbly. Arthritis," she said, wincing as she rubbed her knobby hands together. "After I get moving they're okay, for a few hours. Then it seems like they seize up on me again. Anyway, repairing this quilt is going to take a little time. Are you sure you want to do it yourself?"

"If you'll talk me through it."

"Happy to. I never mind passing my wisdom on to the next generation of quilters," she said with a twinkle in her eye. "Plus, I like hearing myself talk."

I laughed.

Virginia smiled as she got up from her chair and scooped Petunia up in her arms. The cat opened one eye and made a grumbling sound in his throat before snuggling close to Virginia's chest.

"Spoiled," she murmured lovingly.

"You said something about using antique fabrics for the binding. Like a vintage fabric, a reproduction?"

"No. I'm talking about actual antique fabric that was loomed in the period. You *could* use a reproduction, but it'll never look quite right. You can buy antique fabric online from specialty vendors. The only problem is, they are pricey."

"How pricey?"

"Well," she said, narrowing her eyes, "that depends. For turn-of-the-century fabrics, I'd guess anywhere from thirty-five to sixty-five dollars a yard."

Thirty-five to sixty-five dollars a yard! To restore a quilt that belonged to a woman who gave every appearance of hating me? Was this really a good idea?

Not so long ago, I could spend that kind of money without giving it a second thought, but things were different now.

Lee and I have taken a scalpel to our budget and trimmed it to the bone. We've canceled the cable and Internet, and the newspaper, raised the deductibles on our insurance, and turned the thermostat down to sixty-four.

I don't mind. There's nothing as cozy as a wool sweater and a roaring fire on a winter night. And it's not like we were going hungry or anything. About ninety percent of what appears on our table these days has been grown and harvested on our farm, and there's something very satisfying about that. When we sit down to eat, Lee grins and says, "Look at this, would you?"

But that's just about the only time he smiles now. He's constantly worried about money.

We never go out anymore; restaurant meals aren't in the budget. That's fine, but I don't understand why that has to mean the end of our Saturday "date nights." There are all kinds of free concerts and lectures held at the library and the community center, but Lee isn't interested. He says he's too tired to go out. And to all appearances, it's true. He usually goes to bed, and to sleep, right after dinner.

We haven't made love in a month. And I miss it. I miss the passion, the playfulness, the touch of his hands. Most of all, I miss the intimacy of lying next to him afterward, the quiet talk and lingering looks. I need that. I think he does, too, now more than ever.

I tried to talk to Lee about it, but my comments were less than well received. The conversation, if you could call it that, ended with Lee storming out to the barn and staying there until I gave up on him and went to bed alone.

It doesn't make sense to me. We'd been making love, passionately and enthusiastically, for thirty-four years. We'd never had a problem doing it. So what was so wrong with talking about it? Are all men like this?

Virginia was widowed, but she'd been married, happily from all reports, for fifty-one years. Had she ever encountered this problem?

"Virginia?"

"Yes, dear?" She looked at me with bright, birdlike interest, her big blue eyes made bigger by the magnification of thick eyeglasses.

"I was wondering if you'd . . ." I started to speak. Reconsidered. Blushed. "I was wondering

218

if you'd mind ordering the fabric for me. I wouldn't know what to buy, and anyway, I don't have an Internet connection."

"No problem. We can do it right now. You want to give me a credit card?"

I took a mental inventory of my wallet, trying to remember if I had any cards that weren't already maxed out. "Would a check be okay?"

"Sure. I can just use my card and you can pay me back. I'm glad you're going with the antique fabric. It's a special quilt, worth the investment. Your friend will love it."

"I hope so."

"Quilting isn't a cheap hobby, but," the old woman said with a wink, "it keeps you out of trouble. If I didn't spend my money on fabric, I'd just waste it on beer and cigarettes."

I laughed. "Somehow I don't believe that, Virginia. Evelyn already told me that you're a teetotaler."

"She did?" Virginia clucked her tongue in mock regret. "Well, don't go telling anybody else. There's been some rumors going around town about me having a mysterious and wicked past.

"I know because I'm the one who's been spreading them. I like the idea of having a reputation. Makes me seem more interesting."

23
Madelyn

T he past is not a package one can lay away."
Emily Dickinson said that. I'm starting to
think she was on to something.

I came in the back door, threw my keys and my
purse on the kitchen counter, then sat down at the
kitchen table and buried my head in my arms and
thought about the ghosts from the past that
refused to stay buried—Jake, Tessa, Abigail, and
Woolley.

The past is not a package one can lay away.
Sooner or later, whether you want to or not, you
have to open the box and take a look inside.

If I had been born with a different set of genes,
particularly the genes that determine breast size,
my entire life would have been different. When I
turned thirteen, the year after my friendship with
Tessa ended, my chest went from pancake flat to
a 32C. By the time I left high school, I measured
a 34DD.

At first, I was embarrassed by those two
melons on my chest. I wore baggy sweaters and
sweatshirts to camouflage them, but it was no
use. Boys who hadn't known I was alive before
were suddenly interested in getting better

acquainted with me. Sort of. They didn't give a rip about me. They were, however, deeply interested, even obsessed, in getting acquainted with my breasts, preferably by touching them. Initially, I didn't get it. All I knew was that I was popular, pursued, and wanted, loved even. At least that's what they told me.

And I liked that. I liked it a lot. I liked the whispered endearments, the attention, and, yes, I liked being touched. I'd be a liar if I said otherwise. But mostly, I liked how their caresses made me forget everything—the slights and rejections of other girls, my grandmother's slaps and harangues, my disappointing grades, and my disappointment with myself. In the arms of the boy of the moment, I didn't think about anything. I just felt. And it felt good.

And the power! The power I had over almost every boy I met was exhilarating! They competed for my attention, followed me around like lovesick pups. In my sophomore year, every sports team captain asked me to the prom, except Jake Kaminski.

Deciding that the attentions of Jake Kaminski were essential to my happiness, I hung around outside the ice rink before practice one afternoon. When Jake showed up, lugging his enormous hockey bag, I thrust out my hip and my lower lip and asked why he hadn't invited me to the dance.

"Me? Well . . . I . . . every guy in school has already asked you. I didn't think you'd want to go with me. Would you?"

"Well," I said coyly, tossing my head so my hair fell over my shoulder, "not if you don't ask me."

When Jake came to pick me up, he drove a shiny red Camaro, borrowed from his uncle, and he opened my door for me. The band was awful and Jake's dancing was worse, but we had fun. The evening ended with us on a back road in the state park, in the backseat, with the windows steamed up.

But—and this I remember distinctly—when we pulled up in front of the house sometime after midnight, Jake hopped out of the car and ran around to my side to open the door for me.

None of my other dates opened the door for me at the *end* of the night.

Needless to say, my dating life was busy, but not only because of my physical attributes. It hadn't taken me long to figure out that there were ways to keep a man coming back for more. I was willing to do everything—everything *but*. I might not have been smart, but I wasn't stupid. I had no intention of repeating my parents' mistakes. Every now and then one of my boy beaux would press for more, but if he did, I dropped him like a hot potato. News travels fast among high school boys. After a couple such incidents, nobody pushed me to give them more.

I didn't enter into any exclusive relationships during high school, but Jake Kaminski was my favorite and most frequent companion. I liked him a lot. But our time together was short-lived.

Jake was a year ahead of me in school. His grades were nothing special, but he was a terrific hockey player. Everyone assumed he'd be offered a college athletic scholarship, probably several. It didn't happen. Instead, he went to work at his uncle's car dealership in Fairfield in a part-time job as a car washer and errand boy and took classes at the community college. Jake wasn't exactly raking in the dough, but being in college granted him a deferment from the draft and his uncle promised to promote him to sales if he worked hard and learned the business.

Jake's departure made me realize I needed to think about moving on myself, but there was no way I could do so working for minimum wage at the drive-in. I'd already dropped out of school, so college wasn't in my future. One day, I spotted a newspaper ad for a secretarial job that paid a dollar fifty more per hour than I was making. The ad requested an employment history and a photograph, a common practice back then. I sent in both.

Within six days, I was working for Woolley Wynne. Within six months, I'd fallen in love with him.

Word around town was that Woolley Wynne was "a ladies' man." The rumors were true.

He received a lot of phone calls from sultry-voiced women who purported to be his cousin, his dentist, his insurance agent, etc. When I transferred the call into Woolley's office, he'd get up from his desk and close his office door. He never closed his door when a man was calling. He also made frequent daytime sojourns to the city, and when he did, he usually had me book a suite for him at the Waldorf. I didn't suppose it was because he was planning on taking a nap in the middle of his day.

None of this surprised me. Woolley was charming, sophisticated, and handsome, with brilliant white teeth and a thick shock of white hair to match. He was also very, very rich. Of course women found him attractive. I certainly did, even though he was more than twice my age. What did surprise me was that he showed absolutely no interest in me. Not so much as a pinch.

I set out to change that. I began leaving an extra button undone on my blouses and dropping my pen when Woolley walked by and bending down to pick it up, giving him ample opportunity to get a good peek at what he was missing. Nothing. Next, I tried coming into his office while he was working, ostensibly in search of some misplaced file, then bending low over his desk and allowing my breast to "accidentally" brush his arm. Again, nothing.

I couldn't believe it. I had practically sent Woolley Wynne an engraved invitation to seduce me, but he didn't even bother to open the envelope. I began to worry that I was losing my appeal.

On my eighteenth birthday weekend, Jake came up from Fairfield to take me out. Grandma Edna had gone to visit her sister in Albany and wouldn't be back until Tuesday. I hadn't told her about my date with Jake.

The drinking age was eighteen back then. My birthday wasn't until Monday, but Jake and I decided to celebrate a little early. Nobody checked our I.D. I don't remember how many bars we went to, but I do remember a tree branch coming through the windshield and the flashing lights of a squad car.

We didn't die. We could have, maybe we deserved to, but we didn't. That was the good news. The bad news was that the whole front of the car was smashed in and that Jake got a citation for driving under the influence. The penalties for that were a lot more lenient back then, but it still wasn't good. I remember Jake sitting in the waiting room of the hospital with his head in his hands and mumbling over and over again, "He's gonna kill me. Uncle Sal is gonna fire me and then he's gonna kill me. Then my dad's gonna kill me again."

On Monday, I went into work as usual, black eye and all. Woolley was scheduled for a meeting in Litchfield and lunch with his wife. I didn't expect to see him in the office before two or three. I tried to type up a few letters so they'd be ready for him to sign in the afternoon but couldn't concentrate.

At noon, I locked the office door and walked back to Beecher Cottage for my lunch break, surprised to see Edna's car in the driveway. I was even more surprised to see that my bedroom window was open and that a small mountain of my possessions—clothes, bedding, books, stuffed animals, stockings—was forming on the lawn.

Cursing a blue streak, Edna stuck her head out the window and tossed an armful of my things onto the pile below, including one of my slips. As it fell, the sun shone through the cheap rayon and machine-made lace, making it appear finer than it was. For a moment, it seemed suspended in midair, hovering indecisively overhead, before falling earthward and landing in a puddle of brackish rainwater.

I fished it out of the puddle, muddy and

bedraggled, and I looked up at the window at Edna, who was about to throw another armful of my things onto the lawn.

"What are you doing? Have you lost your mind?"

"I'm helping you move out, you little . . ." she shouted, using a word to describe me that she'd never, ever used before, not among years of insults.

She knew.

She'd had a fight with her sister and come back from Albany a day early, arriving just in time to take a call from Jake's father, who was screaming at her about me. She told me all about it, shrieking insults from the window ledge to the lawn. Then she was downstairs, outside, standing on the grass, looming over me, red-faced and furious, as I bent down to gather up my things.

"I want you out of here, you little tramp! Today!"

She couldn't have wanted that any more than I did, but where was I to go? I had no car, no place to live, no friends, and one hundred and seventeen dollars in the bank.

"You can go to the devil for all I care!" she screamed. "You're headed there anyway! You're just like your mother, just like I always said you'd be. You're a tramp, just like she was. A man-trap. You ruin everything for everyone!"

"It was an accident!"

She grabbed me by the shoulders and shook. "An accident? An accident? You went out and drank until you couldn't see straight. That was no accident!"

She pulled her arm back before swinging it forward to slap me as hard as she could on my bruised cheek and blackened eye. "Idiot! Don't you ever stop to think how this affects me? Everyone in town is talking about this!"

I was used to Edna slapping me, but this was different. She swung her arm back and forth, again and again, like a scythe cutting a swath through tall grass, accenting each crack of her hand against my face with another curse. With the fifth blow—or perhaps it was the sixth, I'd lost count by then—the edge of her diamond wedding ring hit my face, tearing the flesh at the corner of my lip.

My ears rang. I felt a line of blood drip down my chin, a big hand on my arm, shoving me aside, a big-shouldered man stepping between me and my grandmother—Woolley Wynne.

There was a scene between Woolley and Edna, a lot of shouting and insults. The details of it don't matter now.

I do remember Woolley getting in Edna's face, eyes flashing and furious as he called her a crazy old kook who'd driven away her son and whose husband had died just to get away from her nagging and then ending his tirade with a long string of very descriptive epithets. Edna was speechless. I don't think anyone had ever spoken to her like that before.

I wanted to jump into the air and cheer. It's possible I did; my memory of that scene is a little fuzzy now. But I do know that at the end of it, I rode away in Woolley's white Cadillac with all my worldly goods in the trunk.

Woolley's eyes were dark and angry as we drove away. I thought he was angry with me.

"I'm sorry."

"For what?"

Big question. With so many answers. I was sorry for myself, for one thing. Sorry that I'd become exactly what Edna had always said I would—worthless. Something to be tossed out the window and into the mud. Eighteen years old and I'd already managed to screw up my entire life. And Jake's too. I was a completely sorry excuse for a human being and I knew it. But, at the time, that was too much to explain, especially to my boss.

"I've made you late for lunch with your wife."

"I'll call the restaurant and tell her I've been delayed." He took his eyes off the road for a moment, frowned, and pulled a snowy handkerchief from the breast pocket of his jacket.

"You're bleeding." He glanced back and forth from my face to the road as he dabbed my lip, staining the pristine white square with angry dots of crimson. "That's better."

He stuffed the handkerchief into his pocket, then reached out with his hand and touched my lip, my cheek, the purple swelling under my eye, one after the other, briefly but methodically. Woolley had the softest hands of any man I'd ever met. His nails were trimmed close and buffed to a shine. His fingertips were a velvet caress on my bruised cheek. I lifted my chin toward his touch, closing my eyes as his fingers strayed from my face to slowly stroke the flesh of my throat.

"Poor baby. Shall we take you to a doctor?"

"No. I'm fine. I just had a rough night is all."

"Ah, yes," he said, smiling a little. "It was your birthday weekend, wasn't it? You're eighteen now." His smile widened.

"We should take the day off and celebrate," he said. "Where do you want to go? What do you want to do?"

"I don't know."

"No? Well, in that case, I've got an idea."

He turned the car around and drove north, to a little inn just over the New York state line, where the rooms had low, roughbeamed ceilings, tiny, mullioned windows, fireplaces, and wide white beds with fine-loomed sheets that felt like silk on my bare back, the room where I learned that, unlike boys, men cannot be put off by teases and temptations and promises of everything but.

Woolley had rescued me, plucked me up from

the side of the road, defended me, carried me far away to a beautiful place. His voice was sweet in my ear and his hands were soft on my body. There was no hesitancy, no uncertainty in his touch. He knew what he was doing and he knew what he wanted—everything.

By the time he slipped off my skirt, picked me up in his arms, carried me across the room, and laid me down on that wide white bed, that's what I wanted as well.

Everything.

I loved him, the way only a very young girl who has never loved before can. I believe he loved me, too, a little, but not enough. Not enough to give Abigail up for me.

Woolley didn't love anybody the way he loved Abigail. He was obsessed with her—the way only a man who is used to getting everything he wants can be when presented with the one thing he can't have.

I loved Woolley and he loved me, but not enough. Woolley loved Abigail and she loved him not at all. And Sterling? Sterling loved no one, not ever.

Life is so ridiculous. And so very, very lonely.

For four years, until Abigail told him that either I had to go or she would, Woolley took care of me and helped me forget my loneliness. And just like that, it was over. He put me on the train to New

York with a check in my wallet, a kiss on my cheek, and a job offer from Sterling Baron that we both knew would involve very little typing.

"You'll be happier with someone nearer your own age. And Sterling is utterly infatuated with you."

"He barely knows me," I argued. "He only saw me that one time in New York."

"And spent the rest of the night staring at you from across the room, like a cat watching a canary. He couldn't take his eyes off you all night. When I called, it didn't take him two seconds to say you could come work for him."

"We haven't exchanged ten words."

Woolley blinked, clearly confounded by my observation. "What difference does that make? Listen to me, Madelyn. In a few years Sterling Baron will be one of the most powerful men on Wall Street. A man like that needs a woman who'll do him credit. Play your cards right and you'll be that woman."

"But I don't love Sterling Baron! I don't even know him. I love you, Woolley. I want *you*. How can you pass me off as if I were an outgrown sweater? I love you."

Woolley's laughing eyes became hard. He didn't return my endearment or try to defend himself. That wasn't his style. Woolley never lied to me. Sometimes I wished he would.

"Madelyn, you can get on that train, go to New

York, be nice to Sterling, and live in the style you've become accustomed to, or try to make a go of it somewhere else on your own. Accept my help or don't; it's up to you. But what you *can't* do is stay here. We've had a good time, but I'm not going to lose Abigail over a good time."

"Abigail doesn't love you," I spat.

"We don't get to pick who we love, Madelyn. Nor who loves us. Sterling Baron might not be your idea of Prince Charming, but he's rich and he's going to be even richer. And he wants you. You're a lucky girl," he said with a thin smile. "So, no more tears. Say good-bye and get on the train. In a year or two, you'll be set for life. Well set. And you'll be glad you listened to me. No matter what they taught you in school, money can buy happiness, Madelyn. It can even heal a broken heart."

I was wrong. Woolley lied to me after all.

I lifted my head from the cradle of my arms and wiped away the tears with the back of my hand before going to the sink to splash cold water on my face. That's when I remembered that I'd left the bag with the quilts in the coffee shop. Damn!

Well, I hoped whoever found them put them to good use, because I wasn't going back to retrieve them, not today. I wasn't going anywhere today. Tomorrow was a different story. Ghosts or no ghosts, come the dawn, I had to get up, go out, and go on.

To paraphrase an old love, I had a choice: I could go to the left or I could go to the right, but what I couldn't do was stand still.

24
Tessa

November

I shouldn't have told him. I just should have lied.

We've always had a joint checking account. Lee used to leave the job of balancing it to me. Now he calls the automated teller line every night to see which checks have cleared. And he questions me on every purchase.

"Madelyn Baron? You spent sixty-seven dollars on fabric to make a quilt for Madelyn *Baron?*"

"When I knew her, she was Madelyn Beecher. And she was my friend."

He choked out a laugh that was really an accusation. "First of all, no, she wasn't. You stopped speaking to her when you were twelve years old."

"And that was a mistake."

"And second, I don't care if she's your long-lost twin! We're broke, Tessa! Do you get that?

I'm going to have to let the health insurance lapse so we can pay the mortgage this month!"

This announcement pulled me up short. I didn't know. He hadn't told me. That made me angrier, but in a different way. Why hadn't he told me?

Leave it. One argument at a time.

"I'm sorry."

"You're sorry? Do you have *any* appreciation for the kind of trouble we're in here? We're one heart attack away from bankruptcy!"

"Which you're going to give yourself if you don't stop shouting at me!"

I'm not a screamer. I never have been. Neither is Lee. What's happening to us?

"Lee, I'm sorry. What else do you want me to say? It's done."

"I want you to start acting like an adult!"

"How about if you start treating me like one? You're not my father, Lee. Quit treating me like a kid who's overspent her allowance. I'm working my behind off, trying to make a go of the shop—"

"And I'm not, I suppose? I'm just sitting at home playing gentleman farmer?"

"Do you really want to do this? Do you just *have* to fight?"

I laid my hand flat over my eyes, breathing deeply for a moment, listening to the drum of my own heart, willing it to slow before lowering my hand and looking at my husband.

"That's not what I meant and you know it," I said in a deliberately even tone. "We're both working, doing everything we know how to do to get through this. And we will. It'll get better. We've just had a run of bad luck, that's all."

Lee's face colored red and his eyes turned black, hard and bitter as coal. "Bad luck. Is that what you call this?" he shouted. "Bad luck? Bad luck is something that happens that can't be helped. This could have been helped. It didn't have to be like this, Tessa. And I don't just mean for us!"

"What are you talking about?"

"I'm talking about the bubbles and the bankruptcies, the foreclosures and the bank failures, the layoffs and the bailouts, and the fact that every day, just when you think it can't get any worse, you wake up and find out that it is! I'm talking about the Madoffs and the Barons and all the people like them. The ones who started all this, the ones who don't make anything, or do anything, or add anything to this world but somehow think that their fair share of the pie is one hundred percent!

"So you'll have to excuse me if I go a little crazy when I see that you're spending your time and our money to make presents for your old friend Madelyn Baron. But I think she's already taken enough from us, Tessa! And I can't figure out how to pay the insurance!"

He slammed his hand so hard against the table a pen jumped and dropped onto the floor. His anger still unspent, he took aim at it with his big boot and kicked it so hard that it sailed through the air to the other side of the room and bounced off the wall.

"I know it's not fair, Lee. Not to anybody. But you can't take this out on Madelyn. She was just married to him, that's all. You can't hold her responsible for the decisions he made. It's not her fault that we're struggling."

He let out a noise that would have been a laugh except there wasn't a drop of humor in it.

"Oh, I know that. Believe me, I get it. It's my fault. I should have seen this coming. I should have known better! That's what you're thinking. Why not say it?"

"Stop it. Nobody is blaming you for anything."

He wouldn't look at me. I moved toward him, tried to touch him, but he jerked his shoulder back quickly, as if trying to dodge a blow.

"Why not?" he asked as he strode toward the back door. "I sure as hell blame myself."

I don't know what time Lee came to bed. I considered following him out to the barn but then thought better of it, figuring he needed some time alone.

The next day, Sunday, I woke up while it was still dark. I rolled over on my side to see Lee sitting on the side of the bed, getting dressed. His shoulder muscles flexed and rolled under his bare skin and he reached down to pick up his discarded jeans from the floor.

I stretched out my arm and ran my hand down Lee's back, fingers bumping sleepily along the ridge of his spine.

"Hey."

"Hey." He stood up and started to put on the flannel shirt he'd left hanging on the bedpost the night before.

"What time is it?"

"Almost five."

"You want breakfast?"

"Later. I'm going to make coffee." He turned around, looked me in the eye, letting his gaze linger. An acknowledgment. An apology. "Can I bring you a cup?"

I smiled sleepily, relishing the normalcy of a new morning. He sounded like himself again. "That would be nice."

I grabbed Lee's abandoned pillow, added it to mine, and wedged both under my head and shoulders to prop myself up. I blinked a couple of times, easing myself into wakefulness. "I'm going to church later. Do you want to come?"

"Can't. I've got to feed the animals."

"I know," I said through a yawn, "but that won't take more than an hour. I can mix up some pancakes while you're in the barn. We could have breakfast together and drive into town for the ten o'clock service."

He tucked his shirt into his jeans. "Why? So you can pray we win the lottery?"

I pushed myself higher up on the pillows. "That's not why I go."

"Well, that'd be why I was going. And somehow," he said, bending over to lace up his work boots, "I think God would see right through that. I never asked God for help when things were going good for me. Don't you think it'd be hypocritical asking him for help now that things aren't?"

"But I don't go to church just to pray for things," I said. "When I'm there I feel better, like everything is going to work out somehow."

Lee frowned. "Well, of course it is. I'm going to do whatever I have to do to keep us afloat. I've never let you down before, have I?"

"That's not what I meant, honey. I was just—"

"We're going to be fine," he interrupted. "You'll see. If God wants to help, good. Let him. But I'm not going to sit around waiting for him to do it. I got us into this mess. I'll get us out. 'Fear God and take your own part.' That's in the Bible somewhere, isn't it?"

I pushed back the covers and perched myself on the edge of the bed. "I think that was one of the presidents, a Roosevelt. Teddy or Franklin. I'm not sure which."

"Well. My dad always said it, and it always worked for him."

Lee cleared his throat and sat down next to me on the bed. "Tessa? Listen. About last night. I'm sorry. I just . . ."

I leaned to the left, bumping his shoulder with mine. "It's okay. You're just tired and stressed. We both are. It's fine. You know what else is fine?" I asked, running my hand slowly down his muscled thigh and letting a slow smile spread across my face.

Lee raised his eyebrows, questioning. I leaned toward him, kissed him long and slow on the mouth. He wrapped his arms around me, returning the favor. My palm moved up his back, stroking the ridges of his shoulder blades, then down his side along his rib cage and lower, feeling that familiar thrill I had missed so much. Lee groaned and pushed me gently backward onto the bed, moving with me, shifting his body to cover mine.

A rooster crowed.

Lee made a groan of an entirely different sort and lifted himself up, resting his weight on his elbows. "Darren's awake. Which means the hens are up too."

"Let 'em wait," I said, trying to pull him back down.

"If I don't get out there, Darren will just get the girls all worked up over nothing."

"Better them than me. Come on. Stay here. Ten minutes. Five."

Lee grinned as he got to his feet and tucked in his shirttail. "Can't. Besides, you deserve more than five minutes, way more."

"How about five minutes now and more minutes later?"

He laughed. "I'm flattered by your optimism." He kissed me on top of the head. "Tonight. I promise."

I sighed petulantly. "Fine. But do you know how long it's been? I'll tell you how long. You know the guy who runs the produce section of the market? The one with the paunch and the bald spot? He was starting to look good to me."

Lee grinned. "Tonight. It'll be worth the wait, I promise."

"I'm holding you to that." I sat up and reached for my bathrobe. "Do you want pancakes or scrambled eggs for breakfast?"

"Both. Need to keep up my strength to keep up with you." He gave me another quick peck and walked away, pausing at the bedroom door. "Hey. If you think about it, when you're in church today, say a prayer for me, will you?"

I smiled and cinched the belt on my robe. *You can count on it.*

25
Madelyn

"If you say six hundred is the best you can do, Mr. Levitt, then I'm sure it is." I switched the phone to my other ear as I steered onto Oak Leaf Lane. "But I'm on a budget and I've got another quote for four seventy-five. . . . Five hundred? Hmm. That's still a bit more than the other fellow, but . . . you've got such a good reputation," I mused, pretending to weigh my options.

"All right, then. It's a deal. Five hundred. I'll see you first thing Tuesday."

I snapped the phone shut, entirely pleased with myself. Four fireplaces cleaned, broken bricks replaced, and a new damper installed in the living room for five hundred. I really hadn't expected him to go lower than five fifty. Either I was a better negotiator than I'd realized or Mr. Levitt was desperate for work. Probably a bit of both.

My self-satisfied smile faded when I pulled into the driveway and saw Jake Kaminski sitting on my front porch steps.

What was he doing here? After our last encounter, you'd think he would have figured out I never wanted to see him again, but there he was, grinning like the Cheshire cat as he pulled himself to his feet. I turned off the engine and smiled as he approached. What else could I do? It was too late to back out and pretend I hadn't seen him.

Jake came around to the driver's side of the car and opened the door for me. "You can unglue that fake smile from your face, Madelyn. I know you're not happy to see me. But you will be, when you see what I brought you."

He jerked his chin toward the front porch and the two big cardboard boxes that were sitting there.

"Paint," he said. "Twenty gallons of premium interior eggshell white. Enough to paint the whole house, and I'm going to sell it to you at cost because I am a good guy. And because the company has repackaged the line and I've got to get rid of all the cans with the old labels."

"Really?" I did a little calculation in my head. Jake had just saved me about three hundred dollars.

"Really. Now are you happy to see me? Let me help you with your bags," he said, walking to the back of the car. He opened the hatchback before I could stop him and stood there, shaking his head. I felt the color rise in my cheeks.

"Home Depot," he said flatly, then made a tsking noise with his tongue. "Madelyn, how could you? And after I gave you my whole 'doing business with your neighbors' speech."

He threaded his muscular arm through four of the plastic shopping bags, leaving nothing for me to carry.

"Jake. Wait. You don't have to . . ."

Ignoring my protests, he walked to the porch and climbed the steps. "Do you have any coffee?"

Jake put his hand over the top of his coffee mug. "Three is my limit. Otherwise, I don't sleep. But I wouldn't say no to another one of those muffins. I didn't know you could cook, Madelyn."

I put the carafe back into the coffeemaker, sliced another raspberry muffin in half, spread it with butter, and carried it over to the kitchen table.

"Neither did I. But since I'm opening a bed-and-breakfast, I figured I'd better learn the breakfast part at least. I found an old recipe box that belonged to Edna up in the attic. At least, I think it was Edna's. Looks like her handwriting, but I never remember her being much of a cook. She never made anything besides overdone beef and underdone potatoes. And I never saw her bake, not so much as a cookie."

"Maybe she did before. Back when your dad was still alive."

"Maybe." I sank down into the chair opposite Jake's and shrugged.

"What? You don't think it's possible that once upon a time, Edna was a kind, young, muffin-baking mom?"

"Somewhat hard to picture."

"Well, people can change—sometimes for better and sometimes for worse, but they can. I did," he said.

It was hard for me to return his gaze for more than a moment, to pretend not to notice the unseeing stare of his glass eye. Did it hurt him? I wondered. I supposed it didn't, not now. But at the time the pain must have been excruciating.

Over the course of the previous two hours and three cups of coffee, we'd filled each other in on most of what had happened since the night of the accident. After his uncle fired him and his parents refused to let him move back home, Jake had been forced to drop out of college and go to work. He found a job as a bartender, but quickly lost it for drinking up the profits. About a week later, he got a draft notice and soon found himself patrolling jungles in Vietnam. Shrapnel from an enemy grenade explosion ended up in his eye and cost him half his sight.

"Jake," I said, looking down at my hands. "I'm just so sorry. . . ."

He tipped the kitchen chair back onto two legs and crossed his arms over his chest, staring at me. "Why? You didn't do anything."

"If you hadn't gone out with me that night you

wouldn't have wrecked the car, lost your job, your deferment, and your eye."

Jake's mouth split into a grin and he shook his head. "Boy, you sure think a lot of yourself, Madelyn. Sure, I was crazy about you, but I was perfectly capable of destroying my own future, thank you, and I was hell-bent on doing it. You didn't hold me down and pour liquor down my throat that night; I did that all by myself. Then, drunk as a skunk, I got behind the wheel of a brand-new borrowed sports car and I crashed it into a tree.

"After that I got myself fired from a bartending job for drinking too much. Do you have any idea how much you've got to drink to make that happen? A lot. Next, I went to Vietnam, drank a lot more, did a lot of drugs, and practically got my brains blown out. If I hadn't been stoned out of my mind when the grenade was lobbed, I'd still have my eye. Instead, I probably stood there for a full three seconds before I reacted. You'd think I would have figured out that alcohol, drugs, and me were a bad combination a long time before, but nope.

"Took a grenade blast to finally shake some sense into me," he said, rapping his head with his fist. "Maybe I got hit with too many hockey pucks as a boy. Or maybe I'm just stubborn. Probably that. But whatever I am, whatever I've done, I've done myself. So quit trying to hog all the credit, will you? Besides, I'm glad things happened the way they did."

Seeing my open mouth, he laughed. "Don't look at me like that, Madelyn. I mean it. I like my life. I wouldn't change a thing about it."

"Oh, come on," I scoffed. "Not even your eye? Given a choice, wouldn't you have preferred to go through life with two of them?"

"Yes, but it couldn't be that way. I told you, I was absolutely hell-bent on destroying myself. Sooner or later I'd have succeeded. But, lucky for me, God arranged for a grenade to drop into my path and get my attention. I don't think anything else could have. All told, living with one eye seems like a small price to pay."

"God. You think God threw a grenade at you. And you're grateful for this." Now it was my turn to laugh. "Right."

Jake shifted his weight forward, letting the two front legs of the chair hit the floor with a thunk, and tore off a piece of muffin before going on. "Well, I don't think God was crouching in the bushes and throwing grenades, but I do think he used the situation to help me realize that my life had become unmanageable, that I was powerless to restore myself to sanity, and that I needed to turn my life and will over to God."

"Oh, Jake, you sound like a walking AA commercial."

"Only because I am," he said and popped the

last piece of muffin into his mouth. "Alcoholics Anonymous changed my life."

"Yeah," I said and rolled my eyes. "That and the lucky grenade."

"Everything depends on your outlook. I was spiraling out of control way before the accident. Took my first drink at fourteen and didn't stop. I was never loud, never a real troublemaker. I wasn't looking to rebel, I just wanted to drink and I did it quietly. The teachers never took much notice of me. Wrote me off as shy, none too bright, and passed me along. But my coach knew what was up. If I hadn't been such a good hockey player, he'd probably have kicked me off the team, but instead, he kept giving me 'one more chance.' That just made things worse, made me feel like I could get away with it. But it cost me.

"The college coaches wouldn't touch me. That's why I didn't get a scholarship; they found out about the drinking. My uncle gave me a couple of chances, too, but the car was the last straw. I don't blame him for firing me, though I felt plenty sorry for myself at the time. I made quite a habit of blaming everybody else for my mistakes. But when I ended up in the hospital after the blast—that kind of forced me to dry out."

I smiled. "The army doesn't supply martinis to recuperating soldiers?"

"They don't even supply olives. Lucky for me,

I had a doctor who saw right through me. He'd gone through AA himself, so he knew the signs. Of course, that time I got caught trying to steal extra pain pills may have given him a clue too. Anyway, he got me off the pain meds but quick. Then he read me the riot act and forced me to admit the truth: I was an alcoholic. I joined an AA group while I was still in the hospital.

"When I got out, I came home to New Bern and moved in with my folks. They weren't exactly thrilled about having me back, just waiting for me to fall off the wagon. I came close, plenty of times. I got a job on a construction crew, carpenter's apprentice. Let me tell you, the guys on that crew could pound them down. Every night, as soon as we'd close down the job site for the day, they'd head to the bar and razz me for not coming along."

"Didn't they know you were an alcoholic?"

"Sure they did. A couple of them were, too, they just hadn't admitted it. That's part of why they tried to lure me back to it, so they would feel okay about their own drinking."

"That must have been so hard. How did you resist the temptation?"

"I almost didn't. But my AA sponsor suggested I find something to do at night, something that would give me an ironclad excuse for not going to the bar with the rest of the guys. So I enrolled in night classes up at the community college. I was nervous about going back to school. I'd barely made it through high school, and my first stint at college hadn't gone too well. I was on academic probation when I dropped out. Even if my uncle hadn't fired me, I'd probably have flunked out anyway."

He leaned forward, pressing his stomach against the hard edge of the table to get closer, his voice low but intense. "But this time, it was different. I did really well, got Bs. At first I thought it was the teachers, that they were better, or that the material was more interesting. But one day, while I was sitting in my algebra class, listening to and actually understanding a lecture on the quadratic formula, the lightbulb went on. It wasn't that the teachers were better or that I'd suddenly gotten smarter. It was that, for the first time in years, I was sitting in a classroom and I was sober!"

He threw back his head and laughed. He had nice teeth.

"Yes," I said. "I can see how it'd be hard to get through algebra with a buzz on."

"Yeah. Funny how I didn't figure that out before. I thought I was stupid. Partly because I wanted to. It was easier to give up on myself than make any effort. But I . . ."

He stopped himself in mid-sentence, looked at his watch. "Sorry, Madelyn. I've been going on and on. You must have a million things to do."

I did, but I wasn't anxious to see him go. This was the first real conversation I'd had since coming to New Bern. And I was intrigued by Jake's story. He was the Jake I remembered, but there seemed to be more of him, and better. He really had changed, and, as far as I could see, all for the good.

Jake brushed the stray crumbs from the table onto his plate and took it to the sink.

"Jake? One more thing. The hardware store. Did you go into business with your dad?"

"No," he said, rinsing off his plate and cup. "After I came back, Dad lived six more years. I wanted to come into the business with him, but he never did trust me."

"Even after six years? That's so unfair."

He pulled the dish towel off the refrigerator door handle, turned around, and leaned against the counter, drying dishes as he talked. "Oh, I don't know, Madelyn. He had reason to be wary. For alcoholics, sobriety is one day at a time. Even after I got sober, I still had issues. Especially with women. I have terrible luck with wives."

"Oh. You're married?"

He shook his head. "Was married. Three times. First time was to one of my nurses in the hospital, Janie. That lasted six months. She ran off with an orthopedist. I met Number Two at an AA meeting in New Bern. She was the jealous type, always accusing me of cheating on her."

"And were you?"

"No, ma'am. I have very many bad qualities, but infidelity isn't one of them. But every time a woman looked at me sideways, Rhonda thought the worst."

Looking at Jake, even more handsome than he'd been in high school, it was hard not to feel for Rhonda, at least a little. I bet Jake Kaminski had all kinds of women looking at him all the time. And, now that I was used to it, I decided that the glass eye lent Jake a sort of roguish charm. He looked like a man who had lived hard and had stories to tell.

"One day when we were out to dinner, some woman I'd never laid eyes on sent a drink over to the table. I tried to send it back but before I could, Rhonda grabbed the glass and downed the whole thing, then started screaming at me. She went off her rocker and on a bender, drove off in my truck and left me to walk. The next day, when I was at work, she drove it right through the plate glass window of the store."

I winced. "Bet your dad loved that."

"Yeah. You can see why he wasn't excited about bringing me into the business. But we made our peace with each other before he died. After that, I went to the bank, got a loan, and bought the store from the estate."

"You mean he didn't even leave it to you in his will?"

"I've got two brothers and a little sister. He couldn't leave the store just to me. That wouldn't have been fair."

I looked at him, searching his face. He seemed to harbor no bitterness toward his father. That amazed me. In his shoes, I never could have managed that.

"So, what about the third former Mrs. Kaminski? Was she the jealous type too?"

"Nope. Beth was a wonderful woman. She had a good heart, but not a strong one. She died in my arms. The ambulance didn't get there fast enough."

"Oh, Jake. I had no idea. I'm so sorry."

"Yeah. So was I. We were very happy together. But," he said in a deliberate tone, "life goes on and we have to go on with it."

He looped the dish towel back through the handle of the refrigerator door and changed the subject. "Madelyn, I know you want to start painting, but I think we'd better do the floors first. I've got the sander out in the truck. Between the two of us, I think we'll be able to carry it inside."

"You brought me a floor sander?"

"You said you wanted one, right? It can be a little tricky, but you'll get the hang of it. I'll help you tape up the doors with plastic to keep out the dust, then teach you how to work the sander."

I didn't know what to say.

He frowned. "Unless you've changed your mind. Doing it yourself should save you some serious money, but it's going to take a lot of time and sweat. . . ."

"No, no! It's not that. It's just . . . this is just so nice of you, Jake. How can I thank you?"

He grinned and headed toward the back door. "Well, for starters, you can stay away from Home Depot."

26
Tessa

She let you in? She actually let you come inside? And gave you coffee?"

Jake Kaminski nodded as he bagged up my canning jars and gave me my change. "And muffins," he confirmed.

I stuffed the bills in my wallet and dumped the coins in the bottom of my purse. This is why my purse weighs fourteen pounds and my shoulder always aches.

"I've been over there a couple of times, helping her with the remodeling. When she'll let me. She likes doing things her own way," Jake said with a grin.

"Wow. When she saw me in the coffee shop, she turned tail and ran. Wouldn't say a single word to me."

"Running into you probably came as a shock. You should call her."

"I have. Five times." I held my hand up flat with my fingers spread wide. "She won't return my messages. I can't believe you were able to get her to talk to you, to invite you inside and make you breakfast!"

"Muffins," he said dismissively. "And she'd already made them before I showed up. She's experimenting with recipes to feed her guests.

"Look," Jake said, "she turned tail and ran the first time she saw me too. I don't think she's too happy about being back here. New Bern doesn't exactly hold a lot of good memories for her. Maybe seeing you reminds her of things she'd rather forget. Don't give up on her. She doesn't know it, but she could really use a friend right now. The only reason she talked to me is because I showed up on her doorstep unannounced and bearing gifts—twenty gallons of paint and a floor sander."

"A floor sander? You sure know how to charm a girl, Jake."

"Yeah, well. It's a gift."

"So, you think she'll really be able to turn Beecher Cottage into an inn? The house is such a wreck. I can't imagine anybody paying good money to stay there."

"It's a big job," he acknowledged. "But she's making progress. She's finished sanding the floors and is just about done painting the trim. I wanted to help, but once I showed her how to work the machinery, she insisted on doing it all herself. She's determined."

"You mean stubborn," I said. "Always was."

"Yeah," Jake said in a tone of undisguised admiration. "You should see what she's doing with some of that old junk she found up in the attic. She took a bunch of old, ugly paintings, ripped out the canvas, cleaned the frames, repainted them silver, then took an old wallpaper sample book I gave her, picked out papers she liked, glued them onto cardboard backings, and put them in the frames. She created about twenty brand-new pieces of artwork that cost virtually nothing. And they look great! She hung a group of six up on a big white wall in the dining room. I swear, it looks just like something you'd see in one of those expensive boutique hotels in Manhattan."

"She always had an eye for that kind of thing," I said. "But I have a hard time picturing Madelyn as an innkeeper. Warm and welcoming never seemed to be quite her style."

"People can change. Not that she has." He laughed. "But I think she wants to. Deep down, I think there's a finer Madelyn fighting to get out. I always thought so, even when we were kids."

"And running an inn is going to reveal that finer person?"

"Could be. She doesn't have a lot of other options. Beecher Cottage is the only asset she has left, that and some money she'd saved before she got married. And she's using every dime of it to remodel the house. Other than that, she's dead broke."

Lee walked up to the counter carrying a package of hinges. "Who's dead broke?"

"Madelyn Beecher," I answered.

"Yeah. Sure she is." He snorted and pulled his wallet from the back pocket of his jeans. "You can't make me believe that she doesn't have something stashed away, offshore bank accounts or something."

Jake took the five-dollar bill Lee handed him, put it in the till, and started to count out the change. "I don't think so. The government seized everything, from bank accounts and real estate to dishes and Madelyn's jewelry."

"That's right," I added. "They auctioned off everything on eBay, including a box of monogrammed stationery. It went for almost three hundred dollars. Isn't that crazy? Who'd pay that much for someone else's stationery?"

"Weird," Jake agreed.

"Well, I don't feel sorry for them," Lee said and shoved his change into his pants pocket. "That guy ruined the lives of hundreds of innocent people. It's only right they sell off the stuff and divide the money among the people he cheated.

Maybe his wife didn't have anything to do with his scam, but she lived pretty well from it."

"For a while," Jake agreed. "Not anymore. All she got out of that marriage was a tarnished name and the clothes on her back. And she's selling those."

"She's selling her clothes?" Lee asked.

"The designer stuff—clothes, shoes, bags, luggage, what was left of her jewelry. She sent it off to a consignment shop in New York. She said she needed a new roof and a working furnace more than she needed Vuitton luggage."

Lee raised his eyebrows. "Huh."

27
Tessa

It's a nice day, cool and crisp but still warm for November. That early October snowstorm was a fluke. It snowed four inches and melted the next day. We haven't had so much as a flurry since.

When we got back from the hardware store, I decided to go putter in the garden a bit. Not that there's much to be done this time of year. The lavender was harvested early in the summer while the flowers were just buds, laid to dry in the sun on clean white sheets, then put into glass jars or alcohol tinctures to be used in potpourris, sachets, soaps, and creams. The rest of my summer herbal bounty—flowers, seeds, stems, and leaves—were similarly harvested long ago, back when the garden was lush and the sun shone warm every day.

Now the garden is brown and stark, trimmed back tight, the tender plants covered with sheets of opaque plastic or bell-shaped glass cloches. If I had my way, I'd use nothing but cloches, but I only have a few and they're expensive. The plastic does the job, though far less prettily. Because they're hardy enough to endure the New England winter, I left the rosemary bushes uncovered except for a generous blanket of mulch at the base. Rosemary is so strong a scent that I don't often use it in my products, but it rivals lavender as my favorite herb. It's got so many uses, both culinary and cosmetic, and I just love the smell. Something about that sharp, resiny scent wakes up my senses and makes me think that something good could happen soon.

I pulled a pair of garden clippers from the pocket of my barn coat, snipped off a few sprigs of rosemary, and thought about our conversation with Jake Kaminski.

Can people change? And I've decided to believe they can.

I've changed. I came to New Bern in search of a new lifestyle, but what I've found is a new life. Not an easier life, definitely not. So much of what I'm facing now is unexpected, even frightening. But I have to believe, I do believe, that these changes and this new life are leading me to something truer and better.

I pray now. When I began it felt awkward, forced, like those stumbling, start-and-stop conversations you have when meeting someone for the first time, full of uncomfortable silences as I racked my brain for the next question, the proper terminology. I picked up a book on prayer but found it just confused me.

Then one day, while I was in the shop, repairing some stitching on Madelyn's quilt (quilting during business hours, I have found, helps me fill the sometimes long stretches of time between customers), I started praying. I prayed for Lee, for Josh, for Madelyn, for Margot, Virginia, Evelyn, and all the new friends I've made at the Cobbled Court Quilt Shop, where I am now a regular, and for myself, for all my doubts and worries, as well as all the things I'm grateful for.

Somehow, as I was praying, rocking that needle back and forth the way Virginia taught me, I forgot to be awkward. Prayer flowed from me naturally, in a plain and continuous pattern that mirrored the motion of my needle; simple, rhythmic, thought by thought, stitch by stitch, forgetting to be worried about the outcome, focused only on *that* stitch, *that* inch, *that* curve, until I came to the end of my thread and myself, and pulled my gaze back to discover the bigger picture, the pattern that had emerged through the honesty of my prayers and workings of my needle—and I liked what I saw.

I doubt there are any books out there titled *Quilting Taught Me to Pray*, but maybe there should be. Praying—and quilting—has taught me that there's a little more to me, and a lot more to life, than I had realized.

I knelt down on the ground by the rosemary bushes, flattened my hands into shovels, swept the mulch up, and pressed it closer around the base of the bushes, like pressing damp sand into the shape of a castle, a fortress to protect these hardy but not invulnerable plants from the winter that is sure to come, feeling peaceful and so thankful for everything—the day, my garden, the smell of rosemary. Now that the pump has been primed it seems that everything I do brings forth a stream of prayer: quilting, gardening, breathing. And I've noticed that the more I give thanks for what I have, the more I notice how much I have to be thankful for. Strange how that works.

I clapped the mulch from my hands before running them along the silver-green branches and lifting my palms to my face, breathing deeply. Maybe something good will happen. Maybe soon.

As I rose from my knees, I suddenly knew how I was to help it happen.

I stood at the kitchen sink, washing my hands. Lee came in and grabbed an apple from the blue bowl on the counter.

"Lee, do you know where we put the pictures when we moved?"

"The albums? They're on the bookshelf in the living room. Bottom shelf, right next to the atlas."

"No," I said. "I mean the box with the pictures. The old ones. You know, the box with my high school yearbook, my diploma, and that shoe box with all the pictures we always say we're going to put in an album but never do."

Lee chewed a bite of apple and nodded as I spoke. "Guest room closet. Top shelf. It's pretty heavy. Do you want me to get it down for you?"

"Would you? Thanks." I dried my hands on a kitchen towel. "Hey, I need to run back into town. I won't be long, but dinner might be a little late. Is that all right?"

"No, it isn't," Lee said with one definite shake of his head. "I'm starving. I'll start working on dinner. We're having Glenda, right?"

"Sadly, yes. I'm feeling a little bad about that. Aren't you?"

"This is a farm, Tessa, not a retirement home for chickens past their prime. You can't think of the stock as pets."

"If you'd quit naming them maybe I could. Glenda was a good old girl."

"And now she'll be a good old dinner," Lee said matter-of-factly before taking another bite of apple and walking slowly toward me. "But if your conscience won't permit you to partake of the dinner I'm planning, the crispy fried chicken and gravy, potatoes mashed with cream fresh from this morning's milking, sautéed apples with cinnamon, baked acorn squash with rosemary, brown sugar, and pecans . . . well, I guess I can eat it all myself and make you a peanut butter sandwich or something."

I turned around and smiled. Lee smiled back and moved close, pressing his hips to mine.

"Didn't your mother ever tell you not to talk with your mouth full?"

"Uh-uh. I was raised by wolves. Here. You have some." He bit off another piece of apple, held it partially clenched between his teeth, and leaned down to feed me the other half, his lips touching mine.

"Mmm. Lee, you grow a good apple."

"Didn't your mother ever tell you not to talk with your mouth full?" He stopped my retort with a kiss, a long one, then buried his face in my hair.

"You smell good," he murmured.

"It's the rosemary. I was in the garden."

"Are you sure you want to go to town?"

No, I'm not. And you're just making that harder.

"I won't be long."

Lee sighed dramatically. "All right, but you don't know what you're missing."

"Oh, yes I do. That's why I'm going to hurry back as quickly as I can. Now," I said, rocking up on my toes to give him a quick peck, "would you be an angel and get that box down for me?"

28
Madelyn

With an expression that was almost a wince, Chico handed me a folded piece of pink paper, his bill.

I opened it and gasped. "Chico! This is almost twice the original estimate!"

"I know, Miss B. But when I bid the job we didn't know that the shower pan was cracked and that the subfloor was rotted *or* that the pipes were corroded."

I sighed, looked at the figure again, sighed again.

Chico twisted his lips into an apologetic expression. "I sold you the pipe at cost and I didn't charge for ripping up the subflooring."

Nodding, my eyes still on the pink paper, I said, "And this includes all the work for the sprinkler system?"

"Yeah, and all the other changes the inspector wanted."

"Okay. I guess I'd better get my checkbook."

After walking Chico to the door and thanking him, I poured myself a second cup of coffee and sat down to balance the checkbook and look over the bills. It wasn't pretty.

The biggest single item had been the exterior painting. If I could have done it myself I would have, but it was too big a job for me, and even if I'd had the skills to do it, I didn't have the time. I had to get it done before the snow. Otherwise, especially if we had a rainy spring, it could have delayed my opening. Luckily, we'd had a week-long stretch of unseasonably warm weather. It gave us time enough, but only just, to get the painting done. Good thing Mr. Jorgensen had a big crew. And the end product really was beautiful.

The bright yellow siding looked a little flashy sitting among its more sedate neighbors, clad in the standard New England white clapboard with black shutters, but the brighter paint palette is historically fitting for the Victorian period and very pretty. It looks like the perfect spot for a romantic weekend in the country. Mr. Jorgensen did a good job, but the bill . . . ouch! It just about wiped me out.

Fortunately, the consignment shop had sold three more of my designer bags and two of my Chanel suits. If not for that, I wouldn't have been able to pay Chico and the others.

The carpenter would want to be paid after he

finished installing the two new cabinets in the bathroom; then Chico would be back to connect the water and drains to the sinks. Hopefully, we wouldn't run into any more surprises.

Thankfully, the cabinets had cost me almost nothing. I'd salvaged two antique dressers from the attic and had the carpenter cut holes in the tops and install two ceramic sinks I'd bought for ten dollars at a barn sale. They looked good, too, very much in keeping with the age and style of the house. And the claw-foot tub we'd brought down from the attic was free. Once the new tile was in—a discontinued style I'd bought for fifty percent off at the tile shop; "discontinued" was becoming one of my favorite words—the bathrooms would look great. I hoped.

I'd checked a DVD out from the library, *Tile Installation for the Do-It-Yourselfer.* The video made it look easy; hopefully the video was right.

Jake had volunteered to install the tile for me, but I'd already let him do too much. He was certainly a handy man to have around. And surprisingly easy to talk to.

Another thing about Jake? He hasn't made the slightest move on me. He hasn't tried to fondle me, or kiss me, or even flirt with me. A few years ago, that would have bothered me, but now it's a relief. I can be myself with Jake. And, as I said, he is a handy man to have around. If I so much as hinted that I wanted help tiling this floor, he'd be on my doorstep with a trowel and a bucket of grout before I could hang up the phone.

But I don't want his help. I want to do it myself. There's something nice about collapsing into bed at the end of the day, exhausted, knowing you've accomplished something. If not for all the bills (and my ever-shrinking bank balance) I might have said I was enjoying it.

If not for that.

Sighing, I flipped through my check register and looked at all the entries: checks written to the plumber, the electrician, the carpenter, the heating and air-conditioning company, the various supply companies—nearly all of them for more than I'd budgeted when I sat down to work out my original business plan.

Chico found me a deal on faucets and showerheads—fixtures his other customers had ordered before getting laid off and having to cancel their remodeling plans. That helped make up some of the cost of the shower pan, but there was still so much to be done. But my biggest worry was the roof.

Dwight Sparks, a white-haired man with a Santa Claus beard and smile to match, the owner of A-1 Affordable Roofing, had come to inspect the roof and give me an estimate the week before. The verdict? The whole thing needed to be replaced. It was going to cost thirty-three thousand dollars.

"Thirty-three thousand! Are you sure? Couldn't we just patch the bad spots? Replace some of the shingles?"

His smile faded and he shook his head sorrowfully. "I know, Madelyn. It's a lot of money, but that roof is shot. I'm gonna have my boys come over tomorrow and tack on some big blue tarps, real heavy-duty ones, that should keep the wet out of your attic for now, but come spring, you've *got* to replace that roof. One big storm and the whole darned thing could blow off. But you seem like a nice lady. I'll tell you what; I'm going to give you a ten percent discount. I'll do it for twenty-nine thousand seven hundred. That's just the best I can do."

"Thank you, Mr. Sparks. I appreciate it. I'll call you as soon as I get the money together."

Twenty-nine thousand seven hundred dollars. Where was I going to get that kind of money? How was I going to pull this off?

I penciled a reminder to myself to check out the cost difference between twenty-year and thirty-year shingles, then paused and scribbled one word—"Gene?"

His message was still on my voice mail. I'd first listened to it two days before, while deleting all but one of the several messages left by Sterling, some cajoling, some pleading, mostly angry, and always with the same aim—to get me to testify at his sentencing, now just days away.

Gene's voice was a smooth contrast to Sterling's desperate tone, but his request was the same, though he'd added a wrinkle that got my attention.

"I understand why you don't want to do it, Madelyn. You're safely out of the spotlight now and I'm sure you want to stay that way, but it's just one day. Sterling tells me that you're remodeling your grandmother's house into an inn. That must be an expensive venture. The firm is prepared to help with any—well, shall we say expenses—within reason, of course, that might be required in association with your court appearance on Sterling's behalf. If you'd like to discuss that further, please give me a call at the office. I'll talk to you later, Madelyn."

I saved the message and, in the last two days, had played it at least five times.

Why was Gene so interested in having me testify for Sterling anyway? Maybe it was some sort of desperate PR move on the law firm's behalf, a last-ditch attempt to make it look like the people they represented weren't complete crooks. Or maybe Gene hoped that I'd be a good diversion for the press, that a picture of me arriving at the courthouse to "stand by my man" would prove more interesting to the media than pictures of him taking the same route. Maybe that. Maybe Gene thought that keeping the name of Blackman, Janders, and Whipple out of any news reports about the notorious Sterling Baron was worth a grand, or five, or ten. I wouldn't put it past him.

Ten thousand dollars. That would make a big dent in my roofing bill. Would that qualify as "expenses within reason"?

I hated Gene, hated the cool assurance in his voice, the certainty that I would return his call, as if he'd somehow managed to sneak a peak at my bank balance and knew how desperate I was.

Did Gene know how badly I needed more money? Or did he just assume that everyone needed more money? In Gene's world, Sterling's world—the world that had been my world—there was no such thing as enough, only more. More than enough.

I remember a cocktail party we threw years before, Sterling standing in a corner with a martini glass in his hand, surrounded by sycophants, including Gene, telling the story of the reporter who had asked John D. Rockefeller, the wealthy industrialist, how much money would be enough. Squinting and pinching the thumb and forefinger of his drink-free hand together until they were nearly touching, Sterling leaned toward his listeners and delivered the famous mogul's response.

"Just a *little* bit more."

The audience howled, partly because of the

mischievous look on Sterling's face and partly because they understood exactly what the old tycoon had been talking about.

That was what they wanted, wasn't it? What Sterling wanted? What I'd wanted? A little bit more. Just a little bit more.

Look what it had gotten us.

I sat there, staring at the paper, and then crossed out Gene's name.

I rinsed my coffee cup and left it to dry on the counter, put on my jacket, then walked back to the table to collect the outgoing mail. At the bottom of the pile lay a large manila envelope containing the forms required for my do-it-yourself divorce. They were all filled out and ready to go. All I had to do was get them into Sterling's hands to begin the proceedings. Easy. Since all of our assets were gone and we had no property or children or pets to fight over, divorcing Sterling required little more effort than filing these forms, paying some fees, and signing some papers.

There was one more message on my voice mail, from Sterling, the last of the dozens he'd left, and the only one I had saved.

"Madelyn, it's me. I know you're not coming to the hearing. It's okay. I get it. Wouldn't have helped anyway. I was kidding myself." He expelled a single, sharp laugh. "I'm never going to see the outside of a prison again, I know that.

But it would have been nice to see you again. I know what you're thinking, but I'm not trying to lay a guilt trip on you. I'm not. I've put you through enough already and . . . well, I just wanted you to . . ." His voice cracked, like he was trying to keep from crying. In all our years together, I had never seen Sterling cry, not once.

"I'm sorry, Madelyn. I know you won't believe me, but I am. I wish I'd done things differently, but even if I had another chance, I don't think I'd have known how. I'm not a good man. I never was. I know I used you, Madelyn. We used each other, didn't we? But I didn't want it to be like that. Everything that was supposed to make me happy never did—except you, for a while. In my entire life, you were the only thing that brought me any happiness, the only person I ever came close to loving."

For a moment the line was quiet except for the sound of his breathing.

"Anyway," he said. "I just wanted to tell you that, while I still had the—"

That was the end of the message. An electronic beep cut him off, signaling his time was up. I don't know why I saved it. I guess I felt sorry for him, for us. Guilty.

I hadn't stolen anything from anybody and I hadn't known that's what Sterling was doing, but that didn't make me innocent. Sterling was right, we had used each other.

We were not good people. I am not a good person.

I picked up the mail and my grocery list, stuffed them into my coat pocket, and went out to run my errands. I left the manila envelope on the table.

I'd heard that a mattress factory in Norwalk was going out of business and having a big liquidation sale, so, after finishing my errands in New Bern, I drove down. It was worth the drive.

I bought five brand-new mattresses for seven hundred and fifty dollars, delivery included. The truck will bring them tomorrow afternoon. I also bought a dozen excellent-quality pillows for seven dollars each. It was a really good deal—too good.

By this time next week, everyone at the factory will be out of a job. Will they be able to find another? That factory would close whether I bought mattresses or not, but I felt guilty, benefiting from the misfortune of others.

Impulsively, I shoved a twenty-dollar bill into the hand of the young man who helped me carry the pillows to the car. He took it, but he wouldn't look me in the eye. I spent half the drive home debating whether I should have done that or not. Not because of the money. He needed it as much as I did, maybe more. Maybe he has a family. But I wish I'd handled it a little more subtly. I didn't mean to embarrass him.

It was dark by the time I got back to New Bern. My gas tank was almost as empty as my stomach. The money I'd given to the man who loaded my car had been earmarked for a drive-through cheeseburger and a fill-up on the way home. Thankfully, I made it home with an eighth of a tank to spare.

I turned onto Oak Leaf Lane, considering the merits of apple-walnut muffins versus cheddar-jalapeño scones as an accompaniment to my dinner omelet, and saw a crowd of cars and people on the street.

No. Not cars, vans. News vans. And reporters, dozens of them, all crowded in front of Beecher Cottage.

What were they doing here? Obviously, it had something to do with Sterling, but his sentencing was a week off. Surely they weren't on the story already. And even if they were, why would they be bothering with me? How had they found me?

I took my foot off the gas and pressed the brake, but gently, slowing the car gradually, considering my next move. My first thought was to turn around and drive away, but I'd dealt with the media before. One of them was bound to spot me and follow me, and when they did, the rest would follow. Besides, where would I go? I didn't know anyone in New Bern, except for Jake, but I couldn't go to his house trailing this horde of camera-wielding locusts. I considered going to a hotel but then remembered that I had no cash and had used my last check to buy the mattresses. My credit card wouldn't do me any good; I'd maxed it out buying a new washing machine. My only refuge this night was Beecher Cottage.

As soon as I opened the car door, I was surrounded by a press of bodies, the flash of camera bulbs, and a barrage of shouted questions. The din was so loud I couldn't understand what they were saying. I heard my name shouted over and over as the mob competed to get my attention, hoping that I'd look up just long enough for them to snap a shot of me looking scared, or guilty, or angry, or sad, any expression that would look good with a headline.

With my head down, face blank, and keys in hand, I ran for the back door, stopping only long enough to grab a big white shopping bag that was blocking my entrance, shove it inside, and slam the door behind me.

What did they want? Was there some new development in the case? It had to be something big. Charges dismissed on account of some legal technicality? A mistrial? But there hadn't even been a trial. Sterling pled guilty. What could have happened?

I walked around the house, quickly closing the drapes, thankful for the sheers that obscured my features from the cameramen lurking outside, and double-checking the locks on the doors. In the kitchen, I saw the message light blinking on my phone. A quick check of the caller identification menu showed several calls from numbers I didn't recognize and others listed as "private"—probably reporters—and three calls from the Metropolitan Correctional Center.

The phone rang before I could listen to the messages. The caller identification read "Eugene Janders, Atty."

"Gene? What's going on? There's a swarm of reporters outside my house."

"Madelyn, where the hell have you been?"

"Out. Buying mattresses. I just got home."

"You went shopping? Now, of all times, you went shopping?"

Gene's voice was shrill and loud. He reminded me of Sterling when he got angry. I screwed my eyes shut and silently counted to three, determined not to be sucked into a shouting match.

"Gene, I'm asking you again: What is going on? Was there a mistrial? Is there some new evidence? What?"

"No one from the prison called you?"

"They did, but I was out, I told you that. I haven't listened to the messages yet. Tell me what happened."

A pause. "Sterling is dead."

My hand flew to cover my mouth. I didn't want

to believe it, but the tone of Gene's voice told me it was true. I closed my eyes, trying to take it in, lowered my hand to my breast, feeling my heart beat through my blouse and sweater.

"How? Was it a heart attack? He's been under so much stress, with the sentencing coming." I pressed my lips together hard, thinking about that last phone message he'd left for me, the message I never returned.

"It wasn't a heart attack. . . . Madelyn . . . Sterling hanged himself from the bars with his belt. He committed suicide."

29
Madelyn

Why aren't I crying?
My conversation with the warden of the prison was short and to the point. Sterling's death was self-inflicted. He'd been a cooperative, even cheerful prisoner. He hadn't shown any suicidal tendencies, so there had been no reason to put him on a special watch. In fact, Sterling had checked out two library books just that morning.

The warden seemed to genuinely believe that Sterling had acted on impulse, but I knew better. Sterling never did anything without a plan. Checking out the library books, his cheerful and cooperative attitude, I was sure it was part of that plan, a ruse to keep the guards from suspecting anything. Deception was Sterling Baron's stock in trade.

"We've transferred the remains to the morgue. Have you made any funeral arrangements?"

"Oh . . . yes. I mean, no. I haven't had time. . . ."

"Let me give you the number for the morgue. I believe the office is closed, but you can call them directly in the morning."

"Thank you."

"Oh and, Mrs. Baron? I am sorry for your loss."

My loss.

I sunk weakly into a kitchen chair. The pile of muffins I'd baked last night was still sitting on a plate on the table, covered by plastic wrap, but I wasn't hungry now. I tipped my head back and closed my eyes.

Why wasn't I crying? I didn't love Sterling, but he was my husband. We were married, for better or worse, mostly worse, but we *were* married. For thirty years, I had been Mrs. Sterling Baron. Who was I now?

He couldn't be dead. His voice was there on my saved messages. If I punched in a few numbers I could hear him, that deep bass voice. Talking. Breathing. Alive.

I wish I could have talked to you one more time, Madelyn.

Now I wished it too. He'd called to say good-bye. I wished I'd called him back. I wished I'd known what he was planning. I wished I could have talked him out of it. Sterling was cruel to me and faithless, but what we'd done, we'd done to each other.

I opened my eyes. Outside I heard voices, someone laughing, the throaty purr of the car engine that suddenly stopped as a late-arriving news crew joined the scrum.

He couldn't be dead, but I knew he was.

That's why they were here laying siege to my house, to me, lying in wait on my lawn, my sidewalk, my door, with microphones and cameras at the ready. I had to get out of here. But how? I couldn't just get in the car and drive off. The reporters would only follow me. I needed someone to *get* me out of here, secretly, and a place to lie low until the frenzy died down.

And I needed to bury Sterling.

Dear God. Why wasn't I crying?

I didn't remember that Jake wasn't home until the third ring. He'd gone to a hardware convention in Pittsburgh. If I called him on his cell phone and told him what trouble I was in, I knew he'd drive back, but I didn't have his number. What hotel was he in? I didn't have a computer so I couldn't look up the location of the conference.

I put the kettle on to boil and pulled a tea bag out of the canister, hoping a cup of tea would help me focus. Leaning against the counter, I considered the feasibility of phoning every hotel in Pittsburgh until I found Jake. I couldn't very well ask an operator to give me numbers for every hotel in the city. Could I? It might come to that.

The sugar bowl was empty. I walked toward the pantry to refill it and noticed the white bag sitting on the floor by the back door, the one that had been blocking my way when I came in. Curious, I walked over and looked inside. There was an envelope on top with my name written on it in purple ink. The handwriting was loopy, feminine. Definitely not Jake's.

I picked up the envelope, pulled back several layers of white tissue paper, and saw the quilt. My quilt! The one I'd left behind that day I'd run into Tessa. Someone had brought it back.

I pulled it out of the bag, picking it up by two corners and letting the thick, soft folds of fabric open fully. Someone had repaired it, beautifully.

I stretched it out over the back of two chairs so I could examine it more carefully. The torn seams had been resewn, the pulled quilting restitched, and the whole thing had been cleaned. The brown spot, left when Tessa and I had accidentally spilled our hot chocolate, was gone. I ran my fingers over the place where the stain had been, in the second row of blocks, feeling a little twinge of regret. My loss.

It was a beautiful quilt, there was no denying that. It had a whole new binding. No, not new. Not quite. The blue fabric was soft and slightly faded with age, which looked entirely right with the rest of the quilt. It was a new binding, but the fabric was old, possibly antique. Someone had gone to a lot of trouble to restore this quilt. Who would have gone to such trouble for me, a stranger?

I went back to the bag, picked up the envelope, and opened it. There was a card inside, a picture of two red poppies that I recognized from a Georgia O'Keeffe painting. I opened the card. A black-and-white photograph fell out. I looked at it and gasped.

30
Tessa

We'll talk about all that later. What matters right now is finding a way to get you out of there. Try to get some sleep. I'll talk to you first thing tomorrow morning. Do you need anything? You sure? Okay. Good night. Madelyn? . . . I'm so sorry for your loss."

I hung up the phone. Lee came out of the bathroom with a towel wrapped around his waist.

"Who's calling this time of night? Is Josh all right?"

"It was Madelyn Beecher," I said quietly.

"Really." He dropped his towel and climbed back into bed. "Well, that's nice. I guess. She liked the quilt?"

"And the picture, yes. But that's not why she called." I rolled onto my hip to face my husband. "Madelyn's in trouble. Sterling hanged himself in his jail cell and now the press is surrounding her house. She can't get out and nobody can get in, not without running through a gauntlet of cameras and microphones."

"He killed himself?" Lee's expression changed from astonishment to disgust. "Sounds like something he'd do, though, doesn't it? Take the easy way out. Coward."

I couldn't bring myself to think of suicide as the easy way out for anyone, but it was hard to disagree with Lee's assessment of Sterling Baron's character. He was a coward.

"Honey, Madelyn is trapped in that house. We've got to find a way to get her out without the press knowing. I said she could stay with us until things calm down."

"You said what?"

I didn't bother repeating myself. He'd heard me the first time; he just didn't like what he'd heard. But I know Lee as well as I know myself. And I knew that, in the end, he'd do the right thing. Lee is a good person.

"Tessa, you've got to be kidding."

"She's got nowhere else to go."

"You mean her other friends aren't jumping up and down at the prospect of having Madelyn Baron, and the national media, come for a sleepover? I wonder why?"

"She doesn't have any other friends, Lee. Not now. All her old friends dropped her. She doesn't know anybody in New Bern, except Jake, and he's out of town."

"Yeah. To a hardware conference. He told me."

Lee was still frowning but he'd lowered his voice, a sure sign that his resolve was weakening. "I still don't see what this has to do with us. Why does she have to come here? What's wrong with a hotel?"

"It wouldn't take five minutes for the press to track her down at a hotel. But no one will think to look for her here."

"Assuming we could get her away without anyone knowing," Lee mused. "It'd take some pretty elaborate plan to pull that off." He stared off into space, his lips working as if he were chewing over the options. After a moment, his shoulders twitched and his eyes refocused.

"No, Tessa. This is crazy. I'm sorry for her troubles. She's gotten a raw deal. But that's not our problem or your fault. Why should you be the one to bail her out?"

"Because. Someone has to. And because I'm her friend."

"That was a long time ago."

"I know, but she's alone and her husband is dead. I know he wasn't exactly a model citizen, but she needs help. I think I should give it to her. I think I owe it to her."

"So this is about assuaging your guilty conscience?"

"A little," I admitted. "But it's also the right thing to do and the right time to do it. Think about it. Is it a coincidence that Madelyn and I both came back to New Bern now? Or that she left her quilt behind in the coffee shop and that, having just taken up quilting, I found it and decided to restore it? Was it chance that I happened to leave that quilt, and a note with our phone number, on her doorstep exactly at the moment she was facing a huge crisis?"

Lee narrowed his eyes. "So," he said slowly, "you think you're some kind of divine instrument? That the Almighty is using you to reach out to Madelyn Baron?"

Or her me.

I felt a flush of heat on my cheeks. I knew how crazy this sounded to him.

"It just seems like an awful lot of coincidences, that's all. But more than that, helping Madelyn is just something I want to do. Since coming back here, I've realized that friends are important, as important as family, even, but in a different way. And Madelyn was the best friend I ever had."

Lee shifted his weight onto his hip and ran his hand down my arm before interlacing his fingers with mine. "Baby, that was so long ago. You and Madelyn have lived whole lives since then. After so many years, you may have nothing in common. People change. Sometimes friendships die. Sometimes with good reason."

I nodded. "I know. Maybe that's how this will turn out. But I can't just turn my back on someone who needs my help." I squeezed my husband's hand and looked into his eyes. "I don't think you can either."

Lee sighed, unlaced his fingers from mine, and reached up to push his hair off his forehead. "Do you see it?"

"See what?"

"The big letter 'S' on my forehead. Stands for 'sucker.' "

I grinned. "You're a good man."

"Yeah, yeah." Lee pushed himself into a sitting position and threw off the blankets.

"Well, if we're going to smuggle your long-lost friend out from under the nose of the paparazzi, we're going to need a plan, and reinforcements. Might as well get up and start working on it."

"Lee? I love you."

He grinned. "I love you, too, babe. But that doesn't mean I'm not a sucker."

• • •

By morning we had a plan and by lunchtime we were ready to put it into action. Jake Kaminski was in on it.

It hadn't been easy to find him, but after we telephoned Josh in Florida (he turned out to be an expert computer sleuth) we were able to find the location of the hardware convention, the hotel it was being held in, and finally, Jake, who had driven from Pittsburgh to New Bern in the middle of the night to help us. The rescue team consisted of Lee, Jake, and Matt, one of Jake's clerks. I was supposed to stay behind.

"Why can't I come along?"

"Because you'll attract attention, that's why. We don't want them getting suspicious, Tessa. These aren't small-town reporters we're talking. These are the big guns—the networks, Fox, CNN. . . ."

"*Entertainment Tonight*," Jake offered as he zipped a pair of white coveralls over his jeans and T-shirt. "They're going to be on the lookout for just this kind of thing and if they see a woman in the truck, they'll know something is up."

"My UPS man is a woman. Women can deliver things."

"They can," Lee agreed, "but they usually don't, not big things like furniture. You don't want to endanger this operation, do you? We'll be right back."

"The operation? Why do I suddenly hear the sound track to *Mission: Impossible* playing in the background?"

"Well," Lee grinned, "you have to admit, this does have a 007 feel to it."

He checked to make sure his coveralls were zipped, then settled his baseball cap squarely on his head. He looked at Jake, then Matt, and nodded. "Gentlemen? Let's roll!"

They were gone five hours. I was worried sick.

In spite of their attempts to look as much like a mattress delivery company as possible, a couple of the reporters eyed them suspiciously as they carried in the five large mattress boxes. After delivering the mattresses that Madelyn had bought the day before—she'd called and had them sent to my house instead of Beecher Cottage—and carrying the "empty" boxes back out to the plain white panel truck Jake used at the store, two of the news vans had followed them.

They had no choice but to drive the truck, which had a top speed of about fifty miles an hour, down the highway and all the way back down to the mattress factory in Norwalk.

"You should have seen those guys." Lee laughed. "They wouldn't give up. But Jake brazened it out. He drove up to the factory gate, told the guard we had a return to make, and sailed on through like he owned the place. Jake, you are one cool customer."

"I sure wasn't feeling cool. I was beginning to think it wasn't going to work. But after we went through the gate, the reporters decided we were legit. Good thing the guard bought my story. Nice work, fellas."

Jake and Lee high-fived each other and then did the same to Matt, who was grinning like the cat who ate the canary. Boys.

"Did it occur to any of you to pick up the phone and tell me what was taking so long? I just about wore a hole in the rug with all my pacing."

"We didn't want to take the risk. We thought they might have had some kind of special listening equipment or something, you know. Something that could tap into an unsecured line."

I looked at Jake and raised my eyebrows, silently questioning the logic of this, but he just nodded.

"Lee's right. They do have things like that. I saw them when I was in Washington, DC, at the Spy Museum."

I rolled my eyes. "Whatever. The main thing is you're here and nobody followed you. Thanks, guys. Where is Madelyn? You didn't leave her locked in the truck, did you?"

"She's outside," Jake said. "She said she needed a minute."

"Do you think she'd like a cup of tea? Or a sandwich?"

Jake nodded. "Good idea. I'm sure she hasn't eaten."

I turned to head for the kitchen. The front door opened and Madelyn walked in carrying a beige overnight bag.

Without thinking, I walked toward her with my arms open, ready to comfort her, give her a hug, but she shrank back. I felt a twinge of disappointment but told myself it didn't matter. She'd had a hard day, a hard life. And, I reminded myself, she wasn't here to bury the hatchet and catch up with an old friend who had treated her poorly. She was here because she had no one else to turn to and nowhere else to go. I dropped my arms to my sides.

"It's good to see you, Madelyn. It really is. Lee, can you take Madelyn's suitcase to the guest room?"

"Sure." Lee smiled as he took her bag and headed down the hall.

Jake said he and Matt should get going, then said his good-byes, telling Madelyn not to worry and he'd see her soon. She gave him a half-smile and nodded.

When everyone was gone, I turned back to Madelyn. "Are you hungry? I've got sandwiches in the kitchen. Have you eaten today?"

She blinked a couple of times, as if surprised by

the question and trying to remember the answer. "Um. No. I don't think so. But I'm not really hungry."

"Well, then I'll just make you a half sandwich," I said, using the technique my mother had always employed when dealing with her picky eater— me. Don't give them the option of saying no. "Come on into the kitchen."

I smiled and began walking toward the door, hoping she'd follow. Instead, she reached out and grabbed at my elbow, stopping me.

"Tessa? I just want you to know, if the press finds out I'm here, I'll go. I don't want to cause you any more trouble than I already have. I won't stay long."

"Stay as long as you want to. I meant what I said; it's good to see you. I only wish it weren't under such sad circumstances."

She let go of my elbow and stood there for a moment, pressing her lips together. "Thank you. I . . . Well . . . I don't know what else to say, Tessa. Just . . . thanks."

"You don't need to say anything else. Not tonight. We've got plenty of time for that."

31
Madelyn

A very sensible choice," Mr. D'Amato, the funeral director, said. This was all new to me, but he had a smooth bass voice and manner of speaking that made me feel that I was doing well, making all the right decisions.

"For environmental as well as economic reasons, many people prefer direct cremation to burial now. However, I do think having a brief memorial service beforehand is a good idea. It brings a dignity to the occasion and a sense of closure to the family. The difference in cost hardly makes it worth considering anything else."

"Yes," I agreed, though he had yet to tell me what the difference in cost would be. Whatever it was, it was more than I had. But I couldn't let Sterling go without at least some sort of . . . I don't know . . . ritual, I suppose. Some acknowledgment, however small, that he was a person. Anything else would have been too sad.

"Very good, then," Mr. D'Amato continued. "I'll see you tomorrow at eight o'clock. It will be dark, so no one will see you come in. I will be here to greet you at the side door, as we discussed. Again, I am so sorry for your loss, Mrs. Baron. But be assured that we're taking every precaution to maintain your privacy in this time of grief."

"Thank you."

"Mrs. Baron, one more thing. Would you like a guest book at the service? So Mr. Baron's friends may express their condolences? Under the circumstances, I wasn't sure. . . ."

"No. Thank you, Mr. D'Amato. That won't be necessary."

I'd intended for Sterling's funeral to be small and private, but it turned out to be even smaller than I'd envisioned. I had made a few calls to Sterling's closest friends and associates. No one wanted to come.

Angela Radnovich, wife of Mike Radnovich, the famous basketball player who had been Sterling's favorite golfing partner, sounded the most sincere in her refusal.

"Madelyn, I'm so, so sorry. What a terrible thing. I wish we could be there—I told Mike we should go—but the publicity . . . He said that we couldn't. . . ."

"No, no," I interjected. "It's all right, Angela. I understand. Mike is probably right. If the press were to find out . . . It was kind of you to even consider it."

"Well, you've always been kind to me, Madelyn. You were the first woman in New York, the first of Mike's circle anyway, who actually talked to me. I'm so sorry about everything."

Everyone I contacted was sympathetic, though far less sincere than Angela. One or two said that they'd like to see me when "things calm down"— but they also said they were unavoidably otherwise engaged. Most had long, rambling excuses. I didn't pause long to listen, just said good-bye and hung up. I didn't have to be polite. I would not be seeing any of them again.

Gene said the press was staking out his office and apartment and that he didn't want to take the risk that they'd follow him and disrupt the services. His excuse was legitimate, but I sensed he was glad to have it.

"I'm sorry, I can't make it, Madelyn, but you understand."

"Of course."

"What funeral home have you chosen?"

"I haven't. Not yet."

I'm not sure why I lied. Maybe all this cloak-and-dagger I've had to resort to is making me paranoid. I feel like I've been spirited away to a safe house.

Strange, but I do feel safe here. No one bothers me, no one asks me questions. I'm grateful to Tessa and Lee for taking me in. And for coming to Sterling's funeral. Yes, it will be a very private service, just me, Tessa, Lee, Jake, and Reverend Tucker. That's all.

No, Mr. D'Amato. No guest book will be necessary.

. . .

I agonized over the casket. The direct cremation "package" came with what Mr. D'Amato referred to as an "alternative container," but it was really just a cardboard box shaped like a casket. It was the most practical choice. After all, the casket would be cremated along with Sterling's remains. But . . . it was a cardboard box.

The next step up, a fiberboard container embossed with blue-gray cloth, was also designed for cremation, but at least it *looked* like a casket. I would have preferred to go with that, but it would have added another thousand dollars to the bill.

"A cardboard box," I said after hanging up with Mr. D'Amato. "It's just so sad. Everything about this is so sad."

Tessa knit her brows together sympathetically and handed me a glass brimming with red wine. "Don't be hard on yourself, Madelyn. You're doing the best you can."

"I suppose. But I wish . . ." I lifted the glass to my lips and drank deeply, giving myself time to think. "I just wish I could afford something nicer, with flowers and music. I owe him that much, surely."

"Do you?"

Tessa had this way of asking the questions no one else dared to, of cutting through the bull and to the chase. I had forgotten.

"Not any more than he owed me, so I guess we're even. I just want to do the right thing. It should have been better, you know? It all should have been better."

No one knew where I was.

The reporters were still staked out in front of Beecher Cottage, hoping to catch me coming in or going out. Even without me, they were having a field day, filming stand-ups on my lawn, dredging up the details of Sterling's meteoric rise and fall and the grisly minutiae of his last days. One reporter went so far as to find an exact replica of the belt Sterling hanged himself with. He held it up to the camera and, in somber tones, speculated as to what Sterling's thoughts had been when he'd expelled his final breath and gone, far from gently, into that good night.

"Did he think of redemption? Of relief? Of the many lives he'd ruined and crimes he'd committed? Or . . . of Madelyn? His wife of thirty years who, according to Baron's attorney, Eugene Janders, had refused to testify as a character witness at his sentencing. Was the rejection of the woman he'd loved the straw that finally broke the spirit of the man who had once been known as 'the Prince of Wall Street'? The world will never know, and Madelyn Baron," he said, pausing dramatically as the camera panned the exterior of Beecher Cottage, "the Wall Street

Widow," another dramatic pause, "isn't talking."

Gene. That snake. He couldn't resist one last chance to make my life miserable. And it would be his last chance. I was never going to speak to him again, never. Good thing I'd followed my instincts and lied when he asked about the location of the funeral parlor. Otherwise, there was no doubt in my mind that a cadre of reporters would have been stationed outside of D'Amato's Mortuary, awaiting my arrival.

As it was, things went according to plan. Jake borrowed a van from his sister, one of the old, full-sized numbers that don't have windows on the sides, and drove me to the funeral home. Lee and Tessa came separately and picked up the Reverend Tucker along the way. The reverend was standing next to Mr. D'Amato when I arrived.

The funeral director shook my hand and ushered us into a white-walled, industrial-looking room with a large metal furnace at the end—the crematory.

Not far from that, there were a few chairs set up in a row—very few, but still more than we would need. In front of that was a long table draped with a white cloth that held the "alternative container." Lying on top of that was an enormous blanket of white roses, so large it entirely covered the cheap cardboard casket that held my husband's body.

I turned around to look at Tessa, Lee, and Jake.

"You didn't even know him."

Tessa looked at Jake, who shook his head.

Reverend Tucker cleared his throat. "The flowers are from Abigail Spaulding. I believe her first husband, Woolley Wynne, knew your husband. She wanted to pay her respects and she asked me to tell you how genuinely sorry she is—for everything."

I felt a catch in my throat. "Please tell her I said thank you and that . . . I appreciate her condolences."

There was no eulogy. How could there be? I was the only person present who knew Sterling well enough to deliver one. Reverend Tucker led a prayer, read something from a worn black Bible, one of the psalms, I think. I don't remember his words, just the sound of his voice, clear and rhythmic, his pitch leaning toward treble, mournful and keening. Even if he didn't mean it, I was glad that someone besides me at least seemed to be mourning Sterling's untimely death and wasted life.

When I die, who will mourn me?

When he finished reading, the reverend closed his Bible, leaving a finger in the pages to mark his place. Mr. D'Amato, assisted by Jake, Lee, and a somber-suited associate, lifted the rose-camouflaged casket and carried it to the crematory.

None of this seems quite real. I know it is, it must be. But it doesn't seem that way. Maybe it will in a day or two, after I get some sleep . . . if I'm ever able to sleep again.

The bed in Tessa's guest room is comfortable, but when I lie down on it, I can't sleep. Instead, I lie there thinking, trying not to think, not crying, and wishing I could cry. Last night, around three, worn out and sick of myself, I got up and crept down the hallway past Tessa and Lee's bedroom quietly, but not as quietly as I could have. Part of me hoped that Tessa would hear me and get up to keep me company, but she didn't. They are sound sleepers, those two. Why wouldn't they be? Their consciences are clear.

But I couldn't sleep.

I made myself a cup of tea, carried it into the living room, and curled into Tessa's easy chair, the one that belonged to her mother, the old blue velvet now replaced with beige chenille. Thinking I'd read for a bit, I picked up the Bible Tessa left on the table. I flipped through it, hoping to come across something dry and dull enough to induce sleep. Instead, I happened upon a story about a rich man who, as any rich man would, inquired about the price of admission to heaven and found it too high.

As I stood before the open door of the crematory and watched the pallbearers slide the casket into the narrow brick-lined chamber that would soon be fired to a temperature that would reduce Sterling's body to fragments and memories—my memories—I found myself thinking about what I'd read the night before, one line in particular. "It is easier for a camel to go through the eye of a needle than for a rich man to enter the kingdom of God."

That was the most depressing thing I'd ever read, but even worse was what came after: "With people it is impossible, but not with God; for all things are possible with God."

I don't know if I believe in God, much less heaven or hell. But I'd like to believe that during our lives, we're not—that I'm not—doomed to endlessly repeat my mistakes, to live and die and disappear. Those words, if they are even a little bit true, seem to say that it's at least possible, hard but not hopeless.

But not for Sterling. Not now.

In choosing to end his life, he also chose to sever himself from even the barest hope that someday, somehow, things might be better, that even from the inside of a prison cell, he might yet have made his life count for *something*—or someone. It's hard to imagine how that might have played out, but surely there was at least the slimmest of possibilities of something better to come, as slim as a camel that could thread itself through the eye of a needle, which sounds impossible, but . . . what if it's not?

What if?

Tessa plucked a single rose from the blanket covering the casket and handed it to me. Mr. D'Amato shut the heavy metal door and nodded to his assistant to ignite the flame as Reverend Tucker began to intone the words "Ashes to ashes, dust to dust . . ." and tears for the death of hope flowed down my cheeks.

Right now I've got more questions than answers, but I'm certain of one thing: I do not want my life to end without at least the possibility of hope.

I want something better. I want to change.

32
Madelyn

It was decided that Lee and Tessa would take the reverend home and I'd drive with Jake. "You really didn't have to do this," I said as I buckled my seat belt. "I could have gone in the other car."

Jake turned the key in the ignition and pumped the gas a couple of times. "I don't mind."

"Well, thanks. I didn't relish the idea of riding back with Lee. I'm sure the feeling is mutual."

Jake checked his rearview mirror before pulling away from the curb. "Yeah?"

"Don't get me wrong, he hasn't said anything

or been rude. But I get the feeling he holds me personally responsible for the banking crisis, the housing slump, the Wall Street meltdown, and the decline of Western civilization."

"All that, huh? Wow." Jake glanced over at me. "Lee's all right. He's just having a hard time right now. Lotta people are."

"I know. It was nice of Lee and Tessa to take me in."

I turned my head and stared into the darkness as we drove past rows of houses, peering past curtains into warmly lit living rooms, like sets in a play, some peopled with performances in progress, others vacant and expectant, waiting for the actors to make their entrance. In the glow of lamplight every home we passed looked safe and peaceful. I wondered if they were.

Jake broke the silence. "Do you miss him?"

"No. Not really. I know that sounds terrible, but we'd lived separate lives for so long. I talked to Sterling's secretary more often than I talked to Sterling."

"There had to be something between you," Jake said. "You were married for a long time."

"We were. After a fashion."

"Did you love him?"

"I don't know anymore. We were definitely attracted to one another, especially at the beginning. I mean, we both understood what we wanted out of the relationship—I wanted security

301

and he wanted a beautiful woman by his side—but that wasn't all. I admired him, I suppose. Sterling was handsome, powerful, charming. Woolley was, too, but Woolley was married. We had to sneak around, meet at hotels far off the beaten path, eat our dinners from the room-service menu rather than risk being seen together in the restaurant.

"It wasn't like that with Sterling. He seemed proud of me, as if he wanted to show me off. He took me places—parties, restaurants, concerts—and introduced me to people, important people, celebrities and politicians and socialites, as if I were some sort of prize he'd won." I smiled bleakly, remembering my younger self.

"It wasn't all bad, you know, being a trophy wife. Not at first. It was wonderful to be prized, paraded about in front of glamorous and celebrated people, becoming glamorous and celebrated myself. Of course, a lot of people didn't like me. They only tolerated me because of Sterling. Even so, it was exciting. And Sterling was . . . I thought he . . . Well, he wasn't so hard in those days.

"There *was* something between us," I said, sounding a little more defensive than I'd intended. "Something more than the money. If it had been only about money, then I'd have been satisfied with what I had, wouldn't I? There was certainly enough money, more than enough.

Sterling never denied me anything that could be paid for by cash or credit." I sniffed and looked down, pressing my chin into my shoulder. "I wanted more. I wanted love. But Sterling didn't love me, not ever."

"Then why did you stay with him?"

"Money. Status. Lack of imagination, I suppose. By that time I couldn't imagine living any other way. You'd be surprised what you can learn to put up with, what you can convince yourself not to see, in the name of self-preservation. Also, I was afraid. Afraid of being alone, of reverting gloriously to type, of becoming what everyone always thought I was, a gold digger reduced to grasping divorcée, the stuff of courtroom dramas and sensational stories in the tabloids." I let out a hollow laugh. "Which is what happened anyway.

"But," I said, "and, believe me, I know how naïve this sounds, there was also a part of me that just kept hoping that it would get better. Even at the very end, during our last weekend together, I wondered if it might not be possible."

Keeping his eyes on the road, Jake said, "That sounds human, not naïve. I mean, if you don't have hope, what's the point? Nobody wants to end up divorced. Even after my first wife cheated on me, I considered taking her back. People thought I was crazy, but if she'd been willing to work things out, I'd have tried."

"And your second wife?"

"Rhonda? Well," he said, drawing out the word, "it's hard to patch things up after your wife tries to run you over with your own car, but . . . yeah, if she'd wanted to try again, I might have. At least half of what was wrong with us was really what was wrong with me."

"Like what?"

"Like I didn't listen. Or put my dishes in the dishwasher," he said, smiling faintly before his expression turned serious again. "And I didn't make her feel safe. She was a jealous woman, but I gave her reason to be. I didn't cheat, not ever, but when other women flirted with me, I'd flirt back. I told myself it was just harmless fun, that I wasn't hurting anybody, but I hurt Rhonda something awful."

"Did you know it at the time?"

"I should have. But I blamed her, said she was the problem. We'd fight. I'd end up sleeping on the sofa, feeling sorry for myself. I was an incredible jerk."

As he talked I found myself nodding; I could have written that script myself.

Sterling and I after a party, him a little drunk, me screaming at him for flirting with some Flavor of the Week, him screaming at me for being jealous, not trusting him. Insults, denials, curses, slamming of doors. Sterling storming off in search of more genial female company. Me waking the next day and seeing his side of the bed with sheets unrumpled and pillow undented.

"You sound pretty enlightened now, Jake. How did that happen?"

"Beth," he said, as though the mere mention of her name made everything clear.

"We met on a blind date; friends introduced us. We went to a movie at the Red Rooster, dinner after. It was nice, you know, but not spectacular. I was dating several women at the time."

"I've heard that about you. Word around town is you're quite the ladies' man."

He grimaced. "Don't believe everything you hear. I like women. They like me. But that doesn't necessarily mean I'm a 'ladies' man.'"

"Doesn't necessarily mean you're not."

He shot me a look. "Can I finish my story?"

"Sorry. Go on."

"Anyway, Beth seemed nice and I found her attractive, so when I walked her to her door after dinner, I asked if I could come in."

"As in come in and stay the night?"

"Yeah, pretty much. She said no. Didn't even think about it before answering, didn't even *pretend* to think about it. Didn't flirt or invent a story about not wanting to wake up her roommate, something that might have salved my bruised ego. She just said no."

"And you weren't used to hearing that?" I said with a teasing smile, already knowing the answer.

Jake wasn't just handsome and a good conversationalist, which is a pretty rare combination all by itself. He could also operate a floor sander and fix a leaky faucet. Of course women said yes to even his most suggestive suggestions.

He shook his head. "She wasn't mean or unpleasant about it. In fact, she said she would love to see me again but that I was not invited in, not that night or any night.

"Well, I was ticked. I wrote her off—so I told myself. But I couldn't get her off my mind. I called and asked her out again. By the third date, I was hooked."

I groaned and rolled my eyes. "And that's what hooked you? The fact that she wouldn't sleep with you?" It was Woolley and Abigail all over again. Men are such morons, such easily manipulated morons.

"No," he said firmly, "it wasn't that. It was her confidence that drew me. So many women are so desperate, willing to agree to anything because they think having a man will validate them as a woman. Desperation is *not* attractive. Not to me.

"Beth wasn't looking to me or anybody else to 'complete' her. She was already complete and she knew her value. She made me court her and, in the process, taught me about romance, and intimacy, and respect, and what real love looks like."

The headlights of an oncoming car illuminated Jake's face and I glanced over to see if he was crying, but his eyes were dry.

"She helped me realize that the real thing is worth the wait."

I looked out the window, relieved to note we were nearly there. I wasn't in the mood to hear any more about Saint Beth. It was nice that Jake's third marriage had been happy, but weren't we supposed to be talking about *my* grief?

Jake made a right turn onto the street that led to the farm. "Beth didn't let me get away with anything, but she was also very gentle. She showed me how to be her hero, then treated me like I already was that guy—even when I fell short."

"She sounds wonderful," I said brightly, hoping to bring the subject to a close. I was starting to suspect that Jake's mental trip down memory lane was really a subtle tactic to bring the conversation around to my own shortcomings and perhaps he had a point, but really? Was this the time? I'd just cremated my husband.

I shifted in my seat and crossed my left knee over my right. "You were very lucky." I sighed. "Sterling was never supportive. All he knew how to do was—"

Jake kept talking as though he hadn't even heard me. "I was lucky, very. You know, Madelyn, it's the easiest thing in the world to tell somebody what they want to hear, but it takes a real friend to tell somebody what they need to hear."

There it was. I knew it.

I should have driven back with Lee and Tessa after all. I didn't care for this conversation and was trying to communicate that through my words and body language, but Jake wasn't taking the hint. So much for subtlety.

"All right, Jake. Come out with it. What are you trying to say?"

Jake frowned as he turned the van onto the farm's gravel driveway. "Nothing," he said with an utterly unconvincing expression of innocence. "I was talking about Beth."

"Oh, you were not. I mean, yes. You were talking about Beth, but your message was directed at me. All that 'somebody who cares says what you need to hear, not just what you want to hear' stuff. That's your lead-in for trying to say what's wrong with me, isn't it? Okay, so fine." I crossed my arms over my chest. "You want to point out my faults, go right ahead. I'm listening."

Jake pulled the van up to the side of the house, turned off the engine, and yanked the handle of the parking brake. "Madelyn, I swear I don't know what you're talking about. But if I had planned on listing possible areas for your character improvement, I might begin with your realizing that every conversation isn't about you."

"See? I knew it. All right. Go on. What else is wrong with me?"

With his mouth slightly open and his head shaking, Jake looked up at the ceiling of the van. "I don't understand women, I swear I don't. Madelyn, nothing is wrong with you."

"Well, we both know that's not true," I puffed. "I'm broke, miserable, alone, and friendless. My life is a complete train wreck. The only people who care what happens to me are the ones who read the tabloids hoping I'll implode."

"Madelyn. You are not friendless. I'm here, aren't I?"

"Well, all right then!" I exclaimed in exasperation. "You say you're my friend, then *be* my friend. Quit avoiding the issue and tell me what's wrong with me!"

Jake took in a big breath, puffing his cheeks out to the size of Ping-Pong balls before blowing it out again, then pulled reflectively on his nose.

He looked at me skeptically. "You really want to do this?"

I bit my lower lip and asked myself the same question.

"Yes," I said quietly. "I need help, Jake. I've been so miserable for so long that I can't remember what it feels like not to be miserable. When I was standing there today, watching them load Sterling's body into that furnace, I . . ." I stopped to catch my breath, pressing my fist against my lips.

"I don't want to end up like that. But I don't want to go on living like this either. Tell me what to do," I begged. "I just want somebody to tell me what to do."

"Maddie," Jake said. I've always hated for people to call me Maddie, but somehow, I didn't mind it coming from him. "Are you trying to tell me that . . ."

"No. I'm not planning anything desperate. But there are an awful lot of days when I wake up and wish I hadn't. I just want things to be . . . different."

"Things happen, Maddie. Life isn't always fair and there isn't a whole lot you can do about that. But I don't think that's the problem." He paused for a moment, reading my expression. "Are you sure you want to hear this?"

I nodded.

"All right," he said doubtfully, "but remember that everything I'm about to tell you is something I've had to tell myself too. You and I are a lot alike. There are shelves of books written about what's wrong with people like us. I've read a bunch of them and I'm glad I did. They helped me understand a lot about who I was and why I did some of the things I did. They just didn't help me do much about it."

"What did?"

"At the risk of sounding simplistic, not focusing on it so much," he said, rushing ahead to stem the tide of protests he saw forming on my lips, clarifying his point.

"Not focusing on *myself* so much. Beth helped me realize how much energy I wasted feeling sorry for myself. I'd stopped drinking years before, but one day I realized that I'd just exchanged one addiction for another, alcohol for self-pity, and the one was making me just as miserable as the other. So"—he shrugged—"I gave it up."

My face felt hot, flushed with equal parts annoyance and embarrassment. "So you're saying I'm the problem? That my misery is of my own making? You don't know what I've been through, Jake. Your parents may not have been the Cleavers, but at least you *had* parents! You didn't have to live with a—"

"Hang on!" Jake raised his hands to stop my barrage. "I know you've had some tough breaks, Madelyn, but you've had a lot of things your own way too. Look around you, Mrs. Baron," he said, inclining his head toward the darkened windows of Lee and Tessa's house. "A lot of people have had a lot of tough breaks lately."

"What? If that's what you thought, Jake, then why did you bother to drive me home? I might as well have ridden with Lee, or Aaron Fletcher for that matter! Well, don't worry," I said coldly. "You won't have to do it again."

I wrenched open the door and was about to jump out of the van, but Jake grabbed my forearm and wouldn't let go.

"Hang on a minute, Maddie."

"Don't call me Maddie!"

"Fine, Mad-e-lyn," he said impatiently, enunciating each syllable of my name. "But before you go getting pissed and running off, you're going to sit still and listen."

I tried pulling away again, but Jake wouldn't release his grip on my arm. With my eyes blazing and my arms crossed over my chest, I sat still and listened; I had no choice.

Jake took a breath and let it out.

"I am not laying all the misery of the world at your doorstep. I'm saying that stuff happens. It happens to everybody. Sometimes it's our own fault and sometimes it's not. What I'm trying to tell you, because I care and because you *asked* me," he said with a pointed look, "is that you're not the only one who's suffering at the hands of other people. You're so busy blaming everybody else for everything that's wrong with your life that you can't see anything else. You're selfish and self-absorbed, Madelyn, and it's making you miserable. Just like it did me.

"You want to know how to change?" he asked. "Be grateful for what you've got instead of constantly focusing on what you don't. Quit keeping score. Forgive people and the past and let it go. Start looking for ways to make others happy. If you make a habit of that, you won't have time to be miserable."

He loosened his grip on my arm. "That's it— my CliffsNotes prescription for life. It's not real deep, but it works for me."

I glared at him. "Are you done now?"

"Yeah."

"Good." I reached up and removed his hand from my shoulder, brushing him off with deliberate disgust before climbing out of the van. "Go to hell, Jake!" I spat and then slammed the door.

I stormed off toward the empty house. Behind me, I heard the mechanical hum of a car window rolling down and Jake's voice, laced with laughter.

"No thanks, Maddie. Already been there and back. I'm not planning a return trip. Never again."

I went into the guest room and lay down on the bed without bothering to take off my black funeral dress. A few minutes later, I heard the popping sound of tires on gravel and got up to close my door and turn out my light. Tessa whispered something to Lee as they passed my door on the way to their room, but I couldn't make out what she said.

Eventually, after the sound of murmuring

voices and running water stopped coming through the walls and the house settled into silence, I took off my clothes and got in under the covers, but sleep eluded me for many hours. My dreams were muddled and nonsensical. I only remember part of one, a bearded image of my father standing before me, gripping my shoulders with both hands and saying, "That's the deal, Maddie. That's the deal."

33
Tessa

I dumped my purse and the mail onto the bench near the back door and paused for a moment to sniff the air. Something smelled good.

"Madelyn?"

"In here!"

I slipped off my shoes, kicked them under the bench, and padded toward the kitchen in my stocking feet, following the scent of orange peels and baking butter.

Madelyn pulled a baking sheet from the oven. "I made scones."

She set the pan on the stove and I broke a point off one of the hot, crumbling scones and blew on it before popping it into my mouth and groaning with pleasure. "Oh my gosh! Fabulous. Is that rosemary I'm tasting?"

"And orange." Madelyn nodded. "You had all that rosemary in the refrigerator and a half jar of marmalade. I figured it was worth a try."

"You figured right."

Madelyn smiled. "I made a pot of minestrone soup too. You had quite a few vegetables in the crisper that would have gone bad in a couple more days. I couldn't sit around here doing nothing. I figured I might as well make dinner. You don't mind, do you?"

I pulled two glasses out of the kitchen cabinet and filled them with merlot and handed one to Madelyn. "Are you kidding? Keep this up and I'll be begging you to move in permanently."

"Busy day?"

I shook my head. "Absolutely dead. It was exhausting. Much more exhausting than a day spent on my feet waiting on long lines of customers. At least, I think it is. I've never had long lines of customers. When you ring up only three sales in eight hours, you've got plenty of time to sit around and worry. That *will* wear you out. I know this for a fact."

"Is it that bad?" Madelyn asked and then went on without waiting for an answer. I think my face said it all. "I just don't get it. I tried some of the lavender hand cream you left in the bathroom and it was incredible. How much do you charge for that?"

"Fourteen dollars."

"Is that all?" Madelyn puffed in disbelief. "The hand cream I used to buy from a little boutique in Manhattan cost four times as much and it wasn't half as good. If you were selling this in the city . . ."

"But I'm not."

"If there was some way to get the word out," Madelyn mused. "Do you have an advertising budget?"

"I did. My original business plan included a three-thousand-dollar advertising budget. But when the price of display shelving turned out to be more than I'd bargained for, it got cut." I tipped my glass up sharply and took a good-sized gulp.

"I *do* make good products," I said defensively. "I *know* I do. But the things I sell are seen as expendable, luxuries. And in times like these . . . Let's face it. I picked a lousy time to open a business. If he were trying to start up today, I doubt Bill Gates could make a go of it. It's just impossible. . . ."

I clamped my mouth shut, suddenly remembering the task Madelyn was about to undertake. "Don't listen to me. The wine has gone straight to my head."

"It's all right. I know the odds are against me. But I don't have a lot of other options. And who knows? Maybe I'll get lucky. Sterling always said if he had to choose between smart and lucky, he'd pick lucky every time."

Madelyn's eyes started to fill. I grabbed the wine bottle and made a move to top up her barely touched glass, but she waved me off.

"It's all right. I'm not crying about Sterling. I'm just crying. I have been all day. First I couldn't cry and now I can't stop. It's really irritating." She laughed and wiped away a tear on the back of her hand.

"Enough of that," she said. "Speaking of husbands—yours, by the way, is a really sweet guy. You may have won the husband lottery, Tessa."

"I know, but don't tell him. I've convinced him that I picked him out of a crowd."

"Right. Anyway, he's out there hammering away on a project, so I told him I'd handle dinner. Do you think soup, salad, and scones will be enough?"

"Plenty," I assured her. "But you didn't have to go to all this work."

"I didn't mind," she said. "I wanted to do it. There's something else too. Come on. I'll show you."

I followed Madelyn to the back of the house, and I took a deep breath as we entered the workroom, relishing the sweet perfume of dried herbs, flowers, and essential oils. I could pick out the scent of rose petals and rosemary, calendula and peppermint, orange and lemon peels and, of course, lavender. Too much lavender. Usually the smell soothed me. Today it just added a deeper shade of purple to my already darkened spirits.

Lavender hung from the ceiling beam in bunches and sat on the tables in sealed jars, waiting for me to do something with it. But what was the point? My store was already stocked with lotions, balms, and soaps that no one was buying. Why make more?

Madelyn led me to the far side of the room, to the corner cabinet where I kept my small stash of quilting fabrics and notions. The cabinet has a lot of empty space I'd love to fill with more of that gorgeous fabric I drool over every time I go into the quilt shop, but I can't afford to buy more fabric. Not now. Maybe it was a waste of time anyway.

I doubt I'll ever be a really good quilter. My quilts are tidy and neatly pieced and, thanks to Virginia's tutelage and a lot of practice, my hand-quilting isn't bad for a beginner. But my quilts lacked something. I'd said exactly that to Madelyn when I showed her my most recent project, a basket quilt that I was sure I'd love but didn't.

Madelyn stopped in front of the cabinet. "I hope you don't mind," she said as she opened the door. Without explaining further, she reached inside the cabinet and pulled out my quilt, my dull, uninspired, by-the-book, stitch-by-numbers basket quilt that I'd worked on so hard and been so dissatisfied with.

Not anymore. Madelyn had transformed it.

Doing that thing that she does better than anybody, Madelyn had gathered up little bits of this and that from here and there, castoffs and toss-outs that most people wouldn't have given a second glance, and turned them into something beautiful.

My dull little basket quilt was now a one-of-a-kind creation. The previously empty patchwork of purple and green baskets brimmed with an assortment of flowers, as varied and vibrant as a display window in a florist shop.

One held a bouquet of blue and bluer morning glories veined with long silver beads I recognized as coming from an old and out-of-fashion necklace that I'd tossed into the Goodwill box in the laundry room, the place we collect unwanted household items before donating them to charity. Madelyn had made ingenious use of that old necklace and many other items I'd thought useless.

Another basket brimmed with pink and yellow dahlias whose ruffled petals seemed familiar but not entirely—until I remembered the dusty basket of silk flowers I'd recently removed from the guest bath. Madelyn had washed them off, layered them one on top of the other, and stitched the layers together with a pink pearl in the center that I recognized as coming from an old earring that was missing a mate. The other blocks were similarly adorned and embellished with sequins and sparkles and buttons and bows, but my favorite was the lavender: four fat, fuzzy purple patches tied into bunches with bright celery-green ribbons at each of the four corners of my beautiful, utterly delicious, and entirely unique quilt. There wasn't another one like it in the whole world. Madelyn had seen to that.

"Madelyn, this is . . . well, I just don't know what to say."

"You don't have to say anything."

"I just love it! Especially the lavender—where did you ever get the idea? And how did you do it?" The downy stalks of lavender were gorgeous and full, stitched from lengths of fluffy, wispy yarn in variegated shades of purple and pink.

"Oh," she said. "Those are from an old sweater I brought along."

"You unraveled your sweater to embellish my quilt?"

"Just the sleeves. I'll turn the edges under and make it into a shell to go under jackets."

I laughed. How very like Madelyn to figure out a way to remake her old sweater even while she used it to embellish my quilt. "I can't believe you went to all this trouble for me."

"I was glad to, and anyway, I was going crazy sitting around here doing nothing." Her smile faded and she sank down into my easy chair.

"Every time I turn on the radio I hear another 'Widow of Wall Street' story. It's been five days! When are they going to get tired of me and go pick on someone else?"

I wished I could answer her question. I'd driven by Beecher Cottage on my way home and the news vans were still parked out front.

Madelyn growled in frustration. "I shouldn't be hanging around your kitchen baking scones. I should be home sanding woodwork and painting walls, tiling floors and sewing curtains and arguing with contractors!"

I pressed my lips together, suppressing a smile and a secret. I was bursting to tell her, but I couldn't. I'd promised not to.

She closed her eyes for a moment, took in a deep breath, and blew it out slowly. "Don't mind me. It's just hard to have my plans delayed. I'm very grateful to you and Lee for letting me stay here."

"Oh," I said dismissively, "it's all right."

"No!" she said emphatically, slapping her hand on the arm of the chair. "It's not all right. It's much more than that, so let me just say this, okay?

"I'm an idiot. I've been angry for so long. But when I opened that bag and saw the quilt and the pictures, I remembered, for the first time in a long time, some of the good things I've had. And so, as hard as all this has been, a part of me is happy it happened this way. I don't think anything less than a crisis would have convinced me to talk to you again."

Her eyes teared again, but this time she made no move to wipe them. "And so I'm grateful to you and Lee. And to fate, or God, or whatever it was that brought me back here and forced me to see the truth. I'm grateful. Truly I am."

34
Tessa

Madelyn and I were sitting at the kitchen table going through stacks of old pictures and photo albums when Lee came in from the barn. We had progressed from blubbering to sniffling, but our eyes were still red. Lee eyed us nervously as he filled a plate with salad and scones, then ladled soup into a bowl.

"Ahem . . . I'm just going to take this back out to the barn with me. I'm kind of in the middle of something."

Madelyn and I skipped salad and the soup and went straight to the scones, spreading them with a thick layer of butter and a slathering of honey. I took cocoa powder and sugar from the cupboard and made hot chocolate.

"This takes me back," Madelyn said. "Remember your mother's banana bread?"

"Best in the world," I said. "She always served it with about an inch of butter."

"And big cups of cocoa. Your mom was always so nice to me."

"She liked you."

"She felt sorry for me."

"Well, yeah. But she liked you too. Mom always said you had spunk."

Madelyn made a face. "I wasn't spunky, I was a pain. I never knew when enough was enough and I never knew when to go home." She took a quick slurp of cocoa and shook her head.

"Actually, that's not quite true. I knew I was overstaying my welcome, but I couldn't help myself. The best times I ever had were with you and your family. Did you know that, in my head, I used to call you 'the regular family'?"

I laughed. "Why?"

"Because you were! You were all so regular! Your mom wore an apron and made banana bread and meat loaf, and helped you with your homework, and belonged to the PTA. Your folks never missed a parent-teacher conference. Your brother was an Eagle Scout and you took ballet. Your dad left for work every day at seven and came home every night at five. On Saturday morning he mowed the lawn and sprayed down your driveway with a hose. And you all lived in that nice house with carpets on the floor and those plastic covers on the sofas. . . ."

"In the living room!" I gasped. "That's right. I'd almost forgotten about that. Mom didn't want the upholstery getting ruined. Do you remember how, in the summertime, we'd sit on the furniture with our shorts on and the plastic would sweat and stick to our legs?" I squashed my mouth into what Madelyn and I used to call "fish lips" and made a sucking sound. Madelyn cracked up.

"See what I mean?" Madelyn said. "When I was a kid, I thought everybody, except me, was living on the set of *The Dick Van Dyke Show.* Whenever I was at your house, I was sure of it. You were all so normal! And happy. You all seemed so happy."

I couldn't argue with her. We were a happy family, by and large. Certainly I'd had a happy childhood. And we were normal, or at least we fit the image of what somebody somewhere, Frank Capra or some other purveyor of American mythology, had decided a normal family should be.

"We had our issues too," I countered. "I often wonder if my parents didn't want more out of life. Mom made a great loaf of banana bread, but they don't hand out a lot of trophies for that, do they? And Dad . . ." I shook my head. "He was so smart. Do you know he rebuilt the engine of our Buick all by himself?"

Madelyn smiled as she dunked a piece of scone into her cup. "There were car parts laid out all over your front yard for days, and he spilled oil on the driveway."

"That's right," I said, tipping my head back and grinning as I remembered how many Saturdays he'd spent standing on the driveway, frowning and grumbling while he sprayed the oil stain with his hose. "He never was able to get it clean again."

"You had the nicest yard in town."

I picked up a black-and-white photo from the pile on the table, a picture taken on Easter Sunday, 1964. My family stood in front of the house, dressed in our best, posed in front of flower beds filled with daffodils.

"Dad made sure of that. He was a good man, a good father. I'm not sure he was happy, though. He could have done anything. Instead, he spent his life working at the plant, doing the same job day after day and year after year to pay the bills. All Mom and Dad had was that house, this town, the day in and day out of our so-called normal lives. They never flew to Paris, or rode in a hot air balloon, or entered the Iditarod."

"The Iditarod. With the sled dogs? Up in Alaska?" Madelyn drew her brows together and gave me a doubtful look.

"I'm just saying that they never took a risk, that's all. They never did anything out of character. They never took a chance, bet the farm on one crazy roll of the dice. And they taught me to be just the same."

"But you're not the same," Madelyn said. "You're a risk taker. If you weren't, you wouldn't be here, betting the farm on buying a farm, dumping a perfectly good corporate job so you could come back here and make hand lotion and lip balm and potpourri. . . ."

"That no one seems to want to buy." I sighed. "Maybe my dad was right after all. Maybe this was a mistake. Lee thinks so."

"Did he say that?"

I shrugged. "We've had a hard year. We've both been frustrated and discouraged, but Lee seems to express his frustration through anger and withdrawal. For a while we weren't even—" I stopped myself. Madelyn probably didn't need or want to hear all the intimate details of my life.

"Anyway, things are hard right now. We don't talk about it much, but I know what he's thinking. He thinks we should have stayed in Massachusetts, let well enough alone."

"Is that what you think?"

I reached for a third scone and slowly spread it with butter as I considered the question.

"No," I said finally. "Unless something changes, drastically and soon, I'm going to have to close the shop, I realize that. Maybe my timing was off or maybe it was just never a good idea to begin with. But I'm not sorry I *tried*. I'm happy I took the chance."

"Well, there you have it. You're a risk taker.

And you're happy. See? Your parents weren't such bad role models after all."

I raised my eyebrows. "I didn't learn that from my parents. I learned it from you."

"Sure you did," she scoffed.

I picked up another photograph from the pile, the picture of Madelyn and me sitting on the porch, the day after our midnight adventure with the pigs.

"Remember this?"

Madelyn put her elbow on the table and rested her chin in her hand. "Sure. How could I forget?"

"Remember the article they ran about it in the paper? How the trooper they interviewed speculated that the crime might have been perpetrated by a ring of professional livestock rustlers?"

"Oh, if only he'd known!" Madelyn guffawed.

"If only he'd known," I echoed. "But why would he? He could never have imagined such a thing. Until I met you, neither could I. Before I met you, I was pretty short on imagination.

"Everybody I grew up with was just like me, such good little girls, so prudent and obedient and dull, keeping our hands folded in our laps— except you. I'd never met anybody like you!

"You didn't play by anybody else's rules and you didn't give a damn what anybody else thought. You didn't wait an hour to go swimming after you ate. You saw the possibilities! You took trash and turned it into treasures. You ran your own show, refused to walk in lockstep with anybody else. You smoked cigarettes and stole sex books from the library. . . ."

"I didn't *steal* them," Madelyn countered. "I just didn't check them out because I knew the librarians wouldn't let me. I snuck them back onto the shelves after I found out what I wanted to know."

"And shared that information with me," I said. "If not for you, I might still be laboring under the misconception that French kissing can make you pregnant. And that's my point. You taught me a lot of things, gave me a kind of . . . courage, I guess.

"But for a long time I forgot how good it felt to take a chance on myself. Do you know when I remembered? When I opened up an old box and found this."

I laid the picture down on the table and pushed it toward Madelyn.

"You're not the only one who's grateful, old friend. You've changed my life—a couple of times now. And all for the good."

It was after ten when Madelyn and I packed it in for the night and close to eleven before Lee came in from the barn.

"I didn't think you'd still be awake," he said as he pulled his sweater off over his head.

I yawned and closed the book I was reading. "In another five minutes I wouldn't have been. What were you up to out there?"

He slipped out of his jeans, tossed them over the back of a chair, and climbed into bed, scooting all the way over to my side. Lee likes to sleep close. So do I.

"I told Madelyn about how Charlie had offered me a good price for any microgreens I could grow for him in the winter, and she gave me a great idea: Take those old storm windows and use them to build cold frames. I built six big frames, enough to grow lettuces for the Grill on the Green plus a couple of other restaurants. Chefs will pay a good price for organic, out-of-season greens. And the frames didn't cost me a dime, just my labor and the materials I had on hand."

"Sounds like you had a good day."

"I did. You?"

I just looked at him. He frowned sympathetically and lifted his arm so I could lay my head on his shoulder.

"It'll get better," he said.

"Maybe. But maybe not."

"Well, we'll just cross that bridge when we come to it. Won't we? In the meantime, here's something that'll cheer you up: I was wrong. You were right."

I smiled. "Is this a blanket admission or do you have something specific in mind?"

"You were right about having Madelyn here—it was the right thing to do. Rich or poor, I guess everybody has their struggles. She's nicer than I thought she'd be and pretty handy to boot."

"She is," I agreed with a yawn, thinking of my beautiful new quilt and how I planned to hang it on the wall of the shop, right behind the register.

Lee stretched out his arm to turn off the light. We lay there in the darkness.

Just when I was on the edge of sleep, he said, "George called me today."

I stirred sleepily. "Oh? Did he have another job lead for you?"

Lee shook his head. "No, he wanted to know if I had one for him. They're closing the company, letting everybody go."

My eyes flew open. "What? Everybody? Why? Are they moving the headquarters? Was there a buyout?"

"Bankruptcy," he murmured. "Nobody saw it coming, nobody in middle management anyway. The big guys knew. They were trying to find a buyer right up until the last minute, which is why they were keeping it all under wraps, at least that's their story. George showed up to work yesterday and they told everybody they could pack up their stuff and go back home. No severance, no nothing."

"You're kidding!" I gasped. "What's George going to do?"

"Collect unemployment, I guess. And try to find another job."

"Poor George," I murmured. "That's awful."

"He sounded pretty depressed. But it got me thinking. If I'd stayed at the company, I'd be in the same boat. I know things are still touch-and-go for us, but at least we have the farm. We can feed ourselves, which is a lot more than most people can say. And we're doing what we want, controlling our own destiny. I feel pretty good about that. Coming here was a good idea."

He rolled toward me in the darkness and kissed me. "No matter what happens, I'm glad we took the chance."

35
Madelyn

It was day six of my exile. I sat in Tessa's easy chair, stitching closed the openings of some little sachets.

Remembering how much she'd liked making tiny quilts for the dollhouse when we were little, I'd suggested she sew some miniature quilt blocks and fill them with lavender to make drawer sachets. It's a good way to use up the scraps from her quilts and her extra lavender.

Tessa loves quilting, as much for the people it has brought into her life as the actual quilts—

maybe more. She told me all about her friends from the quilt shop. Once the media scrum breaks up and I can come out of hiding, Tessa wants me to meet them, maybe take a quilting class with her. It's a nice idea, but I told her I'd have to take a pass.

"This is me we're talking about. The Widow of Wall Street—remember? I don't think your friends would be all that excited to include me in their sewing circle. And even if they were, I've never been a joiner. Besides, I'm too busy to take up quilting."

And I am. Or I will be once those stupid reporters pack up their cameras and leave. How long can this go on? Isn't there some war or government scandal they could cover?

When Sterling was arrested and brought to trial, the media attention made some sense. I didn't like it, but I understood it. His arrest was part of the larger story of the whole economic collapse and what had led to it. But this hounding! The macabre fascination with every detail about his suicide and our broken marriage—that wasn't news. It was a sideshow attraction.

I'd meant what I'd said to Tessa. I'm glad we've had this time together, but enough already. I want to go home!

Well. I never thought I'd hear myself say, "I want to go home," home meaning Beecher

Cottage. I don't know how, but sometime between throwing Abigail off my front porch and sanding all those endless miles of wood floors, Beecher Cottage became my home. And I want to go back there, now! I've got so much to do.

I wish I'd thought to bring along that bolt of drapery fabric I bought to make curtains for the rooms. Tessa's sewing machine is old, but compared to the old foot treadle model I'd found in the attic, it sews at lightning speed. I could have finished the whole job by now. What a waste of time.

The telephone rang and startled me so that I nearly jammed the sewing needle into my finger. I couldn't find the scissors, so I quickly bit off the thread, laid aside the finished sachet, and ran into the kitchen to answer the phone.

"Woodruff residence."

"Madelyn? It's Tessa. Turn on the television!"

"Why?"

"Just do it!"

Cradling the phone between my shoulder and ear, I turned on the little television Tessa kept on the shelf with her cookbooks. It only gets two fuzzy channels, but I found the local midday news was on one of them.

The screen showed a tall, scruffy man wearing a baseball cap pulled down low to obscure his face, pushing through a sea of reporters who were all shouting questions at once. A trail of text ran along the bottom of the screen saying, BREAKING NEWS! NY BASKETBALL STAR MIKE RADNOVICH SCANDAL! BREAKING NEWS!

Mike Radnovich? Sterling's old golfing buddy?

"Madelyn? Are you watching? Mike Radnovich was caught in some sort of love quadrangle. He has four girlfriends. One is pregnant. So is his wife."

"Angela? Oh, no."

"Do you know her?"

"Oh, yes. Yes, I do."

Angela Radnovich, the only person who'd expressed any real sympathy for Sterling's death and the only one who seriously wanted to attend his funeral. I'd met her at a charity event two years before. She was standing alone next to a potted plant and looked a little lost, so I crossed the room to talk to her.

Angela was nice but young; I'm sure she couldn't have been more than twenty-two or twenty-three. She was blond, pretty, large breasted, and seemed a little out of her depth. And why wouldn't she be? Until recently, she'd worked at a car rental counter in Tacoma, Washington—that's how she'd met Radnovich, renting him a Cadillac Escalade. Now she was the celebrity wife of the wealthiest, most famous basketball player in the country. It was the fairy-tale story that millions of would-be Cinderellas dreamed about. But from the way her eyes darted around the room, nervously watching her husband talking and laughing with any number of women just as pretty as she, I guessed Angela hadn't gotten the happy ending she'd counted on. I understood, only too well.

"Poor Angela. I didn't know she was pregnant."

"Three months," Tessa said. "That's what the news reports said. I didn't realize you were friends."

"Not friends. More like acquaintances. She's a sweet girl. Very young. This must be so awful for her."

"I know but . . . well . . . you know what this means, don't you?"

I did. The sideshow had moved on, just as I'd wished. But I wouldn't have wished it on Angela Radnovich. I wouldn't have wished it on anyone. Still, that's the way things are. The sideshow pitches its tent anywhere crowds gather—last week on my doorstep, this week on Angela Radnovich's.

"Are the reporters gone?"

"Nearly," Tessa said. "Jake says they're packing up right now."

"Jake? What's he doing over there?"

"Um . . . I'm not sure. Maybe he just decided to drive by when he heard the news. You can go home whenever you want."

"How about now?"

Lee had gone to Great Barrington to drum up

customers for his microgreen business. I needed a ride. "Let me call the quilt shop. Maybe I can talk somebody into covering for me so I can come and pick you up."

Tessa arrived ninety minutes later. It felt like an eternity, but I used the time to clean the guest bathroom, strip the sheets off my bed and put on a clean set, then write a thank-you note to Tessa and Lee. I left it on the kitchen counter next to a plate of cookies I'd baked earlier that morning. After that, I took my suitcase into the front hallway and paced.

I wanted to go straight home, but Tessa insisted we stop by the quilt shop first. She promised it would only take five minutes.

The Cobbled Court Quilt Shop sits in the most charming but worst located commercial space in New Bern, possibly in all of Connecticut. As the name implies, it faces an actual cobblestone courtyard, built back in the horse-and-buggy days, at the end of an alley too narrow for cars to pass through. Thus, the shop has no parking. Anyone who wants to visit the Cobbled Court Quilt Shop must do so on foot.

When I was a girl, the shop was home to the old Fielding Drugstore. Back then, Fielding's was the only drugstore for miles around and so, inconvenient location or no, they did a good business. People had to buy their aspirin somewhere.

That was all well and good if you were selling drugs, something that people had to have, but quilting fabric is definitely not on the list of life's necessities. At least not for most people; the way Tessa had been talking about the quilt shop and all the fabric she was just longing to add to her "stash," I was starting to think she might be an exception to that rule.

We parked the car on the street. Tessa asked if it would be all right to make a quick detour into For the Love of Lavender, which sits a few doors from the entrance to Cobbled Court. What could I do?

"Just five minutes. I promise. No more. I want to make sure that Ivy's fine, let her know I'll be back soon. She was sweet to cover for me. You'd like her."

I'd walked by For the Love of Lavender a score of times since I'd moved back to New Bern but had never been inside. It was a charming space, cheerful and inviting, with large-paned windows that let in the light, and white walls and, of course, it smelled heavenly, just like Tessa's workroom at the house. Tessa had already hung "our" quilt up on the wall behind the cash register; it really had turned out well. Ivy thought so too.

"Are you sure you don't want to try quilting?" she asked. "You have a natural talent for embellishing."

"Can't. I just don't have time right now, not while I'm trying to get my business off the ground."

Ivy nodded sympathetically. "There are never enough hours in the day. Between my kids, my job at the shop, and my other job at New Beginnings—"

"New Beginnings? Over in the old elementary school, right? A friend was telling me about some of your programs."

"That's right. I started as the liaison between the quilt shop and New Beginnings, coordinating vocational internships, but now I split my time between the two," she said. "And just in case two jobs and two kids weren't enough, I'm studying for my GED. We've got preparation classes at New Beginnings. Someday, when my kids are older, I'd like to go to college, but first I've got to get a high school diploma. This is the first step."

Tessa was right; I did like Ivy. Our five-minute visit stretched to twenty. I left with Ivy's business card in my pocket and a promise that I'd stop by New Beginnings very soon.

Our arrival at the quilt shop was announced by tinkling from an old-fashioned set of bells that hung on the knob.

Within seconds of coming through the door, I was encircled by women, some customers, some employees, all of them smiling and shaking my hand, saying how glad they were to meet me, and how much they loved what Tessa and I had done with her quilt. Tessa, it seemed, had brought "our" quilt to the shop to show it to her friends before hanging it.

It was a little overwhelming. They wanted to know about the inn—when was I planning to open? How many rooms would I have? How was the renovation coming along? And the quilt— where did I get my ideas? Had I ever quilted before? Why not? Why didn't I start? And Tessa—how long had we known each other? Where had we met? Was I surprised when I found out that she'd moved back to New Bern too?

What they did not ask about was Sterling, his Ponzi scheme, his suicide, or our relationship. I'm not saying they weren't thinking about it, but they were too polite to ask. That was a relief.

There were seven or eight of them, and they all talked at once and introduced themselves rapidly. It was hard to keep the names and faces straight.

Margot I recognized from our encounter in the coffee shop and because Tessa had talked about her so much. She was the religious one, who had played some role in awakening Tessa's newfound faith. I felt a little uncomfortable talking to Margot, wondering if, behind that wide smile and those sparkling blue eyes, she might be secretly judging me. But if she was, she gave no sign of

339

it. After a few minutes I felt more relaxed in her presence.

Evelyn, who was a few years younger than me and had a very artsy way of dressing, with big earrings and necklaces and fabrics that moved well when she walked, owned the shop. Tessa had talked about her, too, told me how kind and calm she was, with an understated sense of humor. I didn't get to talk to her long enough to tell if Tessa was right in her assessment, but she seemed very nice, welcoming without being overbearing or effusive. Like the others, she urged me to take up quilting, but when I gave her the same answer I'd given to Ivy, she backed off.

"I know what that's like. When you're starting your own business, you barely have time to think, let alone take up a new hobby. Tessa says you're quite a baker. I'll tell you what, if you ever find yourself with a little time and an urge for some company on a Friday, just drop by. No notice or reservation required and you don't have to sew a stitch. But there is a price for admission—the baked good of your choice." She smiled in a way that made her warm eyes even warmer.

"I'll think about it," I said, never supposing I would.

The older woman, perhaps in her late seventies, who carried a very fat cat in her arms, was Evelyn's mother, Virginia. Originally from Wisconsin, she had moved to New Bern the year before and worked as her daughter's assistant manager. She was the one who had shown Tessa how to restore my quilt. She was an expert hand-quilter.

There were two sisters, Bella and Connie, but I never did figure out which was which, and Wendy, the Realtor I'd met on my first day in New Bern, who had the strangest laugh and the gaudiest rhinestone glasses I'd ever seen in my life.

Finally, hanging back at the fringes of the group and a little behind me, was one more, a woman whose presence didn't register until she reached out and laid her hand on my forearm, just as we were getting ready to leave. Turning to see who had touched me, I came face-to-face with Abigail. Abigail wore a dark, serious expression, her eyes like storm clouds ready to split open.

"Are you all right?" she asked quietly.

"Yes," I said quickly, suddenly afraid of the catch in my throat. "Thank you for the flowers. They were beautiful. And they made things . . . easier."

She nodded mutely, accepting my thanks, releasing us both from the need to plow over old ground, then leaned close to my ear, speaking so softly no one else could hear.

"I know what it is like, my dear, to be married to a difficult man. A man who is hard to love and who, perhaps, you never loved, and then to suddenly lose him. We've led strange lives, Madelyn. We know about regrets and private grief that others will never understand. But you mustn't blame yourself or look back—not any longer than it takes to learn what you must learn. After that, let it go. The past is past, Madelyn. But you're still here," she whispered urgently and exerted a gentle pressure on my arm. "And I'm glad. You be glad too."

36
Tessa

I glanced at my watch and decided we'd killed enough time. I tried to extricate Madelyn from the center of the Cobbled Court welcoming committee but couldn't. Not before Abigail pulled Madelyn close and whispered something that made tears well in her eyes and not before Evelyn remembered she had an old sewing machine upstairs that Madelyn might want to borrow.

"It's nothing fancy," Evelyn said. "But it was just tuned up and it has a nice, even, straight stitch. Perfect for sewing curtains."

"You have nice friends," Madelyn said as we loaded the machine into the trunk of my car.

It's just a short drive from the quilt shop to Beecher Cottage, but Madelyn was jiggling her foot anxiously as I drove, as though it was all she could do to keep herself from stretching her leg over to my side of the car and stomping on the gas pedal. She was so impatient to get home.

When we pulled up in front of Beecher Cottage, Madelyn's jaw dropped and her hand flew to cover her surprise. I was glad I'd kept the secret.

She got out of the car and stood on the sidewalk for a good minute before finding her voice. "It's . . . the tarps . . . they're gone! Did someone?"

"Fix the roof?" I asked. "Yes, they did. Looks a lot better now, doesn't it?"

She turned to stare at me with wide, disbelieving eyes. "But how did you do it?"

I laughed. "I didn't, Madelyn. I'm scared of heights, remember?"

"Then who did it?"

As if in answer to her question, Jake Kaminski appeared from around the corner, whistling and carrying an armload of torn-up blue tarps, the tarps that had covered the roof of Beecher Cottage for many months.

"What do you think?" he asked. "Looks a lot better now, huh?"

He turned to look at me without waiting for Madelyn's response. "Thanks for stalling. I just put away the ladders. I'm going to toss these in the back of my truck and put them in the Dumpster over at the hardware store."

Madelyn blinked a couple of times and her cheeks flushed. She didn't look as pleased as I thought she would, but maybe I was imagining it. It was a lot to take in.

"You didn't have to do this," she said.

"I know."

"You've got a business to run. You don't have time to roof someone else's house."

"Really?" he asked, crinkling his brow in mock confusion. "That's weird because I think I just did."

"This is too much, Jake. Especially after I . . . I can't let you replace my roof!"

"Oh," he replied with studied obtuseness. "Well. Do you want me to take it off?"

Jake glanced over at me with a "has she lost her mind?" sort of expression. I pressed my lips together to keep from laughing.

"You know what I mean!" Madelyn answered in an exasperated tone. She threw up her hands. "I have to pay you for all this!"

"No," he said stubbornly. "You don't. When I heard you got your estimate from Dwight Sparks, I decided I needed to get up there and check the job out for myself. Just because somebody calls their business A-1 Affordable doesn't mean it is, Madelyn. Dwight's a cheat. And a liar. You didn't need a new roof. You will in about five years, but right now, all you needed to do was get rid of the moss and replace some of the shingles."

"What? Are you sure?"

He nodded. "I'm sure. I worked on a roofing crew after I got back from Vietnam. I know what I'm talking about. You just needed a few shingles, and since I used the ones you already had stored up in the attic, it was almost free."

"No," she argued. "Your time isn't free. I've got to pay you, Jake. I'm going to." She planted her feet and crossed her arms, a stance that I recognized as immoveable. Apparently, Jake recognized it too.

He opened his mouth wide, almost as wide as a yawn, scratched his beard, and narrowed his eyes, thinking.

"All right, then. How about a trade? My sister Mia's twenty-fifth anniversary is coming up. I want to give her something nice. A weekend at the inn?"

"A long weekend," Madelyn countered. "Four days, three nights. My best room. With flowers and a bottle of champagne on arrival. And for you, a basket of muffins delivered to the hardware store on the first Tuesday of every month for a year. Deal?"

Jake tilted his chin and eyes upward, considered her proposal. "One more thing," he added. "You let me take you to dinner."

Madelyn let out a short exhalation of frustration, shimmied her head from side to side. For a moment, I wondered if Jake had overplayed his hand.

"No, Jake. Thank you but no. My husband just died. I'm not ready for that."

From where I stood it looked like that was that, but Jake regrouped and soldiered on. He certainly didn't give up easily. I wondered if Madelyn realized how much she and Jake had in common.

"Why not? I said I want to take you to dinner, Madelyn, not to bed."

"Jake!" Madelyn protested and shifted her eyes toward me with obvious embarrassment. Determined not to show how much I was enjoying this, I kept my face blank.

Jake shrugged innocently. "Well, that's what you were thinking, wasn't it?"

Madelyn said nothing.

"Look, Madelyn, I'm not asking you to trade your virtue for a roofing job. I just enjoy your company. And I hate eating alone. Don't you?"

Madelyn nodded, but barely.

"Then let's eat together. Nothing fancy. Pizza. How about that?"

"Too many carbohydrates."

"Fine. Mexican."

She made a face. "Sushi," she offered.

"Sushi," Jake agreed. "But I'm not eating raw fish. I want to state that up front."

"And we go dutch. That's the deal. Take it or leave it."

He gripped her outstretched hand. "Guess I'll take it."

Jake smiled, looking like he'd just won a hand of high-stakes poker. I couldn't blame him. I doubted there was another man on the face of the earth who could have moved the Immoveable Madelyn. I shoved my hands in my pockets to keep from giving him a high five.

For a moment, Madelyn looked confused, as if she, too, was surprised that he'd gotten around her, but the bargain was sealed and Madelyn wasn't one to go back on her word. She gave a short nod and quickly changed the subject.

"The roof looks great, Jake. Really great." She took a couple of steps backward to take it all in.

"What are those?" She pointed to the flowerbeds in front of the porch and the mounds of mulch with silvery sage stalks poking out at odd angles.

I smiled. I was beginning to wonder when she'd notice. "Lavender. I had too much, so I did a little transplanting. It doesn't look like much now, but come summer the purple flowers will be pretty against the yellow."

"Oh, Tessa!" She gave me a squeeze and I knew how pleased she was. Madelyn is not a hugger. Never was.

I hugged her back. "I planted a little culinary garden in the back, too, near the kitchen. Rosemary, thyme, sage, and mint. And did you see Lee's present?"

I looked toward the street, next to the sidewalk.

Her gaze followed mine and she laughed when she saw the sign Lee had made to match the house. The background was yellow and the borders and lettering were in blue.

"Beecher Cottage Inn. Established 2009. No Vacancy." She clapped her hands to her chest. "Oh, I love it! Tell Lee I said so."

"Did you see this?" I asked, walking to the sign so I could demonstrate. "He drilled a hole in the 'No' and hung it on a nail so you can remove it when you do have a vacancy."

"Never going to happen," Jake said. "Once the word gets out, everybody is going to want to stay here."

Madelyn turned to face us both and I could see she was fighting back tears, but that was all right. These were good tears, I could tell.

"Thank you. Thank you so much. I don't know what to say. It just looks like I could open for business tomorrow!"

"Not quite," Jake said. "There's plenty to do inside yet. But I did get Barry over here to install the cabinets while you were gone."

Jake's face split into a grin. "Somebody pushed a microphone into his face and started asking him about you, and Barry just about shoved it down the reporter's throat. I had to pull him off the guy. But your bathrooms are done. . . ."

Madelyn frowned and started to say something, but Jake cut her off.

He raised his hands, anticipating her protest. "Except for tiling the floors. I thought you'd want to do those yourself."

Madelyn crossed her arms again and gave him a challenging look. "You thought right."

37
Madelyn

Jake's left eyebrow rose to a skeptical angle as I picked up my chopsticks and dipped a piece of yellowtail into a saucer of wasabi and soy sauce.

"Looks like bait to me."

"It's tuna and it's delicious. You should try it," I said with a deliberate smile before putting the fish into my mouth.

Jake shuddered in disgust. I chewed. My mouth turned to flame and my sinuses cleared from my nostrils to my toenails. My eyes poured tears like water from a spigot. I lunged for my water glass, downed the contents, and coughed.

Apparently thinking I was choking, Jake pounded my back. I waved him off.

"Wasabi," I gasped. "Too spicy."

Jake pushed his water glass toward me and then turned around to find our waitress, miming a pouring motion to indicate our glasses were empty.

"You okay?"

Blinking back tears, I nodded. "Yeah. I forgot how potent that stuff is. It really is good, though."

"Yeah, I can see that. Think I'll stick with my tempura. Thanks anyway, Maddie," he said and then stopped himself. "Oh. Sorry. I'm not supposed to call you that, am I?"

"That's all right. I don't mind."

The waitress approached with the water pitcher and refilled our glasses. I watched her in silence, mentally rehearsing my speech.

After she moved on I took a breath and plunged in. "Listen. Jake. There's something I've been meaning to say to you about that night, after the funeral. I was fairly awful to you. I'm sorry."

Jake was tentatively poking a piece of tempura with his chopstick, as if worried that it might suddenly begin moving. "That's okay. Hey, what is this anyway?"

The light in the restaurant was dim. I had to squint to see his plate. "Eggplant."

"That's what I thought." Jake pushed the offending vegetable to the side. "But this is shrimp, right? And it's cooked?" With surprising dexterity, he picked up a piece of shrimp with his chopsticks and took a bite.

"I mean it," I said earnestly. "I'm really sorry. I had no right to be so angry with you, especially since I asked for your opinion."

"It's all right. Apology accepted. Can you pass the soy sauce?"

I handed him a small ceramic carafe and watched as he poured a stream of soy sauce onto his steamed rice. It was nice of Jake to extend his pardon so readily, but his offhand manner left me feeling unsatisfied. I felt the need to explain myself.

"I wasn't quite myself that night. . . ."

Jake's mouth was full, but he interrupted me with a shake of his head. "Actually, I disagree. I thought you were entirely yourself. At least initially. Though you kind of backed off as the evening wore on. And I probably could have done without the part where you told me to go to hell but, all in all, I thought it was a worthwhile discussion, didn't you?"

He looked up with a teasing smile, daring me to contradict him. I couldn't.

"It was, I admit it. And I'll go even further. You were right."

I quickly took a bite of my dinner, hoping that would be the end of it, but Jake looked at me with an expression that invited elaboration. Fair enough. After all the things I'd said to him that night in the van, I owed him that.

"I've done a lot of thinking about what you said about me being selfish and self-absorbed. You're right. I am. It's all about me, isn't it? It always has been. My comfort, my needs, my desperate compulsion to gather up enough, and more than enough, of anything—things, men, money, possessions. . . ."

Jake didn't contradict me, but his teasing expression was replaced by sympathy. "There were reasons for that. As a kid, you had to be selfish to just survive. Nobody was watching out for you. Edna sure didn't. And you had no one to teach you differently."

"Not entirely," I said. "I had my dad, for a while anyway. He taught me about love, and loyalty, and selflessness. But after he died, I forgot.

"However," I said with a rueful smile, "your somewhat blunt assessment of my character made me start to think about him and wonder if he'd have thought you were right about me. I decided he probably would have. That made me feel even worse than I had before, which I honestly hadn't imagined was possible. But you know what they say about hitting rock bottom. . . ."

Jake winked. "You've got nowhere to go but up?"

"That's right. So, the long and short of it is, I decided to give your advice a try. The next morning I got up and started looking around for ways to make other people happy. You know something? It worked.

"Seeing Tessa's face light up when I embellished her quilt, or how something as simple as cooking dinner can encourage someone who has had a hard day, made me feel better than I had in a long while. And it made me think that . . . maybe I have something to offer the world."

I ducked my head, feeling a little funny about saying that out loud. "Nothing huge, you know. I know I'm no Rhodes Scholar or anything. . . ."

"So what?" he said. "Neither am I. But everybody can do something for somebody else."

"Like fixing their roof?"

Jake didn't say anything to that, just dipped his head slightly. "Or baking some muffins. Or making a quilt. Or whatever. The point is, everybody has something to offer. Even broken-down, recovering, one-eyed hardware guys."

I dipped another piece of tuna into my soy sauce, being careful not to overdo it this time.

"You know something? I'm really excited about the inn. I mean, it's still an economic necessity for me, a way to make a living. But I'm starting to think it could also be a new beginning.

"I want to bring new people, and a new history, to that old house. Think about all the different kinds of people who might show up at my door! Honeymooners, exhausted parents, empty-nesters trying to rekindle romance, girlfriends looking for a weekend away, people who just want to sit on my front porch and do absolutely nothing—I might have an opportunity to do some real good in this town!"

"You could," Jake agreed.

Jake sorted through the rest of his tempura, kept the shrimp, carrots, and sweet potatoes, and then, after looking at me with raised brows to gauge my interest, placed the eggplant and mushrooms on my plate.

I ate a mushroom and then another piece of tuna. My eyes began to fill again and my nose started to run. I sniffled. Jake looked up and shoved his water glass toward me.

"Too much wasabi?"

I wiped my eyes with my napkin and shook my head.

"Jake, why are you so nice to me?"

He grinned and shrugged. "I'm a hardware guy. When I see something broken, I fix it. Can't help myself."

38
Tessa

The Christmas shopping season had brought an increase in business, but more the ebb and flow of an unpredictable tide than the tsunami of commerce I'd hoped for. Exactly one week before Thanksgiving, my traffic was more a dead calm than anything else, emphasis on the word "dead." So when Lee dropped by the shop unexpectedly, I was even more than usually glad to see him.

"This is a nice surprise," I said, coming out from behind the counter.

"I had to drop off Charlie's microgreen order at the Grill, so I thought I'd drop by and say hello." He kissed me. "Hello."

"Hello yourself."

"About Thanksgiving," he said as though we'd just been discussing the subject. "We should get a bigger bird than last year, enough so we'll have some leftovers. I was thinking around twenty pounds."

I stared at him, waiting for the punch line, but he seemed serious. "Twenty pounds? Unless you're planning on eating turkey soup and turkey hash every night between Thanksgiving and Christmas, that seems a bit extreme. With just the two of us, it'd really be more practical to roast a chicken instead."

Lee had been fiddling with some of the tester bottles, nodding absently while I spoke. Now he opened a jar of lemon beeswax hand balm and sniffed it before rubbing some onto his calloused hands.

"Yeah, except it's not going to be just the two of us. I saw Jake over at the hardware store and invited him to Thanksgiving dinner. And Matt too."

"Matt?"

"Yeah, Matt. Jake's clerk, you remember. He was looking a little glum. He just broke up with his girlfriend and he doesn't have any family in town. And then I saw Charlie at the Grill and invited him and Evelyn. Oh, and Evelyn's mother, too, Virginia. That's her name, right? And I was thinking you could invite Madelyn too."

He finished rubbing in the hand balm and flexed his fingers a couple of times, as if testing them out. "Huh. This is pretty good stuff."

I shook my head, not quite sure I'd heard him right. "Wait a minute. Lee? Are you telling me that we're going to have seven people over for Thanksgiving dinner?"

He looked at the ceiling, tallying the numbers in his head. "Eight if you count Madelyn. But I was thinking, why don't we invite a few more? What about that new friend of yours, Margot? And anybody else you can think of who doesn't have plans for the holiday. I mean, if we're going to invite eight we might as well invite sixteen, right?"

"Sixteen? But, Lee . . ." I spread out my hands and paused, waiting for him to draw the obvious inference.

"What?" he asked, mirroring my expression. "You've been moping around for days about your empty nest and how pathetic Thanksgiving will be with just the two of us. . . ."

"I never said that."

"You didn't have to. It was written all over your

356

face. Look, I know how you love having family around during the holidays. So I figured, let's invite some. I mean, they're not our family but they're somebody's. Right? Why don't you invite the quilt circle? You're always saying you want me to meet them."

I had said exactly that on a number of occasions, but I never supposed Lee would take me up on it.

"Well, why not invite them?" he asked. "It doesn't cost any more effort to cook a twenty-pound bird than it does a twelve-pounder, does it?"

"Not really, but it's not extra work I'm concerned about, it's extra money."

"We don't need money," he replied. "We've got a farm, remember? The hens aren't laying as much right now as they were before, but if we skip our breakfast omelets this week, we'll have enough to make deviled eggs for appetizers. We can do a nice microgreen salad with candied walnuts, beets, and goat cheese. The root cellar is loaded with potatoes, squash, and onions. We've got pumpkins and apples for pies. Charlie offered to bring a few bottles of wine. We can bake some loaves of bread over the weekend and let them dry out for the stuffing, and we've got plenty of herbs for seasoning." Lee grinned proudly.

"Do you realize," he continued, "that we can just about feed ourselves right off the farm? We may be broke, babe, but we're not poor. I've been doing a lot of thinking lately. We've had some setbacks, but I feel pretty good about what we've accomplished. Thankful. I'd like this Thanksgiving dinner to reflect that and I'd like to share it with others."

Lee moved toward me, backing me up against the counter and looping his arms around my waist.

"This might be the best Thanksgiving we've ever had. It'll certainly be the most authentic. The only thing we'll have to buy is some cranberry sauce for the turkey."

"Well, what about the turkey? We don't raise turkeys."

"Kevin Heath does. We're going to do a little bartering—apples, greens, and cheese in exchange for one of his birds. So? What do you say, babe?"

I wrapped my hands around the small of Lee's back. "I say the Woodruffs are going to have a Thanksgiving to remember."

And it was.

When we sat down for dinner a week later, our numbers included the original eight invitees plus Margot; Ivy and her two children, Bethany and Bobby; Gibb Rainey, an elderly gentleman who held court in a lawn chair outside the New Bern post office every day except Sunday and was well-known to everyone in New Bern and was a particular friend of Virginia's; as well as Dana, the first woman who'd completed her New Beginnings internship at the Cobbled Court Quilt Shop, now a full-fledged employee; and Wendy Perkins. We were fifteen in all. If Abigail, Franklin, and Evelyn's son, Garrett, hadn't flown to Chicago to spend the holiday with Liza, Abigail's niece and Garrett's girlfriend, we might have been eighteen.

My dining room table only accommodates eight, but Lee took the guest room door off its hinges, set it atop two sawhorses he brought in from the barn, and voila! Instant table! With a white tablecloth, some candles, and a basket filled to overflowing with ornamental squash, you couldn't tell it from the real thing.

Dinner was delicious, though I suspect that may have had more to do with the ingredients than any sudden improvement in my culinary skills. Have you ever had a fresh turkey? If not, you should. One bite and you'll never settle for frozen again.

I did have to buy a few things at the market. Besides cranberry sauce I bought butter, sugar, and flour, and some canned goods. Even so, we fed fifteen people an enormous repast for twenty-two dollars and sixty-eight cents. Not bad.

Amazing what a year can bring. A year ago, Lee and I barely knew a soul in this town, and now? We had to turn doors into tables to find places enough for our friends.

If Josh had been there, it would have been a perfect holiday, but he called at about ten o'clock that morning with a question that brought a smile to my face.

"Mom? You know that green bean casserole? How do you make that?"

Ah, the ubiquitous green bean casserole. It's as much a part of Thanksgiving as the turkey. My mother made the green bean casserole every Thanksgiving, just as her mother did before and I did after. And now the torch had passed to Josh.

"I don't want to show up empty-handed at Ted's place, so I thought I'd bring the casserole. I'm standing here in the kitchen. I've got cans of green beans, cream of mushroom soup, and some of those French fried onion thingies. What do I do now?"

I laughed because at that moment, I, too, was in the kitchen, looking at that exact same lineup of ingredients. Personally, I detest green bean casserole, but some holiday traditions just refuse to die, and that's probably a good thing.

For the next thirty minutes, Josh and I rolled up our sleeves and donned our aprons and worked side by side, albeit long distance. It was nice. Not quite as nice as it would have been to have him home, but nice.

And I learned a few things cooking with Josh long distance that I probably wouldn't have if he'd been home for the holiday. Though Josh was far from home, he still valued our family traditions and my advice. Also, at least some of the lessons I'd tried to pound into him over the years had stuck—he remembered that you never come to someone's home empty-handed. And, in a way, talking him step by step through that awful recipe made me feel closer to him than ever. He would always be my child, but now he was becoming my friend, too, someone I would have been happy to invite to dinner even if we weren't related.

I was proud of him. We had a nice Thanksgiving together.

But the best part came at the end of the day, as I looked down the table, the groaning board, past nearly empty bowls of potatoes and squash and creamed onions and green bean casserole and jellied rubies of cranberry sauce, the bread plates decorated with a confetti of crumbs and brush-stroke smears of butter, beyond the carcass of the noble bird, the bones picked clean, to the head of the table where the head of my heart, my beloved, my husband sat smiling, laughing, attending his guests, presiding over this banquet he had labored to provide and then offered with open hands.

Lee was happy again. That was the best part, the answer to my prayers and the reason for my gratitude, the picture I'll never forget.

39
Madelyn

January 2010

The doorbell rang at ten and, for a moment, I panicked. She wasn't supposed to arrive until four!

I still had to put sheets on the beds and dust upstairs. There were no flowers in the vases, no muffins in the oven, and no curtains at the windows. I wasn't ready!

There was no help for it now. I took a deep breath and told myself to calm down. I couldn't very well leave my guest standing on the porch. Ready or not, the Beecher Cottage Inn was officially in business.

I smiled and opened the front door. "Welcome!"

Margot and Evelyn burst into a rousing, loud, and partially on-key rendition of "Happy Opening to You!" Margot had a beautiful voice. Evelyn, not so much.

Evelyn thrust a bottle of champagne toward me. "We come bearing gifts."

"And good wishes!" Margot chirped.

"Oh! Thank you. What a nice surprise."

"But wait! There's more!" Margot said with all

the gusto of an infomercial pitchman before bending down and picking up one of two large Cobbled Court Quilt Shop shopping bags from the porch. Evelyn grabbed the other bag. I stepped back so they could carry their cargo into the foyer.

"Don't worry. We're not going to stay," Margot assured me. "We just wanted to drop these off. Happy grand opening from the Cobbled Court Quilt Circle!"

Her announcement pretty much gave the gift away, but even so, when Margot and Evelyn pulled out two beautiful pink and blue quilts on a white background, I was completely taken aback.

"Don't cry," Evelyn instructed. "Your mascara will run."

Good point. I didn't have time to redo my makeup, so I blinked a few times and took a few deep breaths to calm myself.

"Well. I . . . Thank you. They'll be perfect for Room Three. It has twin beds. The walls are all white, but the floor has a blue braided rug I found in the attic. It's just that color. I can't believe you went to all this trouble."

"The pattern isn't as hard as it looks. A lot of quilters stay away from the Carolina lily block because of the Y-seams, but I've got a special technique that eliminates that step. Appliquéing the stems takes a little extra effort, but Virginia is a whiz at all kinds of hand work."

I smiled and nodded as Evelyn spoke, trying to pretend I understood but, in truth, she could have been speaking Turkish for all I knew. What I did know was that the quilts, with bouquets of pink lilies bowing gracefully over the edge of sky blue baskets, were beautiful.

"I am so touched. Please tell everyone I said thank you and that as soon as I get a moment to come up for air, I'm going to drop by on a Friday night with a plate of muffins."

Margot cast a delighted glance in Evelyn's direction. "Told you!"

"Margot!" Evelyn chided.

Margot blushed and ducked her head. "Sorry."

"Told her what?" I asked.

A guilty smile tugged at the corner of Evelyn's mouth. "The quilts *are* gifts," she assured me, "no strings attached. We just wanted to get you off to a good start. After all, yours is the first new business to open in New Bern in more than a year. If things work out for you, it could bring more tourists, more shoppers, maybe even more jobs."

"We could sure use a few of those," Margot added.

"But," Evelyn continued, "neighborliness aside, we were sort of hoping you might reconsider our invitation to be part of the quilt circle."

I launched into my list of legitimate excuses,

but Evelyn stopped me before I could get very far.

"I know. I know," she said sincerely. "You don't have time to take up quilting right now. And I completely understand. But there's a lot more to quilting than actual quilting, you know. It's about camaraderie as much as making quilts, making connections and friends.

"When I was growing up in Wisconsin, my mother, Virginia, and her quilting buddies got together every Tuesday for almost thirty years. They were beginners when they started, but by the time I was in high school, every one of them was an expert quilter—everyone but Louise."

"What was wrong with Louise?"

"Nothing," Evelyn answered. "Except Louise didn't quilt. Not a stitch. She liked the women in the circle, and she liked getting together with them every week, and she liked watching the others work on their quilts, but she had absolutely no interest in making a quilt for herself. As it turned out, she didn't need to. The women in Mom's circle were avid quilters. But after a while, they started to run out of beds to put their quilts on, so, like many quilters, they tended to give them away as gifts—often to Louise."

Evelyn spread out her hands. "Look, I know you're too busy to take up quilting right now and I know I don't know you very well, not yet. But I'd like to. We all would. So, what do you say?

Would you like to be our Louise? We've got plenty more quilts where those came from."

She gave an exaggerated wink, making the bribe obvious, and I laughed. I couldn't help myself. Evelyn and I didn't know each other well, but I liked her already.

Margot's blue eyes sparkled and she clasped her hands together in front of her chest. "Does that mean you'll come?"

"It means I'll think about it."

"Fair enough," said Evelyn, raising her hands. "That will do for now. In the meantime, we'll clear out and let you get ready for your guest. Good luck!"

I walked out onto the porch to wave good-bye. "Thank you again for the quilts," I called. "I just love them!"

"It was our pleasure," Evelyn called as she and Margot crossed the street and walked toward town.

Something in her voice maybe, or perhaps the spring in her step, gave me the idea that she was telling the absolute truth.

As soon as they left, I went back to work. I'd stayed up half the night sewing the curtains. The only thing left to stitch was the hems. Evelyn's machine was faster, but I decided to do those final seams on the old foot treadle machine I'd found in the attic. Something about that just felt right to me.

When the hems were sewn and the curtains ironed, I carried them upstairs along with piles of freshly laundered sheets and stacks of quilts.

My reservation book was all but empty. Who knew how long it would be before some of these rooms were occupied? Yet I felt the need to make up every single room just to prove that I really was open for business.

I hung up curtains in each room and made up the beds. The new lily quilts looked like they'd been made for Room Three, which, I reminded myself with a smile, they had. I hung a set of big fluffy white towels in each bath and set out little baskets of miniature For the Love of Lavender soaps, shampoos, and lotions on the counters. Tessa had ordered the tiny bottles just for me. I liked the idea of using locally made bath amenities for my guests. Those little touches make all the difference.

As four o'clock approached I had only Room Two to finish. It was not my biggest or most elegant room, but it was my favorite. It had new paint, new wallpaper, new light fixtures, a new bath, new everything. Of all the rooms in the house, Room Two had undergone the most complete transformation. It was my room. It *had* been my room, when I was a girl. I saved it for last.

Sitting at the front of the house, it had a big bay window that let in plenty of light. I'd added a built-in bench beneath the window and topped it with an upholstered cushion. It made a lovely spot to sit with a book or look out at the garden and the bushes heaped with snow like thickly frosted cakes.

I took off my shoes and stood on the window seat to hang the curtains, then climbed down and stood back to admire the effect. The white eyelet curtains looked fresh and pretty against the yellow walls. The buttercup cotton lining peeping through the eyelet openings pulled the whole room together, making it look cheery and warm even on this cold winter day. And if that didn't do the trick, there was a stack of dry wood and kindling standing at the ready in the recently reopened fireplace. I pulled the blue wingback chair nearer the fireplace and put a basket filled with magazines next to the chair. With the fire blazing, filling the room with the light and warmth it lacked in former days, this would be a cozy haven.

After making up the bed—that beautiful brass and mother-of-pearl bed I'd found up in the attic—with fresh sheets and fluffing the pillows, I added the final touch, the quilt. The clean white background fabric and blue double-chain pattern added just the right touch to the room, giving it a fresh and forward-facing look with a nod of appreciation to the past, just as I had intended.

The quilt was beautiful but, to me, it was more than that. It was a touchstone, a reminder of the person I once had been, an invitation to gather up the best of myself and carry it forward, to pass through the slender door, a difficult feat, but not an impossible one. It was a symbol of restoration, of work in progress.

No one who would stay in this room, no one who knew me, not even Tessa, who had restored the quilt and our friendship, would fully understand that symbol, but it didn't matter. It was a beautiful room now, a place of rest and respite. I hoped that everyone who stayed here would find both.

When the doorbell rang the second time, I was ready.

Even with her blond hair pulled back into a ponytail, her eyes hidden behind dark glasses, and her body swollen by pregnancy, she was still beautiful. But when she pulled off her glasses and I saw the hard, bitter edge in her eyes, I knew things had changed. Angela Radnovich was no longer young. She didn't believe in fairy tales and happy endings, not anymore.

After finishing the chicken sandwich, bowl of vegetable soup, and glass of milk I served for dinner, Angela said she was tired and went upstairs to her room. I washed up the dishes, put the leftover soup in the refrigerator, and followed shortly after. Passing by her room, I heard crying. I came very close to knocking, but thought better of it. She was entitled to her tears.

I couldn't wave a wand and make it all better. I couldn't remove the sting of her husband's betrayal, or the shame of having it played out in public, but I could give her a good meal, a soft bed, a private place to cry and, when tears were spent, mentally prepare her to greet the little life that she carried inside her and face her future as a single mother. Before continuing down the hall to my own room, I paused to lay my hand flat on Angela's door and silently wish her well.

It had been a long day and I was grateful for my bed, but when I turned out the light, I couldn't sleep. My body was tired, but my brain was working overtime.

I kept thinking about what Evelyn had said about Beecher Cottage and what it might mean to the town if I could make a go of it—more tourists, more shoppers, more business, more jobs. I only had five rooms to rent, but in a town the size of New Bern, five rooms filled with tourists ready to shop and eat and spend a little money could make a big difference.

If I was a success. If.

I wanted success; I had from the first. But now I wanted it in a different way, not just for myself.

I wanted it for the town and the people who had welcomed me. For Tessa and Jake and Lee and Evelyn, and all the other merchants in town. For Margot, Virginia, and Ivy, and all the people who worked for them. For the high school kids who needed summer jobs, for the lady at the bakery who looked so tired and told me she was working two jobs since her husband lost his.

I wanted it for Angela and everyone like her, people who needed a peaceful place to recharge their batteries and remember that life was still good, just like I'd told Jake that day at the restaurant. It wasn't all that much, I knew. It wasn't a cure for cancer or the solution to peace in the Middle East, but it wasn't nothing either. For the first time in my life, I might actually be able to help people.

Lying in the dark, my eyes staring up into a chasm of black, I felt a tightness in my chest, like a hand clamped around my heart.

This is what it's like to be a part of something, of someplace. This is what it's like to care. I never knew.

40
Tessa

February

The holiday season had put us in the black for the year, but barely. As I sat next to Lee at the kitchen table after dinner to go over the books, I could see the writing on the wall. The Christmas bump was over. Sales in January were even slower than the year before.

And so I faced a choice: soldier on through the winter in hopes that the spring tourist season would lift our sales and max out my credit line in the process, incurring more debt at sixteen percent interest, or cut bait now, slash the prices on my remaining inventory, use the proceeds and that slim border of black ink to pay off my creditors, then lock the doors and walk away.

There really wasn't a choice, but to help me save face, Lee pretended there was.

"Babe, if you want to keep going, then we'll just figure out a way to do it. Things'll work out somehow."

He said it with such conviction that for a moment, I almost believed it was possible. I certainly wanted it to be. But no amount of wishful thinking could trump the cold reality of my balance sheet. As far as For the Love of Lavender was concerned, I'd reached a dead end. It was sad. I was sad. But it could have been worse.

That holiday sales spike would allow me to pay off my creditors; I would walk away minus the capital we'd invested in the shop but also minus any additional debt—no small thing. And Josh had called the week before to say that Professor Kleypas had chosen him as one of his three summer research assistants. The experience would be a great addition to his résumé and pay enough to cover his tuition for the fall semester. We were so proud—and more than a little relieved. I didn't know what we'd do about tuition for the second semester, but I supposed we'd cross that bridge when we came to it. As my morning devotional recently reminded me, "Do not worry about tomorrow, for tomorrow will worry about itself. Each day has enough trouble of its own."

Each day has trouble enough of its own. You don't have to be a theologian to know that's true. But a thing may be as true as death and taxes and still be hard to put into practice. I'm a world-class worrier. I always have been.

But it was good to know that at least where Josh was concerned, our worries had been put to rest for the next few months. We were very fortunate. The only downside was that we'd be deprived of Josh's company for the summer and Lee would be deprived of his best farmhand just when he needed him most. But if I wasn't working in the shop every day, I'd be available to help in the fields. I'm not as strong as Josh, but I'm capable.

Lee really was going to need an extra hand this summer. His microgreen business has taken off. The farm brings in enough to cover about three-fourths of our most basic bills without having to dip deeper into our savings. We still can't afford to eat in restaurants, or go on vacation, or buy medical insurance, but we're paying the mortgage, the utilities, the taxes—the bare necessities.

And things are looking up for the summer growing season too. Seven of Lee's thirteen restaurant customers have already said they want him to supply their summer produce, including greens, vegetables, eggs, and some of my fresh herbs. And they've been willing to sign contracts for minimum orders between May and October to ensure that they are first in line for Lee's produce. It's a win for everyone. The restaurateurs get the pick of the field at a good price and we get a guaranteed minimum income. With that in hand, Lee thinks we can refinance our mortgage and save almost four hundred dollars a month. There isn't much I like about this economy, but I've never seen mortgage interest rates so low. If we can get that refinancing, we'll benefit for years to come.

And so, there it was . . . I'd been granted a tiny opening, a brief window of opportunity in which I could walk away from the business without burdening myself and my family under a mountain of debt and, with hard work and a little luck, earn enough to keep food on our table and a roof over our heads. And, as my mother always used to say, "Enough is as good as a feast."

Even so . . .

I pushed the pile of papers to the other side of

the table. "Enough," I said. "Time to admit defeat. I have to close the store while we're still more or less whole."

I got up to clear the table, but Lee leaned forward in his chair, looped his arm around my waist, and pulled me down onto his lap. "Hey. Who's been defeated? Not you. Not ever."

"Not until now." I draped my arm over his shoulders and leaned my head against his. "That's what's so hard about this. Not losing the business as much as losing. The business stopped being fun months ago. Now that I've made the decision, it's honestly kind of a relief. But this is the first time I've ever really failed at anything. And it's harder to take because it's also the first time I've ever really taken a big risk. Maybe that's the lesson in all this: Stick to what you know, color inside the lines."

I sat up straighter and sighed. "Nothing has worked out like I thought it would."

"What are you talking about?" Lee scoffed. "When you and I started talking about all this we said we wanted to live in a real community; we wanted to escape the cubicle prison, work for ourselves, preferably outdoors and with our hands, and spend more time together." As he talked, Lee held up a fist, raising one digit for each item on our long-ago wish list until all five fingers were raised.

"We've gotten everything we asked for. And I

know it's probably selfish of me, but I'm kind of happy that we'll be working together this summer. And this last item," he said as he wiggled his little finger. "The part about spending more time together? I meant that. There is no one I'd rather wake up next to, work alongside, and lie down at night with than you, Tessa. I love you, babe. And if I live to be one hundred and ten, there won't be enough hours in the day for us to be together."

I kissed him lightly on the lips. "Back at you, Mr. Woodruff."

I got to my feet and resumed clearing the table, but Lee stopped me again, taking the salad plates from my hands.

"It's Friday. You're supposed to be at the quilt shop. Remember?"

"Oh, I don't feel like going—not tonight. I need to start working out a plan to close the shop. We're going to need to pick a day, notify our accounts, pay off the last of the bills, see about ads and signage for a going-out-of-business sale, find a liquidator to buy the display units and fixtures. . . . Do you have a pen and paper? I'm going to start making lists."

"Uh-uh," he said, pushing me away from the table. "Nothing doing. All that can wait. Right now, you need to go to the quilt shop and see your friends. You'll feel better if you do. You know I'm right."

"But you said you couldn't get enough of spending time with me."

"True," he replied, reaching over to pick up my car keys from the kitchen counter. "And while you're off making your quilts, seeing your friends, and finding your smile, I'll be counting the minutes until your return."

He slapped the keys into my palm with a smile. "Go!"

41
Tessa

One of the things I like about quilting is that if you make a mistake or decide that the block you were working on didn't turn out as well as you'd hoped, you can just rip out the seam and try again. Margot calls it "unsewing."

Wouldn't it be nice if all of life were like that?

Lee told me to forget about the store for the moment and just to go out and enjoy myself. It's good advice. But I don't want to enjoy myself. I want to sit around and mentally unsew all the mistakes I made since arriving in New Bern while eating a whole bag of kettle-cooked potato chips and a quart of chocolate ice cream.

That's probably reason enough to stick to my routine. Things are bad enough without adding any extra inches to my backside.

However, if I wanted to avoid calorie-packed temptation, Cobbled Court Quilts was the last place I should have headed. Now that the inn is open and running, Madelyn has become our "Louise," keeping us well supplied with her home-baked goodies. Though she never sews a stitch, Madelyn makes her presence known, passing plates, filling glasses, offering ideas on fabric combinations and possibilities for embellishing the quilts in progress. She really knows how to work a room, a skill I suppose she picked up during her years as a socialite. And yet, this doesn't feel like that. There is nothing manipulative or obligatory in the way Madelyn interacts with the other women; she just really enjoys their company.

And the feeling is mutual. On those few nights when Madelyn can't attend because she has guests at the inn, she is definitely missed. Of course, it would probably be better for Madelyn if she had to skip quilt circle night more frequently. It's early days yet, but I'm worried about her business—or lack thereof. It must be scary trying to do all this on her own.

What would I do without Lee? Sorry as I'm feeling for myself right now, I know how lucky I am to have him.

By the time I arrived at the shop, Margot, Virginia, and Abigail were already sitting at their sewing machines, their work spaces strewn with a multicolored and messy collage of fabrics measured out in yards, patches, and scraps. Evelyn, Ivy, and Madelyn stood clustered around a television set that someone had set up near the refreshment table, laughing as they watched a video of Mary Dell Templeton, the host of *Quintessential Quilting* and Evelyn's old friend from her old life back in Texas.

Madelyn and I are the only members of the group who haven't met Mary Dell. She filmed an episode of her show here at the quilt shop a couple of years ago and was a big hit with the locals. People are still talking about it. Since we don't have cable, I've never seen the show, but Evelyn had promised to tape the most recent program for me.

After saying hello to everyone, I went to join Madelyn near the television. "Look who's here!" she exclaimed before turning to the refreshment table. "We were beginning to think you weren't coming. Good thing you showed. I brought your favorite."

"Brownies? Yes!"

Madelyn smiled as she drew a knife across the already half-empty baking pan and began cutting the remaining brownies into tidy squares.

Of course, everybody likes brownies and just about everybody makes them, but nobody makes brownies like Madelyn. I don't know what she puts in them, but she's got some kind of secret ingredient that makes these brownies far more irresistible than is usual or reasonable. I've had dreams about these things. No kidding.

While Madelyn fussed with the food, I turned to look at the television.

Mary Dell was just as everyone described her, blond and brash and big, not in person so much as in personality. She had big hair, big earrings, and a big, bold smile to match. Next to Mary Dell sat her son and cohost, Howard. Howard, who has Down syndrome, is in his early twenties.

Evelyn explained that Howard chooses all the fabrics for Mary Dell's quilts because he has all the color sense in the Templeton family—all. And as I caught a glimpse of the neon orange pants that Mary Dell was wearing, I could see what she meant.

"Oh my gosh!" Evelyn laughed and pointed at the screen. "See how Howard's eyes keep shifting over to Mary Dell? He's just dying to rip that leopard scarf off her neck, but he can't. They made a deal: Howard has veto power over quilt fabric, but when it comes to his momma's wardrobe, he has to keep his opinions to himself. Poor Howard! This must make his teeth hurt."

"Well, those pants are making my eyes hurt," Abigail commented. "Last time I saw orange that bright was on a traffic cone. Don't they have people to dress her?"

"Mary Dell doesn't pay any attention. She likes

380

how she looks. I think that's part of her appeal. Mary Dell is happy being Mary Dell and it shows. Plus, she's hilarious. Listen to this. . . ."

Evelyn raised the volume a couple of notches as Mary Dell looked into the camera with her bright eyes and wide smile.

"Now, here's a little gardening tip sent in by Bernice Krueger of Moraga, California. Howard?"

Howard cleared his throat and read from a sheet of pink stationery.

"Dear Mary Dell and Howard: If you're looking for a way to lighten heavy soils *and* shield your spouse from the full scope of your fabric habit, consider shredding your old quilt shop receipts and mixing them in with your garden compost. I've been doing this for years and my rose garden is the envy of the neighborhood. In fact, my 'Mr. Lincoln' hybrid tea roses just won fifty dollars at a local garden show. Know what I did with the prize money? I made more compost supplies, And this wall hanging."

As Mary Dell laughed and as Howard held up a photo, the camera came in to show Bernice Krueger's quilted version of her award-winning rose.

"Well, that's a good tip, Bernice." Mary Dell chuckled. "We're going to send you a *Quintessential Quilting* T-shirt for sharing that with us.

"You know, Howard, back when I was married to your daddy, I had that same problem. I just didn't think it was right to burden him with complete disclosure when it came to my fabric purchases."

Howard nodded solemnly. "You mighta given him a hard attack."

"Indeed I might, honey. I sure might." She smiled at her son's malapropism but didn't correct him.

"So, for his own protection, I decided that every time I wrote a check to the quilt shop, I'd just record it in the register as having been written to the grocery store. Well, one night, Donny was sitting at the kitchen table, trying to balance the checkbook, and he was just grumbling to himself and scratching his head. So I said, 'What's the matter? Won't it add up?' And Donny said, 'Yeah, it adds up fine, but for the life of me I cannot understand how you can be writing four checks a week for groceries when there isn't one blessed thing to eat in this house!'"

Mary Dell threw her head back and laughed at her own punch line. Howard joined in.

"Oh, Momma! He should have known what you were up to! I would have."

"I know you would, darlin', because you know how happy fabric makes me. Now that I'm older and wiser, I wouldn't give the time of day to a man who didn't understand that. A man who can't appreciate a good yard of cotton, can't appreciate me."

Apparently forgetting they were being filmed, Howard turned to his mother and beamed just as the *Quintessential Quilting* theme song began to play in the background. "Hub-Jay appreciates you *and* a good yard of cotton, doesn't he, Momma? He wouldn't have a hard attack on you!"

Mary Dell's smile froze on her lips. Her eyes darted away from her son's face to the camera. "Well, Howard, it's time for us to go. Can't believe how the time flew! Until next time, remember, behind every good quilter . . ."

Howard finished the line. ". . . is a great big pile of fabric!"

"So get to it, y'all!" Mary Dell winked as the music rose up and the credits started to roll down the screen. Evelyn turned off the video. Abigail looked at her with raised brows.

"Well, well, well," she said. "What an interesting slipup."

"Were they taping that live?" I asked.

"Definitely," Evelyn said and walked to her sewing machine. "I called her the minute it aired. Mary Dell has a beau. Hubble James Hollander, Hub-Jay for short. He's nice and he owns his own business. That's all she'd tell me."

"A businessman," Abigail murmured. "That sounds promising. And it sounds as if Howard approves of him."

"Oh, he'd have to or Mary Dell wouldn't give him the time of day. I don't think Mary Dell even had a date since Donny left, not until now. Howard is her whole life."

Abigail, who is always careful about her weight, cut one brownie in half and put it on a napkin before carrying it back to her sewing machine. "Chicks do have a habit of leaving the nest. I think it's good that Mary Dell is doing a little something for herself at last."

"I do too," Evelyn said and took another brownie for herself, a whole one, and brought it to the ironing board. "She sounded really happy. Hey, Madelyn, when you get a moment can you give me some help with my borders? I was just going to repeat the one I did around the center medallion, but now I'm thinking it looks a little dull. I'd like to find something a little more daring."

"Sure. Be there in a minute."

Madelyn thrust a glass of something sweet and bubbly—prosecco, I think—into my left hand and a plate piled with dense, gooey brownies into my right. I took a sip of my drink and then, since my left hand was occupied, bent my head down to the brownie plate and took a bite, sighing with satisfaction.

"Fabulous. Definitely made my night. What do you put into these things anyway? And don't go telling me a pinch of this and a pinch of that.

You've got some strange secret ingredient in there. What is it?"

Madelyn glanced over her shoulder. Everyone else was hard at work. The steady hum of sewing machines and steamy hiss of Evelyn's iron made it impossible for anyone to overhear our conversation. "It's not my recipe, it's one of Edna's. I found it in her recipe file. I won't tell you the ingredients but I will tell you what she called them—but only if you promise not to tell Virginia."

Before I could ask why Virginia would care about what the recipe's title was, Madelyn whispered, "Bourbon Street brownies."

"There's liquor in there?"

"Kentucky bourbon," Madelyn affirmed. "Finest kind."

I fought to keep from laughing. "You're right. We can't tell Virginia. She's a teetotaler."

"So was Edna—that was her story anyway. Did I tell you I found a whole case of empty bottles of 'tonic' in the cellar?" Madelyn said with a conspiratorial grin.

"Well, that explains a lot of things."

"Doesn't it, though?" Madelyn said. "Anyway, don't tell Virginia. There's no actual alcohol in there, it burns off in the baking, but I wouldn't want to upset her. Even Jake said he could have some if he wanted, but he prefers my peach raspberry muffins. I swear I'm going to have to start calling him Muffin Man. He gobbles down at least three every time he comes over. And never gains an ounce. Irritates the heck out of me," she said with a smile that belied her words.

"So," I said slowly, "how often is he over at your place?"

"A couple of times a week," she said casually. "Three or four. If it snows he comes over with the truck to plow my driveway and stays for breakfast. And if I've got guests and need to get out to run errands, he'll come watch the phones for me. And we get together for sushi every other Wednesday."

"Uh-huh."

"Oh, stop it, Tessa. Don't look at me like that. We're not dating. We're friends. I like it that way and so does Jake."

"You sure? I don't know too many men who plow somebody else's driveway out of friendship."

"I'm sure, so let's talk about something else. Like you. When you came in you looked like you'd lost your best friend, which," Madelyn said as she reached for the bottle of bubbly and refilled my glass and her own, "we both know is impossible. You're stuck with me for life."

She touched the rim of her glass to mine before we took another sip. "So, really? How are you?"

"Fine."

Madelyn tilted her head to the side. "You're

going to have to rehearse that a few more times. Not a convincing performance."

"I don't want to talk about it. I came here to eat brownies, quilt, and forget my problems. Okay?"

"Okay," Madelyn said.

An old friend knows when you're lying but also knows when to let it lie.

"But when you're ready to talk, you know I'm always ready to listen. Right?"

"Right," I said with a little smile, knowing it was true.

Madelyn nodded and let it lie. "Until then, I have a little project that might interest you." She walked across the room to the coatrack, picked up a Cobbled Court Quilts shopping bag from the floor, and carried it to the table.

"Actually," she said loudly enough for everyone to hear, "I'm hoping this will interest a couple of you. Remember Angela? She came to stay with me when the inn first opened?"

"The basketball player's wife?" Virginia clucked her tongue. "Poor thing. Somebody ought to take some dull scissors and do surgery on that husband of hers." No one disagreed.

"Her baby is due soon," Madelyn said, "and I was wondering if I might talk some of you into making a baby quilt for her."

She pulled a pile of fabric out of the bag, a collection of green, cream, blue, and yellow cottons patterned with stripes, stars, checks, and polka dots that complemented the anchor fabric, featuring a picnic of smiling, pajama-clad teddy bears flying kites on a background of sea-glass green. I was sure that these fabrics weren't part of a manufacturer's collection, but they went together perfectly, in a combination more interesting than any planned collection could ever have been.

How was she able to do that? I'd tried to pull off that bold, scrappy look when buying fabric for my most recent project, spending over an hour pulling bolts and piling them on the table only to chicken out at the last moment and replace the scrappy patterns with a yawn-inducing collection of safe solids. Maybe I should have asked Madelyn to choose my fabrics. She could play Howard to my Mary Dell.

The moment Madelyn spread out her fabrics, everyone abandoned their sewing and gathered round. The sight of a new fabric attracts quilters as surely as a magnet attracts steel.

"Oh, that teddy bear fabric is so sweet!" Margot exclaimed. "Is it new?"

Evelyn nodded. "Just came in on Monday. But I didn't know we'd sold any yet."

"Madelyn bought it while you were at lunch with Charlie," Virginia replied. "I was sort of hoping she'd decided to start quilting after all. But this is the next best thing. Who wants to help?"

Margot ran her hand over the yardage and said, "I love making baby quilts."

Poor Margot. She was bright, beautiful, cheerful, and, nearing her fortieth birthday, single. She loves children and wants a family of her own, but there seems to be no sign of a husband or babies on her horizon. I remembered what that felt like to want a baby so badly but be afraid you'd never have one of your own.

The wistful tone in Margot's voice pulled me up short. My mom always used to say, "Enjoy the little things in life, Tessa. One day you may look back and realize they were the big things." I was so lucky to have Josh. And Lee. And friends.

"I'll help with Angela's quilt," I said.

"Me too," Margot said in a deliberately cheerful voice.

The others echoed her and, in less time than it takes to unsew a seam, were chattering about the fabric, sketching out patterns, and having a wonderful time. Even me. I told Madelyn that I'd come to the quilt shop to quilt, eat, and forget my problems, and that's exactly what happened.

Sometimes, if you're lucky, you realize that the little things are really the big things. Or, as Lee might say, "Broke I may be. Poor I am not."

42
Madelyn

March

It was March 20, the first day of spring. I wonder if Tessa realized that when she chose that date to close For the Love of Lavender? There was a certain irony, even poetry, to closing a shop devoted to all things herbal just as the earth was stirring, waking to a season of growth. With all she had on her mind, I doubt she'd given much thought to the significance of the date or the fact that our birthdays were coming up later in the week. It didn't matter. I had memory enough for us both.

It was a Saturday morning and two of my rooms were filled—the first time I'd ever had more than one room occupied at a time. At the moment, the most notable feature in my reservation book was a lot of white space, but I hoped warmer temperatures would change that.

So far, I'd experienced a few bumps on the road—the occasional leaking toilet or burned breakfast, a broken coffeepot, the guest who ignored the prominently placed sign on the hearth stating that the fireplace was only ornamental but, using several rolled-up magazines for fuel, tried to light a fire anyway, another who stayed out until two in the morning, lost his key, and was nearly arrested when a neighbor caught him trying to jimmy open a back window and called the police. But those few missteps aside, things were going well. My guest book was filled with praise from my customers as well as promises to come back soon and spread the word. I hoped they were telling the truth.

The easiest way to reach my target audience would be to advertise, preferably in the *New York Times*. But that was way, way beyond my means. Instead, I had to settle for a sixth of a page display ad in *Passport* magazine, which was distributed free of charge at restaurants, museums, boutiques, and anywhere else tourists might frequent—the same magazine my guest had used as fuel for the forbidden fire. Evelyn's son, Garrett, had designed a basic website for me, offering information, pretty pictures, and a phone number to call for reservations. Other than that, I had to rely on luck, word of mouth, and my new brochures, which had just arrived from the printer.

After feeding my guests, doing the dishes, cleaning the rooms, and changing the sheets, I planned to drop off a stack of brochures at the visitor information booth on the Green, then stop in at For the Love of Lavender to give Tessa her birthday present and a big dose of moral support.

Jake said he'd stop by around noon to watch the office for me. The moment I could afford it, I had to hire some part-time help. I couldn't keep imposing on Jake.

I use a back corner of the kitchen for my office. That's where Jake found me when he arrived. He greeted me and grabbed one of the leftover breakfast muffins from a platter on the countertop.

"You're going to get fat if you keep that up."

"Think so?" he asked, glancing down at his stomach with a grin.

I laughed. "You are so irritating."

The phone rang. It was Angela Radnovich, calling to thank me for the baby quilt.

"You're welcome, Angela. But you should be thanking the women over at Cobbled Court. They did all the work. I just bought the fabric."

"I'm sending two thank-you notes, one for you and one to your friends. I love the quilt. It's already in the crib, ready for the big day."

"It'll be here before you know it. How are you feeling?"

"As well as can be expected, considering my husband's publicist just sent out a press release announcing his wedding to the next Mrs. Radnovich. Their timing is good, mid-May. The baby will just avoid being born illegitimate."

"What? How can he do that? Your divorce isn't final yet, is it?"

"It will be at the end of April. Mike wants this wedding to go forward on schedule. He accepted my first settlement offer without batting an eye. I get the apartment in New York, the house in Vail, two million a year in child support, and twenty-five million in cash. After all he's put me through, I should have asked for fifty," she said in a voice dripping with loathing.

"Anyway, it's all but done. I don't want to talk about it. I just called to thank you and, believe it or not, to talk to you about a wedding."

Reading my thoughts, Angela barked out a bitter little laugh and said, "No, not mine. I've sworn off men forever. But my personal assistant, Kerry, just got engaged. I told her not to do it, that all men are lying sacks of scum, but she won't listen. Anyway, I want to throw her a wedding. . . ."

"Angela, that is so sweet of you!"

"No, it's not. This is purely out of self-interest. She wanted three weeks off to go home to California for a wedding and honeymoon trip. I can't spare her that long, not with the baby coming, so I offered to fly her family out here, pay for the wedding, plus a five-day honeymoon in Vermont. This way she won't be gone more than a week.

"We'll need to book all your guest rooms," Angela said. "We can have the ceremony out in your herb garden, assuming the weather is good, and the reception in the living room. I'm willing to pay another thousand for use of the garden and public rooms and five hundred more for helping coordinate the details. We'll need a caterer, florist, and photographer, but I'm sure you have contacts. So? What do you say? Do you have a weekend open in May or June?"

I wedged the telephone between my ear and shoulder and frantically flipped through the calendar, looking for a completely open weekend, mentally kicking myself for letting people book single rooms for single nights during tourist season.

"Wait! What about the third weekend in May? We're wide open."

"The same time as Mike's wedding," Angela said flatly. "How ironic. I'll send a deposit. Kerry will call you on Monday."

I hung up the phone, clapped my hands, and stomped my feet for joy. All five rooms booked for a weekend! Plus fees for public room rentals and wedding coordination! It added up to . . . ? I was too excited to do the math, too excited to contain myself. Without stopping to think, I let out a whoop, flung myself at Jake, and kissed him on the lips.

And Jake kissed me back.

His lips were soft, but his kiss was hard, slow, almost lazy, and so assured. His arms rested at steep angles across the small of my back and the blades of my shoulders. He spread his fingers wide and pressed them gently but firmly to my body, as if trying to leave his imprint on my flesh and in my memory.

It worked.

The certainty of his touch summoned images to my mind, memories of our first date and of a young Jake running through twin columns of light spilling from the headlamps of a borrowed car to open my door; images of Jake older and wiser and handsome, waiting on my porch steps with patience and twenty gallons of paint; of Jake leaning against a wall, watching me struggle to control and conquer the floor sander, muscled arms crossed over his chest, wanting to help but holding back because he knew I wanted to do it myself; of Jake laughing, and frowning, and listening, and telling me the truth no matter what; of the way his glass eye wandered when he was tired, the way he smiled when I entered a room. The heat of his hands warmed me, made me forget myself and my need to maintain control, made me remember myself and the spark of long-dormant desire.

I gave myself up to it, melting into the circle of his arms, leaning in, lifting up, softening my mouth and opening my lips, tasting his tongue with mine. For a few sweet moments, it felt right to forget and safe to remember. And then Jake's arms angled even lower, his fingers closed tight and his hands slid down and around the swell of my hips, and that spark of desire surged inside me, igniting an ancient and instinctual flame, an elemental longing. My hips rocked forward to meet his without permission or precaution.

He responded in kind and suddenly my brain reengaged, overriding the careless cravings of biology. I uncoiled my arms from his body and planted my palms on his shoulders to push myself back as hard and far as I could.

"Stop it," I gasped.

Jake frowned, doubting me. I took a step back and dropped my arms to my side, taking in a deep, slow breath through my mouth and exhaling raggedly but deliberately.

Jake spread out his hands. "Why?"

"Because I know what happens next. I know where this goes. And I'm not going there again, not ever. Every mistake of my life has begun by tumbling into bed with someone. I like you too much to add you to my list of regrets."

He gave me a long, appraising look.

"Wow. That's the smoothest brush-off I've ever received. Did you make that up as you went along? Or have you been practicing? What comes next? Are you going to tell me you 'just want to be friends'? Don't play games with me, Madelyn."

"I don't know what comes next, Jake. I haven't the slightest idea how all this works. But let me ask you something. Where is the 'just' in friends?

I've never wanted to be friends with a man before, *never*. Do you know how big a deal that is for me? Up until now I've only seen men in terms of what they could do for me or buy for me or get for me. I don't feel that way about you."

"Really? Well, for somebody who wasn't looking to get anything out of me, you seem to have taken a lot—a newly roofed house, sanded floors, snowplowed driveway, somebody to watch your phones . . ."

He crossed his arms over his chest defensively. I'd wounded him and so he wanted to wound me back. And he had. His words were cruel and his insinuation was insulting. I'd never have taken that from a man I liked less than Jake, but I *did* like him. I was only just beginning to realize how much. And so instead of throwing him out of my house and my life, I stood my ground.

"That's not fair, Jake. You've done a lot for me, much more than I could ever have expected or asked. But everything you did for me—the roof, the discounts, the snowplowing, and all the rest—was *your* idea and you know it. I never asked you for anything. Even so, I went to some effort to repay you for your unsolicited kindness to me. The muffins? The anniversary getaway for your sister? My insistence that we go dutch on our dinner dates? That was my way of trying to keep our relationship friendly rather than romantic, and I think you know that too. That was the unspoken agreement. In fact, we *did* speak of it—or you did. Be honest. You understood my concerns. When we started going out to dinner together, you assured me that we were just going as friends, that you weren't trying to lure me into bed, remember?

"And I took you at your word, Jake. I was relieved because I value our relationship too much to let it become sexual. Sex always ruins everything."

"I see," he said sharply. "So I should be honored that your feelings toward me are platonic? Now who's not being honest?"

He pointed a finger at me, all but poked it into my chest. "You kissed me first, Madelyn. And don't try to tell me that you didn't mean anything by it, that you just got carried away. You didn't give me a peck, or a smooch. That was a *kiss,* an incredible one. I didn't know you could kiss like that. You sure didn't in high school. So don't try to pretend there's no sexual spark between us, because we both know it isn't true."

"I didn't say that," I retorted, not bothering to let him know I'd been *about* to say all of those things. People who can demolish your arguments before you even give voice to them are irritating enough; it's not necessary to let them know how right they are.

"Of course there's a sexual attraction between us. We'd hardly be human if there wasn't. But that doesn't mean we have to give into it, does it?

Remember what you told me about Beth? About waiting for the real thing?"

"I have been waiting! I didn't want to pressure you. I've been waiting months for you to make a move so I'd know you felt . . ."

"I'm sorry. I shouldn't have done that, but I was just . . . I lost my mind for a minute, okay? Let's not ruin a really good thing because I went crazy for thirty seconds. Think about it, Jake. You've already had two failed marriages and probably five times as many failed relationships in your life. I'm not that far behind you. Do you really want to add ours to the list?"

Jake hooked his thumbs in the belt loops of his jeans and stared at me for a moment, his posture less defensive but no less angry.

"It really doesn't matter what I want, does it? You've decided for both of us."

"I want to keep being friends, Jake," I said quietly. "You matter to me."

"Yeah? Well, I guess that should make me feel better. But somehow it doesn't."

He pulled his truck keys out of the pocket of his jeans and walked to the door. Before he left, he turned toward me and inclined his head in farewell. Or good-bye?

It took all my resolve not to run after him, to grab him by the arm and ask him to stay, to kiss him again. But I was resolved. And I was right. Of that I was sure.

43
Madelyn

After Jake left, I had to sit down and collect my thoughts, or rather, control them. I couldn't take time to think about Jake and me, not just then. Instead, I needed to focus on Tessa. I'd promised to come to the shop and help her get through this last day. She needed me.

Today of all days, Lee wanted to be there for her, but he'd gotten a call from a man who lived in Chicago and owned three big restaurants in Hartford. He wanted to talk to Lee about supplying his restaurants with microgreens and produce but would only be in town today and insisted they meet. Tessa understood. It was too good an opportunity to pass up, but Lee almost did, until I volunteered to stand in for him.

I couldn't let Tessa and Lee down. But I also couldn't leave the inn unattended for hours at a time. I called Tessa. She took several rings to pick up. In the background, I could hear a murmur of voices. It sounded like she had quite a crowd.

"Tessa? Jake can't watch the office, so I can't leave right now, but I'll be there just before five."

"That's fine. Don't worry. I'm too busy to be lonely. Wait a sec, will you?"

I heard a thump as Tessa put the phone down,

then the ring of the cash register, the rustling of bags, and Tessa's voice thanking her customer and, I thought, nearly reminding her to come again before catching herself. When she came back on the line, her voice was almost a whisper, too soft for the customers to hear.

"It's crazy here! I'm knee-deep in bargain hunters. I guess I should be grateful, but still . . . One lady tried to buy my quilt. She took it off the wall without even asking! The vultures are out in force, Madelyn, come to pick the carcass clean."

"I can come over sooner if you need me. I'll find someone to watch the office," I said, wondering who I could call. Maybe Margot? Or Ivy?

"No, I'm fine, really. Margot was here at lunch and Ivy is here now. Evelyn's coming later. She saw the crowd at my door this morning and organized a steady supply of helpers. Abigail came this morning. That was interesting."

"I'll bet," I said, echoing Tessa's soft chuckle. "Are you sure you're all right?"

"I'm sure. Besides, I don't know where I'd put you if you did come now. If there were any more bodies here we'd need lubricant. Gotta run. See you around five."

"I'll be there as soon as I can. Hang in there. I've got a bottle of white chilling in the refrigerator. I'm bringing it, a corkscrew, and two glasses."

"Madelyn," she sighed, "you are a mind reader."

Tessa's remark about the vultures hadn't been far off the mark.

By the time I arrived, carrying a picnic basket over my arm and a bottle of wine in my hand, the shop's bone-white shelving and display cabinets were nearly empty, picked clean as a Christmas turkey. The crowd of bargain shoppers had dissipated, there being no more bargains left to buy, and Tessa was waiting on one last customer, a woman who was buying up the last four tubes of lip balm, all peppermint flavored.

"I'm so sorry to see you close," the woman said. "It's such a lovely shop."

"Thank you," Tessa replied with a weary smile.

The woman looked around as Tessa stuffed a shopping bag with purple and lilac tissue paper, then tied the handles closed with a bow of purple, green, and natural raffia.

I smiled to myself and shook my head. It might be her last customer on her last day in business, but Tessa was going to give this woman (who was getting a seventy percent discount) the same level of service she gave to every customer. She didn't know another way. No wonder she'd been the teacher's pet when we were kids.

"I feel bad that I haven't been in before," the woman said, ducking her head. "But my husband has been out of work for more than a year. Shopping hasn't been on my agenda for a long time. I'm going to save these as birthday gifts for my daughters and daughter-in-law. Just a little something," she said with an apologetic shrug.

"You've got such a lovely shop," the woman repeated. "I'm sorry I'm not buying from you under different circumstances. . . ."

"No need to apologize," Tessa said. "I'm glad you came in today." She reached under the counter, pulled out five silvery tubes of hand cream, and slipped them into the woman's bag. "Here," she said. "Take these. There's enough for your daughters and an extra one for you."

"But . . . I . . . I don't," the woman stammered. "I mean, I can't . . ."

"Sure you can." Tessa glanced at her watch. "There's still five minutes before closing. That means I'm still the boss around here."

"Thank you," the woman replied, accepting the bag that Tessa held out to her over the counter. "Thank you so much."

"You're welcome. I hope you enjoy it. It's lavender. My favorite."

The woman assured Tessa that she would, thanking her three more times as Tessa escorted her to the door before closing and locking it. The woman waved at Tessa through the display window and Tessa waved back until the woman disappeared around the corner, then froze for a moment, her hand still in the air with fingers splayed, before closing them into a fist and letting her arm drop heavily by her side.

I walked up and draped my arm across her shoulders. "If you're going to go out," I said, "that's the way to do it—with style."

Tessa looked at me and smiled, eyes glistening. "You think?"

"Yeah, I do."

"She seemed like a nice lady."

"She did," I agreed. "Just like you. You're a class act, Tessa. What my dad would have called 'a stand-up broad.' When it came to women, that was his highest form of praise. Probably explains why he never married."

"Thanks, Madelyn. Thanks for coming."

She turned and hugged me. I hugged her back, holding on for a long time, not loosening my grip until she did.

"Now," I said, rubbing my hands together. "Let's open that picnic basket, uncork that bottle, and figure out what you're going to do with the rest of your life."

Tessa wiped her eyes with the back of her hand, then laughed. "Is that what's on tonight's agenda?"

"Among other things, my friend. Among other things."

44
Tessa

I like it better this way," I said, twisting to take in the empty shelves and counters cleared of objects, the flickering shadows of flame projected onto naked walls warmed by the glow of fifteen candles.

We'd started with one lavender candle that Madelyn had pulled from the recesses of her basket and set in the center of an old, worn quilt she'd brought for us to sit on during our picnic on the shop floor. Halfway through the bottle of wine, and after cutting into the orange cake she'd baked and decorated with a birthday candle (only one, for which I was grateful), I decided we needed more light, so I got up and lit my remaining stock of vanilla candles. The effect was peaceful and softened the sharp edges of my mood.

"It's clean. Simple. Why did I crowd the place with so much stuff? If I'd just displayed a few items at a time, maybe people would have been able to see more. Maybe I would have . . ."

Madelyn shook her head insistently as she turned her fork backward to lick off a last glob of cream cheese frosting. "The shop was perfect. Your products were fabulous and your service was the best. You didn't do anything wrong, Tessa. It was just your timing that sucked. End of story."

I'd said the same thing to myself a dozen times, but in my heart, I didn't really believe it. Being a victim of the times seems so capricious. I believe things happen for a reason, that there are lessons to be learned even in hardship, and that even when we can't see it, there is always a divine plan at work. But I didn't say any of that to Madelyn.

"Anyway, the candles look nice."

"They do. The older I get, the more I appreciate dim light."

I clinked my glass against Madelyn's. "Can you believe we're about to celebrate another birthday? I thought I'd be smarter by now. Or that I'd at least know what I want to be when I grow up. Seems a little late to be reinventing myself again. And a little pathetic, don't you think?"

Madelyn rolled her eyes. "Will you quit feeling so sorry for yourself? If you insist on continuing to look at this as a failure, then it will be. But if you choose to look at it as an opportunity, then it will be. It's your choice."

"Did you read that somewhere? Or are you just making this up as you go along?"

Madelyn arched her left eyebrow, the way she does when she's pretending to be mad. "That's the second time I've been asked that today."

"I know. I was just teasing you," I said. "But, really, what are you going to do about Jake?"

"I already told you—nothing. I wasn't wrong and I was telling him the truth. He'll either decide to believe me or not. Quit trying to change the subject. We were talking about you. What *do* you want to be when you grow up? I mean, were you really happy working in the shop all day? Because, knowing you like I do, I can't quite see it."

"Why?" I asked, bristling a little. "I was pretty good at retail."

Madelyn lifted her hands. "I didn't mean it that way. I know you were good at it, but did you *like* it? Seems to me you're happiest when you're out in your garden, not cooped up inside a store."

She had a point.

Working in the shop had been fun at first, but as time wore on, and especially as the dreamed-of crush of customers failed to appear, I'd begun to resent the long, lonely hours spent dusting shelves and rearranging stock.

"I don't know. I think what I really wanted was the chance to grow the herbs and create the products. That's the fun part. But I also wanted to share them with people.

"Like this," I said, picking up the center candle. "When I've had a rotten day, walking into a room that smells of lavender, or treating myself to a hot shower with a bar of bergamot and lime soap, or rubbing on lemongrass body lotion makes me feel like things aren't so bad. Peppermint hand cream can't cure a broken heart, but if I can make things that give ordinary people a little bit of luxury, a moment's pleasure . . . I wasn't looking to make a lot of money, just a living. And doing so while helping people enjoy life a little more."

I shrugged. "I know that probably sounds silly."

"No." Madelyn rocked forward so she could reach the wine bottle and refill my glass and then hers, tipping the bottle high to make sure none of it was wasted. "Just the opposite. I think that sounds very wise."

She grinned, reached out to break a crumbly piece of cake off with her fingers.

"And I say that because, believe it or not, I feel exactly the same. Ha! Wouldn't Gene Janders be surprised to hear that? Sterling too."

She looked up at the ceiling, as if Sterling's ghost might be found hovering above, and announced in a loud voice, "But it's true! I, Madelyn Beecher Baron, the gold digger's gold digger, the most mercenary of the mercenary, have come to a clichéd but important realization: Money doesn't buy happiness."

She popped the piece of cake into her mouth and looked at me with a "how do you like that" expression.

"True, but it does come in handy now and then." I sighed. "Now that the shop is closed, I suppose I should look for a job."

"I thought you were going to help Lee on the farm?"

"Yes, but he doesn't need much help right now, not until the weather warms up. If I could bring in some money, even a little bit, it'd be a big help. Plus, I need something to do with myself. I've always worked."

Madelyn looked thoughtful as she licked frosting from her fingers.

"Well, why not come work for me part-time? I mean it," she insisted, reading the doubt on my face. "I can't call on Jake to help me anymore. I never should have in the first place. And with this wedding coming up, I could really use an extra pair of hands."

"You don't want me," I protested. "I don't know anything about innkeeping."

"That's a relief. On my budget I can't afford to hire someone with experience.

"Seriously, Tessa. I'm going to have to hire somebody, why not you? The hours could be flexible, so you could help Lee when he needed it. More importantly, it'd give you a chance to think out what you want to do with For the Love of Lavender."

"What do you mean, what I want to do with it?" I frowned. "That dream's over. It died at five o'clock, after I rang up my last sale and locked the front door."

She shook her head emphatically. "I don't think so. You were doing what you love, creating products you love, that other people could enjoy. You had the right idea. I just think you chose the wrong way to execute it. For the Love of Lavender isn't dead, just on hiatus. You just need to find another way to do what you love, Tessa. You need a Plan B."

"I see."

I appreciated Madelyn's attempts to buoy my spirits, but her newfound optimism and insistence on refusing to do what I'd done, acknowledge my failure and accept the consequences, was a little irritating.

"Where will I find this Plan B? How long will it take to find it? A month? A year? Ten years?"

"I don't know. But why not leave the door open to the possibility? Come work with me for a little bit and see what happens next. What do you say?"

I wasn't sure if it was a great idea to work for my friend. But I had to do something, and Madelyn's offer was tempting. Maybe she couldn't pay me much but, these days, who could? Especially for part-time work with flexible scheduling? And even if I could find a job, I really didn't want to start at the bottom in some new company filled with new people, not now.

"All right," I said and stuck out my hand. "I accept. Thanks, Madelyn."

"Yeah?" Madelyn's face lit up as she grabbed my outstretched hand to seal the bargain. "That's great! It's fun, you'll see. Most of the time, I don't even think of it as work." She lifted her hand, adding a caveat. "Except when I'm dealing with a clogged toilet or a demanding guest. That's definitely work. But most of the time it just feels like . . . life. . . . Like living a satisfying life, more satisfying than the life I lived in New York and *much* less tiring.

"Do you have any idea how exhausting it is to pretend to like people you don't, who are also pretending to like you? What a waste of time and energy. Since coming to New Bern, I've worked harder than I've ever worked in my life. But when I flop into bed at night, I feel like I've accomplished something."

Madelyn paused to take a sip of wine. "I had a sweet couple stay with me a couple of weekends ago. They were celebrating their anniversary, so, as a surprise, I decided to bake them a cake. They must have thanked me ten times."

"Well," I said, inclining my head toward the half-eaten birthday cake, summoning my willpower to keep from taking another slice, "if it was half as good as this one, I can understand their gratitude. That was smart, Madelyn. I bet you made them customers for life."

Madelyn nodded. "You're probably right, but that wasn't why I did it. I was trying to make their visit special. And I did. And it felt great. Of course, I was happy to have that room occupied—I needed the money. But that money is already gone. However, the image of that couple sitting in my dining room, holding hands across the table as they blew out the candles on their cake, will stay with me for a long time. It made me happy to see them so happy.

"And I guess that's my point. I had everything backward. When I was only thinking about money and myself and how to get more money for myself, I couldn't buy happiness at any price. Now that my first focus is on making other people happy, happiness has fallen into my lap like a ripe apple."

"Speaking of happiness," I said, throwing willpower to the four winds as I reached for the knife, "how about another piece of cake?"

"Why not? I have a theory that calories consumed on your birthday don't count toward annual totals."

"My birthday isn't for two days yet and yours is two days after that."

She shrugged and held out her plate. "Birthday week. Close enough. Wait a minute!" she cried. "I almost forgot your present!"

Madelyn put down her plate and started rummaging around the bottom of the picnic basket before pulling out a small package wrapped with turquoise tissue paper and handing it to me.

"Open it!"

I tore through the layers of tissue and gasped as I spied a glint of silver and aquamarine glass.

"The bracelets! Our friendship bracelets! I can't believe you kept them all these years."

"I didn't," she said as she reached over to place one of the bracelets on my wrist. "I smashed those to smithereens years ago. I salvaged the beads from jewelry I found at tag sales and thrift shops while I was doing the remodeling, and restrung them, so these are new. Well, old-new. Like our friendship.

"And *this* time," she said as she put on her own bracelet, "I strung them on silver-plated beading wire instead of fishing line, so it's virtually unbreakable—also like our friendship."

I held up my arm in the candlelight and twisted my wrist back and forth, making aquamarine shadows dance on the walls and ceiling. "I love it. I just love it. Happy birthday, Madelyn."

"Happy birthday, Tessa."

45
Madelyn

May

I came down the back stairs into the kitchen, carrying a laundry basket piled so high with sheets and towels that I didn't see Tessa was on the phone.

"Tessa? When I reorganized the supply closet, do you remember where I put the lightbulbs? A bulb burnt out in Room Four. At least, I think it's just a bulb," I mumbled to myself. "It better be. I'm tired of writing checks to the electrician."

I plunked the basket down on top of the dryer and turned to see Tessa with the phone to her ear, her eyes screwed shut, and her hand held out flat toward me, indicating that this was not a convenient time to talk.

"I'm sorry, but we're full that weekend. We've got vacancies every other weekend in June. I'd be happy to book you for any of those," Tessa said hopefully, then nodded in silent acquiescence as whoever was on the other end of the line spoke.

"I see. Well, I know the other inns are full too. It's a very popular weekend. You might try calling Barbara Jansen at the Goshen Chamber of Commerce. I think she's working on some sort of waiting list for vacancies. You're welcome. Hope you find something. And if you're ever back in the area, I hope you'll come stay with us."

Tessa hung up the phone and sighed.

"Let me guess," I said. "They wanted a room during the Dylan Tyler concert?"

"You got it."

Three weeks previously, it had been announced that Dylan Tyler, the legendary singer who rose to fame in 1968 with the release of his *Starlight at Midnight* album and had been releasing hits ever since, proving that there were still many beautiful songs to be sung with nothing more than an acoustic guitar for accompaniment, would be giving an outdoor benefit concert in Goshen. The concert tickets sold out within three hours. Every hotel room in a fifty-mile radius sold out within six hours.

I growled and shoved the sheets into the washer while Tessa pulled towels out of the dryer and started folding. "Why did it have to be that weekend? The one weekend we're full? And why does the wedding have to be at the same time as the concert? We could have booked those rooms ten times over."

"Look on the bright side. We're at sixty percent occupancy for the last two weekends in June and we've got at least forty percent occupancy for every weekend in July. So you're going to break even for June and July. Not bad."

"Uh, not quite," I admitted. "I just hired Chico's brother-in-law to tear out the old walkway and put in a new brick one."

"And how much is that going to cost?" Tessa tucked a bath towel under her chin and folded it into thirds. "Four hundred?"

"Five," I admitted. "And fifteen hundred more for the arbor in the garden and to replace the picket fence and garden gate in front."

Tessa stopped folding. "I don't know why you decided to do all that right now. Couldn't it wait?"

"I want everything looking great for the wedding pictures," I said defensively. "It's an investment. If we could start doing a lot of wedding business, we'd be set. Wipe that look off your face. I was going to do it eventually anyway. You're such a worrywart."

"I know. It just seems like a lot of money."

Sometimes it felt like I'd hired a loving but scolding older sister rather than a part-time assistant, but it was all right. Tessa worried because she cared—and because she couldn't help it. Some people are born cautious just as others are born reckless. And if you have to think very hard to decide which of us is which, you haven't been paying attention.

Sometimes you just have to go with your instincts. And I had a feeling about this wedding. Something was going to happen, something big.

It wasn't anything I could name, just a sense that the weekend was terribly important, that my future and the future of the inn hung in the balance. But I didn't say that to Tessa.

"It's not that much."

"You're the boss." She shrugged, piling the freshly folded towels in her arms. "I'll go put these up and replace that lightbulb before I leave. Anything else you need?"

"No, that should do it," I said as I measured out detergent and poured it into the washer. "How're things at the farm?"

"Good. Today we're transplanting tomatoes, making goat cheese, and picking the first strawberries. Since it's so early in the season, Lee thinks we can get six dollars a pint for them at the farmers' market. Oh! Speaking of that, I saw Evelyn at the farmers' market on Saturday and she told me that her friend Mary Dell is coming up for a week. We'll finally get to meet her."

"Really? What's the occasion?"

Tessa grinned. "What else? She's got tickets to Dylan Tyler."

"Of course she does," I said. "Doesn't everybody? It'll be nice to meet her, though. I wonder if we should have some kind of little party for her here at the inn? I couldn't do it on the weekend since I'll be too busy with the wedding. But if she's here for a week . . . Maybe a tea? Can you ask Evelyn when you see her on Friday?"

"Aren't you coming? You could ask Evelyn yourself."

"Can't. They're not checking out until Saturday morning," I said, casting a quick glance toward the ceiling and the general location of my currently occupied guest room. "Somebody has to stay on duty."

"Why not me? That's part of the reason you hired me, isn't it? So you could get out every now and then? Have a life? You've been collecting quotes from caterers, photographers, and florists, contacting the justice of the peace, even booking airline tickets for Kerry's relatives from California. What are you? A travel agent? And I can't believe Angela talked you into baking the wedding cake too."

"I volunteered to do that," I corrected her. "I like baking. It's not a huge cake. There will only be twenty-five guests."

"Well, I think Angela's getting a bargain, hiring you to do the wedding coordination. Go to the quilt circle on Friday. You need a break."

"So do you," I countered. "You're working two jobs. You've got as much claim on exhaustion as I do."

"I've got an idea. Why don't we flip a coin? The winner gets to go to the quilt shop and the loser stays here and mans the office. Then, next time we've got guests on Friday, we'll take turns."

Before I could agree or disagree, Tessa fished a

quarter from the pocket of her jeans and, still balancing the stack of towels in one hand, tossed it into the air.

"Call it!" she called out.

Without thinking, I claimed heads. The quarter hit the wooden floor and rolled a couple of feet before tipping over with Washington's face blinking upward.

"You win," Tessa said.

"That wasn't fair," I said. "The coin rolled. And I never agreed to a toss anyway."

"You called it," Tessa replied, as if this settled everything, and then climbed the stairs.

"I don't feel right about you missing the fun on my account."

"Can't hear you!" Tessa trilled from the top of the stairs.

"Yes, you can," I protested. "No kidding, Tessa. I don't feel right about it."

"Get over it. We flipped. You won. End of story." She walked off without waiting for me to respond, her footsteps echoing on the floorboards over my head.

"What's the point of being the boss if nobody listens to you?" I mumbled to myself. The telephone rang. I interrupted my grumbling to answer it.

"Beecher Cottage Inn. May I help you?"

A deep male voice said, "Yes. Do you have availability on Wednesday night?"

"This coming Wednesday?" I opened the reservations book and saw nothing but empty space for that day. "Yes. Yes, we do."

"Good," the voice said, rising to a timbre and tone I recognized. "Then meet me for dinner at the Japanese place at six."

"How are you, Jake? It's good to hear your voice."

"Bored. I've been spending a lot of time with Moira Swanson lately."

I'd heard that. There aren't many bachelors in New Bern, especially good-looking ones with real jobs, and there are five single women for every man who could be considered even remotely datable. When news of the tear in my relationship with Jake spread through the grapevine, you could practically hear the cheers of New Bern's single female population, only to be followed by a collective moan about three weeks later, when he was seen escorting a preening Moira Swanson to dinner at the Grill on the Green.

"Oh really," I said, feigning ignorance. "Moira seems nice."

"She is," said Jake. "As long as you don't want to talk about anything but Moira. So, how about it? Would you like to meet me for dinner?"

Hearing his voice made me realize how much I'd missed talking to him. I did want to have dinner with him, but not if it meant confusing him about our relationship. The fight had been my fault, at least initially, because I let myself get carried away. I wanted to make the ground rules clear—for both our sakes.

"It can't be a date, Jake."

"Yeah," he snapped. "I know that. Did you hear the part where I said we'd *meet* at the restaurant? If this were a date I'd pick you up. And before you bring it up, we're going dutch, just like we always did. And I won't so much as kiss you hello or good-bye. We'll shake hands. Soberly. I promise not to make any sudden moves or slip anything into your drink. I just want to have dinner with someone who doesn't consider *People* magazine her primary news source. Okay? Now, are you coming or not?"

"I'd love to, but not this week. There's just too much to do for the wedding, but how about the Wednesday after?"

"All right. I guess I can wait a week, if I have to."

"Good. I'll see you then. Six o'clock. If you arrive first, order me a California roll. Extra wasabi and pickled ginger on the side."

"How're things coming with the wedding? Do you need help with anything?"

"No," I answered. I would not impose on our friendship again. "We're in good shape. But thanks for asking, Jake."

46
Madelyn

W hat do you mean, no brownies?" Virginia put her hands on her hips and stared at me through the thick lenses of her glasses, glaring at me as if I'd just announced that Christmas would be canceled this year.

"I figured everybody was tired of them by now," I said, setting my basket down on the refreshment table. "You're the one who's always saying that we should try new things, that variety and experimentation is the best weapon for fighting off old age and stodginess."

"I was talking about you, not me," Virginia said. "I've lost the battle against old age. Save yourself. Besides, I get enough culinary experimentation from that son-in-law of mine."

"Oh, Mom," Evelyn said. "You're not fooling anyone. You've loved every new recipe Charlie has made for you."

"Not the oysters," Virginia said darkly.

"Okay, except for the oysters," Evelyn admitted.

"All I'm saying is, if something's not broken, why fix it?"

"Your brownies are pretty amazing," Margot said, looking a little apologetic for siding with Virginia.

"Give me a chance, all right? If you don't like what I've brought at least as much as the brownies, then I promise never to make it again. Deal?"

"Deal," they echoed, but doubtfully.

After I passed around home-baked strawberry shortcakes topped with real whipped cream jazzed with a touch of Cointreau and sweet early strawberries from Woodruff Farms, sprinkled with a touch of fresh mint for looks, the doubts were silenced. Everyone had seconds and a couple of people (including me) went back for thirds. If this kept up, I was going to have to take up jogging or something.

But it was worth it—not just for the pleasure of eating them but the pleasure of seeing my friends enjoy them. Isn't it strange that it took me so long to realize how much I enjoyed cooking and baking? If I'd had even a clue about that as a teenager, my whole life might have been different. Of course, if I'd had a clue about nearly anything as a teenager, my whole life might have been different.

I felt a little guilty for coming to the quilt shop while Tessa was minding the store in my place, but not so guilty that I didn't enjoy myself. The workroom was littered with yards of fabric and half-sewn quilt blocks, but the group was in such a talkative mood, I don't think anyone got much quilting done.

Ivy, normally one of our quieter members, was particularly animated. She'd finished her GED preparation classes at New Beginnings and had just taken her exam on Saturday.

"Do you think you passed?" Evelyn asked.

Ivy snipped some stray threads off the back of a class sample quilt she was making for the shop and shifted her shoulders noncommittally.

"You have to get a certain number of total points in all five subject tests to pass. I feel pretty good about that part. But you can't get less than four-ten on any individual test. I'm kind of worried about the science test. I missed that one by eighteen points on my practice test, but I've been studying hard since then. Hopefully, it paid off." She squinted and bent her head toward the quilt back, searching for hidden threads. "We'll see."

"When will you find out?" I asked as I glopped another dollop of whipped cream onto my shortcake, promising myself it would be my final indulgence of the night.

"Soon. They mail the results."

Virginia was standing at the ironing board, pressing a binding prior to stitching it in place. "How many students were in your class?"

"Counting me? Six. I hope we all pass. We've gotten pretty close over these last months. It'd be awful if some did and some didn't." Ivy nibbled nervously at her fingernail for a moment before banishing this possibility. "It's going to be fine. Bella and Connie did a great job prepping us."

"Bella and Connie?" I asked between bites. "The sisters I met here in the shop? I thought they taught in the public schools."

"They do," Ivy said. "But they also volunteer at New Beginnings. Connie was our math and science teacher and Bella handled language arts and social studies."

"But," Margot said, "I thought Bella was a PE teacher at the middle school."

"She is. She's also certified to teach senior high humanities. She's really good. Bella knows American League baseball stats like the back of her hand, but she knows Shakespeare and Emily Dickinson even better."

Abigail, who was sitting in the corner farthest from the temptations of the refreshment table, ripping a seam, looked up with obvious surprise. "Really?"

Ivy nodded. "Bella loves the classics. And you know what's even crazier? She's got me loving them too. Not just reading them but *reading* them, because I want to. I never thought I'd be able to understand books like that, but I was wrong. It's like Bella always says, 'Ignorance isn't a chronic condition, unless you allow it to become one.'"

I choked so hard that I thought whipped cream was going to come out my nose. Margot jumped up from her sewing machine and started pounding me on the back.

"Are you okay?"

"Fine," I assured her in a raspy voice. "It just went down the wrong way. Ivy, do you know where Bella grew up?"

"Manhattan, I think. She's got a New York accent. Why do you ask?"

"No reason. I was just wondering if we knew some of the same people."

New York is a big city. There was no reason to suppose that Bella had picked up that proverb from the redoubtable Millicent Fleeber, but wouldn't it be something if she had? Clearly, I was going to have to spend more time talking to Bella.

"Connie and Bella are really something. They spend all day working in a classroom and then show up weekends and evenings at New Beginnings and do it some more for free. Until I moved here, I never knew people like that existed."

Abigail squared her shoulders and said, "New Bern has always been very community minded. In good times and bad, we stick together. That's what makes this town special."

Considering her civic involvement and generosity, Abigail's pride was not undeserved. And it was hard to disagree with her observation. It seemed like everyone I'd met since returning to

New Bern did something to help others, and all without expectation of receiving anything in return.

During his lifetime, Sterling gave away lots of money, but there was always an angle. He did it to be noticed, to get his name on a wall, for social prominence, for tax breaks, for all kinds of reasons, none of them charitable. And I had been no different, no better, and had come to believe that everyone was that way. Or rather, I had chosen to forget that everyone wasn't that way—that there were good people who did good things without stopping to consider what was in it for them.

My father, who had put aside his own aspirations in pursuit of "the right thing," was one of those people. So was Evelyn, and Virginia, and Margot, and Abigail. And Jake. Definitely Jake. True, that unexpected and unforgettable kiss in the kitchen had complicated our relationship, but I knew that he hadn't been kind to me because he expected anything in return but because he was who he was: a hardware guy with a genuine desire to help fix what was broken. He was good at that.

And then there was Tessa. Here she was, beset with financial worries, yet she'd sheltered me, planted lavender in my yard, and restored my quilt, and pursued my friendship even after I'd cut her cold in the café.

What was it about this town? How had it managed to transform itself in the years of my absence? I thought about the evil Edna, and Mrs. Bridges, the teacher who had despised and dismissed me, about the gossiping girls who had made me feel like an outsider, and the sleazy boys I'd dated in high school, whose delinquency I'd contributed to so carelessly, Jake's included. That was the New Bern I'd known as a child, full of cruel people who'd hurt me and made me feel small. Where were they now? Had they all moved away, been crowded out by a sudden influx of the kind and generous? No, that couldn't be it. Aaron Fletcher was still here, and Candy Waldgren, and Dwight Sparks, who'd tried to sell me a roof I didn't need at a price I couldn't afford. If I went out looking, I was sure I would find some other less-than-lovely souls—philanderers, liars, cheats. They were still here, they had to be.

But it wasn't as if the New Bern of my childhood was entirely devoid of the generous and well intentioned. What about Mrs. Kover, who doled out hot chocolate and gentle advice? And Mr. Walters, the old janitor who treated every little girl like a princess and every boy like a son? And Mr. Kaminski, Jake's father, who gave me wallpaper and carpet samples for the dollhouse? And what about the people who'd changed their stripes and ways? Abigail? Jake? And me, I hoped.

Maybe the New Bern of the 1960s wasn't all that different from the New Bern of today, populated with the good and the not-so-good. In the end, maybe it all comes down to where you choose to look and what team you decide to play for.

Ivy resumed biting her nails. "I just hope I passed. I'd hate to let Bella and Connie down."

"You passed. I'm sure of it." I got up from my chair and walked to the refreshment table. "There's one more shortcake here, Ivy. Do you want it?"

"I shouldn't," she said and held out her plate.

Virginia finished ironing her binding and sat down to start stitching it. Though her glasses were a testament to her less-than-perfect eyesight, Virginia's hand stitches were just as tiny and even as they could be and she could still thread a needle without help, which was more than I could say for myself. Tessa and I were always joking that, pretty soon, we'd need arm extensions just to read the paper, but it wasn't far from the truth. As soon as I could afford it, I was going to go see Virginia's eye doctor.

"So how are preparations coming for the wedding?" Virginia asked as she closed one eye, threading her needle on the first try. "It's coming right up, isn't it?"

"The guests will check in exactly one week from today and the wedding will take place the next day. It's been a little crazy, but we're ready—I think. The flowers have been ordered, the minister and photographer and the musicians are all booked and, with Evelyn's help," I said with a nod in her direction, "I've booked the best caterer in New Bern for the reception."

"Charlie loves doing weddings," Evelyn said. "He's really a romantic at heart. He'll knock himself out making sure everything is perfect."

"Kerry was thrilled with his menu. She's so sweet and so excited about everything. I didn't realize how much fun this wedding was going to be."

"Hopefully," Margot said as she moved to take Virginia's spot at the ironing board, carrying a stack of finished blocks, "this will be the first of many. Destination weddings could be a good business for you."

"Oh, I've thought of that, believe me."

As I scooped the last of the berries and whipped cream onto Ivy's plate, I heard footsteps pounding on the wooden staircase up to the workroom and Tessa's voice calling, "Madelyn? Are you up there?"

She was in the room before I could answer, puffing from the exertion of climbing the stairs. "Good! You're here. I've been calling your cell for the last half hour."

"The battery must be out. What's wrong?"

"Kerry called," she gasped. "In tears. She's calling off the wedding."

It felt like somebody had kicked me in the stomach. All my plans, all my work, all the money I didn't really have but decided to invest, believing that this wedding was *the* event that would put Beecher Cottage Inn on the map—it was all for nothing.

"Oh, no. Poor Kerry. How is she?"

"Pretty torn up," Tessa said. "She didn't say for sure, but I think her fiancé got cold feet. Another girl? Anyway, she was definite. The wedding is canceled."

"Poor Kerry," I repeated. We'd never met, but I must have talked to her twenty times in the last month. She sounded so excited and so young. Too young to have her heart broken, but isn't everybody? And if that's the kind of man her fiancé was, it was better she found out before the wedding than after. I'd call her tomorrow. And after that, I'd have to call the florist and musicians and everybody else who'd been involved in the ceremony. Damn.

"So much for my instincts." I put Ivy's plate down on the table and sank into a chair. "And my first sold-out weekend."

"But isn't that the same weekend as the Dylan Tyler concert?" Abigail asked. "I'm sure there are all kinds of people who need rooms then."

"Of course!" I exclaimed, wondering why I hadn't thought of that myself. "I'll call Barbara

Jansen at the Goshen Chamber and see who she has on the waiting list."

Tessa shook her head. "No go. I phoned Barbara at home first thing after I hung up with Kerry. They put out a call for local people who would be willing to rent rooms that weekend. The response was so big that they were able to accommodate everybody on the wait list. I tried to talk her into moving people to the inn, but she can't do it. The deposits are already in."

Frustrated, I smacked my fist against the table and cursed. Margot frowned with concern but didn't say anything.

"It's not all bad news," Tessa reminded me. "You've got deposits too. At least you won't lose money on the rooms."

"No. Not on that," I grumbled, thinking about my new brick sidewalks, the garden arbor, and the other improvements I'd made in anticipation of the wedding.

I closed my eyes and let my head flop back. It was my own stupid fault. I shouldn't have counted my chickens before they were hatched. And I shouldn't have let myself get so emotionally wrapped up in this wedding. In my mind, I'd begun to think of it as the grand opening we never had, a good omen, the first of many celebrations to be held in the Beecher Cottage Inn. I hated the idea of canceling the weekend.

Then don't.

The words came into my mind out of the blue, without any thought on my part, as if someone else had spoken them into being.

My head popped up like it was on a spring. My eyes flew open and moved around the ring of faces, starting with Tessa and ending with Ivy.

"Ladies? What are you doing next weekend?"

47
Tessa

The greenhouse Lee built this winter is nothing fancy—just thick opaque plastic sheeting stretched over a wooden frame—but it has served its purpose, giving us a small crop of early strawberries that brought premium prices, and now letting us get a jump on tomato season as well. We moved the berries out of the greenhouse and planted them in the garden a couple of days ago, and today we're moving the tomato seedlings out from under the grow lamps in the cellar to the unheated greenhouse to harden off before planting.

"Why so many?" I asked as I ducked my head to make it in through the greenhouse's low door and then set a tray of seedlings down next to Spitz, who was curled up on the floor. She opened one eye to see what was going on and then went back to her nap. "You must have three hundred tomato plants here."

Lee was on his knees, scooting the plastic pots together into more or less orderly rows. "Three fifty," he said. "I'm going to sell a hundred and fifty plants at the farmers' market, three dollars each, then plant the rest."

I knelt down on the opposite end of the greenhouse and started organizing the plants like Lee was, being careful to keep each variety in its own group and leaving a walkway in the center. It really is amazing how many tomato plants you can fit into a ten- by twelve-foot space.

"How many pounds of tomatoes will you get from each plant?"

"Depends," Lee said. "Could be five, could be twenty-five. I wish I'd done more. Next year I'm going to expand the greenhouse. The restaurant business has come on so strong, I bet I could have used five hundred plants this year."

"Or more," I said as I unloaded another tray of seedlings.

Lee shook his head. "No, that's about as many as I'd want to do. Best to keep things small. I'm looking to do three things: support us decently, provide quality products to our customers, and enjoy doing it. That's all. I didn't escape the corporate rat race just to enter an agricultural rat race."

"Sounds like a smart plan." I sat back on my knees and breathed in the scent of rich, loamy earth, taking a moment to enjoy the sea of green surrounding me and the feathery leaves of the tomato vines, most already flowering, many already sporting tiny green globes.

"You know, I don't miss the shop as much as I thought I would. It wasn't that different from being tied to my desk back in Massachusetts. I like having control over my own schedule and more variety in my work. Working at the inn is fun, but I wouldn't want to do it full-time, and helping you is fun, too, but I wouldn't want to spend forty hours a week planting tomatoes," I said, grimacing as I circled my shoulders to work the kinks out of my back.

Lee got to his feet and, after dusting his hands off on his jeans, came up behind me and started to massage my neck. "Well, I appreciate your help. It was lonely around here before. Nice to have some company." He bent down and kissed the top of my head. "Better?"

I nodded. "Thanks, babe."

"My pleasure." Lee got on his knees next to me and helped me finish the job.

"Hey, are you sure you'll be okay on your own this weekend? There's such a lot to do right now. If you need me here, I can bow out. Madelyn would understand."

"And have you miss the greatest girls' weekend

ever? Complete with luxury accommodations at New Bern's most elegant inn and quilting instruction from a real live television star? Uh-uh," Lee said with a grin. "Nothing doing. That's the kind of sacrifice a guy can spend the next ten years paying back."

I elbowed him good-naturedly. "Very funny. Seriously. If you need help . . ."

"I'll be fine. It's just for two nights. Besides, I've got it covered. Since Madelyn is going to be busy, too, Jake and I decided to retaliate and have our own weekend here. Of course, we'll be picking strawberries and milking cows instead of making quilts, but I imagine there will be a little cigar smoking going on too. . . ."

"Not inside my house, there better not be."

Lee rolled his eyes. "No, not in the house. That's why I put those chairs out on the porch. Charlie is coming over, too, on Saturday night, and he's bringing Abigail's husband."

"Franklin Spaulding?"

"Yeah, and Evelyn's son, Garrett. We're going to make chili and play poker."

"Oh, good. That sounds like fun." I smiled as I bent over my work. It was nice to hear that, like me, Lee was finally making friends. Knowing he'd be occupied over the weekend made me feel less guilty about leaving him on his own.

"So, how are the plans coming for the big quilt retreat?" he asked.

"Good. Does it sound silly if I say I'm kind of proud of Madelyn? I mean, here she's faced with this big disappointment with the wedding being canceled, and instead of feeling sorry for herself, she decides to turn the situation on its head and use it to do something nice for others. I don't think she'd have thought of that six months ago, do you? She's invited Ivy and all the women in her GED prep class, plus Connie and Bella, the teachers, and everyone in the quilt circle. Wasn't that generous of her? An all-expense-paid weekend of quilting, complete with food and . . ."

"A bag of luxurious herbal goodies from you," Lee added.

"Oh, but that's nothing." I sat up to wipe my brow with the back of my hand. "I had stock left over from the store. I might as well put it to good use."

"It was still nice of you."

I shrugged. "Anyway, everybody is very excited about the quilt retreat. Of course, Evelyn's friend from Texas, Mary Dell, has something to do with that. A couple of the women from the shelter were on the fence at first. Some of them have little kids and were worried about finding sitters, but once they heard that Mary Dell was going to be the teacher for the weekend, they all said they'd figure out something."

"I'll bet." Lee laughed. "It's not every day you

get to go on a quilt weekend with a celebrity. I bet they're all starstruck."

"I am, too, a little. I hope I don't say something stupid when I meet her."

"You won't," Lee assured me. "She's just a person. Puts her pants on one leg at a time and has to rip out seams now and then, just like everybody else."

I nodded and told myself that what Lee said was undoubtedly true. "Evelyn says she's very down-to-earth. I'm sure we'll have fun. We've just got one problem—not quite enough room at the inn. There are fifteen women coming, but Madelyn only has five rooms with capacity for twelve guests total, and we can only squeeze in that many by bringing rollaway beds into the larger rooms. I'm not sure where we're going to put everybody," I said as I lined up the last tomato plant in the last row and then stacked up the empty trays in the corner.

Lee got to his feet and then reached down to help me up. "Five rooms? I thought there were six."

I groaned as I got up—all that bending over hurts my back. "Nope, just five. Madelyn has *plans* to create a sixth room up in the attic, actually a suite. There's plenty of room. But she doesn't have the money to do it right now. Even if she did, there's no time to do it before Friday night."

Lee narrowed his eyes and sucked on his teeth, the way he did when he was thinking. "What's she got up there in the attic anyway?"

"Right now? A bunch of junk." I stopped myself, grinned. "No, wait a minute. I meant a bunch of treasures. To you and me and anybody else, it'd be junk. But to Madelyn, every rusty bedstead, every broken lamp, every bookend that's lost its mate is a potential treasure. She'll figure out a way to put all that stuff to good use— one of these days. But at the moment, it's just taking up space. Good thing she's got so much storage. You know . . ."

Lee nodded quickly as I spoke, the way he does when he's trying to be polite but is really hoping I'll cut to the chase. "Yeah, yeah, but is it full as in there's no room to move? Or full as in there's just a lot of stuff lying around?"

"Just a lot of stuff lying around. Why do you ask?" He ignored my question and volleyed off more of his own. I was starting to feel like I was on some sort of quiz show.

"Is there lighting up there? What about outlets? How low are the ceilings?"

I closed my eyes, trying to picture the attic. "There's a light, an overhead bulb in the middle of the room. And there's some natural light that comes in from the side windows. I don't know about outlets. The ceilings are low on the sides, but there's plenty of room to walk around."

"Huh. That just might work. Better talk to Jake and see what he thinks." Without explaining further, Lee opened the door to the greenhouse and strode across the grass toward the house.

Sensing his absence, Spitz opened her eyes and got to her feet, looking at me for an explanation.

"Your guess is as good as mine. But I guess we'd better go see what he's up to."

I patted my leg and Spitz fell in beside me, casting a longing glance at the goat pen as we passed the barnyard and went inside.

Three hours later, I was standing on a ladder, hammering long lengths of muslin, painter's canvas from Jake's store, onto the attic beams of the Beecher Cottage Inn so they hung about eight feet from the floor. Madelyn stood at the bottom of the ladder, supporting the weight of the still-unattached canvas with one arm and handing me gold upholstery tacks with the other. Ivy was there, too, with her little girl, Bethany, who was about nine years old and absolutely precious. They were sweeping the floor, Ivy handling the broom while Bethany held the dustpan. Lee and Jake were busy carting off the furniture, boxes, and miscellaneous junk that wouldn't be needed for our current project and stowing it behind the newly constructed canvas walls, where the ceiling was too low to walk upright.

"Lee," Madelyn called out as my darling husband walked past carrying three cardboard boxes, "you're a genius! The light color of the canvas makes the whole room look brighter."

"It does look pretty good," Lee said in a muffled voice. His mouth was hidden behind the stack of boxes and only his eyes and forehead peeked out over the top. "Anyway, it'll do in a pinch, until you've got time and money to put up real walls."

"Well, I like the effect so much I'm thinking that even when we do get real walls, I might hang canvas curtains over all of them. It just creates such a nice, modern background for all these antiques. Very eclectic. I'm telling you, Lee. If you ever decide to give up farming, you could make big money as an interior designer."

Lee didn't say anything to that, just laughed from behind the canvas wall where he was stowing the boxes. Jake came out from an opening between the canvas, holding strings of little white Christmas lights in his hands.

"Look what I found," he said. "We could string them down the center beam."

Madelyn frowned. "And plug them in where? I don't want to overload our one sad little light fixture."

"I found two outlets, one on each wall. They were hidden behind some cartons. I took a good look at the wiring. It's sound. It'll easily handle these. It's not a permanent solution, but it'll do through the weekend."

"I think they'll look nice," Bethany piped up. "Pretty. Like Christmas."

Madelyn smiled at the little girl. "I think you're right. Let's give it a try."

The lights did look pretty; so did the rest of the room.

When we were finished, Ivy stood gazing at the three iron bedsteads (Madelyn had sanded the rust off and spray-painted them white)—a double with a twin on each side, lined up in front of the muslin wall and sitting atop a multicolored braided rug that we'd found rolled up in a corner. The beds were made up with white sheets and blankets, with a quilt lying across the foot. The quilts were torn and worn in spots but when they were folded properly, you couldn't see that. A trunk sat at the end of each bedstead and there were small tables sitting between the beds, to give the occupants a place to lay a book or a pair of reading glasses.

"It looks like a dormitory," Ivy said. "An attic dormitory in a girls' school. Like in *A Little Princess*."

"Or Jo's room in *Little Women*," Bethany added. "That's my favorite book."

"Have you already read *Little Women*?" Madelyn asked. "You're a clever girl."

Bethany smiled. "Mommy read it to me. We read together every night."

"Ah, I see. Then I guess your mommy is a clever girl too." Madelyn smiled at Ivy, who blushed.

"We'll see about that in a few days, won't we? I wish I knew if I passed the exam or not. It feels funny, you giving a weekend to celebrate us getting our diplomas when we don't even know if we passed yet."

"We're not celebrating your exam," I said. "We're celebrating *you* and all those other gals, and the fact that you're working so hard and being such great examples to your children."

"And to all of us." Madelyn looked down at Bethany. "Aren't you proud of your mommy?"

Bethany nodded soberly before asking her mother, "Can't I come to the party too? You said it was a girls' weekend. I'm a girl. And I know how to quilt too. I'm a very good quilter."

Ivy ruffled her hair. "I know, but this weekend is just for grownup girls. Besides, where would you sleep? All the beds are full."

"Not quite," Madelyn said. "If you slept up here, Tessa and I could take the twin beds and you could have the double—you and Miss Bethany. That is, if you don't mind sharing."

Bethany looked up at her mother, eyes wide with hope, clasping her hands together under her chin like a cherub at prayer.

Ivy looked at Madelyn doubtfully. "Are you sure you wouldn't mind?"

"Mind? I'd love it. She must come. I insist."

Ivy looked at her daughter and said, "I guess that settles it. You can come." Bethany whooped with excitement and galloped around from one end of the room to the other like a frisky colt.

Ivy laughed and called to her, "All right, Bethany. Calm down and get your coat. We've got to run by the market before we pick your brother up from soccer. Come on."

Bethany found her coat and followed her mother down the stairs, stopping to wave at Madelyn before she left. "See you on Friday!"

"See you on Friday, darling!" After they'd gone, Madelyn turned to the rest of us. "Oh, isn't she just the sweetest little thing? I've heard that Abigail and Franklin are sort of surrogate grandparents to Ivy's children, but do you think they'd mind sharing the title?"

"Why not?" Jake said. "But I didn't know you liked children so much."

"Neither did I," Madelyn replied. "But then, I've never spent much time with children. I sure like that one.

"Thank you, Lee, for coming up with the dorm idea. There'd be no way we could have found room for Bethany otherwise. And thank *you* too," she said, looking at me and then Jake, letting her eyes linger on his face in a way that made me wonder if her feelings for Jake were quite as platonic as she claimed. I knew she said she'd never love again and I understood why, but never is a very long time and Jake was a very special, and very patient, man.

"Everything looks wonderful. I can't wait until Friday!" She clapped her hands together under her chin, looking almost as excited as little Bethany.

"Glad it worked out," Lee said. "It's the least we can do after you helped get my microgreen business running. That little idea just about saved our skin. Is there anything else we need to do up here? I've got to get back to the farm and take care of the stock."

"And we've got to clean up and get over to the sushi place," Jake said, nodding to Madelyn. "I don't want them giving our table away."

Madelyn turned in a circle, looking the room over with an appraising eye. "I think we're all set . . . except for . . . Oh, never mind. It looks great. I don't want to keep you."

"What is it?" Lee asked. "We've got a little time yet."

"Well," Madelyn replied apologetically, "it's just that there's no place to hang up clothes. We don't need a lot of hanger space but . . . maybe I could rig up a dowel on wires and hang it behind the curtain."

"Why not just use that armoire that I saw under the back gable, that big mahogany piece? Lee and I can move it over there by the end wall, right under the window."

"Are you sure?" Madelyn asked innocently. "It's so heavy. I wouldn't want you two to hurt yourselves."

Lee and Jake exchanged glances, their expressions half insulted, half disbelieving that she could so doubt their strength. Lee hooked his thumbs in his belt. "Step aside, ladies. My partner and I will have this done in no time."

They marched off toward the back gable. Madelyn looked at me and winked.

"Oh, you are bad," I whispered out the side of my mouth. "You played them like a couple of cheap violins."

She looked at me, eyebrows raised. "Well, I had to. We couldn't move that thing. It weighs a ton. Besides, look how cute they are together. They're practically preening, they're so proud of themselves. Any second now they'll flap their wings and start to crow."

"If they don't give themselves a hernia first," I said.

Judging from the grunting sounds they were making as they tried to move that monster, I started to think it might not be a joke after all. After a couple of attempts that moved the armoire only inches, Madelyn and I joined in, but it was still slow going.

"Hang on," Jake said, holding up his hand and panting. "I think there's something inside there." He wiped sweat off his forehead.

"There can't be," Madelyn protested. "I've gone through everything up here, opened every cabinet, drawer, and box." She stopped herself, putting a finger against her lips. "Oh, wait a minute. Except this one. The door was stuck."

Madelyn shrugged sheepishly. Jake let out a little growl before pulling out a pocketknife and using one of the blades to pry open the door of the armoire.

Inside, we found a box with a complete tea service for twelve, a long silver barbell and a box of weights to go with it, and a pile of heavy wool blankets that, when pulled back, revealed something I'd never thought I'd see again.

"Oh, my gosh," I said, turning to look at Madelyn, who was standing with her hand to her mouth, fingers splayed out over her lips. "Will you look at that?"

"The dollhouse," she breathed. "Our dollhouse."

48
Madelyn

It was Friday, hours before the guests were due to arrive for the weekend. Tessa and I had been cooking all morning making muffins for tomorrow's breakfast, and two enormous lasagnas for Saturday dinner, and washing and chopping vegetables for salads. Tonight's dinner, a big pot of chicken noodle soup, was simmering on the stove. Now we were getting ready to fill gift bags with goodies that Evelyn had sent over from the quilt shop—a pink tape measure, a spool of thread, and six-packs of fat quarters in a variety of colors—and all kinds of treats that Tessa had donated from the leftover stock from For the Love of Lavender—citrus shampoo and soap, lavender hand cream and body lotion, and the little quilted drawer sachets we'd made together, one for each guest.

"This is quite a haul," Tessa said as she lined the bags with lavender- and sage-colored tissue paper while I cut lengths of raffia for bows. "It's almost like Christmas."

"We've got sixteen bags, right? We can't forget Bethany."

Tessa's eyes circled the table and her lips moved as she mentally counted the empty bags. She shook her head. "Fifteen. We're short one. That's okay. Bethany can have mine."

"No, she can have mine." Tessa gave me a look, that stubborn one she has when she's about to argue with me. "Okay, how about this? We'll share a bag. You're already up to your ears in herbal goodies, so I'll take the soap and lotion and such, and you take the quilting notions. I'm sure not going to use them. Deal?"

"Deal." Tessa smiled. "You really like Bethany, don't you? Did you ever want children of your own?"

I hesitated. With anyone else, I'd have been embarrassed to admit the truth—it sounded so selfish, so unnatural—but this was Tessa. I knew she didn't judge me.

"Not really. I just never wanted the responsibility. Does that make me sound awful? And Sterling had very definite opinions on the subject. It's probably just as well; we'd have made terrible parents. But Bethany is a sweetheart. Ivy brought her over yesterday afternoon. She was in rapture over the dollhouse," I said, tilting my head in the direction of the living room, where we'd set the dollhouse up on a table in back of the sofa.

Tessa smiled. "Well, why not? We were when we were her age. It's a shame all the furniture was missing."

"I know, but I still have that sofa I bought at the church fair. Now I have someplace to put it—"

The phone rang, interrupting my thought. Angela was on the line.

"I'm so sorry about the wedding being canceled after you went to so much trouble."

"Don't worry about that. How is Kerry doing?"

"She's pretty broken up. I gave her some time off. She went out to see her parents for a few days."

"That's good. Poor thing, but better she found out now than later."

"That's what I told her. But I do feel badly

about canceling on you. You can keep my deposits," she said in a tone I supposed was meant to sound magnanimous. "So you shouldn't be out too much. I wish I could afford to just pay you for everything, but now that I'm on my own and with the baby coming . . ."

And only twenty-five million to your name . . .

The words almost bubbled up from my mind to my lips, but I stopped myself. I was the last person who could afford to throw stones. In Angela's world, that world and mind-set that I had inhabited myself not so long ago, twenty-five million wasn't enough. In that world, there was no such thing as enough.

"I've got to preserve my capital. You understand, don't you, Madelyn?"

"I understand, Angela. Don't worry about it. Anyway, we're putting our unexpectedly vacant rooms to good use."

I told her all about our plans for the quilt retreat, about Ivy and all her friends from New Beginnings who were trying to get their high school diplomas, about Bella and Connie and how they'd volunteered their time to teach them, about Evelyn and Mary Dell, who were volunteering their goods and time to make the weekend a success.

"Madelyn! What a wonderful story. Have you called anyone about it?"

"Called anyone?"

"Magazines, television stations. This is a great human interest story—very heartwarming. And since you're a celebrity . . ."

"Angela, I'm hardly a celebrity. Just someone who married a very rich man and lived to regret it."

"A rich and *famous* man," she corrected me. "And whether you like it or not, that fame spills over to you. Madelyn, I've started seeing someone. He's a senior producer at *Good Morning America*. I think he'd jump all over this. Let me call him."

"Oh, I don't know, Angela. . . ."

"What's to know? Just the other night Steve was telling me how hard it's been for them to come up with upbeat stories these days. *GMA* is all about happy endings, but these days, it's hard to find many."

"But I wasn't looking to generate publicity here, just do a little bit of good for a town that's been good to me."

"Think, Madelyn. One good story on *GMA*, seen by millions and millions of people, and you'd not only rehabilitate your damaged reputation, you'd get more free advertising for your inn than you could buy in a lifetime. You'd be booked solid for the next year. You're trying to do something to benefit mankind, fine. Very generous. But why shouldn't *you* benefit from your generosity too? That's the way things work, Madelyn. What could it hurt?"

She had a point. A story about my altruism on *Good Morning America* would show the world that I wasn't the heartless witch that the tabloids had made me out to be. That would be nice, but I was more intrigued by the positive publicity a warm, fuzzy television report would generate. Maybe my hunch had been right after all! Forget the wedding; maybe this was the reason I'd felt such an urge, spent money I didn't have, to make sure the inn looked its best. A picture is worth a thousand words. Millions of people would see Beecher Cottage Inn and think, "That looks like a great spot to celebrate our anniversary, birthday, wedding, honeymoon." My financial worries would finally be behind me! And it wouldn't just be me who would benefit, of course. I'd be sure to tell the television people about Cobbled Court Quilts, too. And they'd undoubtedly want background shots of New Bern and that would bring in more tourists, more business, more money. Everyone would win. I had to take advantage of this opportunity not just for myself, but for the town. It'd be selfish not to.

"And you're sure they'd be interested?" I asked.

"Absolutely! I'll call Steve right now. Steve Straub. Don't go anywhere. I'm sure he'll call you right away. Fingers crossed."

"Thank you, Angela. I really appreciate this."

"I'm happy to do it, Madelyn. You've always been so nice to me."

When I hung up the phone, my hands were actually shaking. I was that excited.

"Did you hear that?" I asked Tessa.

She stuffed a piece of tissue paper into the mouth of a gift bag with such force that it tore. "I heard."

Disapproval was written on every line of her face, and, I had noticed, when Tessa disapproved of something, the number of those lines increased significantly.

"What?" I spread out my hands, confused by her response. "Angela has a friend at *Good Morning America*. She thinks he'll be interested in sending a camera crew out here to do a story on our quilt retreat. This is *good* news. And good publicity, for the inn, for New Bern, for the quilt shop. . . ."

She wouldn't look at me, just kept stuffing tissue into the bags as if she had something personal against them.

"Good publicity for New Beginnings too."

Tessa's head popped up like it was on a spring. "Good publicity for Ivy? And Dana? And all the other women in their class?"

Clearly I had pressed some sort of hot button, but I still didn't understand how. "Well . . . I guess. Tessa, if you're worried that they might portray the girls in a negative light, don't be. Angela told me that they're looking for happy endings. This would be a 'feel good' story."

"I don't care if they crown them all Mothers of the Year and get them a spot on *Oprah*! There is no such thing as 'good' publicity for these women! Don't you get it? Don't you ever listen?"

"Hey!" I shot back, blindsided by Tessa's ire and furious at being scolded like some irresponsible adolescent. "I don't recall asking for your opinion."

"Too bad! When a friend sees you about to do something dumb, something that will hurt you and others, they get to speak up anytime they want to. Somebody who only tells you what you want to hear isn't a friend, Madelyn. Don't you remember what happened to Ivy when she accidentally stepped into a background shot on Mary Dell's television show? Somebody saw her, told her husband about it, and he tracked her down and attacked her!"

I blanched, remembering Ivy's left hand, the jagged white scars on her knuckles, the way her fingers refused to straighten completely. She'd told me about her husband, her flight from abuse, about unknowingly walking through the background when Mary Dell filmed a video at the quilt shop; about how her husband found her, threatened to take her children, and her life, had slammed the car door on her hand while she screamed in agony, and how much worse it would have been had not Evelyn, Margot, Abigail, and Liza arrived on the scene and fought him off.

How had I not remembered that? How could I have forgotten that story, the history that had drawn me to Ivy on that first day we met at For the Love of Lavender, the testimony of her courage in the face of dangers and hardships that far outweighed my own and made me curious about the women who had come to her aid, curious enough to allow Tessa to drag me into the quilt shop for a five-minute visit that stretched to half an hour, because I had to see for myself if people like that existed, people who'd put themselves out and even into harm's way to protect one of their own? How could I?

How could I? By thinking only of myself, that's how. By becoming so focused on my desires, my lacks, my quest for more, my "needs," needs that didn't even come close to meeting that description, that I never stopped to think how my actions might affect others. By listening to the voices, internal and external, saying, "Everyone does it," and "What can it hurt," and "That's the way things work," by convincing myself of the lies.

Even at the end, even in his prison cell, Sterling clung to the lie that he'd done nothing wrong, that he'd "made millions for his clients." Even with twenty-five million dollars and a paid-for penthouse, Angela had convinced herself that she was just scraping by, that generosity was a luxury beyond her means. Even with a house all mine, left unwillingly to undeserving me, a house with fresh paint on the walls and new shingles on the roof, a reservation book that showed every sign of breaking even my first summer in business, when I'd heard that silken rhetoric, the voice of seduction asking why I shouldn't benefit from my own generosity, I'd been quick to take the bait, to wrap my arms around the generosity that isn't generous at all.

"That's the way things work," or so the story goes. And that's true, if we allow it to be. But the needle is narrow, so narrow. A small shift to the left, a little lean to the right, and you'll swing wide and miss the mark without even knowing it, so distracted by lies that you don't recognize the truth—not unless you have someone to shout down the voices, to tell you the truths you need to hear, whether you want to hear them or not. Not unless you have a Tessa, a friend.

What was I thinking? What's wrong with me?

I must have said that last thought out loud because in a moment, Tessa was at my side with her arm over my shoulder.

"Nothing, Madelyn. Nothing. You're all right. I shouldn't have jumped on you like that. I just . . ." She shrugged, as though admitting the inexcusability of her actions. "I should have engaged my brain before opening my mouth. I should have realized that you'd never purposely put someone else at risk for your own gain. I know you too well to think you'd be capable of something like that."

I closed my eyes for a moment, unwilling to let her go on. "No, you were right to call me out. I'm glad you did. You know what I think? I think *everyone* is capable of something like that. You can be my conscience any time, Tessa, because mine has clearly atrophied from lack of use. But, next time," I said, wincing a little at the memory, "maybe straighten me out without raising your voice? I just can't take it, especially from you. The last time you yelled at me, I lost you for a long, long time." I laughed, not because I found this funny, but because the sudden film of tears that blurred my eyes made me feel silly. "I don't even like to think about that happening again."

She laughed at her own tears, swiped them away, too, and squeezed my shoulder. "You don't have to worry about that, Madelyn. We may disagree sometimes. We may argue. Once in a while, we may even yell at each other. But you're not losing me, my friend, not ever again. That's the deal. And anybody who doesn't like it? Well, you know the rest."

When Steve Straub called from *Good Morning America*, I said thanks but no thanks to his offer to send a film crew to New Bern. Ours was a private party.

49
Madelyn

Even after we'd moved the furniture out to the garage (excepting the dollhouse, which we moved near the front window), we still couldn't fit eight eight-foot tables in the living room, so we tucked one in the foyer and one under the stairs. We had four ironing boards, three in the living room and one in the foyer, and a portable "design wall" (really just a white flannel sheet stretched and hammered into place on a wooden frame) in the dining room. Orange, black, and white extension cords were plugged into every available outlet, snaking along the floors to provide electricity for the irons and sewing machines. When we were done setting up, Tessa and I stood at the doorway between the living room and foyer and surveyed the scene.

"It looks so crowded," I said.

"Because it is," Tessa replied.

"Can't we get rid of one of the tables? After all, I'm not going to be sewing."

"It's two quilters to a table. We need just as many for fifteen as sixteen. Besides, you might change your mind."

"I'm going to be too busy taking care of the guests, making meals, cleaning rooms, that sort of thing." This was true, but it was also a convenient excuse and Tessa knew it. But she also knew when to back off.

"Well. All right," she said reluctantly, "but in case you change your mind, I've set up your sewing machine at the table under the stairs. You're sharing with Mary Dell."

"I'm not going to change my mind. Look, Tessa, I like hanging out with the quilters, but I have no desire to quilt and I never will. Why can't we all just be good with that?"

"Never is a long time. I'm just saying."

I rolled my eyes. "Tessa, were you this much of a nag when we were kids? Why does Lee put up with you?"

"I don't know," she said, grinning. "Maybe he's blinded by lust?"

The doorbell rang. I made a gagging face and went to answer it. "Oh, ick. You've been married for a million years. Shouldn't you two be over that kind of thing by now?"

I opened the door and found my porch crowded with laughing and chattering women carrying suitcases, project bags, and, in some instances, sewing machines, with more streaming up the walkway behind them. I greeted the ones I knew: Margot, Virginia, Abigail—whose luggage was Vuitton, the same style as the pieces I'd sold to pay for the plumbing—Bella, Connie, Dana, Ivy, and, of course, Bethany—who proudly showed off her "Disney Princess" roller-board suitcase, purchased for the occasion—and introduced myself to the ones I didn't, the other students from the GED program, Melissa, Cathy, Lauren, and Antoinette.

I directed everyone to leave their suitcases in the foyer for now, then find the sewing station with their name on it and set up their machine if they'd brought their own before following Tessa into the dining room for tea and cookies and a quick orientation before we handed out keys and roommate assignments.

The last one through the door was Mary Dell. Even if I hadn't seen her on television, I'd have recognized her immediately. One look and you knew she wasn't raised in New England. Her smile was nearly as big as her earrings, her lipstick was the color of a candied apple, her hair was bleached a shade of blond that would have done Marilyn Monroe proud, and her outfit? I'd never seen anything quite like it.

Evelyn had said that Mary Dell liked animal prints. I like them too. I have a pair of leopard pumps and a faux cheetah belt that I just love. But when I do wear one of those items, I make sure that everything else I'm wearing is as plain as possible, a monochromatic outfit in a neutral color: black, cream, perhaps brown. Or, if I'm looking for a casual but fun look, a pair of jeans and a plain white blouse, something simple.

Otherwise, you run the risk of appearing to be "open for business," as Edna would have put it.

Mary Dell, who apparently had not heard or did not subscribe to the "less is more" rule of fashion, was wearing alligator shoes and a belt in two completely different shades of brown, leopard-print jeans, and a tight zebra-striped shirt with a black collar and cuffs embellished by three rows of rhinestones along the edge. She carried a pink cheetah-print project bag with her name emblazoned on the side, also in rhinestones. The woman was a walking menagerie.

I stood at the door, open-mouthed and completely at a loss for words. But that didn't matter. Mary Dell had no problem filling the silence.

"Well! Look at you!" she hooted as she mounted the porch steps. "You must be Madelyn. I'd have known you anywhere. Evelyn said you were as pretty as a picture and had more curves than a Coke bottle. She wasn't exaggerating, was she?

"Tell you what, I'm glad Hub-Jay decided to take Howard off for a boys' weekend in San Antonio instead of coming out here with me. I just might have had to put a brand on that steer to make sure he didn't stray. You're sure a looker!" she exclaimed as she crossed over the threshold and dropped her bag on the floor and took a look around.

"My! Your place is just as pretty as you are. This is nice, real nice. You know, my Hub-Jay is an innkeeper too. He owns the Hollander Hotels. I don't know if you've heard of them?"

The Hollander Hotels? Indeed I had heard of them. It was a small chain that bought up old buildings in downtown areas and refurbished them into beautiful little boutique hotels. Most of their properties were in the Southwest, places like Dallas, San Antonio, Santa Fe, Oklahoma City, and Tulsa, but they'd recently opened a hotel in New York and another in Boston, to favorable reviews.

Hubble James Hollander was *that* Hollander? The one whose hotels had a reputation for excellent service and understated elegance? And he was dating Mary Dell?

Mary Dell looked at me expectantly. When I failed to answer her question she said, "Oh my goodness, where are my manners? I didn't even introduce myself, did I? I'm Mary Dell Templeton."

"Yes. I'm Madelyn Beecher. It's nice to meet you." I stuck out my hand for her to shake, but she ignored that and wrapped her arms around me in a hug that was not quite bone-crushing, but nearly. Mary Dell hugged like she meant it.

"It's nice to meet you, too, darlin'! Evelyn's told me so much about you. I feel like I know you already. You're just so sweet to invite all these gals to stay. We're going to have ourselves a time! Aren't we?"

"Yes," I replied, though I'd already picked up on the fact that most of Mary Dell's questions didn't actually require answers. She used them more as a means of conferring affirmation than seeking information.

I liked her. I don't know that I'd ever encountered anyone with such enthusiasm or energy, and as the weekend went on, I saw that it was entirely genuine. There's something very attractive about that. It helped, too, that I knew her story, how her husband had deserted her upon the birth of their son, Howard, and how Mary Dell had soldiered on alone to raise a child with special needs, eking out a living as a quilt teacher. Mary Dell was optimistic, not because she didn't know hardship but because she had overcome it. Oh, yes. In spite of the fact that any room she was in seemed a little short on oxygen, I liked Mary Dell Templeton. It was impossible not to.

"It was awfully kind of you to volunteer to teach this weekend, especially since you're on your vacation."

"Oh, it's my pleasure," she said sincerely. "These days, Howard and I are so busy with the TV show that I don't get much chance to teach. I miss it."

"Well, everyone is very excited that you're here."

"And I'm excited too. Now, Madelyn, honey,"

463

she said in a more serious tone, "do you have anything to drink? I'm dying for a Dr Pepper. I'm so dry I'm spitting cotton."

"We're just about to serve tea in the dining room."

"Tea?" she said, briefly lifting her eyebrows to a skeptical arc. "Well . . . sure. All right. Tea will do just fine for now."

Some of the ladies knew one another well and some were meeting for the first time, but they seemed to find an almost instant bond, the way I've noticed quilters do. It's interesting.

After tea and introductions, everyone went to get settled in their rooms and then came back downstairs to start quilting. The weekend's project was a wall hanging based on a variation of the card tricks block. An original design by Mary Dell, the "Texas Hold 'Em" pattern would appear in her next book. The ladies were thrilled to be among the first to make it.

While everyone else got to work cutting out their fabric, I cleared away the tea things and then got to work on dinner. Tessa came in a couple of times, wanting to help, but I shooed her out of the kitchen, reminding her that the weekend was my gift to her as well.

"Are you sure you're all right in here?" she asked. "You look like something's bothering you."

"I'm fine. If I look bothered it's only because standing here talking to you is throwing off my schedule. Now, scoot!"

She did, and I went back to my work, setting the table, warming up the soup, dressing the salad, preparing and baking big loaves of garlic bread, opening the wine, and making pots of coffee and fixing platters of brownies to serve for dessert. While I worked, I could hear the sound of conversation and laughter, sometimes gales of it, rising above the whir of sewing machines. I was glad they were enjoying themselves, but in spite of what I'd said to Tessa, I'd admit to feeling a little melancholy, or maybe just introspective. I'm not sure why.

After serving dinner—which seemed much appreciated; I bet they all thanked me ten times each—and cleaning up the kitchen, I went into the living room for a while to chat and see how their projects were coming. But when Bethany started to yawn around nine o'clock, I volunteered to take her up to the attic and put her to bed so that Ivy could keep quilting.

"Are you sure you don't mind?" Ivy asked.

"Not at all. I'm tired too. I was going up soon anyhow. You all stay up as late as you want; just make sure to turn out the lights before you go to bed. Breakfast is at eight. See you all in the morning."

I showed Bethany where the bathroom was and,

after she was washed and had her pajamas on, I tucked her into bed and read a chapter of *Little Women* to her. It was her fourth time reading it. At certain passages, I noticed that her lips moved silently as I read, echoing the dialogue between the March sisters. At the end of the chapter, she snuggled down under the quilts and yawned. I sat on the edge of my bed, took off my slippers, and hung my robe on the bedpost.

"It'd be nice to have a lot of sisters," Bethany said in a drowsy voice. "I have a little brother, Bobby, but that's not the same. Do you have any sisters?"

"I'm an only child. No brothers or sisters."

"I've got a best friend, Erica. She's almost like a sister. Do you have a best friend?"

"Yes," I said as I slipped in between the sheets and pulled up the quilt. "Tessa is my best friend and she's practically like a sister. I've known her since I was about your age." I reached over to turn out the lamp and found a little hand clutching at my wrist.

"Madelyn? Could you leave the light on until I'm asleep? It's nice up here in the attic but it's kind of scary too. It seems like there might be ghosts up here."

I got up and flipped the switch to illuminate the string of white Christmas lights, thinking that they'd be dimmer, before getting back into bed and turning off the lamp.

"Those are nice," Bethany said, looking up at the ceiling. "They look like stars. Good night, Madelyn."

"Good night, Bethany. Sweet dreams."

She was asleep within minutes. I was tired too, but sleep eluded me. I stayed awake for a long time, staring at the ceiling, listening to Bethany's breathing, the soft laughter that emanated from the floors below, and the voices of ghosts.

When we sat down to our breakfast of homemade muffins and fruit the next morning, I learned that about half the group, Mary Dell included, had stayed up and quilted until long past midnight. Mary Dell looked as fresh as a daisy, but some of the others were definitely dragging. Still, that didn't deter them from doing the same thing on Saturday night. I guess they wanted to squeeze every last drop of fun, companionship, and quilting from the weekend. And they seemed to do just that.

The only somber moment came when Janelle, a counselor at New Beginnings, called to say that the results of the GED exams had arrived. Everyone passed, everyone except Ivy. She had gotten excellent scores overall but was two points short of the minimum score needed to pass the science test. When she heard the news, she sat down in a chair and burst into tears. Bella,

Connie, and her classmates immediately surrounded her, murmuring sympathetically and patting her shoulders.

"I'm so sorry. You worked so hard," she sobbed, looking up at her teachers, "and I let you down."

Ivy's eyes were streaming and her nose was running. Dana fished a tissue out of her pocket and handed it to her friend, looking as though she might start crying herself. Lauren ran into the kitchen to get her a glass of water.

"Don't be silly," Bella said. "You didn't let anyone down. You'll pass next time."

"There's not going to be a next time. What's the point? All that stuff about atoms and photosynthesis and whatnot. I don't get it. I'll never get it. I'm too stupid to understand."

Connie got down on her knees, eye level with Ivy, and looked her in the face. "No, you're not. Remember, Ivy, the rest of the girls had taken some science classes before they dropped out, so this was review for them, but it was all new material to you. You've come so far and learned so much. The progress you made in these past few weeks is amazing. I'm very proud of you. We all are. You'll pass next time. You're *not* stupid. The only stupid thing would be to give up after you've come so far. That'd be more than stupid, it would be tragic. You can do this, Ivy. I know you can."

Bethany pushed her way through the circle of sympathy and looped her little arm around her mother's neck. Ivy looked up, her eyes still full of tears.

"Mommy, do you remember when I was trying to learn the multiplication tables and I kept failing the test because I couldn't get the eights and nines? And how mad I was because Mrs. Ramirez made me stay inside at recess to work on them? Remember what you said?"

Bethany began speaking and Ivy joined in, finishing the sentence with her little girl. "If at first you don't succeed, try, try again."

"That's right," Bethany said solemnly. "You can't give up now, Mommy. If you do, how can you help me with my science homework when I go to high school?"

Connie tilted her head to the side. "She's got a point there, Ivy."

"Yeah," Ivy said, sniffling and swiping her fist across her eyes. "I guess she does."

"I've got a chocolate cake out in the kitchen," I said. "I think we should have tea a little early today. Tessa, Margot, Abigail? Would you mind giving me a hand with the plates? We're having a party."

The weekend flew by; I've never known forty-eight hours to pass so quickly. Tessa had insisted on setting up my sewing machine at that table under the stairs, but I never did any quilting and, as near as I could tell, neither did Mary Dell. With fourteen quilters to help, she spent all her time going from table to table, offering encouragement and advice. Though I did spend some time hanging around the fringes, admiring the quilts-in-progress, listening to the jokes and stories, telling a few of my own, most of my weekend was spent making meals, doing dishes, and cleaning rooms, although the girls insisted on tidying up after themselves, reusing their towels and making their own beds, which I appreciated. Even so, it was a big job. But I didn't mind.

Mary Dell and I did have a few moments together, sitting at our table under the stairs, resting our feet.

"Tired?" Mary Dell asked.

I nodded. "A little bit. It's worth it, though. Everybody seems to be enjoying themselves."

"They sure are. Give a quilter a sewing machine, some fabric, and time to stitch it, and she's just as happy as a hog in mud. Madelyn, honey, you spend all this time with all these quilters, you've got an eye for color and fabric, and Tessa told me how good you are with embellishing—how come you've never tried it yourself?"

"I don't have time, Mary Dell. My plate is full as it is. Too—and don't say this to Evelyn, I wouldn't want to hurt her feelings—but I've never seen the point in buying fabric just to cut it apart and sew it back together." I smiled as I said this last bit, but Mary Dell didn't laugh, just looked at me with a soft smile.

Why did I know that she knew there was more to the story than I'd been telling? I took a deep breath.

"And, you know," I said with a shrug, "quilting just doesn't hold good memories for me. My grandmother was a quilter. She tried to teach me how to do it a couple of times. It never went well. I've never been much good at following directions or rules. I kept trying to take shortcuts, change patterns, invent my own blocks. That always made her so mad. One day, we were cutting out blocks—the old-fashioned way, back when you traced around templates, penciled in stitching lines, and then cut out each individual patch with a pair of scissors. Anyway, we were cutting out blocks and I wasn't doing it the way she wanted me to, so she reached across the table with a wooden ruler and smacked me so hard on the hand that it broke. I kind of lost interest after that," I said with a hollow laugh.

"If you think about it, it's kind of a miracle that I ever joined the quilt circle, even as the 'Louise.' Guess it goes to show what a great bunch of women we've got in there," I said, tilting my head toward the living room where most of the group was working.

Mary Dell smiled, not with her customary beaming grin, but with warmth. "Well, that all makes sense and I can see you've got your reasons. Tessa told me a little about your grandmama. Sounds like she was meaner than a whole skilletful of rattlesnakes. But let me ask you something: Just how long were you figuring to let Edna rob your joy? She's been dead for months, hasn't she?"

Before I could respond, Cathy's voice called from the living room, asking Mary Dell to come see why her points wouldn't meet up.

"Be right there!" she called back, then got slowly to her feet. "Maybe it's none of my business, honey, but if it were me, I'd tell that old rattlesnake to hush up and rest in peace."

She gave me a wink and headed to the living room to check on her other students.

By three o'clock on Sunday, everyone had finished their projects. The whole gang lined up on the front porch for a group photo, holding up their wall hangings as I called out, "Ready? Say 'fabric'!"

"Fabric!" they shouted and I snapped the picture. Everyone, including me, was smiling. After that, and over my protests, they all pitched in and helped me change sheets, take down the

472

sewing tables, run the vacuum, and dust the furniture from cellar to dome, leaving everything almost as clean as it was when they'd arrived. We'd have to move the furniture back in from the garage, but Jake and Lee were coming to help with that on Monday morning.

By five, I was standing in the foyer, giving out hugs and kisses, saying good-bye, thinking about doing it again next year.

Mary Dell was the last one out the door. Carrying her pink cheetah bag, she stopped to thank me, locked me in another all but bone-crushing hug, then shoved a pink gift bag tied with orange and blue ribbons into my hands, declaring it was just a little something, before clattering down the porch steps in a pair of zebra-striped platform heels and jumping into Evelyn's waiting car, waving and woo-hooing as they drove off. I stood on the porch and waved until they turned the corner at the top of Oak Leaf Lane, then sat in one of the rocking chairs to open my present.

I untied the bows from the gift bag and pulled out the tissue paper to reveal three pencils, a pad of graph paper, and two books, *Quilting Outside the Box* by Julie Lebreaux and *Scrappy and Happy: Design Your Own Paper-Pieced Quilt Blocks* by Mary Dell Templeton.

"Oh, Mary Dell. You just don't give up, do you?" I laughed and flipped through her book, glancing at the photographs of the different quilts, lingering over some of the more unique selections, until I found a note on the inside cover.

Dear Madelyn,

Thank you for your kind hospitality. You're the Hostess with the Mostess, ma'am. Soon, I'm sure everybody will know it.

In Stitches,

Mary Dell Templeton

P.S. There are more presents for you on the kitchen table. Hope you like them.

P.P.S. When you get a minute, can you send me the recipe for those peach muffins?

Curious, I put the gifts back in the bag and carried it with me into the kitchen, where I found a good-sized cardboard box tied with a bow, and a six-pack of Dr Pepper.

Inside the box were hundreds of fabric scraps in every color and shade imaginable—blue, yellow, red, pink, orange, peach, green, turquoise, brown, beige, purple, and everything in between. They were the scraps left over from the group's wall hangings.

Fifteen sets of scraps from fifteen different quilters made quite a pile of fabric, and quite a world of possibilities.

50
Tessa

June

"That's what you're getting?" I asked. "Black? Plain black? That's it?"

"That's it. Nothing else," Madelyn said. She laid the fabric bolt down on the cutting table and looked at Virginia. "Can I get two yards of this? Oh, and a spool of black thread."

I sighed with disappointment. When I told Madelyn that I needed to run down to the quilt shop after work to pick up some batting for my "Texas Hold 'Em" wall hanging and she'd announced that she was coming along, I'd hoped that this was her way of announcing she'd decided to give quilting a try after all. She's told me ten times that she's never going to become a quilter, but never is a long time. I hoped that hosting the quilt retreat had changed her mind.

But when we walked in the door and she made

a beeline for that plain Amish black, my hopes were dashed. She obviously needed the fabric for some other project. After all, you can't make a quilt out of plain black, can you?

I shuffled off to find my batting and almost ran into Margot, who was trotting out of the back office with a grin a mile wide.

"Well! That was quick!" she exclaimed, beaming at everyone.

"What was quick?"

"The way you two got down here. It wasn't five minutes ago that I left the message."

I looked at her blankly.

"The message," she repeated. "About coming on down here so we could watch together. Mary Dell's producer called and asked me to call Madelyn and tell her to watch today's show. I called the inn but no one answered, so I left a message on voice mail. You didn't get it?"

Madelyn shook her head and took her purchases over to the checkout counter for Dana to ring up. "We just stopped in to get some fabric. Why would Mary Dell care if I watched her show?"

"Don't know. With Mary Dell you never can tell. She likes to surprise people. Anyway, you're here. Come into the office—we've got a television in there. It'll be on in just a couple of minutes."

Forgetting all about my batting, I crowded into

the office with Madelyn, Margot, Virginia, and Dana. Margot told us that Evelyn was over at the Grill on the Green, helping Charlie pick out new tablecloths for the restaurant, but she called Ivy down from the workroom where she was cutting and packing Internet orders.

Margot turned on the television and we gathered around expectantly as the theme music for *Quintessential Quilting* came up and the camera moved in for a close-up of Mary Dell and Howard, who told the audience that on today's show they'd be talking about using color wheels for quilt design and fabric selection, quick and easy tips for paper piecing, and that they were very excited because they had a special guest, Julie Lebreaux, quilt designer and author of *Quilting Outside the Box*.

When she heard this, Madelyn sighed impatiently and sat down in the nearest chair with her arms crossed over her chest. "Okay, Mary Dell. I appreciate the thought, but *enough* already. I get it."

Margot shot me a questioning look, but I just shrugged. I didn't know what Madelyn was talking about either. We followed Madelyn's lead and sat down to watch the show, sort of. I was watching Madelyn more than the show, wondering what was going on and why Mary Dell was so insistent that she watch. Twenty-five minutes into it, I still had no idea. The doorbell on the shop jingled, signaling the arrival of a customer. Dana said she'd take care of it, but after a couple more rings of the bell she stuck her head through the door and, with an apologetic expression, asked if Virginia could give her a hand. After Howard's segment on color wheels, Ivy said she really had to get back upstairs and finish packaging the orders or she wouldn't be able to get them in today's mail.

So, as the interview with Julie Lebreaux was wrapping up, only Madelyn, Margot, and I were left. When that was done and the cameras returned to Mary Dell and Howard for the end-of-show recap, Madelyn grumbled, "Well, that was a waste of time. I've already got the books."

She got up from her chair and started to leave the room just as Mary Dell looked into the camera and said, "Before we say good-bye, I've just got to tell you about a little trip I took to New Bern, Connecticut, where my old friend Evelyn Dixon, owner of the Cobbled Court Quilt Shop, lives."

Everybody froze. Madelyn moved slowly back to her place and, with her eyes glued to the television screen, sank into the chair as Mary Dell continued speaking.

"Just last month, Evelyn and a group of her customers and gals from her quilt circle invited me to join them for a quilt retreat at a beautiful little hotel just a short walk from the quilt shop and downtown New Bern called the Beecher Cottage Inn."

When the picture came up on the television screen, Madelyn leapt out of her chair and all three of us—Madelyn, Margot, and me—started screaming, jumping up and down, and hugging. Dana and several customers came running to see what all the commotion was about. Virginia, who was pretty spry for eighty but couldn't match the others for speed, brought up the rear.

Virginia shouted to be heard over the din. "What's going on here? Did somebody get hurt? See a mouse? What?"

Unable to contain her excitement, Margot waved her hands, squealed, and pointed to the screen. "Look!"

The photograph, taken in full sun that shone through the new leaves of the trees, made the inn look particularly warm and welcoming, an idyllic spot for a weekend getaway. Looking closer, I noticed the brand-new picket fence, and pots of pink and yellow tulips that Madelyn and I had put on the porch just before the quilters had arrived. Mary Dell must have gone outside while everyone was busy quilting and snapped the photo herself. She'd shown me her new digital camera, a present from her beau, Hub-Jay, and had been very enthusiastic about trying it out. Now I knew why.

After a moment, the exterior shot of the inn was

replaced by a montage of interior photos: pictures of the bedroom, fireplace, and bathroom for Room Two, the room Mary Dell had stayed in; of the dining room set for afternoon tea, followed by several shots of the living room, set up with sewing tables and various shots of women quilting, laughing, and generally enjoying themselves. However, none of the shots included images of any of the women from the New Beginnings program. Mary Dell had been careful to make sure that their identities and whereabouts would not be revealed to anyone who might be looking for them. Mary Dell was a smart cookie.

Every new photo unleashed a fresh round of squeals, applause, and commentary from the audience that stood squashed together in the tiny back office. When the camera returned to Mary Dell and Howard, Madelyn waved her hands over her head and shouted, "Hush! Quiet, everybody! I want to hear what they're saying!"

The women settled down and listened as Howard turned to his mother and said, "Looks like you had a good time up in Connecticut, Mama."

"I sure did," she drawled. "Honey, I haven't had so much fun since Patton was a private. Next time you've got to come with me."

"I'd like that, Mama. New Bern is a nice place to visit."

"It sure is, and now that the Beecher Cottage

Inn is open for business, it's even nicer." Mary Dell turned and looked straight into the camera. "If any of you are looking for a place to hold a small retreat for your quilt circle or guild, or just to get away and do a little stitching with your friends, you should check out the Beecher Cottage Inn. We're putting the phone number and Web address up on the screen, so be sure to write that down. Give my friend Madelyn a shout and tell her I sent you. I know she'll treat you right."

Mary Dell winked and the exit music started to swell in the background. "Sounds like it's time for us to say good-bye. Howard, can you take us out?"

"Sure can, Mama." He looked into the camera, grinned, and said, "Thank you for joining us today. Hope we'll see you next time. Until then, remember: Behind every great quilter . . ."

He turned to his mother, who finished the line, ". . . is a great big pile of fabric. So get to work, y'all!"

As the music rose in volume and the credits rolled, everyone streamed out of the office and into the shop, chattering about the program and surrounding Madelyn, patting her shoulders and wishing her well. We all knew what this meant; with that one on-air endorsement to cable television's largest quilting audience, Mary Dell Templeton had put the Beecher Cottage Inn on the map. Quilters from all over the country would want to have retreats at Beecher Cottage. They'd fill Madelyn's rooms and bring lots of extra trade to Cobbled Court Quilts and, for that matter, to every business in downtown New Bern.

Except mine. Because it doesn't exist anymore. It's not fair. I haven't done anything wrong. And I've worked just as hard as Madelyn, harder even. Why should she get all the breaks? Especially when . . .

I stopped myself, even in thought, from going any further. I wasn't going to be jealous of Madelyn; I wasn't. She is my friend. I was happy that good things were happening for her. She had been through such a lot and known very little of the things that had brought the deepest happiness and meaning to my life, the security of growing up in a happy home, a husband's love, the joy of motherhood, the peace of God. These were the things I treasured most, the things that I truly did count as priceless.

And yet . . .

It wasn't easy to take wholehearted pleasure in Madelyn's good fortune, the knowledge that she was standing on the threshold of success, when my own dreams of entrepreneurial achievement had been so recently dashed upon the rocks. I didn't miss working at the shop day after day, not a bit. When we were working in the greenhouse and I told Lee that I preferred the flexibility of my new work schedule and the variety it offered,

I meant that. But I did miss the serenity of working long hours in my herb garden, the pride that came from making a quality product, and the pleasure of seeing people enjoy and appreciate what I had to offer. Not that I couldn't continue to do that, albeit on a smaller scale, for friends and family, but somehow it wasn't the same.

On that last day, when I'd locked the shop door for the last time, Madelyn had said that For the Love of Lavender wasn't dead, just on hiatus, and a workable business model for my dream, a Plan B, would emerge in good time. I had dismissed her words as wishful thinking. But I wanted them to be true.

I'd been on the lookout for a Plan B for weeks, but nothing had happened; not even the tiniest glimmer of an idea or opportunity had appeared on the horizon. And it probably never would. I had tried. I had given it my best and failed—end of story. It wasn't like I was the only one this had ever happened to. Life wasn't fair, but nobody ever promised it would be. That really would have been wishful thinking.

It wasn't Madelyn's fault that I had failed. I *would* be happy for her. I was.

Madelyn pushed her way out from the throng of women and walked toward me, her smile as broad as I'd ever seen it.

"Can you believe it? I'm so glad I listened to you and took a pass on that *Good Morning*

America spot. I feel so much better about this. You know something else? I think it'll be fun to cater to the crafty crowd. Not that I wouldn't be willing to let rooms to people who are non-quilters, but I think this could be a better business model. It's relatively easy to fill rooms in the summer and fall, when the weather is good, but I can book quilt retreats year-round."

"That's true," I said. "Most quilters would drive through a blizzard to get to a quilt retreat."

Madelyn bobbed her head. "You're right. And I think they'll be much more pleasant to work with than the average hotel guest, not that you won't find a crab apple in the barrel now and then. But from what I've seen so far, quilters are some of the kindest, happiest people in the world.

"Hey! I was just thinking, what if we turned the garage into a quilting workshop? Not right away, of course. I can't afford it yet, but it could be a great space. We could add some big picture windows that look out onto the garden, really good lighting overhead, built-in ironing stations, design walls, and cutting boards along the back wall, floor outlets so we wouldn't need all those extension cords. . . . I bet we could fit ten tables with two people each and there'd still be plenty of room. I was also thinking, maybe I'll even change the name of the inn. Instead of Beecher Cottage Inn, what do you think about the Patchwork Place Inn?"

I laughed and shook my head. It was nice to see her so excited. I was happy for her, truly happy. "I think you're getting ahead of yourself," I said. "Not that I blame you, but maybe you'd better take a deep breath and calm down before you go digging foundations and hiring electricians. First things first, right? And at the moment, I think the first order of business is to get back to the inn and check your messages. I'll bet your voice-mail box is full up."

"You're right!" she gasped. She grabbed the shopping bag that held her fabric and thread from the counter where she'd left it, started for the door, and then spun around to face me. "I know you were headed home, but can you come over for a little while and help me update the computer reservations? You're better with that program than I am."

I spread out my hands with exasperation. "It's not that hard. I keep telling you, just remember to do a save after you enter each new record. . . ."

Madelyn looked at me with pitiful eyes, her lower lip pushed out in a pretended pout.

I laughed. "Oh, all right. Let me buy my batting and then I'll come over and show you how it works. Again!"

"Thanks, Tessa. You're the best." She was out the door like a flash, pausing only to say a quick hello and good-bye to Evelyn, who was entering the shop just as Madelyn was going out.

"Somebody looks happy," Evelyn commented as she looked out the front window, watching Madelyn scurry across the courtyard and down the alley. "I guess she saw the show."

"You knew?" Evelyn nodded. "So it was your idea?"

"Nope, it was Mary Dell's. But she told me about it beforehand. No matter how much she likes someone, Mary Dell would never recommend a product or service on the show unless she truly believed it was something her viewers would enjoy and benefit from. Madelyn really has done a wonderful job remodeling the place and she was a wonderful hostess, made everyone feel right at home. Plus, she's got a good setup for quilt retreats. And if I know Madelyn, it probably won't be too long before she'll turn it into a *great* one."

"Before she left, she was already talking about turning the garage into a sewing studio."

"Good," she said. "I'm glad she's excited. This is great news for Madelyn, but it's good news for the town too. It will definitely help our business. Those quilters won't be able to resist coming in and adding a few more yards to their fabric stash." Evelyn bit her lower lip and fiddled with her necklace absently, thinking.

"You know, I should talk to her about putting together some workshops and special classes, retreats people could come to by themselves or

486

with just a friend or two. Of course, she could still cater to groups, but not every quilter belongs to a guild or circle. This would be a nice way for people who don't have time or opportunity to join a quilt group to pick up some new skills and meet some new friends. Plus, it'd be a way for Madelyn to keep her rooms filled during the week. Between Mary Dell and myself, I'm sure we could help her find some first-rate guest teachers," she mused, nodding to herself a few times and then looking up, giving a little start, almost as if she was surprised to see me.

"Sorry," she said with a laugh. "I'm getting ahead of myself but, like I said, this could be really good for business, and not just my business. When they're not stitching, those quilters will walk into town to shop, eat, buy souvenirs for themselves and gifts for the family and friends who couldn't join them. In a town this small, in times like these, an extra couple hundred dollars in sales a week can mean the difference between staying afloat and locking your doors."

"Tell me about it," I said.

Evelyn made a sympathetic face and patted my shoulder. "I know. I'm sorry. You had a lovely shop, Tessa, and you made fabulous products—Mary Dell just raved about your soap and shampoo—but your timing was off. It wasn't your fault."

"I suppose not. I wish it had worked out but . . . anyway, I'm luckier than most. At least I've got a job. And the way things are shaping up, it looks like I'm going to be able to get all the hours I need or want. Madelyn can't run the inn by herself."

"So, you're going to stay on and help her?"

"Sure," I said with a shrug of resignation. "What else have I got to do? I mean, besides help Lee on the farm."

Evelyn tilted her head to the side, her lips bowing into a knowing smile. "Well, that all depends." She reached into the pocket of her skirt, pulled out a folded slip of paper, and held it out.

"What's that?"

"That is the direct phone number for Mr. Hubble James Hollander, Hub-Jay to his more intimate friends, like Mary Dell. After she tried, and loved, your lavender products, she asked if she could have mine too. She didn't keep them for herself, she gave them to Hub-Jay, who loved them just as much as Mary Dell did.

"She didn't have your cell phone number, so Mary Dell tracked me down at the restaurant after she finished the show and asked if I could find you and give you a message. Hub-Jay would like to place a trial order for enough lavender bath amenities to supply one of his hotels for two weeks. During that time, they'll conduct a special survey of their guests to see if they like the products. If they do, Hub-Jay may want to supply all his hotels with For the Love of Lavender bath amenities all the time."

Evelyn's small smile broadened into a grin as she placed the slip of paper in my hand. "He's in his office and would like you to call him before the close of business today. What do you think about that?"

I unfolded the paper and stared at the ten numbers written on it, gripping that piece of paper on either edge, pinching it so tightly between my thumbs and forefingers that it would have taken a crowbar to pry it from my digits.

A slip of paper, a line of numbers, the barest of possibilities—it wasn't much to go on, but in my heart I knew this was more than wishful thinking. It was Plan B.

51
Madelyn

August

That's a lot of zeros, Madelyn."
I pulled off my reading glasses, perched them on top of my head, and looked up at Jake. "You're telling me. Why so much? It cost me less than that to remodel the whole house."

Jake was bending over me as I sat at the kitchen table, going over the initial construction sketches. He straightened up and stretched his back.

"It's a big job," he said and began ticking the evidence of this off on his fingers. "Not only are you remodeling the garage into a quilt studio, which is going to require a complete electrical job, you're also turning the attic into a dormitory for six and adding a full bath with two toilets, and a sprinkler system. That'll require a lot of wiring *and* a lot of plumbing work. It adds up. Remember, most of the work on the first go-round was cosmetic and a lot cheaper because you were the one sanding the floors, installing the tiles, painting the walls. . . ."

"Well? What if I—"

"Uh-uh," he said in a voice that brooked no argument. "No way, Maddie. You've got an inn to run. You don't have time to be a do-it-yourselfer anymore. This is the first day you've been one hundred percent vacant in weeks."

"I know. I almost don't know what to do with myself. The next bunch doesn't check in for two whole days."

"How many?"

"Seven. Four sisters, plus the mother, the aunt, and a granddaughter—three generations of quilters. The two oldest sisters made the arrangements; very nice ladies."

I turned my attention back to the sketches, tapping my pen on the table. "Yeah . . . I guess you're right."

Jake's eyes flew open in surprise and he cupped his hand to his ear. "Excuse me, would you mind repeating that? I'm not sure I heard you correctly."

I made a face and pretended to kick him in the shin. "Very funny," I said and pushed the sketches aside. "It pains me to admit it, but I guess I'm just going to have to shell out the money and hire a real contractor."

"If you want it done in time for a big retreat in the spring," he said, "I don't see as you have any choice. It'll be worth it. Myron will do a good job and he'll give you a fair price on it. Hey, how's the application for your SBA loan coming along?"

"I won't know for sure until next month, but things are looking good so far," I replied, crossing my fingers. "It helped that we've had such a strong summer and are already booking into next year. I don't have a single empty weekend until the middle of November."

"Good for you." He leaned down to give me a quick peck on the cheek. He's started doing that lately and . . . well . . . I don't mind. Jake's a good friend. And friends can kiss, right? It doesn't mean anything.

"We're on for sushi tonight, right?"

"Right," I said. "I'll see you at six. If you get there first, could you order me a—"

"Spicy tuna roll with extra ginger and extra wasabi."

He opened the back door with a grin. "I know, Maddie. See you tonight."

After Jake left, I poured myself another cup of coffee and went back to take another look at the sketches. This project was going to cost a pretty penny, no doubt about it. But the increase in capacity would be worth it. I'd already lost out on a few quilt circle bookings because I didn't have enough rooms. Not counting my room, I really only had space for ten guests, two doubles and two triples. The new dormitory would give me beds for six additional people who didn't mind sharing and wanted more modestly priced accommodations. I liked the idea of having rooms for people on a budget. And if everything went like I hoped it would, in a couple of years, I'd be able to add two more guest rooms, deluxe doubles, over the garage. That would give me capacity for twenty guests, which was about all I thought I could handle and as many as the new quilting studio would be able to hold.

I couldn't wait until spring! I was sick and tired of setting up and taking down sewing tables every weekend. Though, for today at least, having a sewing room in the house suited my purposes.

I picked up the sketches from the table, carried them into the office, and then headed toward the living room, coffee in hand. Just as I sat down to work, I heard the back door open and Tessa's voice calling, "Madelyn?"

"In here! There's fresh coffee in the pot if you want a cup!"

Tessa rattled around in the kitchen while I centered a scrap of purple onto the wrong side of a paper pattern, lined an inch-wide strip of black on the purple edge, and pinned both pieces of fabric to the paper. When I was finished, I heard footsteps coming down the hall and looked up to see Tessa with a cup of coffee in her hand and a quilted project bag looped over her shoulder, beaming like a ray of sunshine.

"Looks like somebody woke up on the right side of the bed today. Did your lottery number come up or something?"

She shook her head. "Nope, something even better. Three something betters, come to think of it." She pulled up a chair and sat down across from me. "Lee went to church with me yesterday morning."

I lifted the presser foot of my sewing machine and positioned my black-purple-paper sandwich underneath, pattern side up, before lowering it again. "Yeah? Well, that's great. I know that's something you've wanted for a long time. Did he like it?"

"Very much. In fact, he's planning on going again next Sunday. Do you want to come too?"

"Thanks, but no thanks," I said, stepping on the foot pedal of the machine as I stitched carefully along the first line of the pattern. "While I'm willing to concede the existence of God, which, as you know, is a major shift for me, I don't believe in organized religion. I told you before, Tessa, I'm never going to go to church."

Tessa mumbled something under her breath.

"What was that?"

"I said, 'never is a long time.'" She took a sip from her coffee mug.

"So you keep reminding me." I lifted the presser foot, pulled out my stitched piece, cut the bobbin threads, flipped to the wrong side of the pattern, and pressed open the seam with my fingers. Perfect. "So, moving on. What's the rest of your good news?"

"Josh called," she said, her smile returning. "He's finishing his internship this week and flying home for a visit. He'll have ten whole days before he has to go back to school!"

"Oh, Tessa, that's wonderful," I said sincerely. "I can't wait to meet Josh. If you need to take some time off while he's here, you can. Lauren is still learning the ropes, but I think she can fill in for you. I'm sure she'd be happy to have the extra hours."

The increase in business had absolutely

necessitated my hiring additional staff. Lauren, who was among Ivy's classmates and had attended the quilt retreat, had just started working for me on weekends. She was no Tessa, but she was working out well so far.

"Well," Tessa said slowly, "I'm glad to hear that because my third piece of good news might mean a little bit of bad news for you."

I frowned, wondering what she meant. Tessa took in a big breath, held it, and then, as if she couldn't hold it one moment longer, blew it back out and exclaimed, "Hub-Jay called! The trials at the Austin hotel went great. He wants me to supply all the amenities for his hotels! Ahhhh!"

Tessa screamed. I screamed. We leapt from our seats, hugged each other, and jumped up and down, as elated as if Tessa really had won the lottery.

"Oh my gosh! This is great news! Incredible! I just . . . I . . ." I gasped, trying to catch my breath as the full impact of Tessa's news came over me. "Well, I . . . that's just amazing. How many hotels is that? Eight? Ten? How are you going to supply that many hotels?"

Tessa laughed a bit giddily and threw up her hands in an exaggerated shrug. "It's actually just eight hotels but, to tell you the truth, I have no idea! You remember what a time we had making product for just one property for a two-week test run."

I certainly did. We'd all pitched in on that one, canceling the usual activities of the quilt circle two Fridays in a row to help Tessa package tiny bars and bottles of lavender soap, shampoo, conditioner, and body lotion. The quilt shop smelled like a garden for days afterward.

"We're going to do it in phases: begin with the first property, in Austin, and then add one more every month until we're supplying all eight. It's a good thing I didn't use my summer crop of lavender this year; otherwise I wouldn't have enough to get started. I'm probably going to have to buy some extra as it is."

"I'll say," I added. "And lease some space for a bigger workshop and warehouse, invest in some equipment, order more containers. Tessa, do you need to borrow some money? I've got a little extra capital at the moment, not much but some. If you need it . . ."

She tilted her head to the side and smiled. "Oh, Maddie. You're the best. That's a sweet offer, but no thanks. Hub-Jay is going to advance us some money to get started and, if that's not enough, I've still got a line of credit from the shop."

"Okay, if you're sure. But if you need my help, you know you just have to ask. Right?"

"I know. Listen, Madelyn . . . there's something else. . . ."

I dismissed her worried look with a wave of my hand. "You don't even need to say it. I understand. You can't work for me anymore, you'll be too busy. In fact, you'd better start looking into hiring some help of your own."

"I already have. I put ads in the paper and on the Internet today. And I went over to New Beginnings and talked to Cathy. We really hit it off at the retreat. She's smart, she's had manufacturing experience, and she really needs a job. She's going to start on Monday. And, fortunately for me," she said with a wink, "I've already got an accountant. Lee is willing to sharpen up his pencils and help me out, at least for a few hours a week."

"That's great, Tessa," I said, giving her one more squeeze before returning to my sewing machine. "I'll miss having you around here, but I'm so happy for you."

"Thanks. I'm going to miss you too, but . . ." She stopped in mid-sentence, frowned, looked at me and then at the sewing machine.

"Wait a minute . . . are you? Is that a quilt block you're making?"

I laughed. "I was beginning to wonder when you'd notice. As a matter of fact," I said, holding up the piece I was working on, "it is a quilt block. So are these." I patted the small stack of finished blocks that sat to the left of the machine.

"You've started quilting?" Her mouth dropped open, her expression a perfect picture of disbelief. "Why didn't you tell me?"

"I wanted to be sure I liked it first. I do, by the

way. Mary Dell gave me these books to read." I picked the books up off the far end of the table and handed them to Tessa, who started leafing through them. "They made me realize that I don't have to quilt according to anybody else's rules. I can make it up as I go along, create my own designs, do it my way."

"And we both know how much you like that."

"Uh-huh," I replied without a hint of apology and picked up one of the completed blocks. "Anyway, the books just opened my eyes to the possibilities. I'm just crazy about this author," I said, pointing to *Quilting Outside the Box*. "In fact, I just booked her for a weekend in April. Julie Lebreaux will be our first guest teacher and the first to teach in the new quilting studio. Assuming it's done by then. Fingers crossed."

Tessa looked up, clearly impressed. "Julie Lebreaux? Really? Wow. I wouldn't mind signing up for that myself."

"Why not? I'll give you the best friend discount—one hundred percent."

"No," she said firmly. "I won't let you do that, but we can argue about that later."

She put down the books and picked up one of my finished quilt blocks, a six-by-nine, paper-pieced rectangle made up of fifteen different-sized scraps with fifteen completely different colors and values, each scrap surrounded and separated by a half-inch band of inky black. That was the neutral element that made all those colors pop and work together. Without that black banding between the colors, the block would have been a big, nonsensical mess. With it, the blocks were beautiful, rich and deep, and no two alike, a stained glass window in abstract.

"Where did you get the idea for these?"

"I was walking to town one day, past the Methodist church—it has that big stained glass window in front—and the next thing I knew, I was running back home to sketch out a pattern."

"It's beautiful," she said with a sigh. "I've never seen anything like it."

"Well, I'm glad you like it because I'm making it for you."

"Really? Oh, Madelyn, really? But you already gave me the flower basket quilt."

"No," I corrected her. "I just helped you with it. That was a collaboration, like our friendship. We each bring something unique to the party and, because of that, the party is a whole lot more interesting—and fun. But this one is just from me to you, because I want to. I've discovered that I like giving gifts."

"That's funny," Tessa said with a laugh as she reached down to the floor to pick up her project bag. "So do I."

The two boxes were wrapped in lavender paper decorated with purple, blue, and green butterflies and tied with green satin ribbons. Tessa did go to a lot of trouble making presents look pretty.

I untied the ribbons on the first box, removed the wrapping, and lifted the lid. "Oh! How sweet! Quilts for the dollhouse. Just like the ones you made before," I said, lifting the first, a teeny-tiny blue and white log cabin quilt out of the box. "Well, not quite like you made before. These are much nicer. Goodness, Tessa! The pieces are so little but they came out perfectly even. How were you able to do this?"

"I followed the directions," she said simply. "And I took my time. I like doing miniatures. It sort of plays to my strengths. Anyway, I'm glad you like them. I started working on them right after we found the dollhouse. And," she said, handing me the next box, "I ordered these at the same time, but there was a mix-up with the delivery company. They just arrived yesterday. Open it!"

Tearing the paper away, I read the words "Dollhouse Family."

I laughed aloud. "No way. Tell me you didn't . . ."

Tessa's face lit up. For a moment, she looked about twelve years old. "Let's try them out."

The dollhouse was another of my remodeling projects.

The sofa I'd bought at the church fair looked so lonely in there by itself that I'd begun looking for replacement furniture at tag sales and thrift shops. So far, I'd found three beds, a kitchen table, chairs, a stove, a grandfather clock, and a claw-foot bathtub. One of these days, I hope to run across a miniature sewing machine. Of course, I could have ordered one from a catalog, but for me the fun has always come from the finding.

Tessa and I pulled chairs to the open side of the little house and sat down. She placed the new quilts on the beds while I opened the box and pulled out two female dolls, which I immediately dubbed Tessa and Madelyn, and two male dolls, who were harder to name.

"This one can be Lee," I said. "But I'm not sure what to call this guy."

"What's wrong with Jake?"

I narrowed my eyes and gave my friend a sideways look. "I don't know. Maybe. But he doesn't live here," I declared. "He's just come for a visit. He's Lee's friend."

"And Tessa's," she insisted as she picked up the Jake doll and posed him on the sofa. "*And* Madelyn's. He's everybody's friend."

I thought about this for a moment. "Fine. He's everybody's friend. And he's here for a visit."

Tessa rolled her eyes. "You're crazy," she said. "And very stubborn. Anyone ever tell you that?"

As she spoke I reached in the box and pulled out one final doll, an old woman with glasses, iron-gray hair, and an expression that looked surprisingly grim for a child's toy. I had no trouble naming this one.

"Indeed, they did," I said, standing the Edna doll up in the kitchen, near the stove. "And much, much worse."

Tessa gasped. "It looks just like her, doesn't it?" She turned the Edna doll around to face the Madelyn and Tessa dolls, who were sitting across from each other at the kitchen table and smiling.

"What are you two doing, sitting there like a couple of lumps!" Tessa said in a croaking imitation of Grandma Edna. "Don't you talk to me like that or I'll wash your mouths out with soap, do you hear me? When I was your age, children were seen and not heard! They respected their elders and they went outside to play, or helped around the house instead of sitting around on their backsides like lazy leeches! And another thing, you two are too big to be playing with dolls! Why aren't you . . ."

For a moment there was a bad taste in my mouth, acrid and sharp, like hatred and humiliation.

But only for a moment.

I reached out for my own doll, stood her up on her feet to face the Edna doll, and said, "You know something, Edna? I think you're tired. Heaven knows I'm tired of you. Hush up, Edna."

I picked Edna up from her place near the stove,

laid her on the white iron doll bed in the attic, swallowed back the bitter taste, and said, "It's time for you to go to sleep now, Edna. Rest in peace."

Tessa reached out, pulled the quilt over the doll, covering its grim countenance, and then rested her hand on top of mine. "I think you're right, my friend. I think that's a very good idea."

DISCUSSION QUESTIONS

1. As a young teenager, Tessa Kover was both intrigued by Madelyn Beecher being "simultaneously cautious and careless" and rejecting of her for being needy and "weird." In what ways could you identify with Tessa? With Madelyn?

2. Madelyn Beecher Baron's upbringing impacted her later life decisions. How have your upbringing and your family affected your decisions? What messages or beliefs have you had to overcome? What values or beliefs from your childhood have worked well for you?

3. Madelyn and Tessa both return to New Bern after being gone for many years. Madelyn returned resentfully because she had nowhere else to go and no other way to live. Tessa moved back to fulfill a dream. Have you ever left a place or situation that you later returned to for one reason or another? How did you feel about returning? How did the return work out for you?

4. Madelyn proves she's determined, resourceful, and courageous, but she doubts her worthiness, intelligence, and contributions. New Bern residents, especially Tessa and Jake, help her see she matters. What are some of your strengths? What are some of your challenges? How have family or friends helped you see yourself differently? How have you supported others to see themselves differently?

5. Financial struggle and fulfilling a dream play key roles in *Threading the Needle*. How has financial struggle led you in a direction you might not otherwise have considered, like Madelyn? Describe a time you had to defer or give up a dream, like Tessa, because of finances. How did this change in direction work out for you?

6. Tessa's mother used to say, "Enough is as good as a feast." How do you feel about "enough"? Is it a feast for you, or do you aspire to more than enough, and why?

7. Jake Kaminski, rumored to be a ladies' man, shares his story of recovery from alcoholism with Madelyn, and he offers her unconditional support. Why does he do this? How does this help Madelyn?

8. Jake tells Madelyn, "You know, Madelyn, it's the easiest thing in the world to tell somebody what they want to hear, but it takes a real friend to tell somebody what they need to hear." Do you agree? Why or why not? Have you ever been in a position of telling a friend something the friend didn't want to hear? What was the result? How did it affect your friendship?

9. Many of the characters in the Cobbled Court series own a business. If you could start your own business, what kind of business would that be? What do you think are the benefits and challenges of working for yourself? Do you think your personality is suited for being a business owner? Why or why not?

10. Thinking about the failure of her retail business, the first time Tessa had failed at anything, Tessa says, "Maybe that's the lesson in all of this: Stick to what you know, color inside the lines." Do you think this is depression talking, or has Tessa's business failure changed her attitude, her outlook on life? Have you ever failed at anything, and if so, how did it change your attitude, your approach to life? Your willingness to take on new challenges?

11. When Tessa was younger, her mother advised her to "Enjoy the little things in life, Tessa. One day you may look back and realize they were the big things." Do you think that is true? If so, what little things in your life have you realized are truly the big things?

12. Madelyn realizes after opening her bed-and-breakfast, which so many New Bern residents supported, that, "This is what it's like to be part of something, of some place. This is what it's like to care." What have you been part of that's been meaningful to you? In what ways have you cared for others?

13. Madelyn finds her childhood quilt in the Beecher Cottage attic. Tessa pays to have it repaired, and then the quilt ends up on one of the beds in Madelyn's bed-and-breakfast. Discuss the symbolism of quilting in the story and to its characters. Near the end of the book, the quilters decide to make a baby quilt for Angela, who was also betrayed by a man. What's the significance of this scene?

Dear Reading Friend,

Whether this is your first visit to the village of New Bern or your fourth, I want to thank you for making the journey. I hope you've enjoyed it as much as I have.

As you may know, when I began work on *A Single Thread*, the first Cobbled Court novel, I had no intention of creating a series. But after completing the manuscript I found myself longing to know more about this place and these characters, and so I invited readers to write and let me know if they, too, wanted to read more about New Bern.

The thousands of wonderful e-mails and letters you sent in response to that question, and that continue to arrive by computer and post on a daily basis, have been an enormous encouragement and blessing to me. Writing tends to be a solitary pursuit, but your letters have fostered a connection between writer and reader, motivating me to give each story my very best effort. I do read every note personally, and every note receives a response.

If you'd like to write to me, you can do so at . . .

Marie Bostwick
PO Box 488
Thomaston, CT 06787

Or you can go to my website, www.marie bostwick.com, and send a note via the contact form.

While you're there you can also read excerpts from my other novels and check out my blog, the Recipe of the Month, my Latest Crush, and an upcoming schedule of appearances. (The only thing I like more than getting letters from readers is meeting them in person!)

And if you register as one of my official Reading Friends (to get to the registration form, click on the "Become A Reading Friend" box on the left side of the home page), you'll get access to special content: You can register for my monthly book giveaway; receive my quarterly newsletter and invitations to my appearances in your area; connect with other readers in the online forum; and download free goodies like the recipes from my Christmas novellas, the Broken Hearts Mending lap quilt pattern from *A Single Thread*, and the Star-Crossed Love table runner from *A Thread So Thin*.

Speaking of quilt patterns, my dear friend Deb Tucker, of Studio 180 Design (www.studio180 design.net), has created another gorgeous pattern inspired by the quilts you've read about in this book. We had so many terrific ideas for this new project that, as I'm writing this, we haven't yet settled on the exact pattern that will be offered. However, by the time you read this, my registered Reading Friends will have another beautiful, free pattern available to download. **Please remember: The patterns are only available via computer and only to registered Reading Friends for their personal use.**

Thank you again for joining me on another journey to New Bern. Until we meet again, I wish you all the best.

Blessings,

Marie Bostwick

Center Point Publishing

600 Brooks Road ● PO Box 1
Thorndike ME 04986-0001 USA

(207) 568-3717

US & Canada:
1 800 929-9108

www.centerpointlargeprint.com